D1448776

URANIA

THE
OTHER VOICE
IN
EARLY MODERN
EUROPE

A Series Edited by Margaret L. King and Albert Rabil Jr.

RECENT BOOKS IN THE SERIES

Giulia Bigolina

URANIA

A Romance

ॐ

Edited and Translated by
Valeria Finucci

THE UNIVERSITY OF CHICAGO PRESS
Chicago & London

Giulia Bigolina, ca. 1518 to ca. 1569

Valeria Finucci is professor of Italian in the Department of Romance Studies at Duke University. She is the author of *The Lady Vanishes: Subjectivity and Representation in Castiglione and Ariosto* and *The Manly Masquerade: Masculinity, Paternity, and Castration in the Italian Renaissance* and the editor or coeditor of three books, most recently of *Generation and Degeneration: Tropes of Reproduction in Literature and History from Antiquity to Early Modern Europe.*

The University of Chicago Press, Chicago 60637
The University of Chicago Press, Ltd., London
© 2005 by The University of Chicago
All rights reserved. Published 2005
Printed in the United States of America

14 13 12 11 10 09 08 07 06 05   1 2 3 4 5

ISBN: 0-226-04877-2 (cloth)
ISBN: 0-226-04878-0 (paper)

The University of Chicago Press gratefully acknowledges the generous support of The Gladys Krieble Delmas Foundation toward the publication of this book.

Library of Congress Cataloging-in-Publication Data

Bigolina, Giulia, d. 1569
[Urania, nella quale si contiene l'amore d'una giovane di tal nome. English]
Urania: a romance / Giulia Bigolina ; edited and translated by Valeria Finucci.
p. cm. — (The other voice in early modern Europe)
Includes text of Novella di Giulia Camposampiero e Tesibaldo Valiani in English and Italian.
Includes bibliographical references and index.
ISBN 0-226-04877-2 (cloth : alk paper) — ISBN 0-226-04878-0 (pbk. : alk. paper)
I. Finucci, Valeria. II. Bigolina, Giulia, d. 1569. Novella di Giulia Camposampiero e Tesibaldo Valiani. English & Italian. III. Title. IV. Series
PQ4610.B58U7313 2005
853'.4—dc22   2004014653

⊗ The paper used in this publication meets the minimum requirements of the American National Standard for Information Sciences—Permanence of Paper for Printed Library Materials, ANSI Z39.48-1992.

To Julie Linehan and Mark Sosower

CONTENTS

ACKNOWLEDGMENTS

I would like to express my gratitude to the many people and institutions that supported this project as the manuscript of *Urania* moved from a critical edition in Italian that I published two years ago to its translation in English today and as "Giulia Camposampiero" was readied for its first modern print.

On this side of the ocean I would like to thank Elizabeth Clark, Giuseppe Gerbino, Julie Linehan, Mary Pardo, Rosamaria Preparata, Mark Sosower, Elissa Weaver, Mary Ann Friese Witt, Ronald Witt, and Naomi Yavneh for their loving support, enlightened discussions, and most of all, for their friendship.

As for the Venetian and Veneto crew of friends and colleagues who have followed my work, helped me during tough times, and made my life cheerful, I would like to thank Paola Modesti, who provided crucial assistance in reading seemingly indecipherable court documents, and Antonia Arslan, Luciano Donato, Annamaria Ferrarotti, and Gianfranco Finucci.

I would have not written this book without the encouragement and the unfailing support of Amedeo Quondam and Albert Rabil, who read more than one version of my work in different stages. Don Guido Beltrame has not lived to see the English version of *Urania* come out, but his assistance has given the term "generosity" a new, fuller meaning for me. I owe also a special debt of gratitude to Margaret King, Virginia Cox, Naomi Miller, and to the anonymous reader from the University of Chicago Press for their generous insights and clarifications.

I am extremely lucky to have been the recipient of a number of grants that allowed me to research through the years, first in Italian and then in English, the real person behind the name "Giulia Bigolina." My thanks go the National Endowment for the Humanities, the Gladys Krieble Delmas Foundation for Research in Venice and the Veneto region, and the Renaissance Society of America. My home institution, Duke University, generously awarded me two Research Council grants and an award for "Planning New Research Initiatives in the International Field." I would also like to acknowledge the help of a Lila Wallace/Readers' Digest Grant from Harvard University/Villa I Tatti that came when I was beginning the translation.

Last, I would like to thank Sharon Brinkman for so effortlessly coming up with idiomatic expressions and Maia Rigas and Randolph Petilos at the Press who saw the book through publication.

Valeria Finucci

NOTE ON TRANSLATION

My translation of *Urania* is based on the transcription of the manuscript of the same title, Codex ms. 98, in the Biblioteca Trivulziana, that I published in a critical edition in 2002 (Bulzoni: Rome).

My translation of "Giulia Camposampiero" is based on the transcription of MS 1451, VIII, entitled "Novella di Giulia Campo San Piero, et di Thesibaldo Vitaliani Raccontata Nello Amenissimo Luogo di Mirabello Da Una Nobilissi. Gentildonna Padovana," which is in the Biblioteca Civica of Padua.

For the transcription in Italian of "Giulia" I confronted the manuscript with the printed Borromeo version entitled "Novella di Giulia Bigolina raccontata nello amenissimo luogo di Mirabello." I have not used the Piranesi version as a guide because of differences in his printed version (these differences will be pointed out in the notes of my translation).

Throughout I have made a few conservative changes in the transcription for the sake of enhancing reading. Specifically,

1. I have given the modern version of proper names when commonly available today, i.e., "Capodilista" for "Capo di Lista," "Camposampiero" for "Campo San Piero," "Tiso" for "Thiso," "Tesibaldo" for "Thesibaldo." I have also provided the modern spelling of some words, i.e., "dunque" for "donche" or "adonche."
2. I have created new paragraphs, made the punctuation uniform, regularized the use of apostrophes and elisions, and eliminated archaic and regional forms when the text presented elsewhere a more precise Italian (Tuscan) orthography.
3. I have substituted "j" or "ij" at the end of a word with "i," as in "studii," which is now "studi," following modern usage, and I have eliminated the vowel "h" at the beginning or in the middle of a word according to modern usage,

i.e., "uomini" rather than "huomini"; "ancora" rather than "anchora," "ono-revoli" for "honorevoli," and "aver" for "haver."

4. I have accented words according to modern usage and corrected the ir-regular use of double consonants by choosing the most used form, i.e., "ra-gionando" for "raggionando," "accortamente" for "acortamente," "valore" for "vallore," and "bocca" for "bocha." I have also changed "et" into "e" and substituted "z" with "t" when followed by "io" as in "ufficio" rather than "uf-fitio" and "orazione" rather than "oratione."

5. I have eliminated capitalization when not justified syntactically or se-mantically, i.e., "novella" instead of "Novella," "giovane" instead of "Gio-vane," "camera" instead of "Camera."

6. Words that have been compressed and shortened, as was typical in the six-teenth century, have been written out in their entirety, i.e., "Imperatore" for "imp" and "repubblica" for "rep."

THE OTHER VOICE IN
EARLY MODERN EUROPE:
INTRODUCTION TO THE SERIES

Margaret L. King and Albert Rabil Jr.

THE OLD VOICE AND THE OTHER VOICE

In western Europe and the United States, women are nearing equality in the professions, in business, and in politics. Most enjoy access to education, reproductive rights, and autonomy in financial affairs. Issues vital to women are on the public agenda: equal pay, child care, domestic abuse, breast cancer research, and curricular revision with an eye to the inclusion of women.

These recent achievements have their origins in things women (and some male supporters) said for the first time about six hundred years ago. Theirs is the "other voice," in contradistinction to the "first voice," the voice of the educated men who created Western culture. Coincident with a general reshaping of European culture in the period 1300–1700 (called the Renaissance or early modern period), questions of female equality and opportunity were raised that still resound and are still unresolved.

The other voice emerged against the backdrop of a three-thousand-year history of the derogation of women rooted in the civilizations related to Western culture: Hebrew, Greek, Roman, and Christian. Negative attitudes toward women inherited from these traditions pervaded the intellectual, medical, legal, religious, and social systems that developed during the European Middle Ages.

The following pages describe the traditional, overwhelmingly male views of women's nature inherited by early modern Europeans and the new tradition that the "other voice" called into being to begin to challenge reigning assumptions. This review should serve as a framework for understanding the texts published in the series the Other Voice in Early Modern Europe. Introductions specific to each text and author follow this essay in all the volumes of the series.

TRADITIONAL VIEWS OF WOMEN, 500 B.C.E.–1500 C.E.

Embedded in the philosophical and medical theories of the ancient Greeks were perceptions of the female as inferior to the male in both mind and body. Similarly, the structure of civil legislation inherited from the ancient Romans was biased against women, and the views on women developed by Christian thinkers out of the Hebrew Bible and the Christian New Testament were negative and disabling. Literary works composed in the vernacular of ordinary people, and widely recited or read, conveyed these negative assumptions. The social networks within which most women lived—those of the family and the institutions of the Roman Catholic Church—were shaped by this negative tradition and sharply limited the areas in which women might act in and upon the world.

GREEK PHILOSOPHY AND FEMALE NATURE. Greek biology assumed that women were inferior to men and defined them as merely childbearers and housekeepers. This view was authoritatively expressed in the works of the philosopher Aristotle.

Aristotle thought in dualities. He considered action superior to inaction, form (the inner design or structure of any object) superior to matter, completion to incompletion, possession to deprivation. In each of these dualities, he associated the male principle with the superior quality and the female with the inferior. "The male principle in nature," he argued, "is associated with active, formative and perfected characteristics, while the female is passive, material and deprived, desiring the male in order to become complete."[1] Men are always identified with virile qualities, such as judgment, courage, and stamina, and women with their opposites—irrationality, cowardice, and weakness.

The masculine principle was considered superior even in the womb. The man's semen, Aristotle believed, created the form of a new human creature, while the female body contributed only matter. (The existence of the ovum, and with it the other facts of human embryology, was not established until the seventeenth century.) Although the later Greek physician Galen believed there was a female component in generation, contributed by "female semen," the followers of both Aristotle and Galen saw the male role in human generation as more active and more important.

In the Aristotelian view, the male principle sought always to reproduce itself. The creation of a female was always a mistake, therefore, resulting from

---

1. Aristotle, *Physics* 1.9.192a20–24, in *The Complete Works of Aristotle*, ed. Jonathan Barnes, rev. Oxford trans., 2 vols. (Princeton, 1984), 1: 328.

an imperfect act of generation. Every female born was considered a "defective" or "mutilated" male (as Aristotle's terminology has variously been translated), a "monstrosity" of nature.[2]

For Greek theorists, the biology of males and females was the key to their psychology. The female was softer and more docile, more apt to be despondent, querulous, and deceitful. Being incomplete, moreover, she craved sexual fulfillment in intercourse with a male. The male was intellectual, active, and in control of his passions.

These psychological polarities derived from the theory that the universe consisted of four elements (earth, fire, air, and water), expressed in human bodies as four "humors" (black bile, yellow bile, blood, and phlegm) considered, respectively, dry, hot, damp, and cold and corresponding to mental states ("melancholic," "choleric," "sanguine," "phlegmatic"). In this scheme the male, sharing the principles of earth and fire, was dry and hot; the female, sharing the principles of air and water, was cold and damp.

Female psychology was further affected by her dominant organ, the uterus (womb), *hystera* in Greek. The passions generated by the womb made women lustful, deceitful, talkative, irrational, indeed—when these affects were in excess—"hysterical."

Aristotle's biology also had social and political consequences. If the male principle was superior and the female inferior, then in the household, as in the state, men should rule and women must be subordinate. That hierarchy did not rule out the companionship of husband and wife, whose cooperation was necessary for the welfare of children and the preservation of property. Such mutuality supported male preeminence.

Aristotle's teacher Plato suggested a different possibility: that men and women might possess the same virtues. The setting for this proposal is the imaginary and ideal Republic that Plato sketches in a dialogue of that name. Here, for a privileged elite capable of leading wisely, all distinctions of class and wealth dissolve, as, consequently, do those of gender. Without households or property, as Plato constructs his ideal society, there is no need for the subordination of women. Women may therefore be educated to the same level as men to assume leadership. Plato's Republic remained imaginary, however. In real societies, the subordination of women remained the norm and the prescription.

The views of women inherited from the Greek philosophical tradition became the basis for medieval thought. In the thirteenth century, the supreme Scholastic philosopher Thomas Aquinas, among others, still echoed Aris-

---

2. Aristotle, *Generation of Animals* 2.3.737a27–28, in *The Complete Works,* 1: 1144.

totle's views of human reproduction, of male and female personalities, and of the preeminent male role in the social hierarchy.

ROMAN LAW AND THE FEMALE CONDITION. Roman law, like Greek philosophy, underlay medieval thought and shaped medieval society. The ancient belief that adult property-owning men should administer households and make decisions affecting the community at large is the very fulcrum of Roman law.

About 450 B.C.E., during Rome's republican era, the community's customary law was recorded (legendarily) on twelve tablets erected in the city's central forum. It was later elaborated by professional jurists whose activity increased in the imperial era, when much new legislation was passed, especially on issues affecting family and inheritance. This growing, changing body of laws was eventually codified in the *Corpus of Civil Law* under the direction of the emperor Justinian, generations after the empire ceased to be ruled from Rome. That *Corpus*, read and commented on by medieval scholars from the eleventh century on, inspired the legal systems of most of the cities and kingdoms of Europe.

Laws regarding dowries, divorce, and inheritance pertain primarily to women. Since those laws aimed to maintain and preserve property, the women concerned were those from the property-owning minority. Their subordination to male family members points to the even greater subordination of lower-class and slave women, about whom the laws speak little.

In the early republic, the *paterfamilias*, or "father of the family," possessed *patria potestas*, "paternal power." The term *pater*, "father," in both these cases does not necessarily mean biological father but denotes the head of a household. The father was the person who owned the household's property and, indeed, its human members. The *paterfamilias* had absolute power—including the power, rarely exercised, of life or death—over his wife, his children, and his slaves, as much as his cattle.

Male children could be "emancipated," an act that granted legal autonomy and the right to own property. Those over fourteen could be emancipated by a special grant from the father or automatically by their father's death. But females could never be emancipated; instead, they passed from the authority of their father to that of a husband or, if widowed or orphaned while still unmarried, to a guardian or tutor.

Marriage in its traditional form placed the woman under her husband's authority, or *manus*. He could divorce her on grounds of adultery, drinking wine, or stealing from the household, but she could not divorce him. She could neither possess property in her own right nor bequeath any to her children upon her death. When her husband died, the household property passed not to her but to his male heirs. And when her father died, she had no claim to any family inheritance, which was directed to her brothers or more remote male relatives. The effect of these laws was to exclude women from civil society, itself based on property ownership.

In the later republican and imperial periods, these rules were significantly modified. Women rarely married according to the traditional form. The practice of "free" marriage allowed a woman to remain under her father's authority, to possess property given her by her father (most frequently the "dowry," recoverable from the husband's household on his death), and to inherit from her father. She could also bequeath property to her own children and divorce her husband, just as he could divorce her.

Despite this greater freedom, women still suffered enormous disability under Roman law. Heirs could belong only to the father's side, never the mother's. Moreover, although she could bequeath her property to her children, she could not establish a line of succession in doing so. A woman was "the beginning and end of her own family," said the jurist Ulpian. Moreover, women could play no public role. They could not hold public office, represent anyone in a legal case, or even witness a will. Women had only a private existence and no public personality.

The dowry system, the guardian, women's limited ability to transmit wealth, and total political disability are all features of Roman law adopted by the medieval communities of western Europe, although modified according to local customary laws..

CHRISTIAN DOCTRINE AND WOMEN'S PLACE. The Hebrew Bible and the Christian New Testament authorized later writers to limit women to the realm of the family and to burden them with the guilt of original sin. The passages most fruitful for this purpose were the creation narratives in Genesis and sentences from the Epistles defining women's role within the Christian family and community.

Each of the first two chapters of Genesis contains a creation narrative. In the first "God created man in his own image, in the image of God he created him; male and female he created them" (Gn 1:27). In the second, God created Eve from Adam's rib (2:21–23). Christian theologians relied principally on Genesis 2 for their understanding of the relation between man and woman, interpreting the creation of Eve from Adam as proof of her subordination to him.

The creation story in Genesis 2 leads to that of the temptations in Genesis 3: of Eve by the wily serpent and of Adam by Eve. As read by Christian theologians from Tertullian to Thomas Aquinas, the narrative made Eve responsible for the Fall and its consequences. She instigated the act; she deceived her husband; she suffered the greater punishment. Her disobedience made it necessary for Jesus to be incarnated and to die on the cross. From the pulpit, moralists and preachers for centuries conveyed to women the guilt that they bore for original sin.

The Epistles offered advice to early Christians on building communities of the faithful. Among the matters to be regulated was the place of women. Paul offered views favorable to women in Galatians 3:28: "There is neither Jew nor Greek, there is neither slave nor free, there is neither male nor female; for you are all one in Christ Jesus." Paul also referred to women as his coworkers and placed them on a par with himself and his male coworkers (Phlm 4:2–3; Rom 16:1–3; 1 Cor 16:19). Elsewhere, Paul limited women's possibilities: "But I want you to understand that the head of every man is Christ, the head of a woman is her husband, and the head of Christ is God" (1 Cor 11:3).

Biblical passages by later writers (although attributed to Paul) enjoined women to forgo jewels, expensive clothes, and elaborate coiffures; and they forbade women to "teach or have authority over men," telling them to "learn in silence with all submissiveness" as is proper for one responsible for sin, consoling them, however, with the thought that they will be saved through childbearing (1 Tm 2:9–15). Other texts among the later Epistles defined women as the weaker sex and emphasized their subordination to their husbands (1 Pt 3:7; Col 3:18; Eph 5:22–23).

These passages from the New Testament became the arsenal employed by theologians of the early church to transmit negative attitudes toward women to medieval Christian culture—above all, Tertullian (*On the Apparel of Women*), Jerome (*Against Jovinian*), and Augustine (*The Literal Meaning of Genesis*).

THE IMAGE OF WOMEN IN MEDIEVAL LITERATURE. The philosophical, legal, and religious traditions born in antiquity formed the basis of the medieval intellectual synthesis wrought by trained thinkers, mostly clerics, writing in Latin and based largely in universities. The vernacular literary tradition that developed alongside the learned tradition also spoke about female nature and women's roles. Medieval stories, poems, and epics also portrayed women negatively—as lustful and deceitful—while praising good housekeepers and loyal wives as replicas of the Virgin Mary or the female saints and martyrs.

There is an exception in the movement of "courtly love" that evolved in southern France from the twelfth century. Courtly love was the erotic love between a nobleman and noblewoman, the latter usually superior in social rank. It was always adulterous. From the conventions of courtly love derive modern Western notions of romantic love. The tradition has had an impact disproportionate to its size, for it affected only a tiny elite, and very few women. The exaltation of the female lover probably does not reflect a higher evaluation of women or a step toward their sexual liberation. More likely it gives expression to the social and sexual tensions besetting the knightly class at a specific historical juncture.

The literary fashion of courtly love was on the wane by the thirteenth century, when the widely read *Romance of the Rose* was composed in French by two authors of significantly different dispositions. Guillaume de Lorris composed the initial four thousand verses about 1235, and Jean de Meun added about seventeen thousand verses—more than four times the original—about 1265.

The fragment composed by Guillaume de Lorris stands squarely in the tradition of courtly love. Here the poet, in a dream, is admitted into a walled garden where he finds a magic fountain in which a rosebush is reflected. He longs to pick one rose, but the thorns prevent his doing so, even as he is wounded by arrows from the god of love, whose commands he agrees to obey. The rest of this part of the poem recounts the poet's unsuccessful efforts to pluck the rose.

The longer part of the *Romance* by Jean de Meun also describes a dream. But here allegorical characters give long didactic speeches, providing a social satire on a variety of themes, some pertaining to women. Love is an anxious and tormented state, the poem explains: women are greedy and manipulative, marriage is miserable, beautiful women are lustful, ugly ones cease to please, and a chaste woman is as rare as a black swan.

Shortly after Jean de Meun completed *The Romance of the Rose*, Mathéolus penned his *Lamentations*, a long Latin diatribe against marriage translated into French about a century later. The *Lamentations* sum up medieval attitudes toward women and provoked the important response by Christine de Pizan in her *Book of the City of Ladies*.

In 1355, Giovanni Boccaccio wrote *Il Corbaccio*, another antifeminist manifesto, although ironically by an author whose other works pioneered new directions in Renaissance thought. The former husband of his lover appears to Boccaccio, condemning his unmoderated lust and detailing the defects of women. Boccaccio concedes at the end "how much men naturally surpass women in nobility" and is cured of his desires.[3]

---

3. Giovanni Boccaccio, *The Corbaccio, or The Labyrinth of Love*, trans. and ed. Anthony K. Cassell, rev. ed. (Binghamton, N.Y., 1993), 71.

WOMEN'S ROLES: THE FAMILY. The negative perceptions of women expressed in the intellectual tradition are also implicit in the actual roles that women played in European society. Assigned to subordinate positions in the household and the church, they were barred from significant participation in public life.

Medieval European households, like those in antiquity and in non-Western civilizations, were headed by males. It was the male serf (or peasant), feudal lord, town merchant, or citizen who was polled or taxed or succeeded to an inheritance or had any acknowledged public role, although his wife or widow could stand as a temporary surrogate. From about 1100, the position of property-holding males was further enhanced: inheritance was confined to the male, or agnate, line—with depressing consequences for women.

A wife never fully belonged to her husband's family, nor was she a daughter to her father's family. She left her father's house young to marry whomever her parents chose. Her dowry was managed by her husband, and at her death it normally passed to her children by him.

A married woman's life was occupied nearly constantly with cycles of pregnancy, childbearing, and lactation. Women bore children through all the years of their fertility, and many died in childbirth. They were also responsible for raising young children up to six or seven. In the propertied classes that responsibility was shared, since it was common for a wet nurse to take over breast-feeding and for servants to perform other chores.

Women trained their daughters in the household duties appropriate to their status, nearly always tasks associated with textiles: spinning, weaving, sewing, embroidering. Their sons were sent out of the house as apprentices or students, or their training was assumed by fathers in later childhood and adolescence. On the death of her husband, a woman's children became the responsibility of his family. She generally did not take "his" children with her to a new marriage or back to her father's house, except sometimes in the artisan classes.

Women also worked. Rural peasants performed farm chores, merchant wives often practiced their husbands' trades, the unmarried daughters of the urban poor worked as servants or prostitutes. All wives produced or embellished textiles and did the housekeeping, while wealthy ones managed servants. These labors were unpaid or poorly paid but often contributed substantially to family wealth.

WOMEN'S ROLES: THE CHURCH. Membership in a household, whether a father's or a husband's, meant for women a lifelong subordination to others.

In western Europe, the Roman Catholic Church offered an alternative to the career of wife and mother. A woman could enter a convent, parallel in function to the monasteries for men that evolved in the early Christian centuries.

In the convent, a woman pledged herself to a celibate life, lived according to strict community rules, and worshiped daily. Often the convent offered training in Latin, allowing some women to become considerable scholars and authors as well as scribes, artists, and musicians. For women who chose the conventual life, the benefits could be enormous, but for numerous others placed in convents by paternal choice, the life could be restrictive and burdensome.

The conventual life declined as an alternative for women as the modern age approached. Reformed monastic institutions resisted responsibility for related female orders. The church increasingly restricted female institutional life by insisting on closer male supervision.

Women often sought other options. Some joined the communities of laywomen that sprang up spontaneously in the thirteenth century in the urban zones of western Europe, especially in Flanders and Italy. Some joined the heretical movements that flourished in late medieval Christendom, whose anticlerical and often antifamily positions particularly appealed to women. In these communities, some women were acclaimed as "holy women" or "saints," whereas others often were condemned as frauds or heretics.

In all, although the options offered to women by the church were sometimes less than satisfactory, they were sometimes richly rewarding. After 1520, the convent remained an option only in Roman Catholic territories. Protestantism engendered an ideal of marriage as a heroic endeavor and appeared to place husband and wife on a more equal footing. Sermons and treatises, however, still called for female subordination and obedience.

THE OTHER VOICE, 1300–1700

When the modern era opened, European culture was so firmly structured by a framework of negative attitudes toward women that to dismantle it was a monumental labor. The process began as part of a larger cultural movement that entailed the critical reexamination of ideas inherited from the ancient and medieval past. The humanists launched that critical reexamination.

THE HUMANIST FOUNDATION. Originating in Italy in the fourteenth century, humanism quickly became the dominant intellectual movement in

Europe. Spreading in the sixteenth century from Italy to the rest of Europe, it fueled the literary, scientific, and philosophical movements of the era and laid the basis for the eighteenth-century Enlightenment.

Humanists regarded the Scholastic philosophy of medieval universities as out of touch with the realities of urban life. They found in the rhetorical discourse of classical Rome a language adapted to civic life and public speech. They learned to read, speak, and write classical Latin and, eventually, classical Greek. They founded schools to teach others to do so, establishing the pattern for elementary and secondary education for the next three hundred years.

In the service of complex government bureaucracies, humanists employed their skills to write eloquent letters, deliver public orations, and formulate public policy. They developed new scripts for copying manuscripts and used the new printing press to disseminate texts, for which they created methods of critical editing.

Humanism was a movement led by males who accepted the evaluation of women in ancient texts and generally shared the misogynist perceptions of their culture. (Female humanists, as we will see, did not.) Yet humanism also opened the door to a reevaluation of the nature and capacity of women. By calling authors, texts, and ideas into question, it made possible the fundamental rereading of the whole intellectual tradition that was required in order to free women from cultural prejudice and social subordination.

A DIFFERENT CITY. The other voice first appeared when, after so many centuries, the accumulation of misogynist concepts evoked a response from a capable female defender: Christine de Pizan (1365–1431). Introducing her *Book of the City of Ladies* (1405), she described how she was affected by reading Mathéolus's *Lamentations*: "Just the sight of this book . . . made me wonder how it happened that so many different men . . . are so inclined to express both in speaking and in their treatises and writings so many wicked insults about women and their behavior."[4] These statements impelled her to detest herself "and the entire feminine sex, as though we were monstrosities in nature."[5]

The rest of *The Book of the City of Ladies* presents a justification of the female sex and a vision of an ideal community of women. A pioneer, she has received the message of female inferiority and rejected it. From the fourteenth

---

4. Christine de Pizan, *The Book of the City of Ladies*, trans. Earl Jeffrey Richards, foreword by Marina Warner (New York, 1982), 1.1.1, pp. 3–4.

5. Ibid., 1.1.1–2, p. 5.

to the seventeenth century, a huge body of literature accumulated that responded to the dominant tradition.

The result was a literary explosion consisting of works by both men and women, in Latin and in the vernaculars: works enumerating the achievements of notable women; works rebutting the main accusations made against women; works arguing for the equal education of men and women; works defining and redefining women's proper role in the family, at court, in public; works describing women's lives and experiences. Recent monographs and articles have begun to hint at the great range of this movement, involving probably several thousand titles. The protofeminism of these "other voices" constitutes a significant fraction of the literary product of the early modern era.

THE CATALOGS. About 1365, the same Boccaccio whose *Corbaccio* rehearses the usual charges against female nature wrote another work, *Concerning Famous Women*. A humanist treatise drawing on classical texts, it praised 106 notable women: ninety-eight of them from pagan Greek and Roman antiquity, one (Eve) from the Bible, and seven from the medieval religious and cultural tradition; his book helped make all readers aware of a sex normally condemned or forgotten. Boccaccio's outlook nevertheless was unfriendly to women, for it singled out for praise those women who possessed the traditional virtues of chastity, silence, and obedience. Women who were active in the public realm—for example, rulers and warriors—were depicted as usually being lascivious and as suffering terrible punishments for entering the masculine sphere. Women were his subject, but Boccaccio's standard remained male.

Christine de Pizan's *Book of the City of Ladies* contains a second catalog, one responding specifically to Boccaccio's. Whereas Boccaccio portrays female virtue as exceptional, she depicts it as universal. Many women in history were leaders, or remained chaste despite the lascivious approaches of men, or were visionaries and brave martyrs.

The work of Boccaccio inspired a series of catalogs of illustrious women of the biblical, classical, Christian, and local pasts, among them Filippo da Bergamo's *Of Illustrious Women*, Pierre de Brantôme's *Lives of Illustrious Women*, Pierre Le Moyne's *Gallerie of Heroic Women*, and Pietro Paolo de Ribera's *Immortal Triumphs and Heroic Enterprises of 845 Women*. Whatever their embedded prejudices, these works drove home to the public the possibility of female excellence.

THE DEBATE. At the same time, many questions remained: Could a woman be virtuous? Could she perform noteworthy deeds? Was she even, strictly speaking, of the same human species as men? These questions were debated over four centuries, in French, German, Italian, Spanish, and English, by authors male and female, among Catholics, Protestants, and Jews, in ponderous volumes and breezy pamphlets. The whole literary genre has been called the *querelle des femmes*, the "woman question."

The opening volley of this battle occurred in the first years of the fifteenth century, in a literary debate sparked by Christine de Pizan. She exchanged letters critical of Jean de Meun's contribution to *The Romance of the Rose* with two French royal secretaries, Jean de Montreuil and Gontier Col. When the matter became public, Jean Gerson, one of Europe's leading theologians, supported de Pizan's arguments against de Meun, for the moment silencing the opposition.

The debate resurfaced repeatedly over the next two hundred years. *The Triumph of Women* (1438) by Juan Rodríguez de la Camara (or Juan Rodríguez del Padron) struck a new note by presenting arguments for the superiority of women to men. *The Champion of Women* (1440–42) by Martin Le Franc addresses once again the negative views of women presented in *The Romance of the Rose* and offers counterevidence of female virtue and achievement.

A cameo of the debate on women is included in *The Courtier*, one of the most widely read books of the era, published by the Italian Baldassare Castiglione in 1528 and immediately translated into other European vernaculars. *The Courtier* depicts a series of evenings at the court of the duke of Urbino in which many men and some women of the highest social stratum amuse themselves by discussing a range of literary and social issues. The "woman question" is a pervasive theme throughout, and the third of its four books is devoted entirely to that issue.

In a verbal duel, Gasparo Pallavicino and Giuliano de' Medici present the main claims of the two traditions. Gasparo argues the innate inferiority of women and their inclination to vice. Only in bearing children do they profit the world. Giuliano counters that women share the same spiritual and mental capacities as men and may excel in wisdom and action. Men and women are of the same essence: just as no stone can be more perfectly a stone than another, so no human being can be more perfectly human than others, whether male or female. It was an astonishing assertion, boldly made to an audience as large as all Europe.

THE TREATISES. Humanism provided the materials for a positive counterconcept to the misogyny embedded in Scholastic philosophy and law and inherited from the Greek, Roman, and Christian pasts. A series of humanist treatises on marriage and family, on education and deportment, and on the nature of women helped construct these new perspectives.

The works by Francesco Barbaro and Leon Battista Alberti—*On Marriage* (1415) and *On the Family* (1434–37)—far from defending female equality, reasserted women's responsibility for rearing children and managing the housekeeping while being obedient, chaste, and silent. Nevertheless, they served the cause of reexamining the issue of women's nature by placing domestic issues at the center of scholarly concern and reopening the pertinent classical texts. In addition, Barbaro emphasized the companionate nature of marriage and the importance of a wife's spiritual and mental qualities for the well-being of the family.

These themes reappear in later humanist works on marriage and the education of women by Juan Luis Vives and Erasmus. Both were moderately sympathetic to the condition of women without reaching beyond the usual masculine prescriptions for female behavior.

An outlook more favorable to women characterizes the nearly unknown work *In Praise of Women* (ca. 1487) by the Italian humanist Bartolommeo Goggio. In addition to providing a catalog of illustrious women, Goggio argued that male and female are the same in essence, but that women (reworking the Adam and Eve narrative from quite a new angle) are actually superior. In the same vein, the Italian humanist Maria Equicola asserted the spiritual equality of men and women in *On Women* (1501). In 1525, Galeazzo Flavio Capra (or Capella) published his work *On the Excellence and Dignity of Women*. This humanist tradition of treatises defending the worthiness of women culminates in the work of Henricus Cornelius Agrippa *On the Nobility and Preeminence of the Female Sex*. No work by a male humanist more succinctly or explicitly presents the case for female dignity.

THE WITCH BOOKS. While humanists grappled with the issues pertaining to women and family, other learned men turned their attention to what they perceived as a very great problem: witches. Witch-hunting manuals, explorations of the witch phenomenon, and even defenses of witches are not at first glance pertinent to the tradition of the other voice. But they do relate in this way: most accused witches were women. The hostility aroused by supposed witch activity is comparable to the hostility aroused by women. The evil deeds the victims of the hunt were charged with were exaggerations of the vices to which, many believed, all women were prone.

The connection between the witch accusation and the hatred of women is explicit in the notorious witch-hunting manual *The Hammer of Witches* (1486) by two Dominican inquisitors, Heinrich Krämer and Jacob Sprenger. Here the inconstancy, deceitfulness, and lustfulness traditionally associated with women are depicted in exaggerated form as the core features of witch behavior. These traits inclined women to make a bargain with the devil—sealed by sexual intercourse—by which they acquired unholy powers. Such bizarre claims, far from being rejected by rational men, were broadcast by intellectuals. The German Ulrich Molitur, the Frenchman Nicolas Rémy, and the Italian Stefano Guazzo all coolly informed the public of sinister orgies and midnight pacts with the devil. The celebrated French jurist, historian, and political philosopher Jean Bodin argued that because women were especially prone to diabolism, regular legal procedures could properly be suspended in order to try those accused of this "exceptional crime."

A few experts such as the physician Johann Weyer, a student of Agrippa's, raised their voices in protest. In 1563, he explained the witch phenomenon thus, without discarding belief in diabolism: the devil deluded foolish old women afflicted by melancholia, causing them to believe they had magical powers. Weyer's rational skepticism, which had good credibility in the community of the learned, worked to revise the conventional views of women and witchcraft.

WOMEN'S WORKS. To the many categories of works produced on the question of women's worth must be added nearly all works written by women. A woman writing was in herself a statement of women's claim to dignity.

Only a few women wrote anything before the dawn of the modern era, for three reasons. First, they rarely received the education that would enable them to write. Second, they were not admitted to the public roles—as administrator, bureaucrat, lawyer or notary, or university professor—in which they might gain knowledge of the kinds of things the literate public thought worth writing about. Third, the culture imposed silence on women, considering speaking out a form of unchastity. Given these conditions, it is remarkable that any women wrote. Those who did before the fourteenth century were almost always nuns or religious women whose isolation made their pronouncements more acceptable.

From the fourteenth century on, the volume of women's writings rose. Women continued to write devotional literature, although not always as cloistered nuns. They also wrote diaries, often intended as keepsakes for their children; books of advice to their sons and daughters; letters to family members and friends; and family memoirs, in a few cases elaborate enough to be considered histories.

A few women wrote works directly concerning the "woman question," and some of these, such as the humanists Isotta Nogarola, Cassandra Fedele, Laura Cereta, and Olympia Morata, were highly trained. A few were professional writers, living by the income of their pens; the very first among them was Christine de Pizan, noteworthy in this context as in so many others. In addition to *The Book of the City of Ladies* and her critiques of *The Romance of the Rose*, she wrote *The Treasure of the City of Ladies* (a guide to social decorum for women), an advice book for her son, much courtly verse, and a full-scale history of the reign of King Charles V of France.

WOMEN PATRONS. Women who did not themselves write but encouraged others to do so boosted the development of an alternative tradition. Highly placed women patrons supported authors, artists, musicians, poets, and learned men. Such patrons, drawn mostly from the Italian elites and the courts of northern Europe, figure disproportionately as the dedicatees of the important works of early feminism.

For a start, it might be noted that the catalogs of Boccaccio and Alvaro de Luna were dedicated to the Florentine noblewoman Andrea Acciaiuoli and to Doña María, first wife of King Juan II of Castile, while the French translation of Boccaccio's work was commissioned by Anne of Brittany, wife of King Charles VIII of France. The humanist treatises of Goggio, Equicola, Vives, and Agrippa were dedicated, respectively, to Eleanora of Aragon, wife of Ercole I d'Este, Duke of Ferrara; to Margherita Cantelma of Mantua; to Catherine of Aragon, wife of King Henry VIII of England; and to Margaret, Duchess of Austria and regent of the Netherlands. As late as 1696, Mary Astell's *Serious Proposal to the Ladies, for the Advancement of Their True and Greatest Interest* was dedicated to Princess Anne of Denmark.

These authors presumed that their efforts would be welcome to female patrons, or they may have written at the bidding of those patrons. Silent themselves, perhaps even unresponsive, these loftily placed women helped shape the tradition of the other voice.

THE ISSUES. The literary forms and patterns in which the tradition of the other voice presented itself have now been sketched. It remains to highlight the major issues around which this tradition crystallizes. In brief, there are four problems to which our authors return again and again, in plays and catalogs, in verse and letters, in treatises and dialogues, in every language: the problem of chastity, the problem of power, the problem of speech, and the problem of knowledge. Of these the greatest, preconditioning the others, is the problem of chastity.

THE PROBLEM OF CHASTITY. In traditional European culture, as in those of antiquity and others around the globe, chastity was perceived as woman's quintessential virtue—in contrast to courage, or generosity, or leadership, or rationality, seen as virtues characteristic of men. Opponents of women charged them with insatiable lust. Women themselves and their defenders—without disputing the validity of the standard—responded that women were capable of chastity.

The requirement of chastity kept women at home, silenced them, isolated them, left them in ignorance. It was the source of all other impediments. Why was it so important to the society of men, of whom chastity was not required, and who more often than not considered it their right to violate the chastity of any woman they encountered?

Female chastity ensured the continuity of the male-headed household. If a man's wife was not chaste, he could not be sure of the legitimacy of his offspring. If they were not his and they acquired his property, it was not his household, but some other man's, that had endured. If his daughter was not chaste, she could not be transferred to another man's household as his wife, and he was dishonored.

The whole system of the integrity of the household and the transmission of property was bound up in female chastity. Such a requirement pertained only to property-owning classes, of course. Poor women could not expect to maintain their chastity, least of all if they were in contact with high-status men to whom all women but those of their own household were prey.

In Catholic Europe, the requirement of chastity was further buttressed by moral and religious imperatives. Original sin was inextricably linked with the sexual act. Virginity was seen as heroic virtue, far more impressive than, say, the avoidance of idleness or greed. Monasticism, the cultural institution that dominated medieval Europe for centuries, was grounded in the renunciation of the flesh. The Catholic reform of the eleventh century imposed a similar standard on all the clergy and a heightened awareness of sexual requirements on all the laity. Although men were asked to be chaste, female unchastity was much worse: it led to the devil, as Eve had led mankind to sin.

To such requirements, women and their defenders protested their innocence. Furthermore, following the example of holy women who had escaped the requirements of family and sought the religious life, some women began to conceive of female communities as alternatives both to family and to the cloister. Christine de Pizan's city of ladies was such a community. Moderata Fonte and Mary Astell envisioned others. The luxurious salons of the French *précieuses* of the seventeenth century, or the comfortable English drawing rooms of the next, may have been born of the same impulse. Here women not only might escape, if briefly, the subordinate position that life in the family entailed but might also make claims to power, exercise their capacity for speech, and display their knowledge.

THE PROBLEM OF POWER. Women were excluded from power: the whole cultural tradition insisted on it. Only men were citizens, only men bore arms, only men could be chiefs or lords or kings. There were exceptions that did not disprove the rule, when wives or widows or mothers took the place of men, awaiting their return or the maturation of a male heir. A woman who attempted to rule in her own right was perceived as an anomaly, a monster, at once a deformed woman and an insufficient male, sexually confused and consequently unsafe.

The association of such images with women who held or sought power explains some otherwise odd features of early modern culture. Queen Elizabeth I of England, one of the few women to hold full regal authority in European history, played with such male/female images—positive ones, of course—in representing herself to her subjects. She was a prince, and manly, even though she was female. She was also (she claimed) virginal, a condition absolutely essential if she was to avoid the attacks of her opponents. Catherine de' Medici, who ruled France as widow and regent for her sons, also adopted such imagery in defining her position. She chose as one symbol the figure of Artemisia, an androgynous ancient warrior-heroine who combined a female persona with masculine powers.

Power in a woman, without such sexual imagery, seems to have been indigestible by the culture. A rare note was struck by the Englishman Sir Thomas Elyot in his *Defence of Good Women* (1540), justifying both women's participation in civic life and their prowess in arms. The old tune was sung by the Scots reformer John Knox in his *First Blast of the Trumpet against the Monstrous Regiment of Women* (1558); for him rule by women, defects in nature, was a hideous contradiction in terms.

The confused sexuality of the imagery of female potency was not reserved for rulers. Any woman who excelled was likely to be called an Amazon, recalling the self-mutilated warrior women of antiquity who repudiated all men, gave up their sons, and raised only their daughters. She was often said to have "exceeded her sex" or to have possessed "masculine virtue"—as the very fact of conspicuous excellence conferred masculinity even on the female subject. The catalogs of notable women often showed those female heroes dressed in armor, armed to the teeth, like men. Amazonian heroines romp through the epics of the age—Ariosto's *Orlando Furioso* (1532) and Spenser's *Faerie Queene* (1590–1609). Excellence in a woman was perceived as a claim for power, and power was reserved for the masculine realm. A woman who possessed either one was masculinized and lost title to her own female identity.

THE PROBLEM OF SPEECH. Just as power had a sexual dimension when it was claimed by women, so did speech. A good woman spoke little. Excessive speech was an indication of unchastity. By speech, women seduced men. Eve had lured Adam into sin by her speech. Accused witches were commonly accused of having spoken abusively, or irrationally, or simply too much. As enlightened a figure as Francesco Barbaro insisted on silence in a woman, which he linked to her perfect unanimity with her husband's will and her unblemished virtue (her chastity). Another Italian humanist, Leonardo Bruni, in advising a noblewoman on her studies, barred her not from speech but from public speaking. That was reserved for men.

Related to the problem of speech was that of costume—another, if silent, form of self-expression. Assigned the task of pleasing men as their primary occupation, elite women often tended toward elaborate costume, hairdressing, and the use of cosmetics. Clergy and secular moralists alike condemned these practices. The appropriate function of costume and adornment was to announce the status of a woman's husband or father. Any further indulgence in adornment was akin to unchastity.

THE PROBLEM OF KNOWLEDGE. When the Italian noblewoman Isotta Nogarola had begun to attain a reputation as a humanist, she was accused of incest—a telling instance of the association of learning in women with unchastity. That chilling association inclined any woman who was educated to deny that she was or to make exaggerated claims of heroic chastity.

If educated women were pursued with suspicions of sexual misconduct, women seeking an education faced an even more daunting obstacle: the assumption that women were by nature incapable of learning, that reasoning was a particularly masculine ability. Just as they proclaimed their chastity, women and their defenders insisted on their capacity for learning. The major work by a male writer on female education—that by Juan Luis Vives, *On the Education of a Christian Woman* (1523)—granted female capacity for intellection but still argued that a woman's whole education was to be shaped around the requirement of chastity and a future within the household. Female writers of the following generations—Marie de Gournay in France, Anna Maria van Schurman in Holland, and Mary Astell in England—began to envision other possibilities.

The pioneers of female education were the Italian women humanists who managed to attain a literacy in Latin and a knowledge of classical and Christian literature equivalent to that of prominent men. Their works implicitly and explicitly raise questions about women's social roles, defining problems that beset women attempting to break out of the cultural limits that had bound them. Like Christine de Pizan, who achieved an advanced educa-

tion through her father's tutoring and her own devices, their bold question-
ing makes clear the importance of training. Only when women were educated to the same standard as male leaders would they be able to raise that
other voice and insist on their dignity as human beings morally, intellectu-
ally, and legally equal to men.

THE OTHER VOICE. The other voice, a voice of protest, was mostly female, but it was also male. It spoke in the vernaculars and in Latin, in treatises
and dialogues, in plays and poetry, in letters and diaries, and in pamphlets. It
battered at the wall of prejudice that encircled women and raised a banner
announcing its claims. The female was equal (or even superior) to the male
in essential nature—moral, spiritual, and intellectual. Women were capable
of higher education, of holding positions of power and influence in the
public realm, and of speaking and writing persuasively. The last bastion of
masculine supremacy, centered on the notions of a woman's primary domestic responsibility and the requirement of female chastity, was not as yet assaulted—although visions of productive female communities as alternatives
to the family indicated an awareness of the problem.

During the period 1300–1700, the other voice remained only a voice,
and one only dimly heard. It did not result—yet—in an alteration of social
patterns. Indeed, to this day they have not entirely been altered. Yet the call
for justice issued as long as six centuries ago by those writing in the tradition
of the other voice must be recognized as the source and origin of the mature
feminist tradition and of the realignment of social institutions accomplished
in the modern age.

We thank the volume editors in this series, who responded with many suggestions to an earlier draft of this introduction, making it a collaborative enterprise. Many of their suggestions and criticisms have resulted in revisions
of this introduction, although we remain responsible for the final product.

PROJECTED TITLES IN THE SERIES

Francesco Barbaro et al., *On Marriage and the Family*, edited and translated by Margaret L. King

Laura Battiferra, *Selected Poetry, Prose, and Letters*, edited and translated by Victoria Kirkham

Francesco Buoninsegni and Arcangela Tarabotti, *Menippean Satire: "Against Feminine Extravagance" and "Antisatire,"* edited and translated by Elissa Weaver

Rosalba Carriera, *Letters, Diaries, and Art*, edited and translated by Catherine M. Sama

Madame du Chatelet, *Selected Works*, edited by Judith Zinsser

Vittoria Colonna, *Sonnets for Michelangelo: A Bilingual Edition*, edited and translated by Abigail Brundin

Vittoria Colonna, Chiara Matraini, and Lucrezia Marinella, *Marian Writings*, edited and translated by Susan Haskins

Princess Elizabeth of Bohemia, *Correspondence with Descartes*, edited and translated by Lisa Shapiro

Isabella d'Este, *Selected Letters*, edited and translated by Deanna Shemek

Fairy-Tales by Seventeenth-Century French Women Writers, edited and translated by Lewis Seifert and Domna C. Stanton

Moderata Fonte, *Floridoro*, edited by Valeria Finucci and translated by Julia Kisacki

Moderata Fonte and Lucrezia Marinella, *Religious Narratives*, edited and translated by Virginia Cox

Francisca de los Apóstoles, *The Inquisition of Francisca: A Sixteenth-Century Visionary on Trial*, edited and translated by Gillian T. W. Ahlgren

Catharina Regina von Greiffenberg, *Meditations on the Life of Christ*, edited and translated by Lynne Tatlock

In Praise of Women: Italian Fifteenth-Century Defenses of Women, edited and translated by Daniel Bornstein

Louise Labé, *Complete Works*, edited and translated by Annie Finch and Deborah Baker

Lucrezia Marinella, *L'Enrico, or Byzantium Conquered*, edited and translated by Virginia Cox

Lucrezia Marinella, *Happy Arcadia*, edited and translated by Susan Haskins and Letizia Panizza

Chiara Matraini, *Selected Poetry and Prose*, edited and translated by Elaine MacLachlan

Eleonora Petersen von Merlau, *The Life of Lady Johanna Eleonora Petersen, Written by Herself: Pietism and Women's Autobiography in Seventeenth-Century Germany*, edited and translated by Barbara Becker-Cantarino

Alessandro Piccolomini, *Rethinking Marriage in Sixteenth-Century Italy*, edited and translated by Letizia Panizza

Christine de Pizan et al., *Debate over the "Romance of the Rose,"* edited and translated by Tom Conley and Virginia Greene

Christine de Pizan, *Life of Charles V*, edited and translated by Nadia Margolis

Christine de Pizan, *The Long Road of Learning*, edited and translated by Andrea Tarnowski

Madeleine and Catherine des Roches, *Selected Letters, Dialogues, and Poems*, edited and translated by Anne Larsen

Oliva Sabuco, *The New Philosophy: True Medicine*, edited and translated by Gianna Pomata

Margherita Sarrocchi, *La Scanderbeide*, edited and translated by Rinaldina Russell

Justine Siegemund, *The Court Midwife*, edited and translated by Lynne Tatlock

Gabrielle Suchon, *"On Philosophy" and "On Morality,"* edited and translated by Domna Stanton with Rebecca Wilkin

Sara Copio Sullam, *Sara Copio Sullam: Jewish Poet and Intellectual in Early Seventeenth-Century Venice*, edited and translated by Don Harrán

Arcangela Tarrabotti, *Convent Life as Inferno: A Report*, introduction and notes by Francesca Medioli, translated by Letizia Panizza

Laura Terracina, *Works*, edited and translated by Michael Sherberg

Katharina Schütz Zell, *Selected Writings*, edited and translated by Elsie McKee

GIULIA BIGOLINA AND ITALIAN PROSE FICTION IN THE RENAISSANCE

THE OTHER VOICE

Giulia Bigolina (ca. 1518–ca. 1569) was a polished writer of prose fiction whose name and work have been recovered only very recently.[1] Although known in her lifetime and admired for her learning, she never published any of her work. Her first printed composition, a novella entitled "Giulia Camposampiero and Tesibaldo Vitaliani," which seems to be part of a longer narrative that was perhaps lost for good, appeared only at the end of the eighteenth century. From then on, there was almost total silence surrounding her persona, and she even began to be confused with a relative of the same name. Yet in the archives of the Biblioteca Trivulziana in Milan and in an eighteenth-century copy at the Vatican Library in Rome, there is the manuscript that was to become her claim to fame, a long prose romance entitled *Urania* that was published for the first time in 2002.[2] Currently, this romance constitutes, together with the novella "Giulia," the first fiction in prose authored by a woman writer in Italian.

Inside *Urania* there is also a short treatise on the worth of women. This is chronologically another first in Italy, predating Moderata Fonte's more complex *The Worth of Women* by perhaps 40 years. Therefore, *Urania* can be studied not only for its fictionalized rendering of a woman writer's peregrination through the country in search of herself, but also because it constitutes

---

1. All contemporary references to this writer are in the feminine form of Bigolina, as usual for women during the Renaissance. This is the form also used in the only writing ever published under her name and the one I am choosing. As was customary for Venetian and Veneto surnames, the family name would have been spelled Bigolino when referring to only one member and Bigolin or Bigolini when referring to all.

2. Giulia Bigolina, *Urania*, ed. Valeria Finucci (Rome: Bulzoni, 2002). I refer the reader to that book for a wealth of detailed information not offered here. The present essay is a much revised and shortened version of my introduction there, "Giulia Bigolina e il romanzo in prosa," pp. 13–68.

the first feminist entry into the debate on a woman's proper place—politically, culturally, and philosophically—in early modern Italian society.

The prowoman development of *Urania* definitively makes Bigolina a resonant "other voice" of the European early modern period. It is unfortunate that the decade in which she did most of her writing, the 1550s, was to become notorious in Italy for the works that were *not* published, as presses became progressively more cautious in bringing out books in light of a powerful Counter-Reformation thrust to control the intelligentsia.[3] But the 1550s was also the decade in which new experiments in long prose narrative by writers like Bigolina from Venice and the Veneto region took place; these set the stage for the development of the Baroque romance—today's psychological novel.

BIOGRAPHY

We know very little about Giulia Bigolina.[4] She belonged to a noble Paduan family whose origins went as far back as 1297 and was the daughter of Gero-

---

3. The number of books in print by the middle of the sixteenth century was in any case limited, even though these were the years in which the editors Francesco Marcolini, Gabriel Giolito, and Michele Tramezzino enjoyed considerable success. A list that is divided into genres in volume 1 of Anton Francesco Doni's *La Libraria* (1550) gives only five hundred titles. See also Salvatore Bongi, *Annali di Gabriel Giolito de' Ferrari* (Rome: Presso i Principali Librai, 1890–95), 2: 39. Concentrating on Venice, Paul Grendler argues that by the end of the sixteenth century it was possible to read all kinds of books, whether printed in Italy or illegally imported, and therefore that censorship had not been very successful. See Paul Grendler, *The Roman Inquisition and the Venetian Press. 1540–1650* (Princeton: Princeton University Press, 1977). For a more pessimistic view of what censorship does to culture and how it determines what an author writes or chooses not to write, see Romeo De Maio, *Riforme e miti nella chiesa del Cinquecento* (Naples: Guida, 1992); Nicola Longo, "La letteratura proibita," in *Letteratura italiana V. Le Questioni*, ed. Alberto Asor Rosa (Turin: Einaudi, 1986), esp. 983–84; and Armando Balduino, "Fortune e sfortune della novella italiana fra tardo Trecento e primo Cinquecento," in *La Nouvelle: Genèse, codification et rayonnement d'un genre medieval*, ed. Michelangelo Picone, Giuseppe Di Stefano, and Pamela Stewart (Montreal: Plato Academic Press, 1983), 155–73. After all, there were 290 forbidden authors listed on the Index of 1554, and Boccaccio was put on the Index in that very decade as well.

4. In fact, until I worked closely at reconstructing her life for my Italian edition of *Urania*, even the official biographical data regarding her were wrong. From the information explaining why a street was named after her in Padua, we learn that she was born in 1563 and died in 1623 and that she was a gentlewoman with surprising skills in writing prose, just as the other most important Paduan woman of the time, Gaspara Stampa, was skilled in composing poetry. See Giovanni Saggiori, ed., *Padova nella storia delle sue strade* (Padua: Piazzon, 1972), 45; and Marisa Milani, "Isabella, Margherita, Perina la Flamenga: Storie di donne fra letteratura e documenti," in *Tracciati del femminile a Padova: Immagini e storie di donne*, ed. Caterina Limentani and Mirella Cisotto Nalon (Padua: Il Poligrafo, 1995), 59. But this reference mistakes Giulia Bigolina, the writer, for the daughter of a cousin's son, Polo, who happened to have the same name, although she did not write. To be sure, the only genealogical tree we have of the Bigolini family does not mention our Giulia, but names the other. Still there are so few women mentioned in the entire tree that one wonders why any importance should be attached to it. See Archivio di Stato di Padova (here-

lamo Bigolin and Alvisa Soncin, who must have been married by 1516, since Alvisa's dowry was paid off that year.[5] We do not know how many children they had, but in addition to Giulia, only a younger son, Socrate, born in 1523, reached adulthood. We do not know the precise dates of Giulia's birth either, but we do know that by 1534 she was married to Bartolomeo Vicomercato because he received her dowry that year.[6] Vicomercato was a lawyer from Crema, Lombardy, and we find him listed as a law student at the Studio (University) in Padua in 1533.[7] Thus, in the absence of any precise documentation, I hypothesize that she married at the usual age for Venetian noblewomen in the sixteenth century, at fifteen or sixteen, and therefore that the year of her birth was somewhere around 1518–19.[8]

Although there are many documents about her mother and her brother, those regarding Giulia are scarce and are mostly dated 1542, when a series of notarized acts chronicled the exchange of some of her farming property,

---

after ASP), *Prove di Nobiltà*, 146, no page number. For the scarcity of data on women in official documents or even in family records (the births and deaths of all daughters were often not entered in the family Bible), see James Grubb, *Provincial Families of the Italian Renaissance: Private and Public Life in the Veneto* (Baltimore: Johns Hopkins University Press, 1996), 55–57. Of this second Giulia Bigolina we have a land tax survey of 1609 in ASP, *Estimo* 1518, 134r–135v. Her death is in *Libro morti*, 2449, as registered in ASP, *Opuscoli*, c. 76, and reprinted in *Genealogia dei Camposampiero*, years 993–1956, which again confuses dates and identities. The fact that this second Giulia was married to a Camposampiero and that the only novella by our writer is entitled "Giulia Camposampiero" has obviously added to the confusion.

5. See ASP, AN, 5208, 245r and 490r. Alvisa's dowry was paid on March 5, 1516. See ASP, AN, 4839, 697r. In a tax survey of 1518 concerned with the property Alvisa brought in dowry, Gerolamo declared that he had five children ("Item ho fioli cinque"), so this probably was not his first marriage. See ASP, Estimo (ES), 1518, busta 34, c. 121r. On the family, see Attilio Simioni, *Storia di Padova. Dalle origini alla fine del secolo XVIII* (Padova: Randi, 1968), 825; and more generally, Vincenzo Mancini, *Lambert Sustris a Padova. La villa Bigolin a Selvazzano* (Comune di Selvazzano Centro: Biblioteca Pubblica Comunale, 1994). Their ancestral place was the town of Bigolino. See Guido Beltrame, *Toponomastica della diocesi di Padova* (Padua: Libreria Padovana, 1992), 22. On the Soncin family, see Biblioteca Civica, Padua (hereafter BCP), BP 1232, f. 445.

6. See ASP, AN, 4830, 827r. Her father Gerolamo was already dead. Dowries were usually given out soon after the marriage took place. See Grubb, *Provincial Families*, 11.

7. See Elda Martellozzo Fiorin, ed., *Acta Graduum Academicorum ab anno 1526 ad annum 1537* (Padua: Antenore, 1970), entry 1962, August 26, 1533, pp. 295–96. Bartolomeo's professor was Mario Socino (Soncino or Soncin), Bigolina's relative from her mother's side.

8. By the sixteenth century, Venetian noblewomen usually married between the ages of fourteen and sixteen, preferably closer to sixteen. See Stanley Chojnacki, *Women and Men in Renaissance Venice: Twelve Essays on Patrician Society* (Baltimore: Johns Hopkins University Press, 2000), 175 and 313. In Florence, women married slightly later, between seventeen and eighteen. See Julius Kirshner and Anthony Molho, "Il monte delle doti a Firenze dalla sua fondazione nel 1425 alla metà del sedicesimo secolo: abbozzo di una ricerca," *Ricerche storiche* 10 (1980): 21–47, esp. 41 and fig. 8. Giulia's brother, Socrate, married at eighteen, quite early for men, so it does appear reasonable to suggest that Giulia could have been married at sixteen. On Socrate's wedding, see ASP, AN, 5206, ff. 303r–304v.

which she brought to her marriage in dowry, with that of her brother in the region of Montagnana and Camposampiero.[9] We do not know when Bigolina became a widow, but her husband was still alive in 1555 because the treatise "A ragionar d'amore," in which she appears as one of the three interlocutors, mentions him, as I shall describe below. In any case, she was a widow by 1559 or at the latest by 1561, because she did not mention her husband in a detailed tax survey of her property at that time. Once widowed, she did not remarry.[10] We know of a son, Silvio, who presented the "estimo" of his mother's property in 1561.[11] He was probably the son to whom Bigolina referred in a letter to the famous mathematician Francesco Barozzi, who invited her to a performance in his house in Padua of a comedy he had written.[12] This letter constitutes the last piece of information we have about Bigolina. We

9. See ASP, AN, 3699, 437r; ASP, AN, 5208, 246r–247v; ASP, AN, 5208, 295v–297v; ASP, AN, 5208, 490r–494v; ASP, AN, 3699, 437v. Although we are not told how much of Bigolina's dowry was in liquid assets and how much in landed property, we know that there was a lack of liquidity in the region in those years and thus it had become customary to dower property rather than money. Restrictions on the use of a dowry on the husband's part (he could administer it and employ the income coming from it for his household expenses but could not alienate it and had to return it to his wife's family if she died) were fully in place. See Grubb, *Provincial Families*, 19 and 98; and for the Venetian case, Chojnacki, *Women and Men*, 132–52. In other parts of Italy, however, dowries included little or no landed property so that the latter could be left to the sons. See Diane Owen Hughes, "From Brideprice to Dowry in Mediterranean Europe," *Journal of Family History* 3, no. 3 (1978): 262–96. Widows were often named tutors of their children till they reached adulthood. See Nino Tamassia, *La famiglia italiana nei secoli decimoquinto e decimosesto* (Milan: Sandron, 1910), 327–34; for the Veneto region, see Grubb, *Provincial Families*, 92; for Tuscany, see Giulia Calvi, *Il contratto morale: Madre e figli nella Toscana moderna* (Bari: Laterza, 1994), 18–29. Sometimes the title was only pro forma and the male relatives of the husband's family, rather than the widow, administered the deceased husband's property in the name of the minors, but this was not the case with Alvisa, who was named cotutor of her son, Socrate.

10. For the date of 1555 as a likely composition time for "A ragionar d'amore," see below, note 29. For the date of 1559 as marking Bigolina's widowhood, see Mancini, *Lambert Sustris*, 132, who cites from ASP, AN, 4446, 275r. I was unable to interpret the document that Mancini mentions. Bigolina's property is listed in "Beni stabili li quali possiedo io Giulia Bigolina," ASP, ES, 1518, busta 34, 142r–143v, dated May 30, 1561. In a tax revision of 1569, there are three more pieces of land listed. According to Grubb, *Provincial Families*, 31, only 11 percent of widows remarried in the Veneto region in those years because the husband usually left the control of property and children to the wife as long as she did not remarry. Were the widow young, she would have been more pressured to contract a second marriage and a second family alliance. When she had no children, she usually returned to her family. For the Venetian custom, see Chojnacki, *Women and Men*, 53–75; for Tuscany, see Calvi, "Reconstructing the Family: Widowhood and Remarriage in Tuscany in the Early Modern Period," in *Marriage in Italy, 1300–1650*, ed. Trevor Dean and K. J. P. Lowe (Cambridge: Cambridge University Press, 1998), 275–96.

11. See ASP, ES, 1518, busta 34, 142r–142v. "A ragionar d'amore" mentions a son as well.

12. Bigolina's letter, which is undated and difficult to date from the context, is her only extant letter and is at the Bibliothèque Nationale of Paris, Fonds Latin, 7218, in an unfinished book manuscript entitled "Lettere missive scritte da diversi a Francesco Barozzi fu del Cl.mo S.or Ja-

know that she was dead by March 21, 1569, because in that tax document she is referred to as "quondam" Giulia Bigolina.[13]

CRITICAL RECOGNITION

Given the confusion until recently surrounding the biography of Giulia Bigolina, one would imagine that she had no name recognition through the centuries, but this is not the case. The first mention of Bigolina as a poet comes from the authoritative pen of Pietro Aretino, who published three letters he sent to Bigolina between September and October 1549. In the third letter, Aretino acknowledged Bigolina's writing skills by thanking her for the lively sonnet she sent him.[14] Bigolina was praised by the historian Bernardino Scardeone in a book published in 1560, in which he noted her *facundia*, the grace of her prose, and her facility with the Tuscan tongue. Scardeone also mentioned that her novellas were in the style of Boccaccio, but without any licentiousness.[15] Most of the early critics referred to Bigolina as a poet, although only one of her sonnets has survived, and all of them followed Scardeone's early assessment of her worth as a writer. In 1589, Hercole Filogenio aligned Bigolina with the best-known Renaissance women writers, such as Vittoria Colonna, Veronica Gambara, Laura Battiferra, and Laura Terracina; a few years later, in 1605, she seemed a new "fecund Sappho" to the historian Andrea Cittadella; and she was the most eloquent composer of fables, come-

---

como et da lui a diversi in diverse materie, et in diversi tempi," 25v. See also Paul Oskar Kristeller, *Iter Italicum Accedunt Alia Itinera. A Finding List of Uncatalogued or Incompletely Catalogued Humanistic Manuscripts of the Renaissance in Italian and Other Libraries* (London: Warburg Institute, 1963–92), 3: 220. On Barozzi, see Gianmaria Mazzuchelli, *Gli Scrittori d'Italia, cioè notizie storiche, e critiche intorno alle vite e agli scritti dei litterati italiani* (Brescia: Bossini, 1753–63), 2: 413; and Michele Maylender, *Storia delle accademie d'Italia* (Bologna: Cappelli, 1926–30), 4: 339.

13. See ASP, ES, busta 34, 143r. I was unable to find proof of the precise date of her death in any document *mortuorum* of the time.

14. The first two letters are in Pietro Aretino (1492–1556), *Lettere sull'arte di Pietro Aretino*, ed. Ettore Camesana (Milan: Edizione del Milione, 1957), 302–3. The third is in Aretino, *Quinto Libro delle lettere di M. Pietro Aretino* (Paris: Appresso Matteo il Maestro, 1609), letter 362, f. 192. None of the letters Bigolina sent to him has survived. Before Aretino, Bigolina was briefly described by a contemporary Paduan as an angel of the heavenly choir, beautiful, rich, and well dressed. The occasion was her attendance at a family wedding. See Giovanni Marie Masenetti, *Il divino oracolo di M. Gio. Maria Masenetti padovano. In lode delli nuovi sposi del 1548. E di tutte le belle gentildonne padovane* (Venice, 1548), 23r. See also Mancini, *Lambert Sustris*, 132. In un undated manuscript chronicle of the most important noble Paduan families, G. Zabarella describes Giulia as a virtuous poet, learned in both Latin and vernacular, and the writer of a number of unspecified works. See *Cronica delle Famiglie di Padova*, BCP, BP 2055, 14r–14v.

15. Bernardino Scardeone, "De Claris Mulieribus Patavinis," in *De antiquitate urbis Patavii et claris civibus patavinis* (Basel: Nicolaum Episcopium, 1560), 378.

dies, and amorous pieces in the style of Boccaccio, indeed without peers in her time, according to Pietro Paolo Ribera, writing in 1609.[16]

The first precise dating of Bigolina's literary activity—1558—a year offered without any supporting explanation, came from Francesco Agostino Della Chiesa in 1620, who in *Theatro delle donne letterate* made of Bigolina's "ingegno" the proof that women could write fiction as qualitatively good as men. In fact, unlike Boccaccio, Della Chiesa argued, even young virginal girls could read her work, because it was written with a sense of decorum, honesty, and modesty.[17] In 1639, Jacopo Filippo Tomasini, the canon responsible for the administration of the newly established library of the Studio of Padua, finally revealed the first title of a novella by Bigolina, "Delle avventure di Panfilo" ("Fabula de Pamphilo"), now lost, written in standard Tuscan and dedicated to the prince of Salerno, a title that recalls Boccaccio's male protagonist of the *Elegy of Madonna Fiammetta*.[18] Three years later, in 1642, Bigolina became a fictional character herself in *Ragguagli di Cipro* by Luca Assarino, where she functioned as a delightfully witty literary "secretary" at the court of love in Cyprus, in charge of deciphering a letter by Boccaccio to his beloved Maria.[19]

We have to wait until 1732 for the romance *Urania* to be mentioned. The citation is in a catalog by Scipione Maffei, an erudite collector, who found

16. Hercule Filogenio, *Dell'eccellenza delle donne* (Fermo: Sertorio de' Monti, 1589), 171; Andrea Cittadella, *Descrittione di Padova e suo territorio,* ed. Guido Beltrame (Padua: Editrice Veneta, 1992), 110, n. 158; and Pietro Paolo Ribera, *Le Glorie immortali de' Trionfi, et Heroiche Imprese d'Ottocento quarantacinque donne illustri antiche, e moderne* (Venice: Evangelista Deuchino, 1609), 287. Women were often identified by their first name followed by the city of origin (in our case, "Giulia padovana") and were indexed by their first name.

17. Agostino Della Chiesa, *Theatro delle donne letterate con un breve discorso della preminenza, e perfettione del sesso donnesco* (Mondovì: Ginaldi and Rosci, 1620), 171–72. Scardeone had already attributed these qualities to Bigolina's work.

18. "Iuliae Bigolinae C. M. Fabula de Pamphilo Etrusco Idiomate Principi Salernitano inscripta," chap. 4 in Jacopo Filippo Tomasini, *Bibliothecae Patavinae manuscriptae publicae et privatae* (Udine: Nicholai Schiratti, 1639), 128. The novella never surfaced, perhaps because the library was badly kept in the early decades after its establishment. Such is the argument that Tiziana Pesenti Marangon makes in *La biblioteca universitaria di Padova dalla sua istituzione alla fine della Repubblica Veneta, 1629–1797* (Padua: Antenore, 1979), 54–60 and 157–84. The prince of Salerno is also one of the characters in *Urania.*

19. In "Ragguaglio IX," Luca Assarino represents Bigolina as working together with two other women writers of the Renaissance, Maddalena Campiglia and Barbara Torelli, to decode a letter written in ciphers by Boccaccio to Maria, the illegitimate daughter of King Robert of Naples. Bigolina is made to say that the enigma could be easily solved following the teachings of Aristotle. But she then facetiously chides Boccaccio for being unable to write, despite his genius, because his letter was indeed too easy to crack: "E sì come lodo il suo Ingegno, il suo ardire, e la sua miracolosa facondia; così sono forzato a publicamente dichiarare, ch'egli non sà per modo alcuno scrivere." See Assarino (1602–72), *Ragguagli di Cipro,* "Ragguaglio IX," 55–60 (Bologna: Monti and Zenero, 1642), at 60.

the work in the rich Saibante collection in Verona.[20] Then in 1794 the Paduan critic and collector Anton Maria Borromeo wrote that he had a copy of *Urania* made for his own use from the Saibante manuscript. He also had managed to acquire a yet unknown novella, which he proceeded to publish in his *Notizia de' novellieri italiani* under the title "La novella di Giulia Bigolina raccontata nello amenissimo luogo di Mirabello."[21] Pietro Piranesi reprinted this novella in Paris in 1823 in a collection called *Bellezza delle novelle* that included twenty-three authors from the fourteenth to the nineteenth century, chosen because they wrote the masterpieces of Italian literature with which, according to him, French readers should be acquainted.[22] Bigolina was then mentioned as having a beautiful style by Melchior Cesarotti in 1796, included in a biography of Paduan writers by Giuseppe Vedova in 1832, written about by the literary critic Bartolomeo Gamba in 1835, and among the ancient novelists listed respectfully by Giambattista Passano in 1864.[23]

The first case of wrong identification, that is, of Bigolina being mistaken for another member of her family, took place in 1741, when in *Della storia e della ragione d'ogni poesia*, Francesco Saverio Quadrio named Polo, Bigolina's second cousin, as perhaps ("forse") her father, because he may have been a writer himself.[24] In 1840, Napoleone Pietrucci, another Paduan biographer, made a certainty of Quadro's uncertain attribution and from that moment

20. Scipione Maffei, *Indice delli libri, che si ritrovano nella raccolta del Nobile Signor Giulio Saibanti Patrizio Veronese* (Verona: Stamperia della Fenice a S. Maria Antica, 1734), 107. The work is registered as "Giulia Bigolina, Urania, nella quale si contiene l'Amore d'una giovine di tal nome. Sec. XVI." In 1753, Mazzuchelli authoritatively confirmed the existence of the manuscript in *Scrittori d'Italia*, 2: 1222–23.

21. Anton Maria Borromeo, *Notizia de' novellieri italiani posseduti dal conte Anton Maria Borromeo gentiluomo padovano, con alcune novelle inedite* (Bassano: Remondini e figli, 1794), 6. The novella was published on pages 119–46. Borromeo also mentions the existence of the novella "Panfilo," although it does not appear that he saw the piece.

22. Pietro Piranesi, *Bellezza delle novelle tratte dai più celebri autori antichi e moderni* (Paris: Teofilo Barrois, 1823). The novella in also in another Piranesi collection that appeared thirty years later, *Scelta (nuova) di Novelle, tratte di più celebri autori antichi e moderni* (Paris: Baudry, 1852).

23. Melchior Cesarotti, *Lettera di un Padovano al Celebre Signor Abate Denina, Accademico di Berlino e Socio dell'Accademia di Padova* (Padua: Fratelli Penada, 1796), 68; Giuseppe Vedova, *Biografia degli scrittori padovani* (Padua: Coi Tipi della Minerva, 1832), 1: 112–13; Bartolomeo Gamba, *Delle novelle italiane in prosa: Bibliografia* (Florence: Tipografia All'insegna di Dante, 1835), 87; Giambattista Passano, *I novellieri italiani in prosa* (Milan: Schiepatti, 1864), 45 and 97.

24. Francesco Saverio Quadrio, *Della storia e della ragione d'ogni poesia* (Milan: Agnelli, 1741), 1: 271. Quadrio mentions the "Sogno faceto sopra le scarpe di Aldo Manuzio," a composition that Polo Bigolin may have written. The manuscript, three pages long, is at the Ambrosiana Library in Milan, codex S93 and codex Q115. According to Mazzuchelli, however, this Polo is perhaps Paolo Manuzio. See *Scrittori d'Italia*, 2: 1223. Quadrio also claims that Bigolina had published, a statement untrue at the time of his writing.

confusion about Bigolina's dates marred her biography.[25] In the twentieth century, Bigolina was included in a detailed catalog of women writers by Maria Bandini Muti, *Poetesse e scrittrici*, which was published in 1941. Then Paul Oskar Kristeller found the eighteenth-century copy of *Urania* that was mentioned by Borromeo in the Patetta Fund of the Vatican Library. Finally, in 1982, Gian Ludovico Masetti Zannini transcribed for the first time short passages from the Patetta copy of *Urania*.[26]

Recently, another work in which Bigolina is present as an interlocutor was found by Kristeller at the Bibliothèque Municipale of Besançon, "A ragionar d'amore."[27] This is a treatise on love in three dialogues that involves two lawyers, Monsignor Perenotto and Monsignor Coraro, and Giulia Bigolina. It may have been written by Mario Melechini, also known as "Il Mutino," who does not participate in the dialogue but names himself in the dedication to his patron, Perenotto.[28] "A ragionar d'amore" includes references to contemporary learned Paduan women of the period around 1550 and names thirteen of them as being able to debate earnestly on love.[29] The two men choose Giulia Bigolina because she reasons and speaks well. But they also establish that she should mostly listen to what is being discussed, a typical trick of trea-

---

25. Napoleone Pietrucci, *Delle illustri donne padovane. Cenni biografici* (Padua: Tipografia Penada, 1840).

26. Bandini Muti, ed., *Poetesse e scrittrici* (Rome: Istituto Editoriale Italiano, 1941–42), 1: 96; Paul Oskar Kristeller, *Iter Italicum* 6 (1962): 403; and 2 (1967): 606, who registers it as being "composed in the sixteenth century"; and Gian Ludovico Masetti Zannini, *Motivi storici dell'educazione femminile: Scienza, lavoro, giuochi* (Naples: D'Auria, 1982), 35–36 and 195.

27. Kristeller, *Iter Italicum*, 2: 202, item 597.

28. I was unable to find anything about Melechini and perhaps, given his nickname of "Little Mute," the real writer of this piece may have been somebody else. But I can identify the two bishops. Monsignor Antonio Coraro was a member of the influential Venetian Cornaro (or Corner) family, which often monopolized ecclesiastical positions in Padua. See Simioni, *Storia*, 919. We first find him as a law student in Padua in 1543. He is subsequently registered in 1551 as a Venetian nobleman witnessing a law degree and in 1559 as a Paduan canon ("canonicus Patavinus"). See Elda Martellozzo Forin ed., *Acta ab anno 1538 ad annum 1550* (Padua: Antenore, 1971), entry 2998, p. 165; and Elisabetta Dalla Francesca and Emilia Veronese, eds., *Acta Graduum Academicorum Gymnasii Patavini ab anno 1551 ad annum 1565* (Padua: Antenore, 2001), entry 91, p. 39 and entry 942, p. 382. "Mons. Perenotto" is Charles Perrenot de Granvelle or, in the Spanish version, de Granvela (1531–67), son of Nicholas, prime minister of Charles V, and brother of Antoine, who was president of the State Council of Philip II of Spain in 1556 and a friend of Bembo, Aretino, Titian, and Tasso. Charles was listed as a law student in Padua in 1551–52 together with his brother Frédéric, as documented in Dalla Francesca and Veronese, eds., *Acta . . . ab anno 1551 ad annum 1565*, entry 53, p. 23; entry 102, p. 43; and entry 145, p. 60.

29. Since Perenotto and Cornaro mention two daughters and a niece of Sperone Speroni, by following the very close dates of these women's weddings and widowhoods, I have been able to date the composition of this treatise to the years 1554–55. For a more precise reconstruction, see my Italian edition of *Urania*, 36.

tises of the time in which women were involved mostly as listeners or to confirm the opinion of men with their presence and required assent.[30] The character Bigolina, most probably modeled on the writer's own personality as was often the case, soon proves that she has a mind of her own and starts to intervene, energetically and repeatedly, in the conversation.

Treatises that included women in dialogues on love in those times were almost always from the Veneto region, and Bigolina may have read them. They include such works as *Dialogo d'amore* (1542) by Sperone Speroni, where Tullia d'Aragona was made to prefer sensual to Neoplatonic love (a position that d'Aragona will refuse when she has the pen in her hand in *Dialogue on the Infinity of Love* (published in 1547); or *Il Raverta* (1544) by Giuseppe Betussi, in which Francesca Baffa was often allowed to intervene. Both women were "honest" courtesans and thus had a blemished reputation in love matters, which the authors fully exploited. This was not Bigolina's case, and her character is allowed to discuss in earnest Neoplatonic philosophy and the power of desire along the lines of Leon Ebreo's *Dialoghi d'amore* (1535).[31] She is also made to cite Homer and from time to time even corrects the two men's assertions. "A ragionar d'amore" was never published, although the text seems complete. Like all documents related to the Perrenot de Granvelle's family, it ended up in their extensive library in Beçancon.

"GIULIA CAMPOSAMPIERO AND TESIBALDO VITALIANI"

The novella "Giulia Camposampiero," which is reproduced here in Italian with facing translation, was first published by Anton Maria Borromeo in 1794 without a title and with just the name of the author and the place in which it was told. Strange as it may sound, no anthology had appeared since the end of the sixteenth century that grouped, however informally, Renaissance novellas, and therefore from the start this collection was an important preliminary assessment of what was still valuable in the genre. "Giulia" was then partially reprinted without the frame and the final sonnet in *Bellezza delle novelle* by Pietro Piranesi (a few other changes were also made within the text, mostly

---

30. For what the silent presence of women accomplishes in discussions on women and love, see Finucci, *The Lady Vanishes: Subjectivity and Representation in Castiglione and Ariosto* (Stanford: Stanford University Press, 1992), chap. 2.

31. Buona Suarda too, a respected woman interlocutor like Bigolina, was allowed to speak seriously in a dialogue by Niccolò Franco, *Dialogo dove si ragiona delle bellezze* (1542). See Virginia Cox, "Seen but Not Heard: The Role of Women Speakers in Cinquecento Literary Dialogue," in *Women in Italian Renaissance Culture and Society,* ed. Letizia Panizza (Oxford: European Humanities Research Center, 2000), 391.

to tone down explicit sexual meanings) as the "Novella di Giulia Camposanpiero e Vitaliano Tesibaldi," in which the first name of the main male character was confused with the last.

Borromeo clearly identified the author of "Giulia" with the Giulia
Bigolina who corresponded with Aretino and was mentioned by Scardeone
in 1560 and not with the Giulia Bigolina who lived more than a generation
later and married a Camposampiero and who, thanks to a striking coincidence, took after her marriage the same name as the main character in this
novella.[32] At that time, in any case, it was not unusual to write novellas using
character names taken from historical or journalistic events.[33]

Borromeo was precise in describing where he found the manuscript: in
the well-stocked library of the Paduan gentleman Giovanni Lazara.[34] The
Lazara (or De Lazara) were the direct heirs of the Bigolini when the family
name died in 1650 at the death of Conte.[35] And it is in the Lazara collection
now housed at the Biblioteca Civica in Padua that I found the novella (MS
1451, VIII), which is classified as an eighteenth-century manuscript. But the
classification is incorrect as the watermark dated 1545 confirms. This is therefore the original sixteenth-century version from which Borromeo had a copy
made for publication, a copy that may not have survived, as was often the
case.[36] The manuscript, which may be in the hand of Bigolina herself and may
have been written shortly after 1545, is composed of sixteen pages (8v. and

32. The connections between the Bigolini and the Camposampiero were in any case old ones,
and Bigolina herself owned land in the territory of Camposampiero, which she brought in
dowry. The same is true for her brother, Socrate. See ASP, *Polizze*, busta 3. The son of the Giulia
Bigolina who was married to Camposampiero, Tiso, married back into the Bigolini family by taking Camilla Bigolina for a wife, once more proving how close the connections between these
two noble families were. On the Camposampiero, see Busta *Prove 3*, 1626 in ASP, *Consiglio di Nobili. Prove di requisiti*, v. 26, *ad vocem*.

33. See, for example, the novellas "Giulia da Gazuolo" and "La contessa di Challant" by Matteo
Bandello; "Teodorica Fiaminga" by Francesco Molza; and "Madonna Gentilina da Bologna" by
Scipione Bargagli.

34. Borromeo, *Notizia*, 6.

35. Conte was the son of Dioclide Bigolin and Giulia De Lazara or, more precisely in the
spelling of the time, of Giulia Bigolina Lazaro Reniera, our third Giulia Bigolina. Dioclide
Bigolin died after 1674, a full quarter of a century after his son, Conte.

36. The countermark, a "chapeau," confirms that the paper was made available in Vicenza in
1545. Examples are in the State Archive of Venice, "Lettere de Rettori," number 224. See Charles
Moise Briquet, *Les Filigranes. Dictionnaire historique des marques du papier des leur apparition vers 1282
jusqu'en 1600*, 4 vols. (New York: Hacker Art Books, 1966), 1: 227, entry 3501. Countermarks
practically disappeared after the sixteenth century. Although we cannot be sure exactly when
Bigolina wrote "Giulia," we might surmise that she did so within the first five years after the paper became available. This fits together with an internal reference in the novella, where Bigolina
states that she is writing a bit more than two hundred years after the events she narrates took
place, in 1347. The *Catalogo dei Manoscritti della Biblioteca Lazara di S. Francesco* compiled in the year

8r.) and is in good condition, with no ink stains but a small correction in the concluding sonnet.

We know that "Giulia" is part of a longer work because the frame refers to other novellas and to a group of ladies and gentlemen gathered in the countryside outside Padua. Here the women tell lively tales under the sponsorship of a "queen." The model is the *Decameron* in which a company of seven ladies and three gentlemen gathered in a *locus amoenus* near Settignano, outside Florence, to tell stories, as well as Bembo's *Asolani*, whose idyllic setting in Asolo, north of Padua, is imitated in Bigolina's choice of the fictional place ("amenissimo luogo") of Mirabello, possibly south of Padua.[37] As the context makes clear, each story seems also to have ended with a sonnet/enigma that the teller recites at the end. The form of the sonnet Bigolina uses is an extravagant one, often employed in burlesque poetry, as in the case of Francesco Berni. It is made up of eleven extra verses following the regulation fourteen—a form called a "sonettessa," in which the coda is repeated more than once.

We do not know how many novellas Bigolina wrote with the intention of composing a book of which "Giulia" was a part, although according to her contemporary Scardeone, she wrote many.[38] None has apparently survived, and the book purporting to collect a number of them may in fact never have been written. Books of novellas were very popular at the time in light of the enduring success and many reprints of Boccaccio's *Decameron*, and Bigolina must have been a voracious reader of them, although, judiciously for a woman of her rank, she shunned the salacious "Boccacceschi" offshoots that contemporary writers often favored.[39]

1786 and housed in the same library, also lists the name of Giulia Bigolina. See BCP, MS 1488, n.p. Bigolina is listed again in *Indice dei Manoscritti dei Fratelli Lazara 1807*, in BCP, MS 1488, in which there is also mention that her novella had been published by Borromeo, although the date is given imprecisely as the year "17. . ."

37. Although the tale does not give any indication as to where a place blandly named Mirabello (literally, "beautiful view," that is, *locus amoenus*) might be, Bandini Muti suggests a location in the Euganea Hills of the Veneto region south of Padua, somewhere close to the hamlet of Luvigliano, in the township of Torreglia, and not very far from Petrarch's villa in Arquà. Today the area still has pleasant meadows and lovely views. It is also surrounded by a number of villas, some of which, like the Villa dei Vescovi, were already built in the sixteenth century.

38. "Scripsit hactenus complurima lectu dignissima, quae sane a cunctis legentibus magno applausu probantur et summa delectatione leguntur: et in primis quasdam comoedias seu fabulas, ad Boccacij morem (servato tamen ubique matronali decoro) insigni argumento, artificio mirabili, eventu vario et exitu inexpectato." In Scardeone, 368.

39. After the publication of the *Decameron*, the novella had a rather tame fourteenth and fifteenth centuries; the only novellas of that period being those of Franco Sacchetti, Giovanni Sercambi, Gentile Sermini, Masuccio Salernitano, and Sabbatino degli Arienti. But then the genre exploded in the first half of the sixteenth century, and the phenomenon was not just a northern

As we would expect, "Giulia" is very much in tune with contemporary public reading tastes, which went in the direction of the pathetic rather than the tragic. A generation after the composition of "Giulia," Girolamo Bargagli offered a list of the characteristics of the most popular tales told during evening social gatherings ("giuochi") in the period: they had to have sound examples of constancy, goodness of heart, and loyalty ("contengano qualche bello essempio di costanza, di grandezza d'animo e di lealtà"); they had to display great honesty and suffering on the part of women ("quelle che grande onestà e gran sofferenza di donne contengono"); and they were to use the exemplary stories of Ariosto's Ginevra and of Boccaccio's Giletta of Narbona and patient Griselda.[40] In creating her characters, Bigolina is deeply indebted to both authors. For example, in the Giletta story (*Decameron* 3.9), Boccaccio had a nobleman make love to his wife, Giletta, thinking that she was another woman with whom he had fallen in love.[41] Reversing gender, Bigolina has a woman make love to a man thinking that he is somebody else, a trick that

Italian one. A list of works published before the Counter-Reformation is substantial, although only a few authors became influential: Machiavelli's "Belfagor" was printed in 1518; Girolamo Morlini's *Novellae et fabulae* in 1520; Luigi Da Porto's *Historia di due nobili amanti* in 1530; Francesco Maria Molza's *Novelle* in 1544; Marco Cademosto's six novellas in *Sonetti e altre rime* and Luigi Alemanni's *Novella* in 1544; Giovanni Brevio's six novellas in *Rime e prose volgari* in 1545; Agnolo Firenzuola's *Ragionamenti* in 1548; Giovan Francesco Straparola's *Piacevoli notti* in 1550 (vol. 1) and 1553 (vol. 2); Girolamo Parabosco's *Diporti* in 1552; and Matteo Maria Bandello's *Novelle* in 1554 (with part four coming out posthumously in 1573). After the 1560s, the stream of publications began to dry up and only Giraldi Cinzio's *Hecatomniti* was often reprinted (seven times between 1568 and 1608). But there were also works that never made it into print in their author's lifetimes, such as Anton Francesco Grazzini's *Cene*, which was not published until the eighteenth century; Pietro Fortini's *Giornate* and *Notti*, which came out (and even then partially) only in 1888; and Giovanni Forteguerri's eleven novellas written between 1556 and 1562, which made it into print in 1871. Enzo Bottasso in fact suggests that one should talk about "noncirculation," rather than circulation, of novellas in the period, given the number of books of novellas that remained unprinted. See "La prima circolazione a stampa," in volume 1 of *La novella italiana: Atti del Convegno di Caprarola, 19–24 settembre 1988,* ed. Enrico Malato et al. (Rome: Salerno Editrice, 1989), 263. For a list, see Bruno Porcelli, "Bibliografia," in *La novella del Cinquecento* (Bari: Laterza, 1979); Giambattista Passano, *I novellieri italiani in prosa;* and Marcello Ciccuto, ed., *Novelle italiane: Il Cinquecento* (Milan: Garzanti, 1982), xxxi–xlvi. For an examination in context, see also Riccardo Bruscagli, "La novella e il romanzo," in *Storia della letteratura italiana. IV. Il primo Cinquecento,* ed. Enrico Malato (Rome: Salerno, 1996), 835–907; Giorgio Barberi Squarotti, ed., *Metamorfosi della novella* (Foggia: Bastogi, 1985); Marziano Guglielminetti, ed. *Novellieri del Cinquecento* (Naples: Ricciardi, 1972); and Armando Balduino, "Fortune e sfortune della novella italiana," 155–73.

40. Girolamo Bargagli, *Dialogo de' giuochi che nelle vegghie senesi si usano di fare,* ed. P. D'Incalci Ermini (Siena: Accademia degli Intronati, 1982), 2: 207. See also Francesco Bonciani, "Lezioni sopra il comporre delle novelle," (1573) in *Trattati di poetica e di retorica del Cinquecento,* ed. Bernard Weinberg (Bari: Laterza, 1972).

41. For the use of Boccaccio in the sixteenth and seventeenth centuries, see Giorgio Barberi Squarotti, "L'instabilità dell'ingegno o l'avventura barocca," *Forum Italicum* 7 (1973): 177–226.

Ariosto had already popularized in the story of Ginevra and Ariodante (*Orlando furioso* 4, 5). Like Ariosto, Bigolina zeroes in on dissimulation, uses the motif of the joust in which a knight fights incognito, emphasizes the element of secrecy in love matters, and ends by cloistering a female character.

"Giulia" is a historical novella that chronicles the tribulations that a couple undergoes until their secret marriage is publicly recognized. The action takes place in the brief period in which Padua was a republic after ousting the Scaligeri in 1347. Giulia, the main female character, actively seeks the love of Tesibaldo Vitaliani, a studious and learned young man from Padua, and ends up marrying him in secret.[42] Quite unexpectedly, Tesibaldo is named the republic's next ambassador to the imperial court in Vienna, where the beautiful Odolania, the emperor's daughter, falls in love with him. But Tesibaldo keeps faithful to Giulia, a choice that his enemy, the Roman Lucio Orsino, decides to use to his advantage. Orsino assures the lovesick Odolania that he can deliver the Paduan ambassador to her room, and that same night he himself makes it to her bed, dressed in Tesibaldo's clothes with the intention of passing for him.

When the affair is discovered and the emperor learns from his daughter about the secret encounters with the man she believes was Tesibaldo, the couple is condemned to death. Giulia hears the unhappy news, refuses to believe that her husband has betrayed her, and goes to Vienna to reclaim him dressed as a man. She fights with the imperial guards but is overcome and put in prison. In the meantime, Odolania and Tesibaldo are freed because Orsino has confessed his crime before dying of sexual exhaustion, and Giulia, who has asked for a meeting with the emperor, has the chance to claim her lawful right to Tesibaldo. The two are reunited, and Odolania is sent to a convent for the rest of her life.[43]

In Bigolina's work, all women are constant in their love, a trait inherent in Boccaccio's Griselda. Constancy is culturally linked to obedience and piety, qualities that Griselda was appropriately made to display in the last novella of the *Decameron*, but Bigolina highlights only the most obvious connection

---

42. The choice of such a last name for a faithful and learned man may coyly refer to the fact that a branch of the Vitaliani family could trace its origin directly from Petrarch. See Paolo Sambin, "Nuove notizie su eredi e discendenti del Petrarca," in *Atti dell'Istituto Veneto di scienze, lettere ed arti*, 255–66 (1951–52) at 260.

43. The manuscript and the Borromeo edition register, respectively, the spelling of "Campo San Piero" and "Camposanpiero" for Giulia's last name. I am modernizing it into the current "Camposampiero." Likewise, I am modernizing the "Thesibaldo" of the manuscript into "Tesibaldo," an adjustment already made by Borromeo. Odolania's name was misspelled in Borromeo's printed version into the German sounding "Odolarica," perhaps because her story was taking place in Vienna.

of constancy with chastity, as well as the less obvious one of constancy with discipline. In this she follows Ariosto, who dressed his chaste woman warrior Bradamante as a man and made her fight, Amazon style, for the right to have the man she chose—just like Giulia and, as we shall see, Urania. Reversing the stereotype, Tesibaldo too displays the same brand of heroic constancy that characterizes his wife. His sublimation of desire and his rejection of the opportunity for male advancement and domination offered him by a regal princess make him a thoroughly lovable figure. Masculine predation and fantasies of power, on the other hand, are severely rebuked in the figure of Orsino.

Giulia escapes the melancholic affliction that will accompany Urania and is always in charge, whether to initiate a love story with Tesibaldo or to become the embodiment of a courtly chivalric hero by putting her life at stake to save her husband. This transference of male aggressiveness to women by appropriating for them the violence that often defines the social relations between men in chivalric romances, although realistically stretched too thin (having presumably never used a sword, Giulia is still able to kill a number of fully armed guards in the emperor's retinue), works to empower women in a way that the narrative that "Giulia" consciously imitates—Ariosto's "Ginevra" episode—did not. All Bigolina's women in fact are fully self-assured. The conflicts come not from their penchant for independence and self-sufficiency, which is rarely castigated, but from the fact that they happen to choose the same man.

In the end, unlawful sex is punished in both man and woman. Orsino dies, and Odolania, who was cast at the beginning as a self-confident sexual figure, is made to renounce her name and rank as she becomes a nun. This seems to be a solution for which Bigolina is thoroughly indebted to Ariosto, who in the Ginevra episode ended a similar story by the maid Dalinda, upon whom Odolania is modeled, with her entry into a convent. But Dalinda and Odolania are characterized differently, although they suffer the same destiny. Odolania made love to Orsino because she thought him to be the man she wanted, Tesibaldo, and thus she acted upon her own desire. Dalinda too made love to a man, Polinesso, dressed as someone else, Ariodante. But she knew his identity and even acceded to his desire that she wear the clothes of the woman he really loved, Ginevra, before making love to her as "interposta persona," just to fulfill his fantasy. This makes of Dalinda a quiescent figure quite unlike Odolania.[44]

---

44. For a reading of this episode in Ariosto, see Finucci, "The Female Masquerade: Ariosto and the Game of Desire," In *Desire in the Renaissance: Psychoanalysis and Literature*, ed. Valeria Finucci and Regina Schwartz (Princeton: Princeton University Press, 1994), 61–88.

In *Urania*, Bigolina will reprise at length the main motifs of "Giulia," like disguise and cross-dressing, as well as the theme of constancy in love, often using Ariosto as her most empowering model. It is to this much lengthier and most innovative work that I now turn.

URANIA

Urania is a psychological romance that centers on the monomaniacal love of a female character who falls into melancholia when her beloved leaves her for a more beautiful woman. The text is comprised of a manuscript of 309 pages plus a long dedicatory letter of forty-one pages. The original is in the Biblioteca Trivulziana of Milan, where it is registered as a "codice cartaceo n. 88 in quarto." According to Giulio Porro, who has studied at length the Trivulziana collection, the manuscript could be the one penned by Bigolina herself and sent to Bartolomeo Salvatico, the lawyer to whom she dedicates it and whose initials "B.S." are visible on the cover.[45] We also have a manuscript copy of *Urania* made late in the eighteenth century for the critic Anton Maria Borromeo, as I mentioned earlier. Today this copy is in the Fondo Patetta, n. 358, of the Biblioteca Apostolica Vaticana, and has recently been cataloged and made accessible to the public. Kristeller, who did not know of the original at the Trivulziana, was the first to give information about the copy of *Urania* in the Vatican.[46] The Patetta manuscript, less legible than the original because of the copyist's handwriting, with a few grammatical and orthographical mistakes and ink stains, has a handwritten note from the eighteenth-century copyist confirming that it derives from the original in the Saibante collection.

Bigolina calls *Urania* a little work ("operetta"), a title that recalls the "little booklet of mine" ("piccolo mio libretto") of the *incipit* of Boccaccio's *Fiammetta*. The introductory letter, in which Bigolina explains how this work came to be written, is dedicated to the "Magnificent and Excellent Doctor of Law, Signor Bartolomeo Salvatico," of whom she declares herself taken by honest love. Bartolomeo Salvatico (1532–1603) was a Paduan nobleman and lawyer. He graduated in both canon and civil law at the very youthful age of twenty, on November 21, 1552, and was already teaching "Institutiones" at the Studio two years later, a position that he held for the next fifty years. Salvatico was also an intellectual and a member of the Accademia degli Elevati and the

---

45. Giulio Porro, ed., *Trivulziana. Catalogo dei codici manoscritti* (Turin: Paravia, 1884), 31. My translation of *Urania* is based on the edited version of this manuscript that I published in 2002.

46. He calls it "a prose novel in volg. with a preface to Bart. Salvatico (composed in the sixteenth century)." See Kristeller, *Iter Italicum*, 1967, 2: 606; and 1962, 6: 403.

Accademia dei Ricovrati; in 1584 he was allowed through a papal decree to read books put on the Index.[47] Since Bigolina refers to Bartolomeo as "dottor di leggi" and describes him as a young man of much valor and nobility, we can hypothesize that *Urania* was composed after 1553, given the date when Salvatico became a lawyer.

The name Urania was typical in pastoral literature, following the *urtext* of Jacopo Sannazaro's *Arcadia* (written in 1483–86), where Uranio was the main character. In a female pastoral in verse written in 1588, Maddalena Campiglia's *Flori*, Urania is a nymph. Urania is also the muse of astronomy, often represented in a light blue dress with stars around her head and the globe in her hand, a characterization that allowed the Neoplatonists to play with a distinction between a divine, contemplative Aphrodite Urania, the inspirer of divine love, and an Aphrodite Pandemon, her terrestrial counterpart. As "fixed and constant like the Northern Star," the name is metaphorically appropriate to a woman inclined to marriage, according to the poet Philip Sydney.[48]

But there is another Urania, in English literature, that I would like to mention. I am referring to Mary Wroth's *Urania*, an intricate prose work, whose first part was published in 1621. Here Urania is a shepherdess, later revealed to be the daughter of the king of Naples. As in the case of *Urania* for Italian literature, Wroth's *Urania* too is the first prose romance authored by a woman in English literature. Almost seventy years separate two identically named works in which two women writers of different nationalities and different linguistic backgrounds launch the genre of the female romance—a coincidence that would be unbelievable, were it not true. And like the Italian *Urania*, which was left unpublished until 2002, the English *Urania* too had a contorted history, for although the first part appeared during the author's lifetime, we have to wait until 1999 for the second part to finally come out in print.[49]

---

47. For the graduation date, see Dalla Francesca and Veronese, *Acta Graduum. . . ab anno 1551 ad annum 1565*, entry 200, p. 79. On Salvatico's (or Selvatico's) intellectual activities, see Maylender, *Storia delle accademie d'Italia*, 2: 264; and Vedova, *Biografia*, 2: 197–201. In 1558, Salvatico married Andriana de Lazara and had thirteen children. Through the years he acquired a remarkable medical and legal library, consisting of 34 manuscripts and 1,500 books, which his son, Benedetto, donated in 1631 to the newly established library of the Studio of Padua, an immense donation at the time. See Gilda Mantovani, *Un fondo di edizioni giuridiche dei secoli XV–XVII: Il "dono Selvatico."* *Catalogo* (Rome: Istituto Poligrafico e Zecca dello Stato, 1984). The villa that Bartolomeo built (now Sartori) near Battaglia Terme still commands a striking view of the Euganea hills.

48. See Nesca Robb, *Neoplatonism of the Italian Renaissance* (London: Allen, 1935), 79–80. On Sydney's description, see K. Duncan-Jones, "Sydney's *Urania*," *Review of English Studies* n.s. 7 (1966): 123–32.

49. Wroth's *Urania* is a work divided into four books for a total of 558 pages. It has many characters, and Urania is not the main one, since the romance centers on the story of the constant

In her introduction, Bigolina explains that she wanted to give an image of herself to Bartolomeo to remind him at her death of the love that she "honestly and perfectly" felt for him. In the past she had sent him love letters and poems. But a monstrous pigmy named "Giudizio" suddenly appeared in her room to convince her that she needed to compose something delightful instead. After a long debate, she decided to write a work that demonstrates that women can at times dispense their love better than men, although they are often accused of behaving stupidly in the matter. In fact, she advises Bartolomeo not to fall for the same mistake she deplores in *Urania*, where the main male character is unable to recognize his good luck in love.

The narrative begins with the presentation of Urania as a young woman writer of intelligence and learning, but not of beauty, who receives men of erudition in her home for honest conversation because such is the custom of her city, Salerno (or of Padua for that matter, given that the conversation in "A ragionar d'amore" took place in Bigolina's own home). Men flock to her because the talk is brilliant, but soon the man she loves, Fabio, who used to visit her because he was attracted by the beauties of her mind, begins to absent himself, lured elsewhere by the graces of a seemingly vacuous young woman, Clorina. Extremely saddened at the realization that female comeliness is the eternal glue of man's affection, Urania decides to leave her home and city and to wander throughout Italy, dressed as a man and under the assumed identity of "Fabio," until she either dies or is cured of her passion. Before leaving, she pens a long letter to her unfaithful beloved in which she reflects on the meaning of beauty and on the frustrations that intelligent women suffer when men prefer the body to the mind.

Shortly after, while dejectedly riding in the woods, Urania meets a group of five women who take her for a man and use the occasion to ask him to resolve their doubts on men, love, and relations between the sexes. When she resumes her journey one day later, she meets a group of five men who again, thinking that she is a man, ask him what women want. When she is finally alone, Urania feels suicidal and decides to let herself die. But as the hours

---

love of Pamphilia for the inconstant Amphilanthus. It was denounced as a *roman à clef* when it first appeared. A steady, ever increasing stream of studies on Mary Wroth (1586–ca. 1640) has been published during the last decade or so, such as Naomi Miller, *Changing the Subject: Mary Wroth and Figurations of Gender in Early Modern England* (Lexington, KY: University Press of Kentucky, 1996), and Sheila Cavanagh, *Cherished Torment: The Emotional Geography of Lady Mary Wroth's Urania* (Pittsburgh: Duquesne University Press, 2001). For English Renaissance romances written by women, see Caroline Lucas, *Writing for Women: The Example of Woman as Reader in Elizabethan Romance* (Milton Keynes: Open University Press, 1989), 8–18; and Wendy Wall, *The Imprint of Gender: Authorship and Publication in the English Renaissance* (Ithaca: Cornell University Press, 1993).

go by, she is unable to go along with her decision and starts looking for lodging for the night.

In a hostel that she fortuitously finds, she meets a young Florentine widow, Emilia, on a pilgrimage to Loreto, and the two decide to travel together. After they return to Florence, they take up lodging in the same house. Still thinking that Urania is a man, Emilia refuses to take a new husband and eventually reveals her love for "Fabio." Urania clumsily rebuffs her and argues that she has to return to Salerno right away to see how things stand back home. Only after that, she declares, can she entertain thoughts of love. Emilia decides to accompany her, still unaware of Urania's identity, and the two travel to Salerno cross-dressed as men. At their arrival, Urania finds Fabio in prison because he has stolen a magic garland from the prince's palace and can be freed only if a maiden summons sufficient courage to kiss a wild woman. Urania—whom everybody takes for a man—attempts to complete this task and, to everyone's surprise, is successful. She frees her beloved and eventually reveals her female identity. The story ends with four marriages: Urania to Fabio; Clorina to a Sicilian man, Menandro, who was competing with Fabio for her affections; Emilia to Hortensio, Fabio's brother; and the prince to the unnamed woman of his dreams, after he had declined the chaste advances of a beautiful duchess who had sent him a painting of her naked body and the magic garland I mentioned above as enticements to love.

The peregrinations in the text are preceded by a long love letter on the model that the abandoned women of Ovid's *Heroides* sent to their faithless beloveds.[50] Urania first excuses herself for her inadequacy and then embarks on a long discussion about why women should be loved and what are the advantages for men of a relationship based on respect and intellectual esteem. Showing that she can discuss Neoplatonic arguments better than her character was allowed to do in "A ragionar d'amore," Bigolina makes Urania com-

---

50. Renaissance women had available manuals on how to write letters for all occasions. These books were bestsellers in their own right, catering to a new bourgeois class that was discovering (and rewriting at the same time) the rules of conduct. The most common books of love letters were by Giovanni Antonio Tagliente, *Opera amorosa che insegna a componer lettere, et a rispondere a persone d'amor ferite* (Venice, 1533); and by Andrea da Zenophonte, *Formulario / nuovo da dittar / Lettere amorose missive et / responsive* (Venice, 1535). The anonymous *Componimento di parlamenti nuovamente stampato* (Venice, 1535) taught women how best to communicate in writing with their families. Even fake books of women's letters were popular, such as Ortensio Lando's *Lettere di molte donne valorose* (Venice, 1548). Men too had their manuals on love letters, as, for example, in a later decade Francesco Sansovino's *Delle lettere amorose di diversi huomini illustri* (Venice, 1574). On the variety of books of letters that constituted the phenomenon, see Amedeo Quondam, ed., *Le 'Carte Messaggiere.' Retorica e modelli di comunicazione epistolare: Per un indice dei libri di lettere del Cinquecento* (Rome: Bulzoni, 1981), 13–157; and Nicola Longo, *Letteratura e lettere: Indagine nell'epistolografia cinquecentesca* (Rome: Bulzoni, 1999).

pare the beauty of the soul to that of the body and to assert that her beauty is to be found inside her poetry, specifically "in the rhymes and prose I composed and gave you." Although Bigolina describes Urania as sentimental and self-punishing in this letter, fully committed to an agenda of unrequited constancy, she also has her fight for a world of intellectual parity between man and woman.

FROM THE NOVELLA TO THE ROMANCE

The prose romance was invented in Italy in the middle of the sixteenth century, although some critics still consider the romance a Baroque phenomenon born in the 1620s.[51] The new genre's literary ancestor was undoubtedly Boccaccio, who first experimented with the two themes that would be exploited in the romance: the journey in search of the beloved, as in *Filocolo*, the *Amorous Vision*, and some novellas of the second day of the *Decameron*; and the journey in search of a mythical, uncontaminated place in the woods, as in the *Nymphs of Fiesole* and the frame of the *Decameron* itself.[52] Boccaccio's erotic and exotic adventures in *Filocolo* (but also in *Theseid* and *Filostrato*) were fully exploited in

51. Unlike novellas, which sprouted all over Italy, there are no Tuscan or Roman romances in either the sixteenth or the seventeenth century, only Veneto ones. The Baroque romance flourished between 1624, with the publication of *La Eromena* by Giovanni Francesco Biondi, and 1662, with *La peota smarrita* by Girolamo Brusoni. See Alberto Asor Rosa, "La narrativa italiana del Seicento," in *Letteratura italiana III. Le forme del testo II. La prosa*, ed. Alberto Asor Rosa, 715–57 (Turin: Einaudi, 1985); Giovanni Getto, "Il romanzo veneto nell'età barocca," in *Barocco in prosa e poesia*, ed. Giovanni Getto (Milan: Rizzoli, 1969); and Albert Mancini, *Romanzi e romanzieri del Seicento* (Naples: Società Editrice Napoletana, 1981). I offer here an incomplete but representative chronological list of sixteenth-century prose romances, many of which are still unread today but which had frequent reprints at the time: Ascanio Censorio, *L'aura soave* (Venice, 1533); Anonymous, *I compassionevoli avvenimenti di Erasto* (Mantua, 1542), a moral romance with eight reprints; Niccolò Franco, *La Filena* (Mantua, 1547), on Sannio's love for the Venetian Filena; Giulio Landi, *La vita di Cleopatra* (Venice, 1551); Cristoforo Armeno, *Il peregrinaggio di tre giovani figlioli del re di Serendippo* (Venice, 1557), which was most probably written by Giuseppe Tramezzino and his collaborators; Antonio Minturno, *Amore innamorato* (Venice, 1559) on the adventures of Amore, son of Venere; Alvise Pasqualigo, *Lettere amorose* (published anonymously in 1563, and with the author's name in 1569), also known as *Lettere di due amanti* (Venice, 1569), an erotic romance; Lorenzo Selva, *La metamorfosi cioè trasformazioni del virtuoso* (Orvieto, 1582), a moral romance with many reprints; Gabriele Pascoli da Ravenna, *La pazzesca pazzia de gli Huomini e donne di Corte Innamorati o vero Il cortigiano disperato* (Venice, 1592), an erotic romance of star-crossed lovers; Ludovico Arrivabene, *Il Magno Vitei* (Venice, 1597), a romance that takes place in China; and Giovanni Maria Bernardo, *La Zotica* (Bologna, 1598).

52. Some critics indeed think that *Filocolo* (1336–38) can be rightly called the first romance of Italian literature. See Salvatore Battaglia, "Il primo romanzo della letteratura italiana," in *La Coscienza letteraria del Medioevo*, ed. Salvatore Battaglia, 645–57 (Naples: Liguori, 1965); and Giancarlo Mazzacurati, *All'ombra di Dioneo: Tipologie e percorsi della novella da Boccaccio a Bandello* (Florence: La Nuova Italia, 1996), 117.

the following centuries by the verse chivalric romance, the most widely used narrative form of the Renaissance. When, after the middle of the sixteenth century, the chivalric romance began to abandon the digressions that had punctuated its endless adventures à la Ariosto in favor of a unified and heroic epic development à la Tasso, and a new interest in historicizing the fantastic and the natural developed, the verse romance began to lose some steam.[53]

In the meantime, by the 1540s in any case, Boccaccio's realistic form, which was modeled on the anonymous *Novellino* and fully developed in most novellas of the *Decameron*, although still very much admired, had begun to appear old, and novella writers began experimenting with a less transgressive and less dramatic narrative, one in which the characters' psychology became fundamental. In the novella, individual nature was played out in two ways following Boccaccio: through references by the narrators themselves, with the consequence that the frame would grow in length; and inside the story, by complicating the plot, with the result that the frame would become useless, as with Bandello or, more to the point, as with Bigolina's "Giulia."[54] The prose romance was born out of a confluence, as well as of a disruption, of all these elements: it was a realistic narrative, like the novella, although it dilated adventures in time and space, without a narrator and a frame; and it preferred complicated and adventurous plots and extraordinary events, like the verse chivalric romances, although it borrowed a good deal from Boccaccio's successful love narratives of *Fiammetta* and *Filocolo*, which had enjoyed a surprising number of reprints during the century.[55]

To be sure, the sixteenth century heavily experimented with genre forms as testified by the virulence of the *querelle* between the supporters of ancient versus modern narrative, which exploded in Italy after the middle of the century—the first literary critical confrontation on what kind of literature, if

---

53. The genre was in any case so well established and recognized that the first prose romances too were printed in two columns, as if they were chivalric romances in octaves, to make them more attractive to the reading public. See Grendler, "Form and Function in Italian Renaissance Popular Books," *Renaissance Quarterly* 46 (1993): 475.

54. See Hermann Wetzel, "Premesse per una storia del genere della novella: La novella italiana dal Due al Seicento," in *La novella italiana* (1989), 1: 280. For the reasons that motivated Boccaccio's decline, see Guglielminetti, "Introduzione," in *Novellieri del Cinquecento.*

55. *Fiammetta*, written in 1343–44, was reprinted after a long hiatus in 1472 and had a further dozen reprints in the sixteenth century; the success of *Filocolo* followed along the same lines. See Adolfo Albertazzi, *Il romanzo* (Milan: Vallardi, 1902), 38. A critical history of the sixteenth century romance novel still needs to be written. A good starting point is Albertazzi's *Romanzieri e romanzi del Cinquecento e del Seicento* (Bologna: Zanichelli, 1891), and *Il romanzo*, chap. 3. See also Bruscagli, "La novella e il romanzo," 888–98; and Porcelli, *La novella del Cinquecento*, 96–103. For Wetzel, the romance is one of the three forms, together with the *exempla* and the "essays," in which the genre of the novella developed in the sixteenth century. See "Premesse per una storia del genere della novella," 1: 265–81.

any, the Italians had invented or perfected beyond the classical forms they had inherited from Greece and Rome. A fascination for hybridization brought not only new theorizations of the tragedy, the comedy, and the epic, but also the production of mixed forms such as the tragicomedy (as in Guarini's famous *Il Pastor Fido,* 1590), the happy tragedy (as in Giraldi Cinzio's *Hecatommithi,* 1565), or the treatise inserted in the comedy (as in Piccolomini's *Raffaella,* 1539).[56] The popular novella started to become more voluminous (by adding, for example, a repertoire on love questions), inserted new genres (like sonnets and enigmas, as we saw in "Giulia," but also songs, theatrical pieces, and material from treatises), or was itself included in chivalric romances (in which case it was written in octaves) and conduct books. In light of this bubbling creativity, many critics have recently spoken of the impossibility of categorizing the nature of narrative in the 1540s and 1550s.[57]

The type of prose narrative that was being written around the 1550s in Italy is indeed notoriously difficult to classify: the *Diporti* by Girolamo Parabosco (1550), the *Piacevoli notti* by Giovan Francesco Straparola (1550 and 1553), the *Vari componimenti* by Ortensio Lando (1552), the *Raverta* by Giuseppe Betussi (1544), and the *Dodici giornate* by Silvan Cattaneo (written in 1553 but published as *Salò e la sua riviera* only in 1745 for lack of a printer) or his yet unpublished "La barca di Padova" show that the narrative genre put forward by these Veneto authors was in a phase of radical transformation. For example, Cattaneo gave importance to the conversation of his male speakers about the behavior of women in public, a choice common to conduct books. His approach was eclectic to say the least: on the fourth day he talked of horticulture; on the eighth day, of Padua; and on the twelfth day, of elephants and music. Betussi's and Lando's works contained treatises, novellas, and love letters. Parabosco inserted love doubts on the second day of his narrative and madrigals and a list of illustrious women on the third, a choice that recalls Betussi and Lando, as well as Boccaccio's *Fiammetta* and *Filocolo,* Agnolo Firenzuola's *I Ragionamenti,* Baldassare Castiglione's *The Book of the Courtier* (1528), Pietro Bembo's *Gli Asolani* (1517), and Giambattista Giraldi Cinzio's *Hecatomnithi.*[58]

56. See for example Daniel Javitch, "Pioneer Genre Theory and the Opening of the Humanist Canon," *Common Knowledge* 3 (1994): 54–66. Bonciani's "Lezione sopra il comporre delle novelle" will also try to systematize a genre that was moving in so many seemingly inchoate directions.

57. Renzo Bragantini, in fact, speaks of paralysis, although I would say that effervescence, rather than paralysis, marked the period. See *Il riso sotto il velame: La novella cinquecentesca tra l'avventura e la norma* (Florence: Olshki, 1987), 46. See also Bruscagli, "Mediazioni narrative nel novelliere di Bandello," in *Matteo Bandello novelliere europeo,* ed. Ugo Rozzo (Tortona: Cassa di Risparmio, 1982), esp. 82.

58. On the narrative in the Veneto region at the time, see Ginetta Auzzas, "La narrativa veneta nella prima metà del Cinquecento," in *Storia della cultura veneta dal primo Quattrocento al Concilio di Trento,* ed. Girolamo Arnaldi and Manlio Pastore Stocchi (Vicenza: Neri Pozza, 1980), 2: 99–138.

Another major reason for the development of romances in the sixteenth century was the vast circulation and impact of Greek romances after they were discovered, translated, and printed. Greek romances offered new possibilities to the developing genre of prose romance: convoluted plots, new reasons to start journeys, and a more diffuse characterization.[59] Narratives of peregrinations became wildly popular, as testified by the *Libro del pellegrino* by Jacopo Claviceo (1508), an erotic romance with nineteen reprints and translations into French and Spanish, and *La Filena* by Nicolò Franco (1547), an epic-erotic romance of peregrinations more than nine hundred pages long.

And then there was the pastoral genre, both in the classical version of Sannazaro's *Arcadia* and in its archetype, Boccaccio's *Ameto*. Italian critics disagree on the derivation of the romance from the pastoral, as was clearly the case in England, because in Italy the woods were more a place for adventure, as in chivalric romances, than an Arcadian refuge from an alienating city and a competitive courtly life.[60] In the romance, the woods worked to stage the theme of the disappointments of love and not to foster moral or utopian narratives, perhaps because women immediately acquired relevance in this genre and their role was soon to modify the action with their presence, rather than simply to listen to the expression of the others' pain, as in the classic pastoral genre. It is in this sense that *Arcadia felice* by Lucrezia Marinella (the first pastoral romance authored by a woman, 1605) or *La Leucadia* by Antonio Droghi (1598), to give two examples, are considered pastoral romances and not romances.[61] In these texts, following Sannazaro, love slowly loses its importance to the point that the main female character is forgotten as the narrative proceeds—the case of Marinella's Ersilia.

Urania unites all the literary genres that came to constitute the romance

---

59. In *Le avventure pastorali di Dafni e Cloe* (1537), for example, Annibal Caro retold and expanded a story of Longo Sofista to make it a love story; Angelo Coccio translated *Storia di Leucippe e Clitofonte* by Achille Tazio in 1550; and Leonardo Ghini rendered the *Historia delle cose etiopiche* of the omnipresent Heliodorus in 1556. On the impact of Greek narratives, see Achille Tartaro, "La prosa narrativa antica," in *Letteratura italiana III. Le forme del testo II. La prosa,* esp. 706–7; and more generally, Arthur Heiserman, *The Novel before the Novel: Essays and Discussions about the Beginnings of Prose Fiction in the West* (Chicago: University of Chicago Press, 1977); and David Konstan, *Sexual Symmetry: Love in the Ancient Novel and Related Genres* (Princeton: Princeton University Press, 1994).

60. For Norbert Jonard, for example, the romance comes from the chivalric romance and not the pastoral. See "Aux Origins du roman: Positions et propositions," *Studi secenteschi* 18 (1977): 64–65; and Asor Rosa, "La narrativa italiana del Seicento," 724. On the influence of the pastoral on the romance, see Gillian Beer, *The Romance* (London: Methuen, 1979), 1–12.

61. As for the pastoral genre in poetry authored by women writers, Maddalena Campiglia's *Flori* and Isabella Andreini's *Mirtilla* came out in the same year, 1588. Both works, as well as Marinella's *Arcadia,* will appear in this series. For a specific Paduan example of verse pastoral, see Valeria Miani, *L'amorosa speranza,* which came out in 1604.

as I have reconstructed it: it is a story of star-crossed lovers, like *Fiammetta*; a narrative of entertainment, like the Greek romances and *Filocolo*; and a pastoral interlude, like the *Arcadia* and *Asolani*. *Urania* has cross-dressed characters, like the court comedies *La Calandria* and *The Deceived*; it has an explicit stance on the position of men and women in society, like *The Book of the Courtier* and *I Ragionamenti*; and it shows the main character engaged in a quest for honor and identity, like the majority of chivalric romances. Bigolina offers multiple narrative strands and plays all the tricks we associate with prose fiction: triangulation of desire, separation of lovers, peregrination, return home to be vindicated, chastisement of the unfaithful beloved, public recognition of the main character's moral values, and a final quadruple marriage.[62] It also shows that the romance was from the very beginning, as has been argued, a perfect arena for the autonomous action of female characters. The motif of the quest, for example—the key romance element—could be easily regendered. Coupled with the ubiquitous theme of androgynous cross-dressing, the quest allowed writers to conceive of women who were able to roam the woods while keeping the man at home, as in Bigolina's *Urania* and "Giulia."[63]

Boccaccio's *Fiammetta* is of course the main source of imitation, because the fertile motif of a lover's obsession for an unfaithful beloved was given a full-blown treatment there first.[64] A more specific Boccaccian source is perhaps the novella of Giletta in *Decameron* (3.9), already used in "Giulia," which has the same narrative strand of an unreciprocated love motivating the main female character to undertake a journey the end of which is positive. More generally, Bigolina is indebted to the Ovidian tradition of the abandoned and eloquent heroines of the *Heroides*, whose voices Ariosto had already successfully echoed in his chivalric romance.[65] She seems also very familiar with the

62. Some or all of these multiple narrative strands were recommended by contemporary critics in order to keep the reader's attention. See Giraldi Cinzio, "Discorso intorno al comporre delle commedie e delle tragedie," in *Scritti critici*, ed. Camillo Guerrieri Crocetti (Milan: Marzorati, 1973), 169–224.

63. On what has been called the femininity of romance, see Helen Hackett, "Wroth's *Urania* and the Femininity of Romance," in *Women, Texts, Histories, 1575–1760*, ed. Clare Brant and Diane Purkiss (London: Routledge, 1993), 39–68 . For the change that an examination of books written by women makes to critical readings of the period, see Elizabeth Harvey, *Ventriloquized Voices: Feminist Theory and English Renaissance Texts* (London: Routledge, 1992).

64. But there are also sizable differences between *Fiammetta* and *Urania*. Fiammetta, for example, remains obsessively centered on her unfaithful beloved, Panfilo, who had seduced her, while Urania, described as virginal and bright, is able to move on and start a journey in search of herself, untainted by gossip about her sexual reputation, although the journey begins under suicidal conditions.

65. Bigolina may have also known the short romance by Enea Silvio Piccolomini, written originally in Latin, *The Tale of Two Lovers, Eurialus and Lucretia*, in which there are letters exchanged be-

Paduan and Venetian literature of the period: like Cattaneo, she reasons about women's behavior; like Betussi and Parabosco, she explores and solves love doubts; like Betussi and Lando, she includes the love letter and material from treatises; like Franco, she employs the motif of the dream; like Mantova Benavides, she introduces jealousy among men.[66]

THE GENRES OF THE "QUESTIONS OF LOVE" AND THE "WORTH OF WOMEN"

The genre of the "questioni d'amore" was much practiced from the Middle Ages to the early modern period, following the examples of Boccaccio's *Filocolo* and Bembo's *Asolani*, and was also used in the new genre of the prose romance by writers such as Parabosco in *Diporti*. The background for a conversation on love usually followed the context offered in *Filocolo*, in which a company of young nobles of both sexes met in a *locus amoenus* in the spring, around noon, and sat in a circle next to a fountain. In Bigolina, Urania meets a group of noblewomen in the woods outside Naples, around noon, in the spring (we can infer the season since she met Fabio one evening at a party the winter before), and they all sit next to a lovely fountain. Urania tells them that she is a poet suffering from love and is taken for a man, a fiction that Bigolina attentively keeps for the entire dialogue. Having women alone talk about love was not a new thing in treatises (although in the fiction Urania is "Fabio"), but often women were involved in a negative way, as for example in Pietro Aretino's *Ragionamento*, in which they counseled each other on the virtues of prostitution.[67]

One of the women asks, What kind of man should women love without fear of being abandoned later? Should one fall in love with young or old men?

---

tween the lovers. Piccolomini's narrative, like *Fiammetta* but unlike *Urania*, posits the sexual encounter of the lovers, Lucretia and Euryalus, a development that is always deleterious to married women in narrative since it leads them to death or madness. Bigolina moves away from such a topos and imagines sexual love in a future outside the text in which it becomes fully legal through marriage. In fact, in women's writing we have to wait for the romantic period to have a woman die for love and lost reputation.

66. Although Mantova Benavides' *Novelle* was not published until the end of the sixteenth century, it is quite likely that Bigolina knew Mantova, given his influential place in Paduan culture at the time. Bigolina also knew Mantova's daughters. See Finucci, "Giulia Bigolina e il romanzo in prosa," 46.

67. In the period in which Bigolina wrote, there were two other treatises with women as interlocutors, both unprinted: *Se è da credersi che [la] donna . . . sia prodotto della natura o a sorte o pensatamente* by Marcantonio Piccolomini (written in 1538) and *Dell'economia o vero del governo della casa* by Aonio Paleario (c. 1555). See Virginia Cox, "The Single Self: Feminist Thought and the Marriage Market in Early Modern Venice," *Renaissance Quarterly* 48 (1995): 570, n. 154.

Should men be poor or rich? Should women trust men? Are men or women more reliable? Urania answers that men and women should choose their counterparts carefully, because in love a man's personality and noble soul are paramount, not his social standing. Men should not be too proud or too mundane. They should know how to joust and hunt and be interested in music and culture. The best men are those learned and respectful. Urania's argument shows that Bigolina has read widely on the subject; in addition to Boccaccio's *Filocolo*, whose thirteen questions on love constitute her model in this section, she knows, for example, the entire debate on the kind of love that it is not moral for men to entertain and whether love is infinite or not, as in *Asolani*. Bigolina also paraphrases the *Dialoghi d'amore* by Ebreo (1535) and *Sopra lo amore* by Marsilio Ficino (written in Latin in 1475 and published in Italian in 1544) and is aware of all the key points in the defense of women by the Magnifico and Cesare Gonzaga in the *Courtier*.[68] Indeed, the ideal man Bigolina describes is modeled on the ideal courtier proposed by Castiglione. Bigolina's argument is well focused: the women in *Urania* are made to say that they would be very happy not to entertain thoughts of love, no matter how much they are solicited by men, and that their reason for wanting to know more about love comes from the fact that they have nothing else more important to do. Given their class, they are not required to do menial jobs but cannot

68. Bigolina does not seem, however, to have read the only other debate on love penned by a woman before her, Tullia d'Aragona's *Dialogue on the Infinity of Love*. The list of love treatises in the Renaissance is a long one. To the names already mentioned I would add Mario Equicola, *Libro de natura de Amore* (1525); Agostino Nifo, *De pulchro et amore* (1531); Sperone Speroni, *Dialogo d'amore* (written in 1528 and printed in 1542), Benedetto Varchi, *Sopra alcune quistioni d'amore* (1554); Alessandro Piccolomini, *Dialogo de la bella creanza delle donne*, known as *Raffaella* (1540); Niccolò Franco, *Dialogo dove si ragiona delle bellezze* (1542), with the second part on love; Giuseppe Betussi, *Dialogo amoroso* (1543), the *Raverta nel quale si ragiona d'Amore e degli effetti suoi* (1544), and *La Leonora, ragionamento sopra la vera bellezza* (1557); Francesco Sansovino, *Ragionamento nel quale brevemente s'insegna a' giovani uomini la bella arte d'amare* (1545); Bartolomeo Gottifredi, *Specchio d'amore nel quale alle giovani s'insegna innamorarsi* (1547); Lodovico Domenichi, "De Amore" and "De' remedi d'amore," both in *Dialoghi* (1562); Flaminio Nobili, *Trattato dell'amore umano* (1567); and Nicolò Vito di Gozze, *Dialogo d'amore detto Anthos* (1581). The majority of these treatises have been reprinted, sometimes partially, in Giuseppe Zonta, ed., *Trattati d'amore del Cinquecento* (Bari: Laterza, 1912). For a critical discussion of love treatises see Mario Pozzi, "Aspetti della trattatistica d'amore," in *Lingua, cultura e società: Saggi sulla letteratura italiana del Cinquecento*, ed. Mario Pozzi (Alessandria: Edizioni dell'Orso, 1989), 57–100. In 1572, Girolamo Bargagli codified the "questioni d'amore" as a game of entertainment in *Dialogo de'giuochi*. Scipione Bargagli did the same in *I trattenimenti dove da vaghe donne e da giovani uomini rappresentati sono onesti e dilettevoli giuochi, narrate novelle e cantate alcune amorose canzonette* (Venice, 1587), where there are four "questioni d'amore." Later in the sixteenth century love treatises became moralistic and falling in love became a dangerous activity. For an examination of this change, see Armando Maggi, "Il tramonto del neoplatonismo ficiniano: L'inedito 'Ragionamento d'amore' di Lorenzo Giacomini la fine dei trattati d'amore," *Giornale italiano di filologia* 49 (1997): 209–28.

spend their time occupied with thoughts of letters and science, because the men around them on whom they depend forbid it, out of jealousy of feminine accomplishments. As a consequence, love is their only possible concern.

The next day Urania meets five Neapolitan gentlemen. This occasion allows Bigolina to examine another frequent literary topic of her time, although no woman had written on it as yet: the excellence and worth of women.[69] Here the author puts aside the gentle tone of the day before and assuredly offers through Urania her thoughts on women's worth and on the need for their education, attributing many conflicts between the two sexes to the fact that women do not have equal access to the political, cultural, medical, and philosophical systems of the time. Bigolina does not concentrate on women abstractly, as other writers had done, but takes men to task for practicing tyranny over this sex for social motives, because "reason does not tolerate that women be unjustly defamed and oppressed."[70] With Bigolina's intervention on the subject, a new chronology of women's production of prowomen treatises in Italy needs to be put forward. Until now, Fonte's *The Worth of Women* and Lucrezia Marinella's *The Nobility and Excellence of Women and the Defects and Vices of Men* (1601) were considered the first texts written in Italian by Italian women writers that argued for the moral and social parity of the female sex—Christine de Pizan's French text, *The Book of the City of Ladies*, was totally unknown, although de Pizan was Italian by birth.[71] In light of Bigo-

---

69. Sources that Bigolina may have had in mind in the writing of this mini-treatise, considering also her intervention in "A ragionar d'amore," are the classical ones on the subject: *Sull'eccellenza e dignità delle donne* by Mario Equicola (1501); *De institutione foeminae christianae* by Juan Luis Vives (1524); *Della eccellenza et dignità delle donne* by Galeazzo Flavio Capra (1525); perhaps also *Della nobiltà et eccellenza delle donne* by Cornelius Agrippa, published in Italian in 1549 and immediately plagiarized by Lodovico Domenichi in his *La nobiltà delle donne* (1549); and *Dialogo delle bellezze delle donne* by Agnolo Firenzuola (1548). Directly from Padua were the *Dialogo della dignità delle donne* by Speroni (1542) and *De la institutione di tutta la vita de l'huomo nato nobile e in città libera* by Alessandro Piccolomini (1542), where male education, universalized to include women, is highly recommended. See also Zonta ed., *Trattati del Cinquecento sulla donna* (Bari: Laterza, 1913).

70. As Moderata Fonte was to write, there is too often a double-edged meaning in men's choices: "You ought to consider the fact that these histories have been written by men, who never tell the truth except by accident. And if you consider, in addition, the envy and ill will they bear us women, it is hardly surprising that they rarely have a good word to say for us, and concentrate instead on praising their own sex in general and particular members of it, as a way of praising themselves." See *The Worth of Women*, ed. and trans. Virginia Cox (Chicago: University of Chicago Press, 1997), 76. I was unable to find any document that would encourage the view that Fonte may have read Bigolina's work, although given that Fonte used to vacation in the region where Bigolina lived, it is possible.

71. I say "in Italian by Italian women writers" in order not to discount fifteenth-century Italian women humanists who wrote in Latin. Isotta Nogarola and Laura Cereta also defended women. Bigolina may have perhaps been aware of the work of the humanist Cassandra Fedele (1465–

lina's *Urania*, we have to move the invention of the first feminist treatise back forty years, to 1553 and thereafter.

At a time in which texts on how to take a wife and how to govern a household were proliferating, Bigolina chose to stress other characteristics of women. This new prowoman militant stance is different, I believe, from that displayed toward the end of the sixteenth century by Fonte and Marinella. These two writers' feminist views may be attributed to the fact, as Virginia Cox persuasively argues, that women were losing their status and identity then as a result of changes in economic and patrimonial assets. In Venice, for example, many upper-class families were putting their daughters in convents in order to leave the family property as undivided as possible for the male line.[72] This is certainly true for the end of the century, but the motivation does not work as well, historically and culturally speaking, for the years in which Bigolina was writing.[73] My hypothesis is that newly enacted Counter-

---

1558), a Venetian who had publicly debated at the Studio in Padua on philosophical and theological issues and had delivered an oration there in 1487. But Fedele embraced no feminist theme in her letters. Fedele's book has been recently published in this series. More generally, on women humanists see Margaret King, "Book-Lined Cells: Women and Humanism in the Early Italian Renaissance," in *Beyond Their Sex: Learned Women of the European Past*, ed. Patricia Labalme (New York: New York University Press, 1980). It has been said that Marinella's book was commissioned to respond to a misogynist but popular intervention on the subject by the Paduan Giuseppe Passi. For an examination of the relationship between Passi's treatise, *I difetti e mancamenti delle donne* (1599) and Marinella's response, see Enrico Zanette, "La polemica femministica," in *Suor Arcangela monaca del Seicento veneziano* (Venice: Istituto per la Collaborazione Culturale, 1960), 211–37; and Adriana Chemello, "La donna, il modello, l'immaginario: Moderata Fonte e Lucrezia Marinella," in *Nel cerchio della luna: Figure di donna in alcuni testi del XVI secolo* (Venice: Marsilio, 1983), 95–170. See also the appendices in Zancan for a bibliography and a chronology of the main books of the *querelle*. Christine de Pizan (1364–1430) was relatively unknown even in France until 1786, when her work was fortuitously discovered by Louise de Keralio, who included it in a collection of women's works in 14 volumes, *Collections des meilleurs ouvrages français composés par des femmes* (Paris: Chez l'Auteur et Lagrance, 1786–89).

72. See Cox, "The Single Sex: Feminist Thought and the Marriage Market in Early Modern Venice," *Renaissance Quarterly* 48 (1995), 557.

73. For example, all three daughters of Speroni married and remarried after they became widows, but things had indeed already changed one generation later, when most of Bartolomeo Salvatico's daughters were made to enter the convent. Bigolina's dowry, as I mentioned earlier, was in landed property and not in liquid assets, but the general trend was toward giving money to daughters and land to sons. In a sense, this required the monachization of most daughters, apart from one or two, a trend that became endemic in the seventeenth century, when not only the nobility but even the classes below them put their daughters in convents in order to assure at least their physical survival at a time of repeated famines and plague. On the impact that changes in the family assets had on social habits after the middle of the sixteenth century, when the system started to pass from the *in fraterna*, in which all brothers had access to property, to one legislated along the lines of a patrilinear indivisible property, which favored the first born, see Marzio Barbagli, *Sotto lo stesso tetto: Mutamenti della famiglia in Italia dal XV al XX secolo* (Bologna: Il Mulino, 1984), chap. 4.

Reformation practices and a limiting atmosphere, as testified by the appearance now of books that blamed rather than praised women, motivated Bigolina to examine the issue of the role of women in society and to focus on education as the way out of marginalization.[74]

Many treatises had denounced the disparity women experienced in society, but often women's superiority was treated facetiously or abstractly. At other times it was hard to see what sort of defense of this sex was mounted. For example, in his prowoman treatise, Speroni made Beatrice degli Obizzi argue that women know that they are naturally and morally inferior to men, servants made to serve them, only to have a man rush to the rescue of women, however awkwardly. For Lodovico Dolce, women's thoughts are "fast, unstable, light, movable, and unable really to fix on anything," a *communis opinio* that could be unflappably written down even in a document that lamented women's social conditioning into objects.[75]

In confuting the arguments adduced to demonstrate a natural and philosophical necessity for female inferiority, Bigolina does not write of superiority but of equality, not of excellence but of worth, and there is not a single humorous element in her argument. For this writer, the virtues women should have in order to live well in society are faithfulness, chastity, and constancy. These are not virtues usually advocated for men—although she does so in the context of both *Urania* and "Giulia"—nor are they virtues that the majority of women would consider the determining characteristics of their sex, although the entire repertory of religious and ancient female figures offered by the church as well as by the literature and culture of the time was modeled on those traits.[76]

Throughout *Urania*, Bigolina argues that if women are faithful and chaste

---

74. See, for example, *Il convito overo del peso della moglie. Dove ragionando si conchiude, che non può la donna dishonesta far vergogna à l'huomo* by Giambattista Modio (1554) and *Despoteia o sia Reggimento . . . Dialogo nel quale si disputa, qual debbia più presto reggere, o l'huomo, o la donna: e per quale caggione la donna de ubidire allo huomo* by Ludovico Niccolò Calusio (1557). Things became worse in the succeeding decades.

75. See Speroni, "Della dignità delle donne," in *Trattatisti del Cinquecento*, ed. Mario Pozzi (Milan: Ricciardi, 1978), 1: 583; and Dolce, *Institution*, 12r (my translation). More generally, see Francine Daenens, "Superiore perché inferiore: Il paradosso della superiorità della donna in alcuni trattati italiani del Cinquecento," in *Trasgressione tragica e norma domestica: Esemplari di tipologie femminili dalla letteratura europea*, ed. Vanna Gentili (Rome: Edizioni di storia e letteratura, 1983), 11–50; and Ian Maclean, *The Renaissance Notion of Woman: A Study in the Fortunes of Scholasticism and Medieval Science in European Intellectual Life* (Cambridge: Cambridge University Press, 1980), 56.

76. For example, after declaring that she does not want to become a woman poet because educated women do not know how to repair stockings or wash clothes, Aurelia Maggi, a fictional female writer in a spurious collection of letters written by a male author, Ortensio Lando, claims that women can be esteemed and honored in the world if they are "chaste, modest, silent, and humble." See Lando, *Lettere di molte valorose donne*.

by nature, as men want them to be, and if they are constant like men (or more so) in their affections, and therefore are morally respectable, then the reason for their social exclusion and submission is inexcusable. The point is not, as Fonte will soon assert as well, that if women were more respected they would cease their complaints—the usual rhetorical mode of submission that has grounded women—but that women should be given an intellectual parity with men because they have demonstrated that they can reach the same objectives when they are allowed to do so. Less nonchalant in her argument than male writers who wrote on the topic, Bigolina makes it clear throughout *Urania* that women's inferiority is political and has its roots in a cultural and philosophical climate that limits women's movements, tempts them into self-deluding narcissism, and controls their means of communication. Therefore, she does not simply praise women's excellence and dignity, as all male prowoman treatises did, but underlines their worth as individuals with a mind of their own.

After refuting the Aristotelian idea that women are anatomically challenged males, an argument often repeated by doctors and clerics, Bigolina has Urania propose a catalog of women competing with men in parallel camps.[77] As Fonte will also do, she insists that many social problems come from men's lack of morality. Countering well-established arguments that women have been responsible for immense destruction, like Helen, or for monstrous acts, like Medea, Procne, and Circe, Bigolina provides through Urania a list of women of the highest morality and then, like the Latin humanist Laura Cereta who had insisted that women have a right to be educated ("nature imports one freedom to all human beings equally—to learn"), she offers her own hymn to female education.[78] Women should have a sense of what goes on in vernacular literature, she argues, and be aware of many ancient histo-

---

77. These lists of exemplary women were everywhere in prowomen treatises, in the wake of Boccaccio's *De claris mulieribus* (1361–75) as, for example, in Vespasiano da Bisticci's (1421–1498) *Il libro delle lodi delle donne*. In men's work the exceptionality of a few women worked to reinforce the sense of the thorough unexceptionality of the entire sex. On this issue, see Constance Jordan, "Boccaccio's In-Famous Women: Gender and Civic Virtues in *De Claris Mulieribus*," in *Ambiguous Realities: Women in the Middle Ages and Renaissance*, ed. Carole Levin and Jeannie Watson (Detroit: Wayne State University Press, 1987). In women's work, on the other hand, as in fifteenth-century women humanists writing in Latin or in Lucrezia Marinella's *The Nobility and Excellence of Women and the Defects and Vices of Men*, ed. and trans. Anne Dunhill (Chicago: University of Chicago Press, 1999), the lists were better contextualized.

78. Cereta, "Letter XVIII to Bibolo Semproni," in *Collected Letters of a Renaissance Feminist*, ed. and trans. Diana Robin (Chicago: University of Chicago Press, 1997), 78. See also Albert Rabil, Jr., *Laura Cereta: Quattrocento Humanist* (Binghamton: Medieval and Renaissance Texts and Studies, 1981).

ries so that, in keeping their minds occupied, they can avoid falling into problems out of boredom and idleness.[79]

THE ROMANCE SECTION

Once the romance proper part of *Urania* starts in earnest, the narrative pace becomes faster. Bigolina invests Urania with a deep melancholy but also with a keen sense of intellectual self-esteem and a voiced determination to have her freedom of choice respected. Urania's sense of loss comes from the fact that no matter how articulate women's minds are, it is the exposed and eroti-cized female body that entices male affections because it suggests female pas-sivity. The lonely journey of self-discovery for the purpose of finding what in fact she already knew—her worth as a woman—through the literal, almost pathological, denial of her femininity, brings Urania back to where she started, Salerno, because it was there that men's respect for women's con-stancy and intelligence was considered important and where a relationship of mutuality could be built. Urania's story demonstrates that women can overcome every problem if they have honest desires, an open mind, and an urge to act on their beliefs. Above all, Bigolina explains, women win if they can create a network of women's relationships.

Like Urania, Emilia—another name borrowed from Boccaccio, who named a narcissistically bent and most striking woman storyteller Emilia in the *Decameron*—is a strong, autonomous woman who uses her widowhood to act freely but not dishonestly and to refute a marriage that she finds uninter-esting for the kind of life she prefers.[80] Emilia is self-sufficient in a house that she administers alone and is able to keep a young man (or so she thinks) next to her without losing her reputation. Her final, altruistic decision to marry Fabio's brother, Hortensio, just to keep close to Urania, even though it comes out as an instance of patriarchal equilibrium imposed to achieve narrative closure, still speaks volumes about the strength of women's ties.

Through Emilia's relationship with Urania, Bigolina consciously reprises

---

79. On the sparse education reserved to women in the period (only 5–6 percent were educated) see Grendler, *Schooling in Renaissance Italy: Literature and Learning, 1300–1600* (Baltimore: Johns Hop-kins University Press, 1989). Only women of a certain social class had a minimum of literary knowledge and could write and read easily.

80. Emilia is the teller of the story of Madonna Beritola in *Decameron* 2.6, which in many ways recalls *Urania* in the woman's peregrinations and the happy end through an eventful reunion. Emilia also tells the story of Tedaldo, 3.5, in which, like Urania, Tedaldo experiences his beloved's rejection and leaves his home, but is able on his return to win back the woman he loves and redress a disastrous situation. Emilia is also in Boccaccio, *Theseid; or, The Nuptials of Emilia.*

the motif of the woman falling in love with another woman disguised as a man that Ariosto had popularized in the episode of the encounter in the woods between his woman warrior, Bradamante, and the Spanish princess, Fiordispina (*Furioso* 25). But in rewriting Ariosto consciously as a woman, Bigolina comes up with a different outcome. The story of Fiordispina's unbound love for Bradamante has been customarily read as a lesbian one. I have argued elsewhere that it is only apparently lesbian, because Fiordispina is made to reiterate *ad infinitum* her desire not for Bradamante, but for what she does not have and for what only Ricciardetto, Bradamante's twin brother, can eventually provide. Be that as it may, the homoerotic implications that the two women's closeness unveiled guaranteed the lasting appeal of the story. In Ariosto, aware that she could not provide a male behavior culturally adequate to the circumstance, Bradamante immediately revealed the truth of her sex so as to avoid keeping Fiordispina in her error.[81] But Bigolina opts to keep Urania's femaleness secret, and Emilia seems to be left to pine ambiguously for the youth in disguise through a series of adventures. This choice could have created plenty of erotic potential, but being a respectable women writer, Bigolina had boundaries to respect. So she constructs an affective, even utopic, but definitely companionable bond between Urania and Emilia based on chastity and compassion as a practical and civic duty. In moving away from the implied male narcissism and homoerotic implications of the Ariostan text, she reclaims the liberating importance of female autonomy and female allegiance.

Another strong woman in *Urania* is Clorina, who is able to have all men fall in love with her beauty. We know what male authors would have made of her, but Bigolina refuses to characterize Clorina as a *femme fatale* and prefers to make her an *ingénue*, so that in the end not only is the topos of the beautiful woman as object of worship turned upside down, but also there are no enemies among women. Like Urania, Clorina too receives men in her home for honest conversations. Like her, she too is allowed to determine her future by choosing the man she wants to marry against the wishes of her father, her relatives, and even her ruler.

Only the Duchess of Calabria who, significantly, is given no proper

---

81. "Gli è meglio (dicea seco) s'io rifiuto / questa avuta di me credenza stolta / e s'io mi mostro femina gentile, / che lasciar riputarmi un uomo vile // E dicea il ver; ch'era viltade espressa, / . . . / parlar con essa, / tenendo basse l'ale come il cucco" ("'My best conduct is to undeceive her,' she decided, 'and to reveal myself as a member of the gentle sex rather than have myself reckoned an ignoble man.' . . . And she was right. It would have been a sheer disgrace . . . if he had kept a conversation with a damsel . . . while like a cuckoo, he just trailed his wings"). *Orlando furioso* 25.30–31 (Waldman translation). For a thorough reading of this episode see Finucci, *The Lady Vanishes*, chap. 5.

name, behaves like a conventional woman in this romance. Her initial presentation as a widow determined never to remarry as a result of a previous negative experience and her inventiveness in trying to get the man she loved characterizes her as a woman of courage, like Urania. But when the duchess opts for passivity for the sake of convention and gives her court painter the responsibility of promoting her case with the prince of Salerno through a portrait of her naked beauty, we know that she is in for a rude awakening. The character "Bigolina" had already taken an anti-Petrarchist attitude in "A ragionar d'amore"; now through *Urania* we are made to understand that the requirement of passivity for the sake of love that constitutes the Petrarchan appeal in culture—staging one's body simply as an erotic signifier—is deadly to women. Once more, it is only when women become dynamic, claim a space for their subjectivity, and look after the satisfaction of their desires—be they carnal as for Clorina or intellectual as for Urania—rather than accept being decorative images for passing Pygmalions, that they obtain their wishes. Thus the duchess, being made to opt not for self-recognition but for a self-deluding and allegorical representation of femininity, is the only woman in our story to fail. As Clorina exemplifies, women's comeliness can temporarily attract men, and in fact the prince is attracted momentarily by the duchess's "supernatural" beauty, but in the end, beauty alone, devoid of a sense of autonomy and self-respect, is worthless. Determined not to act in order to leave her reputation unblemished, our disempowered duchess ends up dying of utter dejection.

Also particularly interesting in *Urania* is the character of the wild woman, who is depicted as horrifying in her display of male rage and predatory attitudes, a demonized figure of generation gone awry. Described with her mouth open, her hair dirty, and her cheeks hairy, the wild woman who kills women after she smells them is a terrifying Medusa figure, the personification of an unbound, sexualized, uncontrollable femininity. She is what Lacan would call the real, that which does not belong to the symbolic order. The episode seems an upside-down version of the story of the Orc in Ariosto, in which the Orc too recognizes women from their "odor di femmina."[82] But if in psychoanalysis Medusa is the self that cannot be looked at, the unrepresentable for the male onlooker, she can be invested with a different function when a woman, rather than a man, does the looking. In Bigolina's rendering, the wild woman ends up accepting a kiss and embracing Urania for, as Hélène

---

82. Ariosto, *Furioso* 17, 40, 42. Although not eaten, women are sadistically punished when the Orc buries them alive, chains them, or exposes them naked on the shore.

Cixous famously put it, "you only have to look at the Medusa straight on to see her. And she's not deadly. She's beautiful and she's laughing."[83]

The wild woman's newfound approachability concludes the traumatic part of *Urania* after which correct gendering, correct social behavior, and even correct naming can be imposed. As our cross-dressed quester "Fabio" now explains to the prince and his court, "I am Urania. I am the one who, led by extreme despair because I felt I was not loved for my worth by my sweetest Fabio, or perhaps to say it better, for my wish to be loved, left these parts with a firm intention never to see them again." By uncovering a feminine self in a highly politicized moment, Bigolina underlines the necessity for Urania to signify her subjecthood as she moves away from inhibitions and reclaims her status in Salerno. The authorial emphasis on the importance of a female-centered sexuality and desire (the problem is not that Fabio did not love Urania, we are told, but that he did not love her the way she wanted to be loved) is predicated on the discarding of woman as lack (the duchess) and on the laughing away of woman as "dark continent" (the wild woman)—the two poles of male fantasy about women that have presided over the creation of the Pygmalion and the Medusa myths.

Bigolina shows less interest in the characterization of men. Fabio becomes a vivid character only when, alone in prison and fearing for his life, he has a premonitory dream that makes him understand in retrospect his amorous failures. His depiction as a passive, womanlike man who needs the help of a motivated, aggressive woman, Urania, to save him from death recalls Tesibaldo in "Giulia." And his acceptance of Urania's love when she—as a smelly cross-dressed brigand—is the least physically enticing, goes a long way in reaffirming Bigolina's point that women should be judged for who they are rather than for what they look like or for how perfectly they embody a male ideal of femininity.

The prince of Salerno, Giufredi, is described as concerned with maintaining a just and even hand in whatever he does and has a good relationship with his citizens, similar to that of a paternalistic, rather than an autocratic, Renaissance ruler. He is also made to remain true to his wish to marry a woman for love rather than for beauty, the ideal for which Fabio should have striven, had he Giufredi's maturity and sense of self. In making him resist a

---

83. Hélène Cixous, "The Laugh of the Medusa," *Signs* 1 (1976): 875–93. A similar episode of kissing ("fiero bacio") by a man kissing a serpent who turns out to be a woman is in Matteo Maria Boiardo, *Orlando innamorato* (Milan: Garzanti, 1978). The *Innamorato* (1482) had been reprinted in 1544. I thank Elissa Weaver for this reference.

courtly love type appeal to fall narcissistically for an imagined woman mirroring him, Bigolina reprises her theme that the ideal woman is not the eroticized and fetishized one, but the chaste maiden next door.

As for Menandro, Clorina's beloved, he is portrayed as having a bad nature, although his characterization is insufficiently developed to make the reader appreciate why. We can easily understand, however, Bigolina's point that male jealousy predicated on violence (Menandro challenges Fabio to a fight, although his opponent is unarmed) is self-destructive. Fathers too seem absent or powerless, leaving daughters able to do just what they like, as long as they do not engage in sexual games.

At times Bigolina is redundant and, like all unpublished manuscripts, *Urania* could have benefited from some judicious cutting. We do not know why the work was never printed. The pressure could have been internal in that the Bigolini belonged to the local nobility, which may have exercised a censure of its own.[84] Or it could have been external, given that it had become difficult for an author to get an imprimatur in Padua after the Inquisition appointed three censors in the 1550s to make sure that unorthodox books were left unprinted and undistributed. After all, a romance written by a woman on a cross-dressed female poet journeying through Italy, unfettered and guilt-free, while considering suicide, was not easy to sponsor.[85]

---

84. Mary Wroth, a noblewoman like Bigolina for example, was publicly satirized and denounced as hermaphroditic and monstrous for publishing her *Urania*: "Hermaphrodite in show, in deed a monster / As by thy works and words all men may conster / Thy wrathful spite conceived an Idell book / Brought forth a foole which like the damme doth look / . . .leave idll books alone / For wise and worthyer women have written none." See Josephine Roberts, "An Unpublished Literary Quarrel Concerning the Suppression of Mary Wroth's *Urania*," *Notes and Queries* 222 (1977), 533.

85. Data are self-evident on the impact that the Counter-Reformation had soon after censors started to look closer at what was being printed: the printing house Giolito, which edited more than a thousand books between 1536 and 1606, published all in all eight editions of Boccaccio's *Fiammetta* and five of the *Decameron*, thirteen editions of Sannazaro's *Arcadia*, and thirty of Ariosto's *Furioso*. But the last edition of the *Decameron* is dated 1552 (the book was put on the Index, as I mentioned, in 1559), and the last of *Arcadia* is dated 1566. Aligning himself with the times, Giolito began to offer more spiritual books. For example, from 1538 to 1564, he published only seven religious works addressed to women, such as the *Specchio di croce* by a writer named Cavalca, but from 1565 to 1589, almost three times as many, that is, nineteen, devotional books dedicated to them came out of his printing press. See Brian Richardson, *Printing, Writers and Readers in Renaissance Italy* (New York: Cambridge University Press, 1999), 145. See also Quondam, "La letteratura in tipografia," in *Letteratura italiana. II. Produzione e consumo*, ed. Alberto Asor Rosa (Turin: Einaudi, 1983), 643; and Vincenzo De Caprio, "Aristocrazia e clero dalla crisi dell'Umanesimo alla Controriforma," in *Letteratura italiana: Produzione e consumo* (Turin: Einaudi, 1983), 299–361. For the paucity of books published in Padua in the sixteenth century, see Marco Callegari, *Dal torchio del tipografo al banco del libraio: Stampatori, editori e librai a Padova dal XV al XVIII secolo* (Padua: Il Prato, 2002), 19; and Tiziana Pesenti Marangon, "Stampatori e letterati nell'industria editoriale

The number of women writers who had published by 1560 in Italy was in any case minuscule, and the other contemporary Paduan *virtuosa*, Gaspara Stampa, today the most famous woman poet of the Italian Renaissance, had died unpublished but for three poems in 1554.[86] *Urania*, like "Giulia," ended up in a drawer or perhaps enjoyed some local circulation among friends and intellectuals. But someone must have cherished the manuscript, or just the memory of the writer, to keep it in a library. Thus it has come to us, no matter how fortuitously, the first in a long line of prose fictions—published or still unedited—written by Italian women in the following centuries.

---

a Venezia e in terraferma," *Storia della cultura veneta*, ed. Girolamo Arnaldi and Gianfranco Folena (Vicenza: Pozza, 1976–), 106–9. For the problems inherent in the passage from manuscript to printed book, see Armando Petrucci ed., *Libri, scrittura e pubblico nel Rinascimento* (Bari: Laterza, 1979).

86. Stampa's work came out a year after her death, thanks to her sister Cassandra. Other women writers published successfully in the period, such as Vittoria Colonna and Tullia d'Aragona, and some published poetry in multiauthored anthologies, but in general women, or at least those of a certain class, were the first to feel that the process of publication may not have been worth the candle.

VOLUME EDITOR'S
BIBLIOGRAPHY

PRIMARY SOURCES

Manuscripts

A ragionar d'amore. Bibliothèque Municipale, MS. 597. Besançon.

Novella di Giulia Campo San Piero et di Thesibaldo Vitaliani Raccontata Nello Amenissimo luogo di Mirabello Da Una Nobilissi. Gentildonna Padovana. Biblioteca Civica, Fondo Lazara, MS. 1451, VIII. Padua.

Urania. Biblioteca Apostolica Vaticana, Fondo Patetta, MS. 358. Rome.

Urania. Biblioteca Trivulziana, codex MS. 88. Milan.

Printed Sources

Alighieri, Dante. *The Divine Comedy.* Ed. and trans. Charles Singleton. Princeton: Princeton University Press, 1973.

Andreini, Isabella. *Lettere della Signora Isabella Andreini Padovana, Comica Gelosa et Academica Intenta, nominata l'Accesa.* In *Women Poets of the Italian Renaissance,* ed. Laura Stortoni New York: Italica Press, 1997.

Aretino, Pietro. *Lettere sull'arte di Pietro Aretino.* Ed. Ettore Camesana. Milan: Edizioni del Milione, 1957.

———. *Quinto Libro delle lettere di M. Pietro Aretino.* Paris: Appresso Matteo il Maestro, 1609.

Ariosto, Ludovico. *Orlando furioso.* Ed. and trans. Guido Waldman. Oxford: Oxford University Press, 1983.

Aristotle. *History of Animals.* In *The Complete Works of Aristotle,* ed. Jonathan Barnes. Princeton: Princeton University Press, 1984.

Assarino, Luca. *Ragguagli di Cipro.* Bologna: Monti and Zenero, 1642.

Bandini Muti, Maria, ed. *Poetesse e scrittrici.* Rome: Istituto Editoriale Italiano, 1941–42.

Bargagli, Girolamo. *Dialogo de' giuochi che nelle vegghie senesi si usano di fare.* Ed. P. D'Incalci Ermini. 2 vols. Siena: Accademia degli Intronati, 1982.

Bargagli, Scipione. *I trattenimenti dove da vaghe donne e da giovani uomini rappresentati sono onesti e dilettevoli giuochi, narrate novelle e cantate alcune amorose canzonette.* Venice, 1587.

Barocchi Paola, ed. *Scritti d'arte del Cinquecento.* 3 vols. Milan: Ricciardi, 1971–77.

Betussi, Giuseppe. *Il Raverta.* Milan: Daelli, 1864.

Bigolina, Giulia, *Urania.* Ed. Valeria Finucci. Rome: Bulzoni, 2002.

Boccaccio, Giovanni. *The Decameron.* Ed. and trans. Guido Waldman. New York: Oxford University Press, 1993.

————. *Famous Women* (*De claris mulieribus*). Ed. and trans. Virginia Brown. Cambridge: Harvard University Press, 2001.

————. *Filocolo*. Ed. Antonio Quaglio. Milan: Mondadori, 1967.

————. *The Elegy of Madonna Fiammetta*. Ed. and trans. Mariangela Causa-Steindler and Thomas Mauch. Chicago: University of Chicago Press, 1990.

Boiardo, Matteo Maria. *Orlando innamorato*. Milan: Garzanti, 1978.

Bonciani, Francesco. "Lezioni sopra il comporre delle novelle." In *Trattati di poetica e di retorica del Cinquecento*, ed. Bernard Weinberg. 4 vols. Bari: Laterza, 1972.

Borromeo, Anton Maria. *Notizia de' novellieri italiani posseduti dal conte Anton Maria Borromeo gentiluomo padovano, con alcune novelle inedite*. Bassano: Remondini e figli, 1794.

Capra, Galeazzo Flavio. *Della eccellenza e dignità delle donne*. Ed. Maria Luisa Doglio. Rome: Bulzoni, 2001.

Castiglione, Baldesar. *The Book of the Courtier*. Ed. and trans. George Bull. London: Penguin, 1967.

Cereta, Laura. *Collected Letters of a Renaissance Feminist*. Ed. and trans. Diana Robin. Chicago: University of Chicago Press, 1997.

Cesarotti, Melchior. *Lettera di un Padovano al Celebre Signor Abate Denina, Accademico di Berlino e Socio dell'Accademia di Padova*. Padua: Fratelli Penada, 1796.

Cittadella Andrea. *Descrittione di Padova e suo territorio*. Ed. Guido Beltrame. Padua: Editrice Veneta, 1992.

Costa, Margherita. *Istoria del viaggio d'Alemagna del Serenissimo Gran Duca di Toscana Ferdinando Secondo*. Venice: n.p., n.d.

Dalla Francesca, Elisabetta, and Emilia Veronese, eds. *Acta Graduum Academicorum Gymnasii Patavini ab anno 1551 ad annum 1565*. Padua: Antenore, 2001.

D'Aragona, Tullia. *Dialogue on the Infinity of Love*. Ed. and trans. Rinaldina Russell and Bruce Merry. Chicago: University of Chicago Press, 1997.

Della Chiesa, Agostino. *Theatro delle donne letterate con un breve discorso della preminenza, e perfettione del sesso donnesco*. Mondovì: Ginaldi and Tomaso Rosci, 1620.

De Zerbis, Gabriele. *Liber anathomie corporis humani*. Venice: Locatellu, 1502.

Dolce, Lodovico. *Dialogo della institution delle donne*. Venice: Giolito, 1560.

Doni, Anton Francesco. *I marmi*. Ed. Ezio Chiorboli. Bari: Laterza, 1928.

————. *La libraria*. Venice: Giolito, 1550.

Ebreo, Leon. *Dialoghi d'amore*. Ed. S. Caramella. Bari: Laterza, 1929.

Erizzo, Sebastiano. *Le sei giornate*. Ed. Renzo Bragantini. Rome: Salerno Editrice, 1977.

Fedele, Cassandra. *Letters and Orations*. Ed. and trans. Diana Robin. Chicago: University of Chicago Press, 2000.

Ficino, Marsilio. *Commentary on Plato's Symposium*. Ed. and trans. Jayne Sears. Dallas: Spring Publications, 1985.

Filogenio Hercole (Ercole Marescotti). *Dell'eccellenza delle donne*. Fermo: Sertorio de' Monti, 1589.

Firenzuola, Agnolo. *On the Beauty of Women*. Ed. and trans. Konrad Eisenbichler and Jacqueline Murray. Philadelphia: University of Pennsylvania Press, 1992.

Fonte, Moderata. *The Worth of Women*. Ed. and trans Virginia Cox. Chicago: University of Chicago Press, 1997.

————. *Tredici canti del Floridoro*. Ed. Valeria Finucci. Modena: Mucchi, 1995.

Franco, Niccolò. *Dialogo dove si ragiona delle bellezze*. Venice: Antonium Gardane, 1542.

Gallonio, Antonio. *Trattato de gli instrumenti di martirio*. Rome: n.p., 1591.

Gamba, Bartolomeo. *Delle novelle italiane in prosa: Bibliografia.* Florence: Tipografia All'insegna di Dante, 1835.

Giraldi Cinzio, Giambattista. "Discorso intorno al comporre delle commedie e delle tragedie." In *Scritti critici*, ed. Camillo Guerrieri Crocetti, 169–224. Milan: Marzorati, 1973.

Kristeller, Paul Oskar. *Iter Italicum Accedunt Alia Itinera. A Finding List of Uncatalogued or Incompletely Catalogued Humanistic Manuscripts of the Renaissance in Italian and Other Libraries.* 6 vols. London: Warburg Institute, 1963–92.

Lando, Ortensio. *Lettere di molte valorose donne.* Venice: Giolito, 1548.

Livy. *A History of Rome: Selections.* Ed. and trans. Moses Hadas and Joe Poe. New York: Modern Library, 1962.

Luigini, Federico. *Il libro della bella donna.* Milan: Daelli, 1863.

Maffei, Scipione. *Indice delli libri, che si ritrovano nella raccolta del Nobile Signor Giulio Saibanti Patrizio Veronese.* Verona: Stamperia della Fenice a S. Maria Antica, 1734.

Marinella, Lucrezia. *Arcadia felice.* Ed. Françoise Lavocat. Florence: Olschki, 1998.

———. *The Nobility and Excellence of Women and the Defects and Vices of Men.* Ed. and trans. Anne Dunhill. Chicago: University of Chicago Press, 1999.

Martellozzo Fiorin, Elda, ed. . *Acta ab anno 1538 ad annum 1550.* Padua: Antenore, 1971.

———*Acta Graduum Academicorum ab anno 1526 ad annum 1537.* Padua: Antenore, 1970.

Masenetti, Giovanni Maria. *Il divino oraculo di M. Gio. Maria Masenetti padovano. In lode delli nuovi sposi del 1548. E di tutte le belle gentildonne padovane.* Venice, 1548.

Masetti Zannini, Gian Ludovico. *Motivi storici dell'educazione femminile: Scienza, lavoro, giuochi.* Naples: D'Auria, 1982.

Maylender, Michele. *Storia delle accademie d'Italia.* 5 vols. Bologna: Cappelli, 1926–30.

Mazzuchelli, Gianmaria. *Gli scrittori d'Italia, cioè notizie storiche, e critiche intorno alle vite e agli scritti dei litterati italiani.* 2 vols. Brescia: Bossini, 1753–63.

Ovid. *Metamorphoses.* Ed. and trans. A. D. Melville. Oxford: Oxford University Press, 1986.

———. *Ovid's Heroides.* Trans. Harold Cannon. New York: Dutton, 1971.

Passano, Giambattista. *I novellieri italiani in prosa.* Milan: Schiepatti, 1864.

Petrarca, Francesco. *Rime sparse.* In *Petrarch's Lyric Poems*, ed. and trans. Robert Durling. Cambridge: Harvard University Press, 1976.

Pietrucci, Napoleone. *Delle illustri donne padovane. Cenni Biografici.* Padua: Tipografia Penada, 1840.

Piccolomini, Alessandro. *La Raffaella, ovvero Dialogo della bella creanza delle donne.* Ed. Giancarlo Alfano. Rome: Salerno Editrice, 2001.

Piccolomini, Enea Silvio. *The Tale of Two Lovers, Eurialus and Lucretia.* Ed. Eric Morrall. Amsterdam: Modopi, 1988.

Piranesi, Pietro. *Bellezze delle novelle tratte dai più celebri autori antichi e moderni.* Paris: Teofilo Barrois, 1823.

———. *Scelta (nuova) di novelle, tratte di più celebri autori antichi e moderni.* Paris: Baudry, 1852.

Plutarch. *Lives.* Ed. and trans. Rex Warner and Robin Seager. Harmondsworth: Penguin, 1972.

Porro, Giulio, ed. *Trivulziana. Catalogo dei codici manoscritti.* Turin: Paravia, 1884.

Pozzi, Mario, ed. *Trattatisti del Cinquecento.* 2 vols. Milan: Ricciardi, 1978.

Quadrio, Francesco Saverio. *Della storia e della ragione d'ogni poesia.* 2 vols. Milan: Agnelli, 1741.

Ribera, Pietro Paolo. *Le Glorie immortali de' Trionfi, et Heroiche Imprese d'Ottocento quarantacinque donne illustri antiche, e moderne.* Venice: Evangelista Deuchino, 1609.

Scardeone, Bernardino. "De claris mulieribus patavinis." In *De antiquitate urbis Patavii et claris civibus patavinis.* Basel: Nicolaum Episcopium, 1560.

Stampa, Gaspara. *Gaspara Stampa: Selected Poems.* Ed. Laura Stortoni and Mary Prentice Lillie. New York: Italica Press, 1994.

Tarabotti, Arcangela. *Women Are of the Human Species.* In *Women Are Not Human: An Anonymous Treatise and Responses,* ed. and trans. Theresa Kenney. New York: Crossroad Publishing, 1998.

Tasso, Torquato. *Jerusalem Delivered (Gerusalemme liberata).* Ed. and trans. Ralph Nash. Detroit: Wayne State University Press, 1987.

Tomasini, Jacopo Filippo. *Bibliothecae Patavinae manuscriptae publicae et privatae.* Udine: Nicholai Schiratti, 1639.

Vedova, Giuseppe. *Biografia degli scrittori padovani.* 2 vols. Padua: Coi Tipi della Minerva, 1832.

Vico, Enea. *Le imagini delle donne auguste intagliate in istampa di rame, con le vite, et isposizioni [. . .] sopra i riversi delle loro medaglie antiche.* Venice: V. Parmigiano and Vincenzo Valgrisio, 1557.

Wroth, Mary. *The First Part of the Countess of Montgomery's Urania by Lady Mary Wroth.* Ed. Josephine Roberts. Binghamton, NY: Center for Medieval and Early Renaissance Studies, 1995.

―――. *The Second Part of the Countess of Montgomery's Urania by Lady Mary Wroth.* Ed. Josephine Roberts. Completed by Suzanne Gossett and Janel Mueller. Tempe: Renaissance English Text Society, 1999.

Zonta, Giuseppe, ed. *Trattati d'amore del Cinquecento.* Bari: Laterza, 1912.

―――. *Trattati del Cinquecento sulla donna.* Bari: Laterza, 1913.

SECONDARY SOURCES

Albertazzi, Adolfo. *Il romanzo.* Milan: Vallardi, 1902.

―――. *Romanzieri e romanzi del Cinquecento e del Seicento.* Bologna: Zanichelli, 1891.

Ambrosini, Federica. "Libri e lettrici in terra veneta nel sec. 16: Echi erasmiani e inclinazioni eterodosse." In *Erasmo, Venezia e la cultura padana del '500,* ed. Achille Olivieri. Rovigo: Minelliana, 1995.

Asor Rosa, Alberto. "La narrativa italiana del Seicento." In *Letteratura italiana III. Le forme del testo. II. La prosa,* ed. Alberto Asor Rosa, 715–57. Turin: Einaudi, 1985.

Auzzas, Ginetta. "La narrativa veneta nella prima metà del Cinquecento." In *Storia della cultura veneta dal primo Quattrocento al Concilio di Trento,* ed. Girolamo Arnaldi and Manlio Pastore Stocchi, 2:99–138. 2 vols. Vicenza: Neri Pozza, 1980.

Balduino, Armando. "Fortune e sfortune della novella italiana fra tardo Trecento e primo Cinquecento." In *La Nouvelle: Genèse, codification et rayonnement d'un genre medieval,* ed. Michelangelo Picone, Giuseppe Di Stefano, and Pamela Stewart, 155–73. Montreal: Plato Academic Press, 1983.

Barbagli, Marzio. *Sotto lo stesso tetto: Mutamenti della famiglia in Italia dal XV al XX secolo.* Bologna: Il Mulino, 1984.

Barberi Squarotti, Giorgio. *Metamorfosi della novella.* Foggia: Bastogi, 1985.

————. "L'instabilità dell'ingegno o l'avventura barocca." *Forum Italicum* 7 (1973): 177–226.

Battaglia, Salvatore. "Il primo romanzo della letteratura italiana." In *La coscienza letteraria del Medioevo*, ed. Salvatore Battaglia, 645–57. Naples: Liguori, 1965.

Beer, Gillian. *The Romance*. London: Methuen, 1979.

Bellomo, Manlio. *La condizione giuridica della donna in Italia*. Turin: Einaudi, 1970.

Beltrame, Guido. *Toponomastica della diocesi di Padova*. Padua: Libreria Padovana, 1992.

————. *Appunti di storia padovana*. Padua: Messaggero, 2000.

Bologna, Giulia. *Libri per un'educazione rinascimentale: Grammatica del Donato*. Milan: Comune di Milano, 1980.

Bongi, Salvatore. *Annali di Gabriel Giolito de' Ferrari*. 2 vols. Rome: Presso i Principali Librai, 1890–95.

Bottasso, Enzo. "La prima circolazione a stampa." In *La novella italiana: Atti del Convegno di Caprarola, 19–24 settembre 1988*, ed. Enrico Malato et al., 1:245–64. 2 vols. Rome: Salerno Editrice, 1989.

Bragantini, Renzo. *Il riso sotto il velame: La novella cinquecentesca tra l'avventura e la norma*. Florence: Olshki, 1987.

Briquet, Charles Moise. *Les Filigranes. Dictionnaire historique des marques du papier des leur apparition vers 1282 jusqu'en 1600*. 4 vols. New York: Hacker Art Books, 1966.

Bruscagli, Riccardo. "La novella e il romanzo." In *Storia della letteratura italiana. IV. Il primo Cinquecento*, ed. Enrico Malato, 835–907. Roma: Salerno, 1996.

————. "Mediazioni narrative nel novelliere di Bandello." In *Matteo Bandello novelliere europeo*, ed. Ugo Rozzo, 61–94. Tortona: Cassa di Risparmio, 1982.

Callegari, Marco. *Dal torchio del tipografo al banco del libraio: Stampatori, editori e librai a Padova dal XV al XVIII secolo*. Padua: Il Prato, 2002.

Calvi, Giulia. *Il contratto morale: Madri e figli nella Toscana moderna*. Bari: Laterza, 1994.

————. "Reconstructing the Family: Widowhood and Remarriage in Tuscany in the Early Modern Period." In *Marriage in Italy, 1300–1650*, ed. Trevor Dean and K. J. P. Lowe, 275–96. Cambridge: Cambridge University Press, 1998.

Cavanagh, Sheila. *Cherished Torment: The Emotional Geography of Lady Mary Wroth's Urania*. Pittsburgh: Duquesne University Press, 2001.

Chemello, Adriana. "La donna, il modello, l'immaginario: Moderata Fonte e Lucrezia Marinella." In *Nel cerchio della luna: Figure di donna in alcuni testi del XVI secolo*, ed. Marina Zancan, 95–170. Venice: Marsilio, 1983.

Chojnacki, Stanley. *Women and Men in Renaissance Venice: Twelve Essays on Patrician Society*. Baltimore: Johns Hopkins University Press, 2000.

————. "Nobility, Women and the State: Marriage Regulation in Venice, 1420–1535." In *Marriage in Italy, 1300–1650*, ed. Trevor Dean and K. J. P. Love. Cambridge: Cambridge University Press, 1998.

Ciccuto, Marcello, ed. *Novelle italiane: Il Cinquecento*. Milan: Garzanti, 1982.

Cixous, Hélène. "The Laugh of the Medusa." *Signs* 1 (1976): 875–93.

Cox, Virginia. "Seen but Not Heard: The Role of Women Speakers in Cinquecento Literary Dialogue." In *Women in Italian Renaissance Culture and Society*, ed. Letizia Panizza. Oxford: European Humanities Research Centre, 2000.

————. "The Single Self: Feminist Thought and the Marriage Market in Early Modern Venice." *Renaissance Quarterly* 48 (1995): 513–81.

Cropper, Elizabeth. "On Beautiful Women, Parmigianino, *Petrarchismo*, and the Vernacular Style." *Art Bulletin* 58 (1976): 374–94.

Daenens, Francine. "Superiore perché inferiore: Il paradosso della superiorità della donna in alcuni trattati italiani del Cinquecento." In *Trasgressione tragica e norma domestica: Esemplari di tipologie femminili dalla letteratura europea*, ed. Vanna Gentili, 11–50. Rome: Edizioni di storia e letteratura, 1983.

De Caprio, Vincenzo. "Aristocrazia e clero dalla crisi dell'Umanesimo alla controriforma." In *Letteratura italiana: Produzione e consumo*, ed. Alberto Asor Rosa, 2:299–361. 6 vols. Turin: Einaudi, 1983.

De Keralio, Louise, ed. *Collection des meilleurs ouvrages francais composés par des femmes.* 14 vols. Paris: Chez l'Auteur et Lagrange, 1786–89.

De Maio, Romeo. *Riforme e miti nella chiesa del Cinquecento*. Naples: Guida, 1992.

Duncan-Jones, K. "Sydney's *Urania*." *Review of English Studies* n.s. 7 (1966): 123–32.

Elwert, W. Th. *Versificazione italiana dalle origini ai giorni nostri*. Florence: Le Monnier, 1987.

Ferrazzi, Cecilia. *Autobiography of an Aspiring Saint*. Ed. and trans. Anne Jacobson Schutte. Chicago: University of Chicago Press, 1996.

Finucci, Valeria. *The Lady Vanishes: Subjectivity and Representation in Castiglione and Ariosto.* Stanford: Stanford University Press, 1992.

———. *The Manly Masquerade: Masculinity, Paternity, and Castration in the Italian Renaissance.* Durham: Duke University Press, 2003.

———. "Giulia Bigolina e il romanzo in prosa del Rinascimento." In Giulia Bigolina, *Urania*, ed. Valeria Finucci, 13–68. Rome: Bulzoni, 2002.

———. "The Female Masquerade: Ariosto and the Game of Desire." In *Desire in the Renaissance: Psychoanalysis and Literature*, ed. Valeria Finucci and Regina Schwartz, 61–88. Princeton: Princeton University Press, 1994.

Frigo, Daniela. *Il padre di famiglia: Governo della casa e governo civile nella tradizione dell'"economica" tra Cinque e Seicento*. Rome: Bulzoni, 1985.

———. "Dal caos all'ordine: sulla questione del 'prender moglie' nella trattatistica del sedicesimo secolo." In *Nel cerchio della luna: Figure di donna in alcuni testi del XVI secolo*, ed. Marina Zancan, 57–93. Venice: Marsilio, 1983.

Garin, Eugenio. "La filosofia dell'amore: Sincretismo platonico-aristotelico." In *Storia della filosofia italiana*. Turin: Einaudi, 1966.

Gentile, Augusto. *Da Tiziano a Tiziano: Mito e allegoria nella cultura veneziana del Cinquecento*. Milan: Feltrinelli, 1980.

Getto, Giovanni. "Il romanzo veneto nell'età barocca." In *Barocco in prosa e poesia*. Ed. Giovanni Getto. Milan: Rizzoli, 1969.

Goffen, Rona. *Titian's Women*. New Haven: Yale University Press, 1997.

Grendler, Paul. *The Roman Inquisition and the Venetian Press. 1540–1650*. Princeton: Princeton University Press, 1977.

———. *Schooling in Renaissance Italy: Literature and Learning, 1300–1600*. Baltimore: Johns Hopkins University Press, 1989.

———. "Form and Function in Italian Renaissance Popular Books." *Renaissance Quarterly* 46 (1993): 451–85.

Grubb, James, *Provincial Families of the Italian Renaissance: Private and Public Life in the Veneto.* Baltimore: Johns Hopkins University Press, 1996.

Guglielminetti, Marziano, ed. *Novellieri del Cinquecento*. Naples: Ricciardi, 1972.

Hackett, Helen. "Wroth's *Urania* and the Femininity of Romance." In *Women, Texts, Histories, 1575–1760,* ed. Clare Brant and Diane Purkiss, 39–68. London: Routledge, 1993.

Harvey, Elizabeth. *Ventriloquized Voices: Feminist Theory and English Renaissance Texts.* London: Routledge, 1992.

Heiserman, Arthur. *The Novel before the Novel: Essays and Discussions about the Beginnings of Prose Fiction in the West.* Chicago: University of Chicago Press, 1977.

Hughes, Diane Owen. "From Brideprice to Dowry in Mediterranean Europe." *Journal of Family History* 3(3) (1978): 262–96.

Javitch, Daniel. *"Cantus interruptus* in the *Orlando furioso." Modern Language Notes* 95 (1980): 66–80.

———. "Pioneer Genre Theory and the Opening of the Humanist Canon." *Common Knowledge* 3 (1994): 54–66.

Jonard, Norbert. "Aux Origins du roman: Positions et propositions." *Studi secenteschi* 18 (1977): 58–80.

Jordan, Constance. "Boccaccio's In-Famous Women: Gender and Civic Virtues in *De Claris Mulieribus."* In *Ambiguous Realities: Women in the Middle Ages and Renaissance,* ed. Carole Levin and Jeannie Watson, 25–47. Detroit: Wayne State University Press, 1987.

King, Margaret. "Book-Lined Cells: Women and Humanism in the Early Italian Renaissance." In *Beyond Their Sex: Learned Women of the European Past,* ed. Patricia Labalme, 66–90. New York: New York University Press, 1980.

———. "Caldiera and the Barbaros on Marriage and the Family: Humanist Reflections of Venetian Realities." *Journal of Medieval and Renaissance Studies* 6 (1976): 19–50.

Kirshner, Julius, and Anthony Molho. "Il monte delle doti a Firenze dalla sua fondazione nel 1425 alla metà del sedicesimo secolo: abbozzo di una ricerca." *Ricerche storiche,* n.s., 10 (1980): 21–47.

Klapisch-Zuber, Christiane. "The 'Cruel Mother': Maternity, Widowhood, and Dowry in Florence in the Fourteenth and Fifteenth Century." In *Women, Family, and Ritual in Renaissance Italy,* 117–31. Chicago: University of Chicago Press, 1985.

Kohl, Benjamin. *Padua under the Carrara, 1318–1405.* Baltimore: Johns Hopkins University Press, 1998.

Konstan, David. *Sexual Symmetry: Love in the Ancient Novel and Related Genres.* Princeton: Princeton University Press, 1994.

Kuehn, Thomas. *Law, Family and Women: Toward a Legal Anthropology of Renaissance Italy.* Chicago: University of Chicago Press, 1991.

Lavarda, Sergio. *L'anima a Dio e il corpo alla terra: Scelte testamentari nella terraferma veneta, 1575–1631.* Venice: Istituto Veneto di Lettere, Scienze e Arti, 1998.

Lenzi, Ludovica. *Donne e madonne: l'educazione femminile nel primo Rinascimento.* Turin: Loescher, 1982.

Longo, Nicola. *Letteratura e lettere: Indagine nell'epistolografia cinquecentesca.* Rome: Bulzoni, 1999.

———. "La letteratura proibita." In *Letteratura italiana. V: Le Questioni,* ed. Alberto Asor Rosa, 965–99. Turin: Einaudi, 1986.

Lorenzetti, Paolo. *La bellezza e l'amore nei trattati del '500.* Pisa: Nistri, 1917.

Lucas, Caroline. *Writing for Women: The Example of Woman as Reader in Elizabethan Romance.* Milton Keynes: Open University Press, 1989.

Maclean, Ian. *The Renaissance Notion of Woman: A Study in the Fortunes of Scholasticism and Medieval Science in European Intellectual Life.* Cambridge: Cambridge University Press, 1980.

Maggi, Armando. "Il tramonto del Neoplatonismo ficiniano: L'inedito 'Ragionamento d'amore' di Lorenzo Giacomini e la fine dei trattati d'amore." *Giornale italiano di filologia* 49 (1997): 209–28.

Mancini, Albert. *Romanzi e romanzieri del Seicento.* Naples: Società Editrice Napoletana, 1981.

Mancini, Vincenzo. *Lambert Sustris a Padova. La villa Bigolin a Selvazzano.* Comune di Selvazzano Centro: Biblioteca Pubblica Comunale, 1994.

Mantovani, Gilda. *Un fondo di edizioni giuridiche dei secoli XV–XVII: Il "dono Selvatico." Catalogo.* Rome: Istituto Poligrafico e Zecca dello Stato, 1984.

Mazzacurati, Giancarlo. *All'ombra di Dioneo: Tipologie e percorsi della novella da Boccaccio a Bandello.* Florence: La Nuova Italia, 1996.

Milani, Marisa. "Isabella, Margherita, Perina la Flamenga: Storie di donne fra letteratura e documenti." In *Tracciati del femminile a Padova: Immagini e storie di donne,* ed. Caterina Limentani and Mirella Cisotto Nalon, 59–64. Padua: Il Poligrafo, 1995.

Miller, Nancy. "Emphasis Added: Plots and Plausibility in Women's Fiction." *Proceedings of the Modern Language Association* 96 (1981): 36–47.

Miller, Naomi. *Changing the Subject: Mary Worth and Figurations of Gender in Early Modern England.* Lexington, KY: University Press of Kentucky, 1996.

Nardi, Bruno. *Saggi sull'aristotelismo padovano dal secolo XIV al XVI.* Florence: Sansoni, 1958.

Padoan, Giorgio. "*Ut pictura poesis:* Le 'pitture di Ariosto, le 'poetiche' di Tiziano." In *Momenti del Rinascimento Veneto,* ed. Giorgio Padoan. Padua: Antenore, 1978.

Pesenti Marangon, Tiziana. *La biblioteca universitaria di Padova dalla sua istituzione alla fine della Repubblica Veneta, 1629–1797.* Padua: Antenore, 1979.

———. "Stampatori e letterati nell'industria editoriale a Venezia e in terraferma." *Storia della cultura veneta,* ed. Girolamo Arnaldi and Gianfranco Folena, 4:93–129. 6 vols. Vicenza: Pozza, 1976–.

Petrucci, Armando, ed. *Libri, scrittura e pubblico nel Rinascimento.* Bari: Laterza, 1979.

Porcelli, Bruno, *La novella del Cinquecento.* Bari: Laterza, 1973.

Pozzi, Giovanni. "Temi, *topoi,* stereotipi." In *Letteratura italiana I: Le forme del testo,* ed. Alberto Asor Rosa, 391–436. Turin: Einaudi, 1984.

Pozzi, Mario. "Aspetti della trattatistica d'amore." In *Lingua, cultura e società: Saggi sulla letteratura italiana del Cinquecento,* ed. Mario Pozzi, 57–100. Alessandria: Edizioni dell'Orso, 1989.

———. "Il ritratto della donna nella poesia d'inizio Cinquecento e la pittura di Giorgione." *Lettere italiane* 21 (1979): 3–30.

Queller, Donald, and Thomas Madden. "Father of the Bride: Fathers, Daughters, and Dowries in Late Medieval and Early Renaissance Venice." *Renaissance Quarterly* 46 (1993): 685–711.

Quondam, Amedeo. "La letteratura in tipografia." In *Letteratura italiana. II. Produzione e consumo,* ed. Alberto Asor Rosa, 555–686. Turin: Einaudi, 1983.

———, ed. *Le 'Carte Messaggiere.' Retorica e modelli di comunicazione epistolare: Per un indice dei libri di lettere del Cinquecento.* Rome: Bulzoni, 1981.

————. *Il naso di Laura: Lingua e poesia lirica nella tradizione del classicismo.* Modena: Panini, 1991.

Rabil, Albert Jr. *Laura Cereta: Quattrocento Humanist.* Binghamton, NY: Medieval and Renaissance Texts and Studies, 1981.

Richardson, Brian. *Printing, Writers, and Readers in Renaissance Italy.* New York: Cambridge University Press, 1999.

Robb, Nesca. *Neoplatonism of the Italian Renaissance.* London: Allen, 1935.

Roberts, Josephine. "An Unpublished Literary Quarrel Concerning the Suppression of Mary Wroth's *Urania.*" *Notes and Queries* 222 (1977): 532–35.

Rogers, Mary. "The Decorum of Women's Beauty: Trissino, Firenzuola, Luigini and the Representation of Women in Sixteenth-Century Painting." *Renaissance Studies* 2(1) (1988): 47–88.

Saggiori, Giovanni, ed. *Padova nella storia delle sue strade.* Padua: Piazzon, 1972.

Sambin, Paolo. "Nuove notizie su eredi e discendenti del Petrarca." *Atti dell'Istituto Veneto di scienze, lettere ed arti* 110 (1951–52): 255–66.

Simioni, Attilio. *Storia di Padova. Dalle origini alla fine del secolo XVIII.* Padova: Randi, 1968.

Snyder, Jon. "La maschera dialogica: La teoria del dialogo di Sperone Speroni." *Filologia veneta* (1989): 113–38.

Stortoni, Laura, ed. *Women Poets of the Italian Renaissance.* New York: Italica Press, 1997.

Tamassia, Nino. *La famiglia italiana nei secoli decimoquinto e decimosesto.* Milan: Sandron, 1910.

Tartaro, Achille. "La prosa narrativa antica." In *Letteratura italiana III. Le forme del testo II. La prosa,* ed. Alberto Asor Rosa, 623–713. Turin: Einaudi, 1982–89.

Turchini, Angelo. *Sotto l'occhio del padre: Società confessionale e istruzione primaria nello Stato di Milano.* Bologna: Il Mulino, 1996.

Vickers, Nancy. "Diana Described: Scattered Woman and Scattered Rhyme." In *Writing and Sexual Difference,* ed. Elizabeth Adel. Chicago: University of Chicago Press, 1982.

Wall, Wendy. *The Imprint of Gender: Authorship and Publication in the English Renaissance.* Ithaca: Cornell University Press, 1993.

Wetzel, Hermann. "Premesse per una storia del genere della novella: La novella italiana dal Due al Seicento." In *La novella italiana. Atti del Convegno di Caprarola, 19–24 settembre 1988,* ed. Enrico Malato et al. 2 vols. . Rome: Salerno Editrice, 1989.

Yavneh, Naomi. "The Ambiguity of Beauty in Tasso and Petrarch." In *Sexuality and Gender in Early Modern Europe,* ed. James Grantham Turner, 131–57. Cambridge: Cambridge University Press, 1993.

Zancan, Marina, ed. *Nel cerchio della luna: Figure di donna in alcuni testi del XVI secolo.* Venice: Marsilio, 1983.

Zanette, Enrico. "La polemica femministica." In *Suor Arcangela monaca del Seicento veneziano,* ed. Enrico Zanette, 211–37. Venice: Istituto per la Collaborazione Culturale, 1960.

NOVELLA DI GIULIA CAMPOSAMPIERO
E DI TESIBALDO VITALIANI

Sì come è bella, ma difficile oltre modo, l'impresa che m'è imposta dalla Signora Cavaliera Conte, nostra regina, nobilissime donne e valorosi uomini, così potess'io ben sperare di condurla a quel debito fine che ricerca la sua grandezza. Meravigliosa per avventura mi darebbe l'animo di far apparere la novella di Giulia Camposampiero, la quale mi commette la reina che io racconti, novella della quale indarno è chi spera di udire né la più bella nè la più adorna. Ma che debbo far io? Certo, se alli comandamenti della cavaliera tenterò di far resistenza, averà giusta ragione ognuno di voi di concludere che io sola, di tanti, sia stata ardita di contravvenire a i dolci solazzi di così soave compagnia, cosa della quale non potrebbe succedere altra che mi travagliasse maggiormente ora e sempre, dove debito officio mio è di far prova se con la debolezza del mio ingegno foss'io bastevole di metter insieme questa non novella, ma istoria. Il che, se piacerà a Dio che succeda, sarà anche per avventura da me, se non illustrata, almanco adombrata la sua grandezza. Se veramente, come temo, non risponderà alla sua altezza e alla vostra aspettazione quello che di quella dirò, sarò io reputata ufficiosa e non disobbediente.

Piacciavi, dunque, graziose donne, poi che in così dilettevol luogo com'è questo di Mirabello ne ha condotto il giudizio meraviglioso della reina nostra, e poi che così grave soma sopra sta l'imbecilli mie forze di far sì che io, donna mal usa a questo, senta dal vostro favorirmi da ognuna di voi ricevere tal giovamento, che ove manca l'ingegno supplisca il vostro favore, nel quale confidata, facile per avventura mi potrà riuscire sì difficile impresa.

Fu dunque già dugento e più anni nella città nostra di Padova, a tempo che, sollevata dalla strage d'Eccelino e non pervenuta ancora alle mani de' Carraresi, ella si governava a repubblica, signoreggiando molti castelli e alcune città circumvicine con molta sua gloria e satisfazione di tutti, un giovane della nobil famiglia de' Vitaliani, chiamato Tesibaldo, al quale, sì come Iddio

NOVELLA OF GIULIA CAMPOSAMPIERO
AND TESIBALDO VITALIANI

Noble women and valiant men, since the task imposed on me by the Signora Cavaliera Conte, our queen, is lovely but inordinately difficult, I hope to carry it to the rightful end that its greatness requires.[1] I may even be able to make the novella of Giulia Camposampiero, which the queen has given me the task of recounting, appear marvelous, so that in vain one would hope to hear a more beautiful or well-turned novella. What should I do in any case? Were I to attempt to resist the Cavaliera's commands, each of you would have just cause to conclude that I alone, among many, have the temerity to flout the sweet pastimes of our lovely company. Nothing else would upset me more; rather, my proper task is to prove that I am sufficiently good, given the failings of my talent, to put together this work, not a novella but a true story.[2] Should God allow this to happen, with luck I shall also adumbrate, if not illustrate, its greatness. If, as I fear, what I say about it does not match the loftiness it requires or your expectations, I shall have obediently, if unsuccessfully, tried.

Since the marvelous judgment of our queen has brought us to such a delectable place as this Mirabello[3] and has placed such a heavy demand on my weak abilities, may it please you, gracious ladies,[4] to allow that I, a woman unused to this, should feel that your kind support overcomes my lack of talent. If I can count on this, such a difficult task may perhaps turn out to be an easy one for me.

So to begin. More than two hundred years ago in our city of Padua, when it was governed as a republic (having recovered from the havoc of Ezzelino and not yet having fallen into the hands of the Carraresi), possessing many castles and controlling a number of cities with much glory for itself and satisfaction for all,[5] a young man of the noble family of the Vitaliani,

e la fortuna erano stati sommamente favorevoli e nel farlo nascere il più bello e grazioso giovane che fosse giamai mai stato per avanti veduto e si potesse sperare forse di vedere per l'avvenire, così avea egli con sì meraviglioso artificio atteso e alla cognizione delle lettere e all'istruzione dell'armi, una e l'altra sommamente convenevoli alla vita cittadinesca, che era riputato di gran lunga avanzare gli altri tutti.

Da queste sue rare bellezze congiunte a così chiare doti di animo procedeva ch'era non pure stimato e onorato da tutti i cittadini, ma era singolarmente amato da ogni condizione di donne, ma da quelle principalmente che erano da marito, ognuna delle quali riputava sè felice oltre modo se avesse potuto ardire di sperare la grazia di così avventuroso giovane. Accompagnava egli la bellezza e dottrina con sì mirabil arte che furno molti che dubitorno che più tosto fosse celeste che umana creatura; e come sempre rimaneva superiore in qualunque delle più ardue disputazioni che molte e frequenti aveva nelle scole e nelle deliberazioni della repubblica, nella quale aveva sempre onorato luogo. Così in danzare, in giostrare, in lottare non era alcuno che più ardisse di seco contrastare, però che era altrettanto destro, agile, forte e gagliardo, quanto dotto, arguto e ingegnoso.

Avea fatto egli fermo proponimento di non maritarsi giammai, benché fosse solo e ricchissimo, però fece lungamente resistenza grande a qualunque donna che per marito lo ricercava. Anzi, essendo da molte vie di continuo combattuto di lasciarsi almeno amare, dimostrò sempre di non aver cosa alcuna che maggiormente lo travagliasse di questo, e in questo suo fermo parer fermato, visse qualche anno lontano da sì gran travaglio.

Avvenne pure che, vinti e superati i Scaligeri dalla repubblica padovana in quella memorabil sempre e sempre gloriosa guerra, giudicarono i padri della repubblica (seguendo in questo le vestigie de' passati) che fosse ben fatto di far publiche feste e di bandire onorate giostre in segno di così grande allegrezza della città. Però, dato buon órdine alle feste, che sempre se hanno fatte grandi e onorevoli per la special grazia che ha avuta questa città di aver sempre copia grande di belle donne, fecero di più bandire per il primo giorno di maggio una publica giostra, il prezzo della quale fu una pezza di panno d'oro foderata tutta d'ermellini, con una colomba d'oro in cima, che aveva in bocca una rama d'olivo carica di smeraldi. Alla grandezza di questra giostra concorsero molti e onorati principi e cavalieri di molte parti.

Frattanto non restavano i gioveni a questo deputati di fare onorevoli feste in corte delli signori, a una delle quali danzando Tesibaldo a caso con Giulia Camposampiero, unica figliuola al cavalier Tiso, non manco bella che artificiosa, avvenne che ora, mirandola fissa quando ragionando con lei che parlava accortamente, s'avvide Giulia ch'era mutato in parte il molto rigore di

named Tesibaldo, was esteemed to far surpass all other young men.[6] God and Fortune had showed him great favor by making him the most handsome and gracious young man that anyone had encountered up to that time and per- haps ever at any time, so well and with such marvelous skill had he attended to learning letters and developing skill in arms, both highly desirable for suc- cess in city life.

All of the citizens esteemed and honored his rare grace and gifts of mind, but women of every condition especially loved him, particularly those of marriageable age, each of whom felt extremely happy just to dare to hope for the grace of such an enterprising young man. His handsomeness and learn- ing were matched by such a marvelous manner that many wondered whether he was a heavenly rather than an earthly creature.[7] Not surprisingly, he won all the most demanding disputations that were frequently held in the acade- mies, and his opinions were highly respected in public forums. No one dared challenge him in dancing, jousting, or wrestling, since he was as adroit, agile, strong, and gallant as he was learned, clever, and ingenious.[8]

He had firmly resolved never to marry, and although he lived alone and was quite wealthy, he long resisted any woman who sought him for a hus- band. And nothing upset him more than being solicited in different ways to at least let himself be loved. Firm in this judgment, he lived for a few years free from this great nuisance.

After the Scaligeri were overwhelmed and conquered by the Paduan re- public in that ever-memorable and still glorious war,[9] the fathers of the re- public judged it proper to hold public festivities and sponsor honorable jousts (following in this the vestiges of the past) as a sign of the city's rejoic- ings. Lavish festivities were ordered, and these were made even more spec- tacular by virtue of the special grace this city enjoyed of always having a con- siderable number of beautiful women. A public joust was announced for the first of May. Its trophy was a piece of gold cloth entirely lined with ermine. At the top it had a dove made of gold with an olive branch in its mouth filled with emeralds. Given the splendor of the joust, a number of honored princes and knights came from many places to compete.

The young men committed to this enterprise took advantage of the oc- casion to enjoy honorable entertainment in the noblemen's courts. In one of these, Tesibaldo danced by chance with Giulia Camposampiero, the only daughter of the knight Tiso, who was no less clever than beautiful.[10] When he looked straight at her as he was listening to her wise words, Giulia real-

Tesibaldo. Però, divenuta animosa, ebbe ardir di dirli che per suo amore fosse contento di dimostrare il suo valore nella giostra. A questo non ebbe vive ragioni di contravvenire il Vitaliano; anzi, convinto e violentato, promise di soddisfare il desiderio di lei, alla quale affermava d'avere obbligo di soddisfare in maggior cosa. Contenta Giulia di questa promessa e finito il ballo, giudicò essere benissimo fatto di sollecitar l'amor suo.

Tesibaldo, veramente, quando combattendo con i studi della filosofia procurava di resistere alle fiamme di amore ora contemplando le bellezze di Giulia, ch'aveano accompagnata alla bellezza una viril dispostezza, si fermava in proponimento di amarla; ora riducendosi a memoria la vita sua passata diliberava di rimoversi dalla sua promessa; ora considerando l'efficacia della fede data di dover giostrare giudicava d'esser astretto a farlo, di maniera che, combattuto da questi dui così gravi pensieri e stando nel fare che questo cedesse a quello, finalmente mirando in quella dubbietà gli occhi di Giulia, conobbe nel vivo raggio di quelli esser descritto: "Dunque mancar tu tratti di quel che sei obbligato?"

E però, risoltosi e d'amarla e di dover giostrare, ebbe ricorso da M. Daulo de' Dotti, suo strettissimo parente, col mezzo del quale, fatta secretissima provisione di cavalli e armadure, ebbe comodità di apparecchiarsi alla giostra che già era principiata e nella quale per giorni tre continui fu da ognuno riputato vincitore Lucio Orsino, gentiluomo romano, col quale oramai non compariva alcuno che ardisse di contrastare. Poco prima che al fine de giorni tre, comparse finalmente Tesibaldo, tutto armato d'armi bianche, con una sopravveste di raso medesimamente bianco, ricamate tutte d'oro, con l'elmo ch'aveva una man d'avorio con un motto che diceva: TU SOLA PUOI. Fu così subito all'apparire conosciuto da Giulia, come dal resto della città tutta fu riputato cavaliere incognito.

Ora, dati i segni della tromba, si vennero l'Orsino e Vitaliano ad incontrare con le grosse lance di tal maniera che, rotte quelle in mille pezzi, alfine fu astretto di cadere in terra l'Orsino. Per la caduta del quale subentrò Tesibaldo nell'obbligo di mantenere la sbarra, e quella sera istessa molti abbattette da cavallo e fece il simigliante il seguente giorno, di modo che fu ragionevolmente pubblicato vincitore della giostra. Per la qual pubblicazione avvenne che, conosciuto da tutta la città, fu senza fine allegra quella vittoria, sì per le condizioni del Vitaliano come per onore universale. Ma come fu di contento questa vittoria a tutti, così fu disturbo e dolore all'Orsino, il quale fra sè medesimo concluse di non lasciar mai senza vendetta quella caduta. Vittorioso dunque Tesibaldo della giostra, ma vinto dallo amor di Giulia, ebbe poco di poi comodità di esser in casa di lei, ove fatte secrete nozze secretamente la fece di donzella donna.

ized that Tesibaldo's forbidding rigidity had somewhat relaxed. Therefore, becoming bold, she dared to ask him to show his mettle in the joust for her sake. Vitaliano had no good reason to contravene this request; on the contrary, strongly persuaded by her manner, he promised to satisfy her desire since he felt he had an obligation to satisfy her even more.[11] Happy for this promise, Giulia judged, after the dance had ended, that she had done very well in soliciting his love.

Tesibaldo tried to resist the flames of love by occupying himself with the study of philosophy. Yet at times, contemplating Giulia's beauty, which united comeliness with a courageous disposition, he would resolve to love her; at other times he would decide to withdraw his promise, remembering his past resolutions; and still at other times, he would decide that he needed to joust, considering the importance of the pledge he had given. The tug-of-war between such opposite inclinations remained unresolved until he looked one day into Giulia's eyes and realized that in their lively ray was written, "Do you want to avoid then what you should be obliged to do?"

Thus, having resolved both to love her and to joust, he appealed to M. Daulo de' Dotti, a relative in whom he intimately confided. Dotti secretly provided him with horses and armor so that he had the opportunity to ready himself for the joust that had already begun and in which, for three continuous days, everyone assumed that Lucio Orsino, a Roman gentleman, was the winner. By now there was no one who dared show up to oppose him. Just before the end of the third day, Tesibaldo finally appeared, entirely armed in white armor, with a satin cloak, also white, embroidered in gold. The helmet had an ivory overlay with a motto that read, "ONLY YOU CAN."[12] Giulia immediately recognized him when he appeared, but the rest of the city took him for an unknown knight.

Now, the trumpet's blast having sounded, Orsino and Vitaliano charged at each other with long lances; these were broken into a thousand pieces, but not before Orsino was knocked to the ground. As a result of his fall, Tesibaldo was now the one obligated to spar, and that same evening he knocked down many on horseback; he did the same the day after, and thus he was pronounced the winner of the joust. Recognized by the entire city as a result of the announcement, his victory brought great merriment, both because of Vitaliano's character and the honor accorded him by everyone. But although this victory made everyone else happy, it disturbed and pained Orsino, who resolved to exact revenge for his fall. Tesibaldo had won the joust, but was conquered by Giulia in love. Soon thereafter the two exchanged secret wedding vows in her house, and Tesibaldo made a woman of a maiden.

Ma mentre che spesso frequentavano questi novelli amanti e sposi questi reiteramenti amorosi, venne nuova alla repubblica che Sigismondo imperatore era giunto a Bologna da Eugenio Quarto e per coronarsi e per dare ordine a molti loro importanti negozi. Giudicorno però convenevol cosa i padri della repubblica di far elezion di quattro ambasciatori, i quali subito andassero e a quella coronazione e a fare ufficio con Sigismondo di rallegrarsi dello imperio poco prima caduto nella sua persona. Furno perciò eletti M. Giacomo Dotto, M. Gio. Francesco Capodilista, M. Roberto Trapolin, uomini gravi e vecchi, e a loro fu aggiunto Tesibaldo per compagno, a' quali fu dato ordine espresso di partirsi subito. Dispiacque questa elezione a Giulia sopra modo, ma con la certezza che presto dovesse ritornare, si consolò molto.

Ora, fatta provision presta e onorata dalli oratori, se inviorno a Bologna, ove giunti ebbe carico Tesibaldo di satisfare al desiderio della repubblica. Perciò, messa insieme una eloquente orazione in lingua latina, in publica audienza, alla presenza di Eugenio e di tutta la città, fece di tal maniera che fu giudicato com'era, uomo superiore a tutti nel parlare eloquentemente. E piacque sì l'uffizio che fece e ad Eugenio e a Sigismondo, che da quello indutti l'uno a l'altro più che dall'onorevolezza dell'ambasceria (che era per il vero sommamente onorevole) e per i vestimenti delli ambasciatori e di tutta la loro corte, e per tutti gli accidenti, come di cavalli, muli e argenterie, volsero far tutti i quattro li ambasciadori loro cavalieri, con molti privilegi.

Venne a Padova fama di così egregio portamento di Tesibaldo e insieme la certezza della cortesia che infinita li usava l'imperatore, di modo che, avendo finito l'ufficio suo l'oratore che seguitava ordinario di continuo lo imperatore, elessero in suo luogo Tesibaldo, e subito li dediorno comandamento che dovesse seguir l'imperatore. Fu di travaglio questa nuova a Tesibaldo, ma di cruccio infinito a Giulia. Questo si doleva che desiderava di ritornare a Padova a dar compimento a' suoi studi, questa si crucciava che, morto il cavalier Tiso, suo padre, intendeva di pubblicar le nozze. Ma astretto dalla viva forza de' comandamenti della sua repubblica, d'animo assai composto ritornò con l'imperatore a Vienna, e accasato appresso il palazzo imperiale faceva sempre operazioni degne di lui, né cosa alcuna mai domandò in nome de' suoi signori all'imperatore, che più ampla molto non la ottenesse. Sigismondo, parte per la sua virtù, parte perché era graziosissimo Tesibaldo, sempre quando li occorreva di ragionar di lui, con vive e vere ragioni concludeva che fosse impossibile che si truovasse vivente alcuno che di gran lunga se li potesse pareggiare.

Udì questi ragionamenti più volte Odolania, sua figliuola, che era a quei tempi la più bella e più graziosa giovane che si potessi ritrovare, e senza

While these newlyweds attended to their amorous relations, news arrived that the emperor Sigismund had come to Bologna to meet Pope Eugenius IV in order to be crowned and to settle other important business.[13] The fathers of the republic thus judged it appropriate to elect four ambassadors to attend his crowning and to convey their congratulations for the empire that had recently come under his rule. They chose signor Giacomo Dotto, signor Giovanni Francesco Capodilista, and signor Roberto Trapolin, all important and old men, and Tesibaldo was added as their companion.[14] They were ordered to depart right away. This decision displeased Giulia enormously, but she consoled herself with the certainty that he would soon return.

The ambassadors were sent to Bologna appropriately provided for, and the fathers of the republic charged Tesibaldo, once there, to formally express the good wishes of the republic. Tesibaldo composed an eloquent oration in Latin and delivered it in a public forum in the presence of Eugenius and the entire city. He performed so well that he was judged a man superior to all others in eloquence. And the function he performed, including both his diplomatic mission and the splendor of the delegation's presence (which was indeed quite honorable), thanks to their clothes, attendants, and accessories like horses, mules, and silverware, pleased Eugenius and Sigismund so much that they decided to make the four ambassadors their own knights with many privileges.

Because of his distinguished behavior, Tesibaldo returned to Padua certain that the emperor would show him great respect. And this he did, for the fathers of the republic, in due course, replaced the current ambassador with Tesibaldo and ordered him, as was customary for one in that position, to follow the emperor. This news troubled Tesibaldo, but it caused untold grief to Giulia. He complained that he wished to return to Padua to finish his studies, and she was worried about making the news of their wedding public, now that her father, Tiso, had died. But constrained by the full force of the orders of his republic, Tesibaldo returned with the emperor to Vienna with a composed spirit. Housed next to the imperial palace, he always acted honorably and never asked the emperor for anything in the name of his noblemen that he did not obtain more than he asked for. Partly because of his virtue and partly because Tesibaldo was very gracious, in his best moments Sigismund judged, with good reason, that it was impossible to find his equal in any man alive.

These opinions were heard many times by Odolania, Sigismund's daughter, who was then the most beautiful and gracious damsel in the kingdom.[15]

averlo pur veduto s'accese talmente che reputò sè beata se poteva acquistare l'amore di sì lodato giovane. Però, deliberata di volerlo vedere, avvenne che il seguente giorno andando Tesibaldo all'imperatore, fu non pur visto da Odolania ma riputato angelo di cielo, di modo che, accese maggiormente le fiamme d'amore, tentò di avere comodità di vederlo quando lei voleva in casa sua, nella quale certe finestre del palazzo potevano guardare comodamente. Era usato Tesibaldo, dipoi i suoi studi, di attendere a molti onorevoli esercizi, quando giocava a saltare, quando ballava, ora maneggiava cavalli; e mentre ciò operava, senza punto avvedersene era non pur veduto, ma ammirato da Odolania.

Frattanto, sendo sparsa per tutto il mondo la fama delle sopraumane bellezze d'Odolania e pervenuta all'orecchie dell'Orsino, riputò sè felicissimo se poteva aver luogo di donzello appresso di lei. Fulli in questo modo favorevole la fortuna, però con lettere semplici d'Eugenio fu non pur accettato ma raccomandato dallo imperatore ad Odolania. Era costume dello imperatore di far molte e solenne feste a consolazion d'Odolania. Però, facendone una sera una più solenne delle altre, a quella invitato Tesibaldo, ma tardando egli a venire con molto dolore di Odolania, fu lei astretta di commettere all'Orsino, suo nuovo donzello, che andasse a levarlo, il quale contento per il comandamento ma dolente per l'odio che portava a Tesibaldo, andò di subito a levarlo e fece sì indusse Tesibaldo ad andarli, che per avventura poco si curava.

Comparse alla festa Tesibaldo a lume di torce con la sua corte avanti che era fornita di fioriti giovani, vestito alla italiana di calze rosse coperte di velluto ricamato d'oro con un robbone di sopra, pur di velluto cremesino, foderato di lupi cervieri, e aveva in testa un cappelletto di pelo guernito di seta e d'oro. Al comparire del quale, le donne tutte che più non l'aveano vedute conclusero che mai più fosse stato veduto il più bello e il più grazioso giovane; il comun parlare delle quali sentendo Odolania, maggiormente si confermava e accendeva nel suo amore.

Ora, principiato il ballo, al quale è lecito alle donne di levare un uomo, piacque all'imperatore e al resto de principi che facesse Odolania questo favore allo ambasciador padovano di danzar seco; la quale non aspettando d'esser molto astretta, con riverente inchino presentossi a Tesibaldo e lo invitò a ballare. Ma cortese egli levato, di subito principiò in germana lingua, da lui benissimo appresa, a ringraziare la signora Odolania di sì gran favore, la grandezza del quale affermava di riconoscere e dalla cortesia di sua signoria e dal rappresentar egli così onorata republica, come quella di Padova.

Da queste parole prese ardire Odolania e subito soggiunse: "Anzi al vostro valore e alle vostre bellezze dovete voi questo obbligo, dalle quali

Without ever having seen him, she started to burn so much with desire that she wanted to win the love of this highly regarded young man. One day, as Tesibaldo was accompanying the emperor, Odolania caught sight of him and judged him to be an angel from heaven. The flames of love being stirred even more, she tried to devise a strategy to watch him whenever she wanted in his own house, into which she could easily glimpse from a window in her palace. After studying, Tesibaldo had the habit of taking part in many honorable exercises, like jumping, dancing, and handling horses, and as he was doing these things, without realizing it, he was not only being observed but admired by Odolania.

The fame of the superlative beauty of Odolania having spread in the meantime to the whole world, it reached Orsino, and he thought he would be fortunate if he could be a page in her retinue. Fortune was propitious in this, because through simple letters from Eugenius he was not only accepted by the emperor but also recommended by him to Odolania. It was the emperor's habit to stage many formal balls to entertain Odolania. On one occasion he organized a most formal ball, to which Tesibaldo was invited. He was late in arriving and that caused much grief to Odolania, who felt obliged to commission Orsino, her new page, to get him. Pleased by the order but afflicted by the hatred he had for Tesibaldo, he immediately went to get him and persuaded him to go, for as it happened, Tesibaldo cared little.

Tesibaldo appeared at the ball by torchlight preceded by his court, which included many handsome young men. He was dressed in the Italian fashion, with red stockings covered in velvet embroidered in gold and a coat of crimson velvet lined with lynx; on his head he wore a little fur-lined hat trimmed with silk and gold. When he appeared, all the women who had not seen him in a long while concluded that he was the most handsome and gracious young man ever seen. Hearing their talk, Odolania was confirmed in her love and burned even more.

The dance in which women are allowed to select a dancing partner began, and the emperor and all the other princes wanted Odolania to request the Paduan ambassador as her partner. Not requiring much inducement, she introduced herself to Tesibaldo with a respectful bow and invited him to dance. Standing up courteously, he began right away in the German language, which he had learned very well, to thank lady Odolania for such a great favor. He asserted that he recognized its importance both because of her ladyship's courtesy and because he represented a republic as honored as Padua.

Odolania took courage at these words and immediately added, "You owe this obligation rather to your worth and your loveliness. Kindled by those

accesa il primo giorno che vi vidi, il primo giorno medesimo me vi donai tutta. E non mi pentisco ora di averlo fatto, anzi, tanto più son contenta quanto che vedo il mio giudizio conforme non pure a quello dell'imperatore, mio padre, che vi ha concluso superiore a tutti in lettere, ma a quello di queste signore, che vi concludono voi di bellezza contrastare con qual si voglia angelo del cielo. Però, onorato signore, piaccia a voi di esser contento ch'io vi servi e d'accettarmi per vostra."

A queste parole mutossi Tesibaldo e più volte dubitò che da altri non fossero state intese, avendo lei parlato altrettanto liberamente quanto arditamente. Pure, avveduto che non erano state udite, principiò egli a rispondere in tal maniera: "Grave offesa fate, signora, alla vostra altezza a ricercare che io per mia accetti vostra signoria alla quale son indegno di servire, e ben mostrate esser desiderosa di favorirmi maggiormente poi che, scherzando meco, prendete gioco di darmi ad intendere che quello diciate col core che con le parole esprimete."

Soggiunse allora Odolania, interrompendo il parlar di Tesibaldo: "Piacesse a Dio che, come parlo io da dovero così foss'io da voi esaudita, che questa notte non tarderebbono ad aver fine i miei tormenti, anzi ora sareste voi mio."

Non sopportò l'accorto ambasciatore che più continuasse Odolania a parlarli in questa maniera, anzi li affermò che ad ogni altra cosa pensasse che a questa, però che a lei nasciuta avventurosamente figliuola di sì grande imperatore conveniva pensare di aver signore e marito conforme alla sua grandezza.

Finì fra tanto il ballo, e rimasa da questa conclusione sopra modo dolente Odolania, pensando ora una cosa ora un'altra, tentò vari mezzi, i giorni seguenti, per indurre al suo volere Tesibaldo. Ma furno tutti indarno, però che ad Emilia, figliuola del duca d'Alba, che di queste cose li parlò molte volte efficacemente, li diede risposta tale che intese che quando fosse egli più di ciò sollecitato, lo propalerebbe al signor suo imperatore. Avvenne poi che Odolania, soprapresa da molta maninconia, gravemente infermò, né truovandosi medicina che la potesse sanar, anzi facendoli ogni cosa nuocimento.

Lucio Orsino, che dell'amore suo s'era benissimo accorto, giudicò questa opportuna occasione e di acquistare la signora Odolania e di vendicarsi col Vitaliano. Però, fatto un giorno animoso e condotto al letto di Odolania, con queste parole cominciò a parlarli: "Sacra Corona, mal si ponno celare le forze de amore, alle piaghe del quale non si trova remedio che basti. So io, e me ne sono accorto, che il mal vostro procede da molto amor che portate al signor orator padovano, né me ne meraviglio punto che voi, savia e accorta donna, l'amiate. Anzi, mi meraviglierei se così non fusse, sendo egli tale qual è. A

the first day I saw you, I gave my whole self to you that very day as well. And I do not regret having done so; on the contrary, I am all the more happy when I see my judgment not only similar to that of the emperor, my father, who has concluded that you are superior to everyone in learning, but also to that of these ladies, who have concluded that you are comparable in beauty to an angel from heaven. Therefore, honored lord, please be satisfied that I serve you and accept me as yours."

Tesibaldo changed countenance at these words, since she had spoken so freely and boldly and he feared that others had heard them. Realizing soon that that was not the case, he answered,"You offend your high status seriously, my lady, in requesting that I accept as mine your ladyship, whom I am unworthy to serve, and you really show that you favor me even more when in teasing me playfully you try to convince me that you express in your words what you have in your heart."

Odolania said then, interrupting Tesibaldo, "May it please God that, since I speak seriously, I could have my wish fulfilled, for this very night my torments would end; indeed you would be mine now."[16]

The wise ambassador could not stand for Odolania to continue talking to him in this fashion; on the contrary, he told her to think of any other subject but this, since she, being born the daughter of such a great emperor, should consider getting a lord and husband fitting to her status.

In the meantime the ball ended, and Odolania remained very much grieved by this conclusion. Thinking now one thing, now another, in the days that followed she tried various means to bend Tesibaldo to her will, but all in vain. He even told Emilia, the daughter of the Duke of Alba, who often spoke skillfully to Odolania of these things, that if he were again solicited about this, he would reveal it to the lord, her emperor.[17] This caused Odolania to fall into a deep depression and become gravely ill, and no medicine could be found to heal her; on the contrary, everything seemed to cause her harm.

Lucio Orsino, who had become very much aware of her love, judged this a timely occasion both to acquire lady Odolania and to take vengeance on Vitaliano. Therefore, turning bold one day as he was brought to Odolania's bed, he said to her, "Your highness, one cannot easily hide the power of love, and there is no adequate remedy for its wounds. I know this and have become aware that your illness comes from the excessive love you have for the lord ambassador from Padua, nor I am surprised that you, a lady wise and sensible, love him. On the contrary, I would be amazed if such were not the case, he

questo amore pensando io, pietade molte volte m'ha astretto a fare questo ufficio, il quale prego vostra Altezza che non giudichi prosontuoso, perché spinto da solo desiderio di servirla mi son mosso a farlo. Voi dunque amate? Il mal vostro è amore? A questo poss'io darvi quel solo rimedio ch'è bastante di sanarvi se così vi piace. Però ditemi liberamente se così volete, e del resto lasciate a me il pensiero."

Piacque ad Odolania l'accorto parlamento dell'Orsino e, desiderosissima d'aiuto, non solo accettò le sue profferte, ma lo pregò grandemente che facesse sì che suo diventasse Tesibaldo, che in ricompenso di questo li prometteva la signora Emilia, figliuola del duca d'Alba, per moglie. Lucio rispose che attendesse lei guarire, che quanto prima a lei bastasse l'animo di venire di notte alla finestra che guarda sopra una corte, allora gli darebbe l'animo di dare Tesibaldo in suo potere. Rimase di questa promessa talmente consolata Odolania, che di là a pochi giorni, non solo risanata ma ritornata al pristino stato di bellezza, fece intendere all'Orsino che facesse quanto aveva detto di dover fare.

Contento l'Orsino fuori di modo, avuto fra tanto l'abito medesimo col quale comparse quella sera Tesibaldo alla festa per via d'un cameriero, di quello vestito, la notte medesima, secondo l'ordine dato, andò a ritruovare Odolania, la quale, credendo che fosse veramente Tesibaldo, non solamente lo ricevette in camera allegramente, ma allegramente lo lasciò diventar possessore e patrone della sua persona. E così, senza punto avvedersene, continuò più notte, una delle quali veduto pure a salire quelle scale con lo abito conosciuto da tutti di Tesibaldo, fu la seguente mattina detto all'imperatore, il quale, non potendo ciò credere per le condizioni di Tesibaldo, si risolse di voler intendere se ciò vero fusse da Odolania; all'appartamento delle camere della quale andò, e seco principiò a trattare di darli per marito Odoardo, figliuolo del re d'Ungheria; il quale per avventura in questa occasione avea mandati suoi ambasciatori a Vienna.

Rispose a queste parole Odolania: "Indarno tenta vostra Maestà di darmi marito alcuno, però che quale m'è stato conceduto da Iddio, tale l'ho avuto io prima che ora. E bene che io sappia che vi debbe esser molesta cosa d'intendere, pure io vi faccio sapere che Tesibaldo è mio signore e marito e con lui ho celebrato secrete nozze."

Travagliorno queste parole lo imperatore talmente che fu più volte per incrudelire contra Odolania, ma pur, vinto dalla ragione, comandò di subito che secretamente fosse lei posta in fondo di torre, il che fu fatto. Ma non si dolse lei tanto di questo, che non si dolesse maggiormente di quello che dubitava che accascasse a Tesibaldo, a casa del quale andò per comandamento

being as he is. Thinking about this love, piety has forced me many times to offer this service, which I pray your highness not to judge presumptuous, because I am moved to act on it only by a desire to serve you. Do you love him then? Your illness is love? I can provide the only remedy that is sufficient to cure it, if this is your wish. Tell me freely what you would like, and leave the rest to me."

Odolania liked Orsino's clever talk and not only accepted his offer, desiring very much to be helped, but also asked him warmly to try to make Tesibaldo hers. As a reward she promised him for a wife lady Emilia, daughter of the Duke of Alba. Lucio answered that she should first attend to her recovery and that as soon as she had the heart to come at night to the window that overlooks a courtyard in the palace, he would have the courage to give Tesibaldo over to her power. Odolania was so consoled by this promise that in a few days, not only cured but also returned to her pristine state of beauty, she let Orsino know that he should do what he said he would.

That same night, following the agreed upon signal and happy beyond belief, Orsino went to see Odolania wearing the outfit with which Tesibaldo had appeared at the ball and which he had in the meantime secured from a servant. Believing that he was truly Tesibaldo, not only did she receive him happily in her room but also happily let him become the owner and master of her body, and she continued to do the same for a number of nights, without realizing in the least who he was.[18] On one occasion Orsino was seen climbing those stairs with the clothes that everyone knew were Tesibaldo's, and the news was given to the emperor the next day.[19] Unwilling to believe it because of Tesibaldo's status, he decided to see whether this was true from Odolania, and went to her apartment. He started to discuss his decision to give her Odoardo, the son of the king of Hungary, for a husband, since he had sent his ambassadors to Vienna on this business.[20]

Odolania answered his words, "It is useless for Your Majesty to try to give me any husband, since I already have the one God has given me. And although I know that it must seem a difficult thing for you to come to terms with, still I want you to know that Tesibaldo is my lord and husband and I have celebrated secret nuptials with him."

These words troubled the emperor so much that many times during her speech he was on the verge of becoming cruel toward Odolania. Still, won by reason, he immediately ordered that she be secretly held in the tower's jail, and this was done. She was grieved only a little about this but much more feared what would befall Tesibaldo, to whose house the city governor went

dell'imperatore di subito il governadore della città, e senza difesa lo ritenne, che a punto studiava, e lo custodì in orribil prigione.

Si meravigliò Tesibaldo assai di questa retenzione, né sapendosi imaginar la causa stando in molto affanno, fulli portata nuova che piaceva alla maestà dell'imperatore che fusse pubblicamente non pur morto, ma arso. Dolente di questa nuova, ma consolato nella sua innocenzia, procurò, ma mai puotè ottenere grazia, di parlare allo imperatore; anzi quanto più procurava, tanto più era repulsato. Dovendosi donque dar esecuzione a questa imperial sentenzia, una mattina, dapoi molto contrasto delli consiglieri cesarei, prevalse finalmente il parer d'uno che affermò non potersi di ragione far morire un oratore se prima il principe da lui rappresentato non intendesse la causa.

Però ottenuto questo parere, sospesa l'esecuzione, furno subito inviati a i capi della repubblica padovana doi oratori con lettere imperiali, nelle quali era dato pieno avviso non pure dell'eccesso dell'oratore, ma della capital condannazione alla quale era piaciuto allo imperatore di condannarlo. Giunti questi oratori a Padova e inteso così orribil mancamento, dalli capi della repubblica fu non pur commendata la condannazione cesarea, ma fatta deliberazione di eleggere oratori che supplicassero l'imperatore e a dare a Tesibaldo maggior pena e a credere fermamente che la Repubblica avesse di questa ingiuria conferita oltre ogni sua aspettazione dolore infinito.

Fatta perciò questa cosa palese nella città e pervenuta con molto rammarico all'orecchie di Giulia (benché si sentisse ella offesa grandemente da Tesibaldo per questa imputazione), argumentando però e concludendo che potesse esser che fosse Tesibaldo innocente di questa colpa, subito si risolse, comunicato questo suo parere con doi suoi cugini della medesima famiglia di Camposampiero, di andar a Vienna vestita da uomo, concludendo sè felice oltremodo se dalle mani di quei che conducevano a morir Tesibaldo fosse lei prima morta. Però, fatta provvisione secreta d'ogni cosa necessaria e principalmente d'arme e di danari, andò a Vienna, a giungere alla quale non tardarono molto gli oratori eletti.

Ma giunti, subito pregorno in pubblico sua maestà e ad incrudelire maggiormente contro il Vitaliano e a perdonare alla signora Odolania, la colpa della quale aveano commissione e d'alleggerire e d'attribuire tutto al troppo ardire di Tesibaldo. Avendo dunque questi oratori eseguito questa commissione, potero bene dall'imperatore ottener la condannazione di Tesibaldo, non già l'assoluzione d'Odolania, contro la quale avea di già publicata la medesima sentenzia, cioè che fosse insieme arsa. Questa sentenzia quella mattina medesima fu dato ordine che fusse eseguita.

right away by order of the emperor. He took him unarmed, since he was studying, and held him in custody in a horrible prison.

Tesibaldo wondered very much about this imprisonment. As he was agonizing because he could not imagine the cause, he got the news that his majesty, the emperor, had decreed not only that he be publicly put to death, but also that he be burned at the stake. Sorrowful at this news but consoled by his innocence, he tried to speak to the emperor, but could not obtain that grace; on the contrary, the more he tried the more he was repulsed. When the emperor ordered that the sentence of execution be carried out, the imperial counselors discussed it, and in the end the opinion of one counselor prevailed. He argued that an orator could not reasonably be put to death if the prince he represented had not been apprised of the reason.

Having reached this opinion, they stayed the execution while two ambassadors were sent to the Paduan republic with imperial letters in which full notice was given not only of the orator's excess, but also of the capital punishment to which it had pleased the emperor to condemn him. When these ambassadors arrived in Padua and the chiefs of the republic heard this horrible judgment, not only did they commend the imperial condemnation, but they also decided to elect ambassadors to beseech the emperor to give Tesibaldo a greater punishment and conveyed the firm sentiment that the republic was also deeply grieved by this injury.

This affair having therefore become public in the city, it caused much sorrow when it reached Giulia's ears. Although she felt very much offended by this charge against Tesibaldo, she concluded that it was possible that Tesibaldo was innocent. Thus she immediately decided to go to Vienna dressed as a man and communicated this decision to two cousins from the Camposampiero side of the family. She felt that she would be lucky if she were killed at the hands of those leading Tesibaldo to death. Having secretly supplied herself with everything necessary, and most of all with arms and money, she went to Vienna, where the elected ambassadors arrived soon after.

Once they got there they publicly begged his majesty to act more cruelly toward Vitaliano and to forgive lady Odolania, whose fault their republic wished to minimize, attributing the entire affair wholly to Tesibaldo's extreme recklessness. The ambassadors succeeded quite easily in obtaining Tesibaldo's condemnation from the emperor, but not Odolania's absolution, for he had already made public against her the same sentence, that is, that she be burned as well.[21] That very morning the order was given for the sentence to be executed.

Però condotta al luogo solito in mezzo la piazza, Odolania, vestita di panni neri, ardita e affermando di aver ciò commesso che l'era l'opposto, ma negando di aver fallato, fu da tutti comunemente pianta, e tanto maggiormente quanto che in lei si vedeva grandissima costanzia. Condotta al luogo del fuoco Odolania e partita la corte per condurvi medesimamente Tesibaldo, acciò che, legati tutti dui ad un medesimo palo, un fuoco medesimo gli ardesse e abbruciasse, Giulia, non pentita del suo proponimento, anzi fatta maggiormente animosa, vestita pur da uomo, non sì tosto vide fuori delle prigioni il suo signore tutto languido e afflitto, che subito, messa mano alla spada, cominciò quando a ferire un officiale, quando ad ammazzarne un altro, di maniera che se non venivano altri in aiuto, lei sola e abbandonata da' suoi cugini avea liberato lo innocentissimo suo consorte dalle mani di venti e più ufficiali.

Ma corsi altri, non solo impedirono la sua liberazione, ma la ritennero e in quella prigion medesima la condussero della quale aveano puoco prima tirato fuori Tesibaldo, il qual, condotto al luogo medesimo ove era Odolania e dovendosi allora dar esecuzione alla sentenzia, corse uno ufficiale a comandare che si soprassedesse. Fra tanto, meravigliandosi Tesibaldo più di vedere nel medesimo travaglio Odolania che se medesimo, cominciò Odolania a così dire: "Mio signore, sarebbe a me questo tormento se non dolce almeno manco noioso, se in questo non vedessi voi ancora, mio unico contento. Ma poiché così piace allo imperator, mio signor e padre, che noi, quali avea congiunti insieme il voler di Dio, insieme corriamo un medesimo tormento nel morire, consolatevi e siate securo che io più compassiono voi che me stessa."

Da queste parole comprese Tesibaldo che qualche falsa demonstrazione intorno ad Odolania avea mosso l'imperatore ad incrudelire così atrocemente e così ingiustamente. Però a lei rivolto così disse: "Fin qui certo, signora, mi ha doluto non pur il morire e il modo del morire, ma anco il non sapere per quale cagione abbia lo imperatore contra di voi e me pubblicata così atroce sentenzia. Se per non aver io voluto assentire alle vostre preghiere ciò è accaduto, mi contento di quello che piace a sua Altezza. Se veramente perché abbi avuta qualche sinistra informazione di me e di voi, questo mi travaglia più del morire e del modo di morire."

Rispose Odolania: "Non accade, mio signore, che neghiate quello ch'è fatto palese a tutto il mondo per mia causa; anzi confessiate, come confesso io, che non merita il nostro amore così crudel fine, e così confessando siate securo d'esser maggiormente compassionato da tutti."

A queste parole rispose Tesibaldo arditamente e affermava che li piaceva il morire, ma che li dispiaceva restasse impressione nell'animo degli uomini

Led to the usual place in the middle of the square and dressed all in black, boldly affirming that she had acted as charged but denying having done any wrong, Odolania was mourned by everyone all the more because of her incredible constancy. After Odolania was led to the place of execution, the court left to bring Tesibaldo there as well, so that both could be tied to the same stake. As soon as she saw her lord all weak and distressed emerging from the prison gate, Giulia, dressed as a man, unrepentant in her resolve, and more spirited than ever, put her hand on her sword. She began by wounding one officer and killing another, so that if others had not come to help, she alone, abandoned by her cousins, would have freed her most innocent husband from the hands of twenty or more officers.

But others arrived, and not only did they prevent his release, but they bound her also and led her to the same prison from which they had earlier taken Tesibaldo. Tesibaldo was brought next to Odolania, and the sentence was in the process of being executed when an official scurried in to stop it. While Tesibaldo was feeling amazed at seeing Odolania in the same trouble as he, Odolania said, "My lord, this torment would be if not sweet at least less horrible to me if I were not to see you, my only happiness, in it. But since the emperor, my lord and father, desires that we undergo together the same torment in dying, inasmuch as we were joined by God's will, console yourself and be assured that I have more compassion for you than for myself."

At these words Tesibaldo understood that some false charges surrounding Odolania had moved the emperor to become so atrociously cruel and so unjust. Turning to her, he said, "Until now, my lady, I was pained not just by the thought that I must die and die in this way, but that I did not know why the emperor publicly enacted such a dreadful sentence against you and me. If this happened because I did not want to indulge your entreaties, I am satisfied that this so pleases your highness. If it happened because he had some sinister information about me and you, this bothers me more than dying and the way of dying."

Odolania answered, "You should not deny, my lord, what I have revealed to the whole world; on the contrary, confess, as I confess, that our love does not deserve such a cruel end, and in so confessing remain confident that you will be more pitied by all."

Tesibaldo replied to these words boldly and affirmed that he did not mind dying, but that he disliked leaving the impression in men's minds that he had

che avesse egli usato tal viltade quale sarebbe stata di domesticarsi con la si-gnora Odolania, sua signora, e sperava che Dio averia dimostrato miracolo di questa sua innocenzia.

Ma intanto che con efficaci parole se affaticava l'innocentissimo e eloquentissimo oratore di persuadere questo a tutti, allora un padre di S. Francesco, uomo di molta religione, affermò alla maestà dello imperatore che, avendo confessato quella istessa mattina l'Orsino, subito poi venuto a morte della infermità guadagnata per le molte fatiche fatte con Odolania, avea egli e palesemente detto a lui e pubblicato a tutti l'orribil tradimento fatto ad Odolania e a Tesibaldo, comprobando la verità di questo tradimento e con l'abito di Tesibaldo che si ritrovava ancora in casa e con molte cose le quali erano successe tra Odolania e lui.

Inteso questo dallo imperatore, e certificato e da altri e dall'aver ritrovato l'abito istesso, comandò subito che fossero non pure liberati, ma condotti l'uno e l'altro alla sua presenza. Giunti i quali cominciò l'imperatore non pure ad escusarsi con Tesibaldo, ma adimandarli perdono, avendo egli creduto che ciò che diceva la figliuola fosse vero.

Tesibaldo veramente, veduti i duo oratori da lui benissimo conosciuti, cominciò in tal guisa a parlare: "Sacra maestà, quello che possa Dio sopra di noi ho apertamente conosciuto in questo affare nel quale ha piaciuto a sua divina maestà ad un medesimo tempo e di fare prova della mia constanza e di mostrarmi la sua pietade, non mi lasciando morire con tal calonnia. Ringrazio dunque sua divina maestà, e all'Altezza vostra affermo che non accade che meco si scusi di questo, che ha piaciuto ad Iddio di provare di me. Ben mi duole che innocentemente abbi non pur patito, ma la signora Odolania in-sieme."

"Anzi," soggiunse l'imperatore, "voi solo altrettanto a torto foste da me condannato, quanto che giustamente Odolania, la quale però rimarrà con-dannata grandemente, quando ch'ella intenda che, credendo d'essere stata vostra, sappi e conoschi esser di Lucio Orsino, come a voi Odolania figliuola non pur affermo, ma col mio grave dolore attesto."

Il che inteso da Odolania e sendosi lei di ciò certificata a' vari segni, de quali ne parlò tra tanto il frate, fu talmente dolente, che manco dolente era prima.

Ma l'accorto imperatore trattò di consolarla, dicendoli pubblicamente: "Odolania, poi che così a voi sono piaciute e piacciono tuttavia le bellezze e condizioni di Tesibaldo, io che sono a voi padre e amorevole mi contento (se così a lui piace) che voi, poi che sete rimasa miracolosamente vedova, siate sua moglie."

A questo rispose Odolania, ringraziandolo grandemente. Ma diversa fu

committed such a vile act as to become intimate with Lady Odolania, her highness. He hoped that God would demonstrate his innocence through a miracle.

While the most innocent and eloquent ambassador was striving with efficacious words to persuade everyone of this, a franciscan, a man of much faith, told his majesty, the emperor, that Orsino that same morning had confessed to him and immediately afterward had died of an illness incurred as a result of his many sexual encounters with Odolania.[22] In his confession Orsino had told him clearly, and revealed publicly to everyone, his horrible betrayal of Odolania and Tesibaldo. Orsino had proved this betrayal by bringing forth Tesibaldo's outfit, which was still in the house, and by recounting many things that had happened between him and Odolania.

When the emperor understood this and was assured of it through others and through the discovery of the outfit, he ordered not only that they be freed, but also that they both be brought before him. When they arrived, the emperor not only apologized to Tesibaldo, but asked for his forgiveness as well, since he had believed what his daughter had told him to be true.

As soon as he saw the two Paduan ambassadors he knew very well, Tesibaldo began to say, "Sacred Majesty, what God can do for us I have realized in this affair, in which it has pleased his divine majesty at the same time both to try my constancy and to show me his grace by not letting me die as a result of a slander. I therefore thank his divine majesty, and to your highness I affirm that you should not apologize to me for this, since it pleased God to try me. It pains me not that I suffered innocently, but that lady Odolania did as well."

"On the contrary," the emperor added, "you alone were condemned wrongly. Odolania instead was sentenced justly. She will understand how great her punishment is when she realizes that, rather than being yours, as she believed, she was in fact Lucio Orsino's, a fact that Odolania, my daughter, I confirm with such deeply felt pain."

Odolania, having understood this and having realized it from various signs about which the friar spoke in the meantime, was more grieved than before.

The perspicacious emperor tried to console her, saying publicly, "Odolania, since you loved so much, and you still love, the grace and learning of Tesibaldo, I, your loving father, would be happy (if he agrees) that you, having become miraculously a widow, now become his wife."

Odolania replied by thanking him greatly. But Tesibaldo answered that

la risposta di Tesibaldo, perciò che disse che non era in termine di accettare così gran cortesia, sendo obbligata la sua fede a donna la quale, se ben non era da aguagliarsi alla signora Odolania, meritava però per le degne sue condizioni di non essere ingannata. Dispiacque questa riposta a tutti, ma ad Odolania più d'ognuno.

Aveano frattanto i consiglieri cesarei comandato che quello che avea non pur violentato, ma ferito e ammazzato alcuni ufficiali, fusse publicamente decapitato. Quando che, trattandosi di eseguire questa sentenzia, intese Giulia, mentre che era condotta al luogo destinato, ch'erano fatti liberi e Tesibaldo e Odolania dalla pena del fuoco per la innocenzia di Tesibaldo, e perciò supplicò lei che fussero contenti quei ministri di fare intendere all'imperatore che avanti morisse intendeva di palesarli importantissima cosa.

Fu ciò riferito all'imperatore, il quale si contentò; e condotta alla sua presenzia Giulia e di tutti i circostanti, e benissimo conosciuto Tesibaldo, cominciò a così dire: "Sacra maestà, sono io non uomo, ma donna; e quella donna, alla quale sola ha concesso Iddio sì maraviglioso signore e marito com'è Tesibaldo. Viva forza d'amore, congiunta ad una certezza che avea della sua innocenzia, m'ha indotto a far questo che ho io fatto. Pregovi dunque o che mi escusiate o ciò recusando il rigore delle vostre leggi, che almanco soprastiate a questa sentenzia per tre giorni, sin tanto che io dia alcuni ordini al mio signor consorte."

Non puotero lo imperatore e gli altri circostanti tutti astenersi dalle lagrime quando conobbero esser quella Giulia Camposampiero, ma sopra tutti Tesibaldo, il quale, corso a lei con licenzia dell'imperatore, non pure la liberò ma condotta in camera della signora Odolania e vestitela da donna, la ricondusse di fuori, ove l'imperatore non pur l'assolse ma la commendò grandemente, e dipoi dato buon ordine, fece per questo solennissime feste. E volendo pur tutti dui ritornare a Padova non solo gli ornò loro e suoi discendenti di molti privilegi facendoli conti, ma li donò molte gioie e alcuni castelli. Per il che non pur ritornorno tutti dui a Padova felici e gloriosi, ma furno a quei tempi e dipoi altrettanto ornamento e splendore di questa città, come amplissimo testimonio della nobiltà delli animi padovani. Odolania veramente visse il restante del tempo assai gloriosamente in un monasterio di venerande monache.

Questa è quella novella, anzi quella istoria, graziose donne e valorosi uomini, la quale ho pur io tentato di raccontarvi. Se tale non è riuscita e quale voi speravate e quale si richiedeva alla sua grandezza, imputate la reina nostra che ha commesso sì grave impresa a me, che mal son atta a fornir compitamente simili uffici. Ma se nel raccontar questa novella ho io mancato, come conosco e confesso apertamente, che debbo dubitare che mi avvenirà se sarò

he was not in a position to accept such a great favor, having given his pledge to a woman who, although she could not be compared to lady Odolania, still did not deserve to be deceived, because of her worthy condition. This answer displeased everyone, but most of all Odolania.

In the meantime, the emperor's counselors had ordered that the person who had not just done violence to but had also wounded and killed some officers, be publicly decapitated. When this sentence was to be executed, Giulia heard, as she was led to the designated place, that Tesibaldo and Odolania had been freed from the stake because of Tesibaldo's innocence. Therefore she begged those ministers to please let the emperor know that she had to disclose a most important thing to him before dying.

This was related to the emperor, who agreed. Led into his presence and that of all those surrounding him and having fully recognized Tesibaldo, Giulia said, "Sacred Majesty, I am not a man, but a woman, and the woman to whom alone God has granted such a marvelous lord and husband as Tesibaldo. The true force of love, combined with a certainty that I had of his innocence, has induced me to do what I did.[23] I pray you therefore either to excuse me or, if the strictness of your laws does not allow this, that you wait at least three days to carry out your sentence, so that I can make some arrangements with my lord husband."

The emperor and all the others surrounding him could not refrain from tears when they realized that she was Giulia Camposampiero, and above all Tesibaldo, who ran to her with the emperor's permission and not only freed her, but led her to lady Odolania's room, dressed her as a woman, and brought her back outside. The emperor not only received her but also commended her greatly and proclaimed the most solemn celebrations. And since both of them wanted to return to Padua, not only did he bestow upon them and their descendants many privileges by making them count and countess, but he also gave them many jewels and some castles. Thus they not only returned to Padua happy and glorious, but they became also the ornament and splendor of this city, the most outstanding witnesses of the nobility of Paduan souls. As for Odolania, she lived the rest of her life quite gloriously in a convent of venerable nuns.[24]

Here is the novella, or better the true history, that I have tried to tell you, lovely women and valiant men.[25] If it did not come out as you were hoping it would and as its greatness required, reproach our queen for having bestowed such an important enterprise on a person like me, for I am unable to accomplish such an assignment properly. But if I made mistakes in telling this story, as I know and openly confess I did, how much greater would my mistake be

io così ardita che tenti di dire all'improvviso in sonetto un enigma, il quale si possa in parte agguagliare a quelli che dopo le savie novelle sono stati detti da ognuna di voi? Chiaramente bisogna ch'io concluda che averete voi giusta ragione di concludere che ardir grande sia stato e il mio e del mio signor consorte a metterci con sì elevati ingegni come sono i vostri tutti.

Ma dirò pure un enigma, e se bene lo giudicherete voi indegno, come che sarà, di contrastare con i vostri, sarò io di questo altrettanto contenta quanto gloriosa, se l'acutezza d'ognun di voi non penetrerà nella sua acutezza, come che mi giova di sperare. Uditelo, dunque, con viso allegro e da niuna parte turbato.

ENIGMA

> Io nasco padre, e meco nasce ancora
> Moglie e cinque figliuoli in un istante,
> E tutti sempre stiam coabitante,
> Nè dall'altro si parte l'un tal'hora.
>
> Diversi son gli uffici; ma allora
> Riposa l'uno quando l'altro avante,
> Stanco d'operare cose sante,
> Manco riposo chiede che d'un ora.
>
> Ma gran disgrazia di sì nati figli
> Che se da me avvien che si riparte
> Mia moglie che fu madre a tutti quegli
>
> Rimangono in tutte le sue parte
> Senza vita, e lei insieme e egli,
> Disgrazia la maggior che s'oda in carte.
>
> Ma avanti che io mi parte
> So che la reina nostra, ella ch'ha ingegno,
> Indovinerà ciò per sì gran pegno,
>
> Se non fate voi segno
> D'esser sì dotti questi versi sciorre,
> Come i vostri sapete ben esporre.

if I were so bold as to pose you an enigma in the form of a sonnet, which can perhaps mirror those that each of you has recited after a good story?[26] In this case, I have to assume that you will conclude that my husband and I have been quite presumptuous in joining the company of such elevated talents as yours.

So I will improvise a riddle, and if you judge it unworthy to compete with yours, as it will be, I will nonetheless be delighted and emboldened if, as I hope, you cannot penetrate its meaning.[27] Hear it then with a good face and in a spirit of fun.

RIDDLE

I am born a father, and with me are also born
A wife and five children right away.
And we live always together,
Nor does one ever leave the other.
Different are the tasks, but then
One rests when the other,
Already tired of doing holy things,
Asks just for a one-hour rest.
But the great disgrace of these children
Is that, if by chance my wife,
Who was mother to them all, leaves me,
They will remain in all their parts
Without a life—and she with them—
The greatest disgrace one hears written down.
But before I depart
I know that our queen, she who has talent,
Will guess this riddle for what is at stake,
Unless you show signs
Of being as learned in unraveling these verses,
As you are in expounding your own.

NOTES

1. It is unclear whether Conte is a real name or a title, count. Given that the noble family of Conti existed in Padua at the time, with property in Noale, close to Padua, I take it as a real name. "Cavaliera" is a title once given to women married to knights.

2. As with *Urania*, the author insists that what she tells is a *storia*, a narration of facts that truly happened, rather than a novella, a fictional narrative. *Storie* using real names and reconstructed, often politicized events, were fashionable in the mid–sixteenth century, as with Matteo Bandello and Luigi Da Porto.

3. For Bandini Muti this fictional place in the Euganea region, being not far from where Petrarch used to live, provided an inspiration to writers and artists. See *Poetesse e scrittrici*, 1: 96.

4. Although the first and last sentence of this novella acknowledge the presence of both men and women at the gathering, here the speaker seems to address herself to women alone.

5. Ezzelino III da Romano (1194–1259) was the worst tyrant the Veneto region ever had, a man, as Ariosto put it, believed to be the son of the devil (*Furioso* 3.33). Dante placed him in the *Inferno*. A Ghibelline leader, Ezzelino (or Exxelino) ruled Padua between 1238 and 1256. The Carraresi took power after 1338 and fortified Padua in ways still apparent today. For a historical overview of this period in Padua, see Benjamin Kohl, *Padua under the Carrara, 1318–1405* (Baltimore: Johns Hopkins University Press, 1998). The Venetian dominion, which greatly benefited the city by making of it a vital part of the "Serenissima," started in 1405 and lasted until 1797, apart from a small interruption in the early sixteenth century.

6. The Vitaliani were among the oldest families in Padua and could claim blood ties with St. Giustina, a Roman saint to whom one of today's largest extant churches in the city is still dedicated, and to Pope Vitaliano (657–72). The family was also thoroughly related to Venetian nobility and to the Borromeo family, which may explain the interest that Anton Maria Borromeo, the first editor of this novella, had for this character and therefore for its writer. Last names could be gendered, thus the occasional "Vitaliano" in the text, along with "Vitaliani."

7. The vocabulary here is Petrarchan with a surprising change in gender, for the rarefied creature is not an unavailable angelical Laura but a restrained Tesibaldo.

8. The echo in these lines is Ariostan, as in the famous description of the well-adjusted Ruggiero who, after his marriage to Bradamante, was described as being able to prove himself in all kinds of enterprises, in and out of bed: "Ruggiero showed greater prowess than the rest; he jousted day and night, and always won. In dancing, in wrestling, in everything he always emerged the honored victor" (*Furioso* 46.100).

9. The Scaligeri were driven from Padua in 1337, and the city remained independent until the Carraresi took over one year later. From the context we can surmise that Bigolina is placing her story in the year 1337 or so.

10. Piranesi's version changes "Tiso" into "Tito." Yet for anyone whose surname is Camposampiero, Tiso comes with the territory, and many male members of the family had this name through the centuries, after the knight Tiso, to whom after the year 1000 the emperor Henry I gave a castle around which the village of Camposampiero was built. The village was later attacked and sacked by both the Scaligeri and the Carraresi and came under the dominion of Venice in 1405. The family became a noble one in 1108, when the male descendants were allowed to call themselves counts. Another Count Tiso invited St. Antony to Camposampiero in 1231 for a time of recollection and meditation.

11. The Borromeo printed version somehow missed this line of the manuscript.

12. In the original Italian, "you" is a feminine pronoun.

13. The editor Borromeo noticed right away a contradiction in the plot, since Bigolina had first stated that the action was taking place when Padua was an independent city, that is, between the second half of the fourteenth century and the first thirty years of the fifteenth, and then she cites the emperor Sigismund, who lived when Padua was already under Venetian dominance. Sigismund of Luxembourg (1368–1437), emperor of the Holy Roman Empire (1433–37), was famously portrayed by Pisanello in a painting of 1433. He was the son of the Holy Roman Emperor, Charles IV, and was crowned in Rome on May 31, 1433, by Pope Eugenius IV, whom he helped avert a schism after the pope issued a bull to dissolve the convocation of the council of Basle in 1431. Eugenius IV was a Venetian noble with monastic habits and a strong dislike for nepotism. He was elected in 1431 and died in 1447. As for why Bigolina mentions Bologna, my guess is that she had in mind the crowning of Charles V in Bologna in 1530 by Pope Clement VII, a momentous event in Italian history, since it marked the reconciliation between the pope and the king following the sack of Rome in 1527 by the imperial troops.

14. The names of these noblemen still circulate in Padua. The Capodilista family is one of the noblest and most influential in the city even today, and as in this story, it is still active in politics. Until recently, this family owned the villa that Bartolomeo Salvatico had built in Battaglia Terme in 1593. The Dotto family funded, among other things, the Oratorio of San Girolamo in Padua in the early seventeenth century. See Guido Beltrame, *Appunti di storia padovana* (Padua: Messaggero, 2000). For the Trapolin family of doctors, see Bruno Nardi, *Saggi sull'aristotelismo padovano dal secolo XIV al XVI* (Florence: Sansoni, 1958).

15. The real emperor Sigismund had a daughter, Elisabeth of Bohemia, whom he married to the Austrian Duke Albert V. When he died, Albert was elected German king of the Holy Roman Empire. This may be the reason for Bigolina's choice to develop the rest of her novella in Vienna.

16. The Piranesi text hass "soon" ("presto") rather than "this night" ("questa notte") perhaps for logical reasons of plot or because, as apparent repeatedly, all sexual innuendos are simply erased in his version.

17. Emilia is a recurring name in Bigolina's fiction as a sort of sidekick to the main character. In *Urania* too she was, among other things, her counselor.

18. True to its chaste aims, the Piranesi version eliminates altogether the reference to the sexual encounters and makes it appear that the two only engaged in some non-consequential conversations at night.

19. The whole scene is indebted to a famous one in Ariosto's *Furioso*, canto 5, where Polinesso, dressed as Ariodante, Princess Ginevra's beloved, is seen climbing up a rope to reach Ginevra's balcony at night. Here too the motif for the ruse is male jealousy. Contrary to what happens to Odolania in Bigolina's novella, Ariosto is able to save Ginevra's reputation (and keep the distinctions between social classes necessary to his audience) by having Polinesso make love not to the princess, but to her servant, Dalinda. Shakespeare, most probably aware of the Ariostan trick through a French translation, uses a similar window scene in *Much Ado about Nothing*.

20. Historically speaking, Sigismund's daughter, Elisabeth, did indeed marry the king of Hungary, Albert. He died in 1484, before his son, Ladislaus, was born.

21. Odolania's sentence, death for having made love to a man not her husband, echoes the one that Ginevra metes out in the *Furioso*, as a result of "the cruel law of Scotland" (4.59). Both women are eventually saved.

22. This comment on Orsino's death as resulting from excessive sexual expenditure is erased in the Piranesi version. It was common opinion in the past that too little sexual control on the part of a man could fatally endanger his health, no matter his age. Such was the reason, for example, that many gave for the untimely death of Raphael or for the timely one of Attila, King of the Huns.

23. The words here echo similar ones in *Urania* that the protagonist addresses to the prince of Salerno who thought, like Sigismund, that the woman before him was a man.

24. Combining the two female figures most prominent in Ariosto's story of Ginevra that Bigolina is imitating, Odolania gets the destiny of the maid Dalinda, who was seduced by Polinesso, and is sent to a convent in Denmark. For a reading of this story, see Finucci, "The Female Masquerade," 61–88.

25. The Piranesi version published in France ends here.

26. "Each of you" is feminine in the Italian original ("ognuna di voi"), and thus we are made to understand that only the women in the group told tales, although men too were present at the gathering in the countryside.

27. Verse compositions containing enigmas placed at the end of a novella were popular in the literature of the period, especially extravagant forms of sonnets like this "sonettessa" (see Elwert, *Versificazione italiana dalle origini ai giorni nostri* [Florence: Le Monnier, 1987], 131). Even madrigals occasionally had in the sixteenth century century the unusual form of "madrigalessa." As for the meaning, I venture that it represents a metaphor of the human being in which the father is the *animus* (that is, the logos, the masculine rational principle) and the mother is the *anima*, the feminine feeling, while the five children are the five senses.

URANIA

DEDICATORY EPISTLE
TO THE MAGNIFICENT AND EXCELLENT DOCTOR
OF LAW, SIGNOR BARTOLOMEO SALVATICO

Were it possible, my worthy and most noble young man, fully to measure all human affections by some objective measure, I have no doubt that many regarded as passionate lovers, once appraised, would be exposed as loving little or not at all. On the contrary, many who seem to love little because they do not know how to show it, or who lack the courage to reveal themselves, would be recognized as faithful and ardent lovers when better assessed. What I say of lovers I could say of every sort of friends. Here originates a great but unacknowledged error, namely, that some are appreciated highly by others who, were they able wholly to measure their affections, would hardly look at them; and many, less regarded and appreciated, would then be held in the highest honor, if their affections could be measured. For this reason I feel that those who consider themselves true lovers or perfect friends somehow wrong themselves by not doing all the deeds sufficient to manifest most fully the perfection of their hearts, because if all who truly love did so, the distinction between true and false lovers would quickly become clear. Since the false ones cannot continue long in the deeds of love, they would hardly have begun to wade the ford before turning back, tired of following it any longer, and thus the truth would become open and manifest quite soon.

I have said this for no other reason than to reawaken your memory, most kind young man, and remind you to count me with your own self as among the few rightly regarded as true friends in the world today. From the first moment I met you and your outstanding worth was revealed to me, I was infinitely pleased by your rare, indeed singular virtues, which ignited me with genuine love; there was born in me likewise a desire, as I said, to find a way to demonstrate my great affection for you. By this I mean that as much as I could (for I will not expound either on your merits or on my desire), I always strove to reveal my honest affection. No one understands this better than you since, as you know, from our first encounter I never failed to visit you often, sometimes by sending loving letters and at other times various kinds of poems.

Were one to say that such acts of mine have been very feeble instruments to persuade a person like you, with his immense merits, that I have so much affection as to make me worthy of your high regard, I would confess that the charge is to some extent true. But at the same time I would like to argue that a heart as noble and worthy as yours values much more the respect and loving affection, even if imperfect, offered with the whole heart, than the affection and respect offered only half-heartedly, for which reason, with due consideration to the act of will, a little affection given in its entirety is worthier than a greater one with reservations attached.

Now then, considering the many times I made clear, as much as my feeble powers would permit, how honestly and perfectly I love you with the affection of my heart and how I respect you with my whole mind, I felt I needed one more act to satisfy my debt toward you, namely, to leave some remembrance of myself with you, so that when I was no longer living you would not lose the memory of the great and pure love I had for you while I was alive.

Pondering time and again what I might do to keep some memory of me alive in you, I remembered that many ancient heroes who had performed quite marvelous deeds in their time left their images after death sculpted in marble, bronze, gold, or some other metal. I believe they did this so that their people, whom they had greatly benefitted and by whom they, when living, had been deeply loved, could, by looking at their images, keep alive in themselves the memory that made them debtors to their lords for the benefits they had received. They could still be loved just the same when dead. Following their lead, I felt I could do nothing better to preserve my memory in you after my death than to leave my own image behind. But since the light of reason in me is not yet snuffed out, I realized that, given my sex and especially the lowly degree of my merits, it would be improper to leave my sculpted image (inasmuch as that is appropriate only for great people). I therefore decided to leave you my image in a painting and needed only to determine how to have myself painted.[1]

One day, while shut in my room alone, walking up and down and thinking about the most appropriate way to have myself painted to show my respect and love for you, I suddenly felt the back of my skirt being pulled quite

---

1. The debate on the artistic superiority or inferiority of sculpture compared with painting was part of a recurring Renaissance discourse on "paragone." Michelangelo, for one, believed in the superiority of sculpture. See Paola Barocchi, *Scritti d'arte del Cinquecento* (Milan: Ricciardi, 1971–77), 1: 455–74. Bigolina preferred painting, although it too, as we shall see, paled in importance with poetry in conveying one's feelings.

strongly. Knowing that there was no other person in the room, I felt my heart beat fast in fright. When I looked behind to see who was pulling my skirt so forcefully, I saw that it was a very deformed little fellow, smaller than a pygmy is said to be.[2] He was completely naked, with a head so large that it would have been almost big enough for a giant. He had only one eye in the middle of his forehead, which was quite large and bright like a mirror, and in turning I saw myself in it entirely from head to toe. It seemed a marvelous and strange thing to perceive myself mirrored in that large eye not, as I was, fully dressed, but as naked as when I was born. I noticed my flesh was so white everywhere (except to the left, where I seemed to spot a stain), that it looked like snow.[3] Seeing that strange little fellow, whom I believed to be a horrible monster, I was full, as I said, of fright, not only from shock but also from the shame of seeing myself naked; I would have liked to be without eyes at that moment. Thus I turned toward the door in order to leave the room, shaking intensely, but he held me quite tightly so that I could not leave, and said to me, "Stop. Do not run away. I do not want to offend you in any way; on the contrary, I tell you I have revealed myself so as to help, not to offend you. When you know who I am, I have no doubt that you will be more pleased at having seen and known me than if you had acquired a large treasure, even though I am deformed. Keep your spirits up and listen to me very attentively."

I could not banish the great fear I had in my heart, although he spoke very reasonably. Still, hearing him talk so humanly, I became slightly more courageous, and thus I answered, "I do not know who you are. Do not be amazed if I fear you and would gladly run away, since I seem to see in you

2. Early modern anatomical books described pygmies as being no more than two feet tall and able to enjoy only a very short lifespan. Gabriele de Zerbis (1445–1505), a Paduan doctor, wrote that they could talk and think a bit, and therefore were human, but were also asocial and lacking in morals. See *Liber anathomie corporis humani* (Venice: Locatellu, 1502), 3–4. Renaissance women writers often used pygmies in the role of confidant. For example, in her chivalric romance, Moderata Fonte (1555–92) makes a little dwarf ("picciol nano"), king of the Kingdom of Pygmies, fall in love with the sunny Raggidora, daughter of king Galbo of Egypt. The pygmy is described as well dressed, although in a strange style, and very handsome ("Di sì rara bellezza è 'l nano adorno"). Endowed with an angelical voice, he is also the most faithful and sensitive of lovers. See Fonte's 1581 *Tredici canti del Floridoro*, ed. Valeria Finucci (Modena: Mucchi, 1995), 2.58–73.

3. Being "spotted" on the side of the heart is a sign of being in love. A similar allusion can be found, for example, in poems of Gaspara Stampa (1523–54): "io son ferita qui dal lato manco" ("I am wounded on my left-hand side"); "Ed avertite che sia 'l mio sembiante / de la parte sinistra allegro e mesto" ("and make sure that on the left-hand side my countenance is always sad and woeful"). The first quotation and translation is from "Capitolo" 243 of Stampa's *Rime* in Laura Stortoni, ed., *Women Poets of the Italian Renaissance* (New York: Italica Press, 1997), 154; the second is from sonnet 56 in *Gaspara Stampa: Selected Poems*, ed. Laura Stortoni and Mary Prentice Lillie (New York: Italica Press, 1994), 50.

parts so ugly, especially when I perceive myself reflected in that large eye of yours. Between the shame I feel for seeing myself naked and the fear you arouse in me for being so ugly, I swear that I shall not feel well until I find myself where I shall no longer see you. Nevertheless, say what you want and I shall listen, but, I pray, be as brief as possible."

Hearing this, the little man said, smiling, "The whole world would be blessed, and you in particular, if you humans were constantly to mirror yourselves in this eye of mine, because then neither injustice nor temerity could be found among you. My name is Giudizio.[4] If you humans knew me, you would not respect me less than I deserve, and these parts of mine, which appear monstrous to you when you look at them, would seem no longer hideous but marvelous, indeed divine, once you were fully apprised of their meanings.

"First of all, you should know that my smallness was given to me not without a larger meaning, since it signifies that all, like me, who are commissioned to be judges in the world, should be neither proud nor righteous, but humble in nature and benign in heart. My being naked shows likewise that judges have to be naked of all hate and affection. This head of mine, so disproportionate in size to my other members, symbolizes that judges need to be well educated and of superior learning, although they must also be, as I said, most humble in nature, so that justice and reason are not stifled when they should be well administered. The reason why I have only one eye is that judges wanting to judge rightly should not occupy their souls with tasks other than judging.

"My eye is also so large as to make you understand that it is not enough for good judges to be well educated and to have no other duties than the troubles of judging; they must also be quite shrewd and on guard. Very often it would be of little benefit to those judged that the judge was most learned and understood the laws well if he lacked caution and did not know the most appropriate ways of administering laws. Believe me, today one can rarely find judges who if learned, are not also self-righteous; and if self-righteous, are not wise; and if wise, do not shut their eyes to avoid looking into mine.

"But I want to leave aside this discussion of judges since, whether good or bad, making judgments is appropriate for them, given that their office is to judge, and talk instead of you humans, for although it does not suit you to judge, still you all want to be judges to the detriment of this and that person. There are some among you who can scarcely see their noses in front of their faces and yet often make a thousand reckless judgments of others. Worse, there are those (and not a few) who, burdened by the most ugly vices, want

---

4. The word could be rendered as "Judgment," "Judge," "Wisdom," or "Justice." I leave it in Italian to catch all the different senses, as the context suggests.

to judge other people with laughter or disdain for any small mistake. But if they were to see themselves reflected in my eye wholly naked, as in a mirror that can show everyone's flesh covered by as many stains as there are kinds of vices in which the soul is kept dirtied (as you have seen in yourself); if in my eye, I say, they would mirror themselves, perhaps they would not be such solicitous investigators of the faults of others. Perhaps, more profitably, they would spend the time now vainly wasted in uncovering and revealing other people's small errors to clean, or at least to cover, their own gross stains.

"Oh, how many usurers, how many impostors, blasphemers, scandalmongers, gamblers, and others stained by the most wretched vices mock or defame that little man or woman in whom they have detected some deficiency! But defects are human, and no one can be free of shortcomings unless protected by the special grace of God. These malignant people denigrate others so much that they themselves deserve not only to be defamed, but also punished, for their serious failings. Many times I laugh at those who do not believe that deceiving or lying is such a great shortcoming. Were they to ponder deeply how lies and deceits constitute vices that can obscure, stain, and soil any good soul (even if they were absolutely clear of any other vice), I believe they would learn to tell the truth more often than they do now and would wear the true image of their hearts sculpted on their forehead better than those who hold the lie on their lips. I speak specifically of some who, by appropriating the worthy name of gentleman, avail themselves undeservingly of a treasure not shared by everyone. They do not consider whence comes the title of gentleman and for what reason it was invented, for they are stupid indeed if they believe that being noble comes from an inequality existing between the blood of a gentleman and that of a plebeian rather than from the habits and virtues by which they live.

"If I were human and the ruler of the world, I would not, as you humans do, allow nobility to be bestowed through inheritance; on the contrary, I would like it to be acquired through virtue. Only the man behaving virtuously would be deemed a nobleman, and degrees of nobility would be assigned according to how a greater or a lesser virtue could be seen shining in one person than in another. Were this done, I can assure you that many would not follow vice and sloth as they do. But I want to leave these persons with their vices—I speak of the wicked and not of the good—and talk about you, the most wretched female sex, so much slandered by the wickedness of many awful men that often I have wondered why your long patience in respecting and serving them is not exhausted.

"There are not many who have respect for you because, as I said, they are stained by so many vices that they continuously work to defame your honor with their poisonous tongues. What do they accuse you of most often?

Of things that when I mull them over astonish me. Perhaps the greatest infamy they bestow on you is that you do not want to obey them or that you show yourselves too reserved and haughty with them or that you are stained by some of the vices by which they are soiled. But even if you had thousands of those vices, I believe all true men would be silent rather than proclaim what they should be mum about. The ungrateful ones disparage you only for the great mistake you commit each time you show yourselves too loving toward them.[5] Such is truly men's pitiless, cruel, and savage nature.

"On the other hand, I do not know what to think myself: since you women are similarly malignant toward each other, I can excuse for the most part men's offenses toward you. Oh, how many women there are—although it does not appear that any other vice can stain a woman but being in love (yet you are not aware that the deliverance that comes from not being accused of any other vice comes from the little consideration men have for you)—how many women there are, I say, who being so stained by such a failing, still do not restrain themselves from continuously accusing with a thousand disgraceful words other women who have perhaps failed less than they. They also do not want to mirror themselves in this eye of mine, which could reveal them better through silence than through words. Moreover, there are others who have additional defects in themselves, but because they have not been stained by this particular one, they arrogantly disdain even to look at those who are free of any fault but this, which is still the most natural and into which women fall either because their destiny induces them to do so or for some other unknown reason.

"But I did not come," he added, "to discuss such a subject with you, although by speaking of it I have entered more than halfway into a sea of trouble. On the contrary, I came to advise you about a decision you made quite foolishly, following your own advice. I would not have come if it were just to advise you alone, but this matter concerns a person who never finds a stain in mirroring himself in my eye and who still never judges anyone. The world would be blessed if there were more young men like him—I am speaking of the one to whom just now you were thinking of making a gift of your image!

"It is a good, indeed an excellent counsel for sure, to give a present to someone worthy of statues and simulacra, were he not so kind and humble in his heart as to shun such honors. It is not surprising that he is the receptacle

---

5. The point that Giudizio expresses here—that the sometimes adversarial relationship of men with women is the result of male fears of losing power (when women do not obey them) or social status (when women betray them)—is reprised at length later on by Urania in her two encounters with noblewomen and noblemen in the woods outside Naples.

of every excellent trait, since nature and heaven, in competition with each other, gave him good looks, grace, and merit at his birth, for which reason all those acquainted with him, competing with one another, are forced to love, desire, and honor him. And yet just now you were using poor judgment when you thought that your painted image, presented to him, was an apt means to keep you alive in his memory after your death, giving little consideration to how much such an image is both too low for him to receive and very unbecoming and unsuitable for you to offer. Let me say how inappropriate it is.

"You must know that all sensible and insensible things that function in themselves or enable others to function—I speak of those that do not have the use of reason—can only do so in relation to the action for which they have been destined by nature. The exception is when man, who often resists and forces nature because of reason's dominance over him, sometimes does violence to nature. This can be seen with sensible things, as when a man uses his talent to train a dog, a bird, or another animal and makes them so contrary to their nature that they seem no longer to belong to their own species, but are transformed into another. The same applies to insensible things such as plants, as when man grafts a species of plant with another and makes the roots of one produce the fruit of the other outside its nature, which would certainly not happen if humans did not violate nature.

"I want to say the same about your image, which by itself would not be a good means to create the effect you wish to achieve in that most virtuous young man because it could not work on its own and without help from something contrary to its nature, the image being a material thing. This would be the case if the image had the power in itself of moving the soul to any passion and altering it. The image being a material thing, as I have said many times, and the soul, that is, the intellect in which it needs to operate, being an essence of the spirit, the one could not work in the other if there was no other mechanism involved in the nature of either one to interpose itself. This mechanism is the sense of sight, which, in its own essence, tends toward the spirit yet comes close to the material image in relation to the act.

"Since the image can then represent only material things to the intellect, through the sight, and since we have two eyes, there are then two things extracted from the image and represented to the intellect, namely, the good and the beautiful. The good, being more appropriate to the nature of the intellect than the beautiful, passes directly through it, whereas the beautiful, more disjoined from its nature, is appropriated for the most part from the imaginative side, which partakes of all the senses more than any other power of the soul. The beautiful stops there only long enough to become able to ascend to the intellect. After having considered the beautiful in itself, the intellect makes of it the concept it most prefers, whether it likes it or not. If it likes the thing known and desired, the intellect sends it to the memory to be kept; if it does not, it banishes it and rejects it.[6]

"Now if the image represents only the beautiful or the good to the intellect, I do not know what beautiful or good thing is in you that you want your image to represent to that young man, since you never have done anything worthy enough to move a noble soul. I do not want to talk of the beautiful any further with you, since I judge that one should leave an image only for the good and never for the beautiful because truly the beautiful is too vain and lewd in itself.[7] Therefore I advise you not to send the image of your face to that gentleman, since it will not make you remembered. Rather, send him an image of your great respect and love, which will constantly keep you in his memory."

I had been silent until then, listening full of great amazement, but since it seemed to me that he had said something so much outside nature that I could not understand it in any way, I replied, "Most wise Giudizio, if I were to praise your great wisdom with my little learning, my arrogance would be no less than the arrogance of one who presumes to enlarge the sea with a cup of water or to make the rays of the sun more resplendent with a small lamp. Therefore, I will be silent about your infinite merits since I am unable to speak adequately. But I must tell you this: that although there is little erudition in me, I have understood very well your reasoning, with the exception of the last thing you discussed. I confess that no matter how much I reflect on it, I cannot understand what you mean, nor do I believe I ever will, when you say that I should send that virtuous young man, whom I honestly love so much, the image of the respect and love I have for him, since I cannot imagine how both can be represented in a painting."

"I am not amazed at your scant learning," he said then, "since it has always been the habit of humans rarely to understand well the things they are told, especially those, I say, that are a bit difficult, if they are not impressed upon their minds with some similes. You will realize that this is true when you learn through similes what seems impossible for you to know now. Tell me then, with what do you love and respect such a worthy young man?"

---

6. This understanding of the relationship between the beautiful and the good comes from Plato, *Symposium* 201, 205d, 206d. See also Marsilio Ficino, *Commentary on Plato's Symposium*, ed. and trans. Jayne Sears (Dallas: Spring Publications, 1985), 49; and Leon Ebreo, *Dialoghi d'amore*, ed. S. Caramella (Bari: Laterza, 1929), 224–26.

7. Giudizio's discourse on beauty, grace, proportion, and the accessibility of reason to spiritual beauty constituted a subject frequently approached by the Neoplatonists as, for example, in Mario Equicola's *Libro di natura d'amore*. Castiglione identified the handsome with the good ("e li belli boni") in *The Book of the Courtier*, 4.58. For an overview and for references to writers such as Agostino Nifo and Benedetto Varchi, see Barocchi, ed., *Scritti d'arte*, 2: 1613–1711.

"Oh," I answered, "I love him with my heart and respect him with my mind."

"Fine," he said. "If then you love him with your heart and respect him with your mind, send him an image of a heart and a mind, or better, send him your heart and your mind."

"God help me!" I answered then. "You confuse me with this shifting talk of yours. To tell you the truth, either I do not understand or you are contradicting yourself. Just a moment ago you reproached the person who leaves a beautiful image of himself rather than a good one, claiming that it is too lascivious, and now you say that I should send him an image of my heart. Yet to send my heart, besides being too lascivious, is also such a childish thing to do that I do not know what to add. Moreover, you advise to send him an image of my mind, and I leave to you to judge how difficult it is to perform this operation, since you yourself have tired of making me understand how much material things are contrary to spiritual ones and how material and spiritual things could never unite if not conjoined by something that takes part in the nature of each. Wherefore I want to say, although I understand very little, that it seems to me that, as the whole world knows, neither you nor nature itself could find an efficacious means through which to paint the mind. You add (and this does not seem to me less strange to hear) that I would do much better to send him my very heart and mind, but you yourself will understand, if you reflect on it, that the first act is no less inhuman than the other seems impossible. Therefore, since it is not in any way possible to paint the intellect, as I have already said, it will also be impossible to send it in any way.

"I readily concede that I could send him my heart, but that most kind young man not only could not in any way make use of my heart, but also, since he is so kind, he would judge me inhuman were I to rip out my own heart. I would not simply be unable to achieve the effect I desire to obtain with such a deed, namely, to perpetuate myself in his memory, but the dreadfulness of such an ungodly act upon myself would precipitate such horror and ill will in him toward me that he would rather retain a memory of death than of me. Therefore, I do not like these counsels of yours and I intend to follow your advice even less."

Giudizio laughed a great deal at these words and then he said, "You have a great mind and for this I praise you very highly. But tell me, I pray, if you had a huge, beautiful pear tree in your garden producing nice, large, and sweet pears, and a dear friend of yours told you many times that he liked that tree a lot and would pay dearly to have it, tell me, would you not, having a great desire to please that friend, dig up the lovely tree from its roots and make it a present to him?"

"Oh, my!" I answered him. "It would be too great a sin to destroy such a beautiful tree to no one's gain, since I know that my friend would not like the pear tree, were it not that it produced such lovely fruits, and would no longer appreciate it once the production of those lovely fruits had been taken away from it. Therefore I say that knowing my friend's pleasure, I would make it appear that he could claim that the beautiful pear tree was his without my destroying it. This would come about by my often giving him some of its fruit, thus satisfying my friend while preserving the tree's status."

"Thanks be to God," he said, "for on your own you have opened the way to understanding me. Oh, sometimes it is a hard and an unseemly thing for us, when because of the disposition of the heavens and in order to advise you humans of some secrets you do not know, we are forced to appear and reason with such ignorant people as you yourself prove to be! You all possess faculties so obscure, lazy, and sleepy that if we want to be understood—we who are divine—it suits us to transform ourselves into such a vile thing as you. I am not speaking of everyone because there are some among you humans who could worthily be called divine were it not for the corruption of their flesh. These few have such great, even outstanding, talent that we do not transform ourselves into them to make them understand us, but they transform themselves to make us more aware, and among those considered the best, there is that noble young man who is the subject of our conversation.

"To return to my earlier intention, I say that you fully reveal your ignorance, since you cannot understand that what I said about the pear tree is a simile for what I was saying earlier about you. Although you have been able to distinguish it very well as a tree, you are not sufficiently clever to adapt it as a simile to the purpose for which I said it. But I want to make this fully clear by telling you that your intellect, with which you said you observe that valiant young man, should be compared to the pear tree of which I spoke, since your intellect can occasion a similar operation in that young man as the pear tree would in the friend you were just now mentioning. But listen to something marvelous: although it seems to you that the intellect cannot be painted and least of all that it can be sent, I will make you understand how you can paint and visibly send it. The heart too, though I know it seems impossible to you that it can be sent without being seen, you will learn how to send invisibly."

"What you are saying is great if you could make me see it as true," I answered, "for I tell you, I suspect you want to drive me to insanity because you confuse me with these doubts and various sayings of yours."

"Oh, silly you!" he then said to me. "Don't you know that the compositions, the inventions, and in the end everything ingeniously created are the fruits that human intellects produce, just as the pears are the fruits that the pear tree produces? If, as you said, by sending some pears to your friend your intention is to make him a gift of the pear tree, why do you not now understand that whoever donates some fruits of his intellect likewise donates his intellect? Therefore, if by drawing some inventions from your mind you compose a little work and send it to that rare young man, you could also say that you have donated to him an image of your intellect and that what was invisible you have made appear visible.

"You could never succeed in doing this without the concurrent consent of your will, and this will stops at the heart. Thus it happens that when, through some compositions of yours, you make the intellect visible, which in itself is invisible by nature, then with the assent of the will, which you have used in composing and sending your message, you have sent the invisible image of your heart, which is by nature visible. One should understand in this respect that the will is always the true image of human hearts. Now you have come to realize how, having determined to leave an image of yourself to that virtuous young man whom you indulge so much, you could leave him an image that will bring more honor to you and will definitely be more pleasing to him than if you had left him the image of your face sculpted in gold."[8]

"Oh truthful! Oh just! Oh divine Giudizio!" I said then. "How my feeble knowledge would have been hindered by ignorance if you had not made me capable of recognizing and understanding with your wise teaching things that I would never have known or understood by myself in a thousand years! But tell me, I pray, since I am of such little learning, how could I do a deed worthy to deserve being kept for a long time in another's memory?"

"Oh," he said, "you are neither Socrates nor Plato and cannot discuss the difficult and obscure steps of deep philosophy, nor are you yet one of those celebrated poets such as Horace or Virgil, who generated in abundance delightfully clever and learned inventions. Everyone knows that you are a woman and possess only whatever virtue and knowledge the heavens thought sufficient for your humble being, although you were given an infinite desire to know (perhaps for your greater penance).[9] Do then what you know how to do, and make it delightful, since you will be excused aplenty for your humble

---

8. To cite the opinion of another woman writer in this context, Tullia d'Aragona—one of the interlocutors in Speroni's *Dialogo d'amore*—also discounted the importance of painting as a faithful way of representing the beauties of nature. She saw the painter's portrait as being able to catch only the color of the skin but nothing further ("solamente il color della pelle ne rappresenta, e non più oltra"). See Pozzi, ed., *Trattatisti del Cinquecento*, 1: 511–63, 547.

9. As has been evident throughout this dedicatory letter, Bigolina affects feminine humility at every turn. This was a common device of both male and female writers of the time, although one could argue that her choice of putting in the same sentence references to Horace and Virgil,

and weak writing because you are a woman. And since the one to whom you will donate your composition is young and most kind, he will be pleased by the delightful subject you select because he is young and he will recognize your good will more than the result because he is kind."

He then vanished from my eyes without my being able to thank him, although I was much in his debt. At his departure I seemed outside myself; still, returning to my senses after a short while and thinking over the deliberation I had made earlier to send you the image of my face so that it would keep the memory of me alive in you, I felt that my first resolution was quite stupid. Therefore, abandoning it completely, I drew near to the second.

Helped by that, I took an image from my low intellect, modeled after my heart's will. This little work, entitled *Urania*, was generated from both and takes the name of the person from whom the whole story originates. I send it to you as a gift. I hope that when you read it you will see sculpted inside the image of my heart with which, because of your great merits, as I have already said, I loved you from the moment we met. If it does not seem to you that my gift is suitable to your excellent merits, consider—you who are so discerning—that the one who does what he can does not do little and the one who gives all he has does not owe anything, even if the present is of the smallest worth.

Take graciously then, my kind young friend, this humble little present of mine, which I freely give you. Were you to deem it worth it to read the whole of my little piece, you would see that wise and shrewd young men sometimes do not know how to dispense their love well, although you men insist that it is always the women who choose poorly in love, as if this were their lot. You will also see that women sometimes, although their luck offers them something good, cling to the worse thing by voluntarily driving the good thing away from themselves, and they do not perceive anything bad until worse comes to worst, as happened to the young man who was so much loved by Urania, named Fabio.

For this reason I pray God to watch over and defend you—you being a young man of much worth and very good breeding—so that you never make such a mistake as long as you live. I also pray God to keep me in your good grace while I live and to revive in you the memory of me after I die, since now that I live and mirror myself in your rare, indeed singular, qualities, he gives me a double life.

---

while claiming to be "not yet" like them, constitutes a sly narcissistic gesture. Dante most famously had employed the same stratagem: "I am not Aeneas, I am not Paul." See *The Divine Comedy, Inferno*, 2.32.

URANIA,

IN WHICH THERE IS THE LOVE STORY
OF A WOMAN BY THAT NAME

THE LETTER[10]

In the time that Giufredi, a prince more handsome and amiable than any other lord living in those days, ruled the state of Salerno peacefully, there was in that city a woman from a very noble family by the name of Urania, who, aside from being properly learned in the vernacular and having the Muses for friends both in prose and in poetry, was adorned with such a noble soul that rather than seeing a single vice come out of such a beautiful soul she would have chosen to die a thousand deaths.[11] Virtue so pleased her that, in talking with others, she could not help becoming radiant with a genuine and virtuous love, no matter how distant those people were from her in virtue.

Thanks more to such virtues than to any great beauty, this woman was loved and desired by many young noblemen of Salerno. But she, who was gratified only by virtue, kept herself far distant from any thought of love, because she did not know among the many who often visited her, both to enjoy her virtues and to follow the custom in Salerno, any who seemed worthy

---

10. Bigolina created sections in *Urania* through a diacritical mark: the drawing of a branch placed horizontally in the text. I have chosen to give them a title to facilitate reading. For reasons of symmetry and content I have also separated out some text into a section (entitled here "The Love Triangle"), which was not set off as a separate section in the manuscript.

11. *Urania's* opening is very close to Boccaccio's *Fiammetta*, although Bigolina places more emphasis on Urania's mind than on her beauty: "At the season when the newly clad earth displays her beauty more than at any other time of the year, I came into the world born of noble parents and welcomed by a benign and generous Fortune" (3). Salerno is a city dear to Boccaccio, and Bigolina might have wanted from the start to link her narrative to that of the Tuscan master by choosing this city over her own, Padua, as the liberal place where women are better educated, more respected, and freer from social controls. From Boccaccio's *Decameron* 2.6 comes also the name of Giufredi (Giusfredi), a southern boy whose name is changed into Giannotto to avoid identification.

of a gift of her heart, although she showed herself very grateful and genial to all and received each with an honorable welcome.[12]

But Love, having decided to wreak cruel havoc with her as he often does with other women (because strength, wealth, and virtue are worth little or nothing against the power of such a potent master), arranged it so that a young nobleman of that city, by the name of Fabio, having heard many highly praise Urania's virtues, became inflamed beyond measure with a desire to know her and have some honorable conversations with her.[13] This great longing to be acquainted with her stemmed from their shared morals and virtues, because he was not only learned in Latin but also greatly adorned with good manners and with a grace given to him by heaven, which made him welcome to every virtuous heart in a way that produced wonder in all who knew him.

Finding himself eager to know Urania, this young man pleaded so ardently with one of her relatives that, to make Fabio happy, he led him to her at an evening gathering in the winter. Fabio was received so graciously by Urania that he dared to ask her to please allow him to come again. Since she was strangely pleased by his genial ways and gentle manners, she answered, with a greater affection and more enthusiastic disposition than she had ever shown toward any other man, that there was nothing in the world that would make her happier than his deeming it worthwhile to come to see her often. The young Fabio seemed to receive an immense pleasure from this answer and acted on it, because he did not let many days go by without visiting her, to the infinite happiness of both. And he did not fail to make up for the days he could not visit with loving and learned letters, which were no less gratefully than learnedly answered (since she knew how to do it well), and many times she added to the letters some very graceful and erudite sonnets with other sorts of rhymes.[14] Within a few months, love grew so strongly between these two lovers that it seemed that they had only one heart, one will, one soul.

I do not know how it came about, but many days after their love reached

---

12. The model for the "honest conversation" between men and women was advocated in many conduct books, most famously in Castiglione's *Courtier*.

13. Fabio was a typical name in the comedy and narrative of the time. For example, Giambattista Girardi Cinzio puts Fabio at the head of the group of men and women discussing love in his *Ecatomnithi*. Although published in 1565, the book was written a few decades earlier, when Cinzio was engaged in writing *Discorso intorno al comporre delle commedie e delle tragedie* (1543), a text that Bigolina may have known.

14. The love story between Urania and Fabio moves along the lines famously traced by writers such as Ebreo, Bembo, Equicola, and Castiglione, in which love is the result of the contemplation of intellectual beauty. Bigolina had talked on the subject in "A ragionar d'amore."

its highest pitch, Fabio turned his eyes, and then his heart, to the love of another woman, although until then he had constantly showed himself a lover
of virtue. Thereafter attributing little value to the many virtues that Urania
had revealed day after day as a result of this love, he forgot the many kindnesses he had received from her. To tell the truth, this woman was much more
beautiful than Urania, but faded in comparison to her in virtue.

As a result of losing his deeply felt love for Urania, Fabio began also to
lose his ardent wish to see her or to hear news of her that earlier had seemed
so important to him. Even when he visited her from time to time, which he
did more for his honor than for love, his conversations were scant and very
different from before. Being very perceptive, Urania was soon aware of the
change, although he roundly denied that he had his heart turned toward any
woman but her. Having become certain from many signs of her lover's inconstancy, but not knowing who could be the one for whom she had been
abandoned (although she was more than certain that no one was her equal in
virtue even if another surpassed her in beauty), she felt such an enormous sorrow for this new turn of events that she believed she would die from the terrible pain.

Therefore, in order not to incur such a great scandal as it would have
been if she had allowed herself to be led to death so cowardly and to avoid
making her pain a cause for the happiness of the woman thanks to whom she
was destitute of all her satisfaction and happiness, she decided to leave
Salerno without delay, dressed as a man and alone, and to wander in the
world until the long suffering and the many discomforts endured along the
way would take from her heart the excessive love—or rather the folly—she
had for Fabio and make her feel pity for herself. She did not know how to
remove the love sculpted in her heart otherwise than through the chance
events that she might encounter.

Having therefore reached such a decision, she had a most faithful servant secretly provide her in a few days with very good men's clothes and a
good horse; the arrangements were secret so that her mother would not be
aware of them, because she would have felt obliged to obey her.[15] That ser-

15. Although the importance of Urania's mother in the narrative is limited, one could argue that
at least Urania has a mother. Many Renaissance authors gave their female characters fathers, but
not mothers. For example, in the *Orlando furioso* Ariosto gives no mother to his major heroines
Angelica, Ginevra, and Isabella. Tasso does the same to Clorinda and Armida in *Gerusalemme liberata*; in fact, in that epic women seem to kill their own mothers at birth. See Finucci, *The Manly
Masquerade: Masculinity, Paternity, and Castration in the Italian Renaissance* (Durham, NC: Duke University Press, 2003), 153. When mothers are present, they are usually ineffective, such as Bradamante's mother in the *Furioso*.

vant pleaded and reasoned with her repeatedly to make her abandon such an ill proposal, but seeing that his words brought no good fruit, he obeyed and satisfied all her wishes. She had firmly decided to leave, for she had no heart to suffer and die a thousand times by seeing the reason for her pain in front of her eyes. But because she did not want her beloved Fabio to impute her departure to any shameful reason and also because she desired to make him know that she had loved only him and still loved him more than all other women loved or could ever love him—and was worthy likewise to be loved and held dear above every other woman—she took paper, pen, and ink and wrote a letter to him in this vein:[16]

"My dear Fabio, desired by me over all others in the world and whom I can call mine with good reason because you cannot take yourself away from me on any grounds if I do not consent, inasmuch as you have given yourself to me of your own free will, I do not know whether I should praise or complain more to the heavens because they made me more perspicacious and of a keener perception than is common among women. When I measure the benefit and the pleasure with the damage and the sorrow I have often received from this ingeniousness and understanding of mine, I find them so equal in scale that I cannot tell the difference between them. But leaving aside all the other benefits and damages I have derived in different ways from my knowing too much, I will speak only of those that, being caused by a greater subject than the others ever were, reasonably produced first a great benefit and pleasure in me and then more damage and sorrow.

"Large, indeed very large, were the benefit and the pleasure I knew I had received when I first came to know you and had the opportunity through my great perception to comprehend each of your inner virtues and recognize their value and merit, knowing that you loved me with a heart devoid of any pretension. This understanding filled my soul and my spirits with an extreme pleasure and later was the reason why my heart grew inflamed with equal love toward yours. But I find now the damage and the sorrow I receive from that same perception not inconsequential, for I soon became aware, from many hidden signs of yours, of the little regard you have for me—on no grounds. Beyond the infinite damage I receive from it, this knowledge causes an unbelievable, boundless unhappiness in my soul and heart.

"To tell you the truth, my dear Fabio, no matter how many times I think

16. As with Ovid's tragic females, like Penelope, Phaedra, Medea, and Ariadne, the letter Urania addresses to Fabio uses the strategy of self-victimization to create a discourse of artistic discovery. Boccaccio's narrative of "furioso amore" in *Fiammetta* is also displayed in the epistolary form. But unlike most literary antecedents, in Bigolina's work it is the woman, rather than the man, who leaves.

of it, I cannot imagine from whence there originated such a sinister thought in you. I say in you, since in any other young man less virtuous than you such an accident would not have seemed a novel thing; but in you, the subject of every excellent virtue, it does not appear only new, but very new. In fact, although I see it openly, it seems almost incredible to me. Considering that not many months have gone by since you came on your own so affectionately to visit me without being sought, and even less for my having desired you, since I did not know you, and that after that you started to love me more, then it can be said that you selected me for your beloved and not I you for my lover, although I tried always to win you with love and kindness after I knew myself loved by you. Nevertheless, I see you inopportunely changed in a few days from your first desire, and I cannot imagine to what shortcoming of mine I could impute such a sudden change in you.

"Since there are two beauties in woman loved and desired by man—that is, the beauty of the body and the beauty of the soul—and the incorruptible and immortal nature of one and the corruptible and fleeting nature of the other make clear how much the one must be kept more dear and esteemed than the other—I would like to know from you how my body, beautiful when you liked it at first, could, in such a short time, become less beautiful or less desirable than it seemed to you then. But let us leave aside all talk of bodily beauty since it should be, indeed it is, the type of beauty less appreciated by virtuous and superior persons like you, and let us talk only of the beauty of the soul. I say that I do not believe that such beauty should appear less evident and less valuable in me now than when you first saw it; indeed, it should rather appear much greater (as it truly is), since my virtue was then without the person who would elevate it and was showing itself almost rusty, like iron far from the whetstone. But after it came near the whetstone of your excellent grace, which I held in such great esteem, I can say (and you should be a good witness of this) that my virtue was already becoming so clear and shining that it would have brought happiness and pleasure to you had you loved me and would have caused others to marvel.

"For what I have said until now and for much more that I am going to say in this letter, you may denounce me for being too bold and arrogant; you may say that it is not proper for a virtuous man and even less for a woman to praise himself or herself so much, as it appears I do. I agree somewhat, but I counter that there are many transactions, wicked and shameful in their very nature, that when done in a specific time and place and for a reason, not only lose the name of wicked and shameful, but acquire instead the name of honorable and just.

"Who can see or hear of a more wicked and shameful thing than a man killing another man, of a murderous hand being so daring as to undo what the supreme God and the great mother Nature have united through harmonious cooperation? Still, we see many times the master executioner take life away in different ways, now from this and now from that man, and no one can be found to reproach him for such an act, nor can it be called wicked. This happens because in such a case the nature of things, constrained by need, changes itself to adapt to circumstances, and such is my case. Although I should not praise myself (indeed I should rather run away when others praise me in my presence), nevertheless I find myself in a situation in which I have to defend and uphold my own reasons. Well, know that you scorn me and flee from me not because I do not deserve you or because I am unworthy to find myself loved by you above any other woman, but because my contrary destiny is such that I met this bitter fate. Thus, this one time, no longer finding myself constrained by circumstances, I should be allowed to talk about those aspects of myself I know are good for the sake of justifying my reasons without being reproached, and I also promise that all I have to praise about myself I will show with good arguments to be true.

"Reasoning with you as a man of virtue and not of the vulgar herd—for those men draw rather near what the senses dictate than toward what reason advises—I say that you should be pleased incomparably more with the beauty of my soul than with the beauty of any woman less virtuous than me. The evidence for my saying this will be made manifest to you by a subtle argument. As you may know, there are two senses through which the virtuous lover delights in his beloved, namely, sight and hearing. The lover feeds and nourishes his eyes and ears with these two senses when he is in the presence of his beloved. When he is absent from the woman he loves, and still wants to savor those sweets tasted earlier in seeing and hearing her, he needs the sight, a sense pertaining to the body, to form in his mind an image of that beauty, and through this he sees and ponders the desired beauty. Without such an interposed means as the sight, he could not rejoice in the absence of that beauty, for material actions and those of the spirit are two extremes that would never unite by themselves if they were not conjoined by some means.[17]

"The same does not happen to the hearing, because as soon as the words emerge from the mouth of the person pronouncing them, since they are pertinent to the soul they move to the hearer's intellect without finding an impediment to arrest them. This intellect, after it has taken as much pleasure as

---

17. This argument was often present in love treatises of the period. For example, the character Raverta (Ottaviano della Rovere) states in a treatise on love, *Il Raverta* (Milan: Daelli, 1864), by Giuseppe Betussi, that beauty is God's gift, which pleases the spirit through the mind or through the eye and the ear (18).

it wants, recommends them to the memory, where they remain. Each time the intellect wants to experience the pleasure of those words, it finds them, and not their images, by going back to the memory, without using any means disjoined from its nature. In recollecting them he experiences the same sweetness he felt earlier in hearing them.

"Now, if the lover cannot look into the bodily beauty of his beloved in her absence unless the interposed means intervene—and the intellect (that is, the words heard, which uncover to him the beauty of the soul) can admire and understand beauty fully by itself without other means—then it is clear that the beauty of the soul should be considered much nobler. It is also clear that, comparatively speaking, a soul has greater beauty than another when it can better fill with its various beauties the intellects and the memories of those observing it and can portray those beauties in various ways.[18]

"I will have you hear miracles now that have perhaps never been heard in the past and my heart tells me that you will think them true. I know that you love another woman more beautiful than me—for I do not regard you as being so blind that I could believe you abandoned me for another woman less beautiful—but I am certain that she is no more virtuous than I am. Now then, if you had to leave this beautiful woman of yours for whom you stopped loving me and wanted to take along with you a portrait to represent her beauty to your eyes, would you not do as Apelles or Zeuxis or any other first-rate painter would do, were they still alive: make more than one portrait, namely, make many and thereby arrive at more than one likeness of your woman?[19]

"Ah, you ungrateful and unappreciative man—for I am forced to say this,

18. In "A ragionar d'amore" Bigolina had already articulated the difference between the beauty of the body and that of the soul along Neoplatonic lines. On the concept, see Eugenio Garin, "La filosofia dell'amore: Sincretismo platonico-aristotelico," in *Storia della filosofia italiana* (Turin: Einaudi, 1966), 2: 681–715; and Paolo Lorenzetti, *La bellezza e l'amore nei trattati del '500* (Pisa: Nistri, 1917).

19. Apelles was one of the most famous painters of the ancient world, known, among other things, for an astonishingly beautiful portrait of Venus. He is said to have portrayed the courtesan Campaspe, Alexander's companion. Alexander liked the artistic creation so much that he most "generously" gave her to him right away since Apelles could enjoy her beauty more deeply than he. Zeuxis too was an admired painter of women. When he was asked to paint Venus, he chose to combine the parts that he judged the most perfect from five of the most beautiful maidens of Crotone and ended with a composite representation of the male ideal of womanhood so satisfying that the painter Nichomachus thought he was seeing a goddess. Both Apelles and Zeuxis were used in early modern texts as spokespersons for the absolute idea of beauty, as in Castiglione's *Courtier* where the story of Campaspe is fully recreated. On the relationship between painting and literature in the representation of female beauty, see Cropper, "On Beautiful Women, Parmigianino, *Petrarchismo*, and the Vernacular Style," *Art Bulletin* 58 (1976): 374–94; and Rogers, "The Decorum of Women's Beauty: Trissino, Firenzuola, Luigini and the Representation of Women in Sixteenth-Century Painting," *Renaissance Studies* 2.1 (1988): 47–88.

and an infinite pain presses my heart not because I say it, but because you have given me reason to say it—tell me, I pray, how many portraits do you have which represent my beauty to you? Here is their miracle, for what your beautiful woman cannot give you for eternity nor the most excellent painters and not even the great master Nature herself, I have already given you, since every time you look and consider the many and various sorts of rhymes and prose I composed and gave to you, you will see as many portraits, even though they are different, which each by itself and all together manifest whatever beauty there is in me.[20]

"Now you see that I have already taught you that the beauties you can observe every day, if you deigned to look at me and at my many portraits with your intellect, are more worthy of being loved and kept dear than any more obvious physical beauty. I know you could reply that you very much like my virtues, but being young—and the nature of young people being not to settle too much on one love or one desire but always to want to see and hear new things—you, as a young man, take delight in changing and seeing new and beautiful things.

"Alas, my dear Fabio, how much I see you led astray along untrodden paths! You will not be able to find as varied, new, delightful, and beautiful things as those you always found when you were with me, no matter how long and in how many places you search. Alas, tell me, I pray, was there ever a time when I was present that you did not see new and pleasant things, such perhaps (and I know you will not deny it) that oftentimes made you marvel? Then if you always find many new, various, beautiful, and delightful things in me alone, why do you bother yourself to look for them elsewhere and where perhaps you could not find any of similar nature and perfection and where you would find fewer so pliant as always to renew themselves to please you? If you perhaps persuaded yourself that this new woman of yours, for whom you make me pitilessly suffer so much pain, were to love you more than I, you can be sure that you are deceiving yourself, because she cannot in any way love you more, and I will make your mistake clear with persuasive arguments.

"I believe you know that the love and favor with which we love this and that person does not extend beyond what we seem to know is the worth of

---

20. As in the dedicatory letter to Bartolomeo Salvatico, Bigolina insists that while woman's beauty is fleeting and no painting can catch every aspect of a woman's personality fully, no matter how brilliant the artist, the poetic "portrait" can do the same quite easily; thus poets are visual artists of the mind. Castiglione expressed the same idea in the dedicatory letter to Miguel da Silva in his *Courtier* when he claimed that his portrait of the Urbino court, although not as refined as one that Raphael or Michelangelo could make, was still sufficiently evocative to readers in its ability to catch reality.

the person we love, and we love more or less according to the value we place on that person's worth, that is, we love on the basis of the knowledge we are able to receive of the significance of that worth. I will give you an example, and it will be one to which you cannot object.

"You know that there are nine choirs of angels of which, as the theologians say, that of the Seraphim is the highest and nearest to the supreme God. Those angels penetrate His great secrets more than all the others and therefore it is said that they are more fervent in loving God, being more cognizant of His infinite knowledge and goodness, than those who do not have such excellent understanding. Now, if the one who has a more perfect knowledge of the beloved loves more, how could you deny that I love you more, and more perfectly, than any other woman when I am more than certain that there is no woman, nor could there be, who could ever have known your inward being as perfectly as I do? Since it is not possible perfectly to love what is not perfectly known, it follows that I alone love you perfectly because I alone know you perfectly, and this you have been able to realize often in the past from many clear signs.

"May God grant that this new love of yours lead you to no worse end than my own has led you up to now—and you could have more readily gained than lost with mine—and I do not believe that you had less pleasure for being loved than I had when I knew I was loved. You should already know, as I know, how worthy I am of being loved and esteemed more deeply by you than by anyone else. Nevertheless, since I cannot nor do I want to please myself beyond what you would allow, I want to let you enjoy this new love of yours in peace. But since I do not have the heart to sustain the enormous injury I receive from you, I have chosen as a lesser evil to leave my own country. Thus you will be the reason why it will be deprived of a person, the likes of which it perhaps will not be able to hold onto again, and for this you will receive the name of ingrate toward the country, and, much worse, you will have done it to yourself.[21]

"To be sure it will be an unbearable pain to chase away—or rather to do

---

21. The loss of a woman poet as a loss for the country comes as a new concept, because it is usually the male hero who is invested in narrative with sufficient political or amorous powers to have his loss mourned by an entire city. Bigolina repeats this statement again toward the end of *Urania*, when she puts it for greater emphasis in the mouth of the prince ruler, Giufredi. A similar example appears in another Paduan woman writer, Isabella Andreini (1562–1604), who reproaches a father for feeling sorry to have had a daughter born to him rather than a son. Andreini argues that this daughter could very well become a great poet or a warrior and bring distinction to her country: "Your country could value her more than Lesbos its Sappho, Scythia its Tamiris and Ithaca its Penelope. Therefore console yourself, celebrate the birth of this daughter of yours, who, I hope, will bring you infinite joy." See *Lettere*, in Stortoni, ed., *Women Poets*, 231.

away—with that deep-seated and perfect love that took root in my afflicted heart when your remarkable virtues gave me reason to do so. I do not know to what other profound pain and affliction my distress might be compared, unless it is the agony of being deprived of a limb, for I consider small any other anguish and grief compared to mine. When I think about the pain that presses us when Fortune takes away our faculties or when death deprives us of some of our friends, it seems to me that we should not be very saddened at those losses if we are guided by reason.

"The justification is this: in regulating our affections and desires within ourselves through reason, always measuring them by their end, there is no doubt that we put affections and love only in what we know could be good to us or would allow us to retain them. Thus, knowing that the power and riches we possess are not ours but belong to Fortune and that it is in her will to take them away from us and give them to whomever she likes, we should desire that love last in us only as long as Fortune wants to leave it in us. Then, any time she should take these things away, we would feel no pain because love would have ended when we are deprived of them.

"Such in fact would be the loss sustained by the death of a friend, assuming that when we started to love him we had in us enough sense and reason to consider that he is mortal and that his death was ordered before our friendship had been contracted. Then we would share our love with his life, that is, with our life, so that if it were to happen that death took him away from us, knowing that death had precedence, and therefore it does not offend us, we would go through this pain very quietly, having shared our love to the end of his life.

"But the same does not happen with the privation of bodily members, which alone it seems to me can be compared for similarity and appropriateness to this disjunction of love you force me to make now. Because Nature adorned these bodies of ours with beautiful and different members with the intention that they remain with us and that we possess them as long as our lives last, it is very proper, having to share love, that love lasts as long as these members do, so that we are secure in the knowledge that they will be with us until death. Thus, if as a result of bad luck it happens that we are deprived of a hand, an arm, or an eye, we can think that the anxiety and pain felt as a result of such privation is incomparable. Since all members are linked to our soul by an everlasting love, we have to believe that no other pain but my own can be equated with the very sharp one we feel in breaking apart, cutting off, and crushing out such a strong and rooted love.

"Such then and not otherwise, my dear Fabio, is my anxiety and pain in eradicating from my heart the most tenacious love I have for you. Having formed in my mind a firm resolution to love you for as long as I recognized the most noble virtues lodged in you, which I knew for certain would never leave you as long as your life lasts, I felt that I would keep such a perpetual love with me as if it were a temple of peace. But realizing now how that great love you had for me is not just broken or cut off but dried at the root, and knowing that it is impossible for me to live too long loving you so much without being loved back, to save my life it is better that I cut down, extirpate, and eradicate, halfway and still fresh, the enormous love I have for you. How much pain I feel and will be feeling I believe the many reasons I related can already make you realize. I will say no more, except to pray that you occasionally remember in your happiest moments that I find myself deprived of any peace because of you. Remember also that you did not disdain to call me your teacher.[22]

"May heaven bring prosperity to everything you do and direct your every desire to a happy end."

QUESTIONS OF LOVE

Her long letter written and sealed, she gave it to her servant to deliver to Fabio without comment. Then, dressed in the male clothes made for her and mounted on a good horse, she secretly left Salerno and set off for Naples, where she had decided to stop for a few days.

She arrived there with the greatest pain any loving heart ever suffered, both because she could not escape the hardship caused by traveling, especially since she was used to having all her needs attended, and because the arrows of love were stabbing her. Realizing that she was going farther away each hour from the one who, despite herself, was her heart and her life, and without whom she felt disembodied, she seemed to find such little rest in Naples that she stayed no more than one day. The next morning, she left that city on a horse, aiming to go first to Rome and then to wander through Italy and see every part of it, thinking—and with that thought deceiving herself—that the sharp passion with which Love had filled her heart would wane in seeing so many and varied things and in much suffering. She was not thinking (although she had seen many occurrences of it) that he would make himself felt in gentle hearts with the greatest force and strength in moments of greatest anguish.

Now, having left Naples, she was so much beside herself that she let loose the bridle, no longer aware of riding, and allowed her horse go at what-

---

22. The word in Italian is "maestra," which has the double meaning of master and teacher.

ever pace and wherever it liked. In spite of herself, her mind had returned to her ungrateful beloved. Crying profusely and opening her mouth, she let out such a pitiful lament that it would have moved any heart, no matter how cruel, to pity. She complained about her destiny and about Love, but even more about Fabio, who had led her to such a costly pass, and among many mournful words, she said,

"Alas, dear Fabio! How is it possible that your heart underwent such a great alteration in such a short space of time? It was so sudden that I can compare it only to lightning; for as lightning makes our eyes blind to one spot with its incredible splendor and departing from that spot leaves us as if blind, so you have worked on my poor self. With the shine of your most excellent virtues and the strength of your grace dazzling my heart, I had hardly become aware of being in your grace before I realized it had abandoned me.

"Alas, why, dear Fabio, could you not see how I became blind when I found myself deprived of your light? Soon I will be like a sightless and unguided person who, not knowing where he goes, whether to a pit or to a river, falls into a pit where he dies. I know that you knew you alone were my light and were aware that your light, reflecting on me, was making my light shine with this double light. Had you persevered in loving me, I would have performed wonderful things for love.

"Where do you think you will ever find a woman willing to do what I would, or who, like me, would be able to praise your excellent virtues on paper in a thousand ways, good examples of which you already have in your hands?[23] It suits me to drink out of this chalice with patience, because I know that such is my destiny; nevertheless, I blame you more than my destiny, since you could have prevented its evil course and instead have let each malevolent influence hurt me. As many wise men say, the stars in the sky are dominated and controlled by learned men, and who is more learned in your profession than you or more deserving of you than me? No excuse could make me forgive you, for you alone are the cause of my every misfortune."

These and other similar loving words the enamored Urania repeated with a large scattering of tears, and she uttered so many fiery sighs that it appeared the air wanted to put itself on fire around her. Having ridden for more than six hours without ever becoming aware of what she was doing or where she was going, she would still not have become alert on entering a pleasant

---

23. In Petrarch's construction, the love for Laura brought the man, Francesco, to acquire the poet's laurel ("lauro") because he endlessly wrote about her. Here the sex of the claimant is switched and the woman poet, rather than the man, inspired by love, is said to be able to achieve greatness. This is the same technique Stampa used in *Rime*.

grove with a lovely fountain protected from the southern rays of the sun by the green and tall trees surrounding it—the midday had just passed—if she had not been stopped by two beautiful women, from among the five who had come down to the fountain. One held the horse's reins, and the other took hold of one of her arms. They shook her so much that she came back to herself. For this reason she was overcome by an infinite wonder and shame, not knowing where she was and aware that she was perceived by those beautiful women as being out of herself. And thus, her whole face reddening out of shame, she spoke with a sweet smile and a broken sigh to those who had stopped her.

"Lovely ladies, if my judgment does not deceive me, I surmise you could easily be in love, for I see you young and beautiful. Were this true, I hope to find in your hearts more pity than mockery for having caught me in such a state, having felt in yourselves how extremely powerful the amorous passions are."

The beautiful women, who wanted him to be such and not otherwise, answered through the boldest one. "Graceful and gallant young man, it is true that pity, which stung the hearts of us all in seeing you reduced to those straits, moved and pressed us first to make you return to yourself. But another reason also moved us, and we will reveal it when you tell us kindly, if you consent, which town are you from? What is your name? Where are you coming from and where are you going? And what is your profession?"

"Most gentle ladies," Urania answered, "to manifest who I am can give me little problem, but I believe it would be of little use for you to know it because I am so obscure that when I have told you who I am you will know me no better than when you simply saw me in front of you. Nevertheless, to make you understand how much I am pleased to obey beautiful women, I will tell you what you asked of me. The town where I was born is very far from here, almost at the borders of Italy in a not too traveled and very humble manor called Geraci.[24] My name is Fabio, and I left the place I just named because love turned against me. I do not know where I am going, since I took only fortune and destiny as guides at my departure, as you may have perceived when you first saw me. My profession was wholly placed in the high study of vernacular letters, and I enjoyed very much composing rhymes and

---

24. The hamlet far away from the center of Italy described here is perhaps Geraci Siculo, an old and historically rich town in Sicily in the Madonie region, which was founded by the Greeks as early as 550 B.C.E. and later dominated by the Byzantines and the Normans. Because of its strategic position, the town was also extensively used by the Arabs to control traffic to the interior. In the fifteenth century, Geraci became a marquisate of the Ventimiglia family. A castle of vast dimensions, whose ruins are still visible today, was then built in the Greek-Byzantine style.

prose, but now all has changed into sorrow, tears, and amorous sighs. If I have anything you think might be of value, I offer it for your use with the same freedom you would use one another."

The gentlewomen took great pleasure in seeing him speak so kindly and the one who had already spoken said again, "It cannot be denied, most kind young man, that the hearts of those who truly love are always courteous and always try to show themselves as practitioners of every virtue, as one sees now in you. We thank you wholeheartedly for your most gracious offer and accept your courtesy in making yourself available to us. We pray you to counsel us regarding a resolution upon which we labored fruitlessly the whole day. If it pleases you to satisfy us with this gift, you may want to dismount and sit with us near this lovely fountain. I hope we do not leave this place until we find ourselves satisfied by you, as by one who could teach us well, given your learning and experience."[25]

Hearing the women's wish, Fabio—this is the name we will call her from now on—dismounted immediately and was received gracefully. After he was seated in their midst, he began, "Lovely ladies, my advice does not deserve to be followed as if it were good, because I have been devoid of any peace and any blessing from bad advice I gave myself. Nevertheless, since there are so many whose nature is to give the most knowledgeable and finest counsel to others while they resort to the worst for themselves, having persuaded myself that I am one of those, I will try (although my comprehension does not extend very far) to give you better advice than I ever gave myself, whatever it is you are soliciting from me. Please tell me, as I have no other wish than to please you."

Hearing him talking to them so agreeably, the noblewomen thanked him from the bottom of their hearts. The one who had previously spoken now continued, "Valiant young man, there are five of us here coming from very noble families in Naples and we love each other no less than if we were sisters by blood. Since we never considered love a necessary thing among human beings (for it could be helpful in some ways but could just as well be hurtful in others), we have kept ourselves until now distant from any amorous thought. Although there are many who labor with their talent and knowl-

---

25. The fact that here only women are involved, although in the fiction of the text "Fabio" is a man, recalls a much longer discussion on love in Fonte's treatise on women's worth where likewise women alone talk about men in a garden, in the summer, and near a fountain with allegorical decorations. There is also a dialogue in Sebastiano Erizzo's *Le sei giornate,* in which a character named Fabio is one of the six male discussants. It takes place just outside Padua, in the summer, in a garden with a fountain, where a meal is served (the year is 1542, when the author was a university student in Padua, but the book was published in 1567).

edge to make us believe that they love us heartily, we have always shown ourselves stubborn and reluctant to each request and entreaty.

"But considering that among us love is a great spur to virtue and that not
being in love can almost be compared to having a body without a mind—
which is especially true of us women—I cannot understand who we are after
we remove ourselves from attending to our familiar chores. For you men prevent us from exercising the discipline of letters and the beautiful arts in order
to keep all the glory for yourselves. Therefore, if love does not awaken our
talents somewhat, we spend our unhappy lives empty and devoid of any
pleasure and knowledge.[26] Worse still, many times men repute us silly because of our excessive goodness.[27]

"But let us stop talking of this, for it is not important at present, and move
to what is of the greatest importance to us. After many varied discussions, we
have agreed on one thing: each of us wants to find a beloved, but we would
like him to be the type of man we would not regret having chosen (as happens to many of us) after we give ourselves to him.

"It is true, as I was saying just a while ago, that each of us is pursued and
solicited by men of different qualities and fortunes. But since we are very
much afraid of making a mistake, inasmuch as we cannot see inside men's
hearts to ascertain whether their amorous demonstrations are real or shallow,
we are unsure about which of them we should cling to for our good. We came
to this place today in order to settle such a weighty question without being
disturbed, but we have done nothing else until your coming than have one
person propose one thing and another add to it another reason, and still we
have not been able to agree or come to a resolution regarding the sort and
status of lover a woman should select.

"Some of us say that a woman should choose an old rather than a young

---

26. Alessandro Piccolomini (1508–78) had asserted through a female character in *La Raffaella*
that for women to live without love is to be dead while alive. Bigolina starts out by repeating the
view that women seem to know more than men about love because they pay greater attention to
their feelings, while men are occupied outside the household. But she soon turns the issue around
and makes her ladies claim that women are preoccupied with love because men are jealous and
do not allow them to receive a proper education so that they can apply themselves to something
else. Later women writers of treatises will return to the same issue more forcefully. See Fonte, *The
Worth of Women*, Marinella, *The Nobility and Excellence of Women*, and Arcangela Tarabotti, *Women Are
of the Human Species*, in *Women Are Not Human: An Anonymous Treatise and Responses*, ed. and trans.
Theresa Kenney (New York: Crossroad Publishing, 1998). Many male authors of the time had
here and there advocated the right, if not the necessity, of women's education, especially for
women of the higher class. An early example is to be found in Castiglione's *Courtier*. But in
women's hands education is right away the *sine qua non* to a normal life for either sex.

27. Much has been made of women's good nature. Francesca Baffa, a female interlocutor in a
male dialogue on love, Betussi's *Il Raverta*, says the same (172).

lover, because he will be stable and faithful (which is something one can rarely see in a young man). Moreover, his many past experiences will make him know fully how to use prudence and reason to save himself and his beloved from danger and even to prevent it from occurring.

"Some say that the lover should be young since, as one can often see from experience in affairs of love, good fortune is more valuable than much wise advice. Therefore it is better that the lover be young, because, thanks to the ardor of his young heart, he will keep his beloved entertained and happy without always waiting for the worst to happen. An old lover will not do this, because his age makes him subject to fear and doubt, and he cries and sighs months and years before encountering the evil he fears, being persuaded that he can have no more good.

"Some among us are of the opinion that the lover the woman chooses should be neither too young nor too old, but in between. By being too young, they argue, there is a great danger that he will dare too much and stumble into things that are less than good; and by being too old he would confuse himself with too much fear. If instead he belongs to both states, he will fear the dangers according to what reason advises and will try to avoid them with all his might; and if they come he will try to confront and overcome them with a bold heart.

"Another then says that, whatever the age of the lover, one should be very careful that he be rich and noble for two reasons. He needs to be noble so that if at any time a woman's fall (as often happens) is discovered, she will not receive that double shame common to women who have given their love to ignoble and vile men. He needs to be rich so that he can protect and defend his beloved with money and gifts in thousands of bad situations.

"Finally, one among us is very much opposed to the above opinion and thinks that any wise woman who desires a lover for her own satisfaction and pleasure rather than to please others should devote her entire care and utmost diligence to flee from the problems that this unstable Love often plants in loving hearts, namely, jealousy, doubt, fear, and suspicion. Such a woman should select a young lover of a lower condition than her own, poor rather than rich. Thinking himself unworthy of that noblewoman because of his humble status, and seeing himself loved by her, such a young man will feel so gratified by her love that he would prefer to die a thousand deaths rather than give her even the slightest offense, fearing that he could lose her or that someone worthier could take away so much happiness from him. Thus this woman, assured of not losing such a devoted lover, will enjoy her love peacefully and for a long time.

"Now, my gallant friend, we wanted to leave this place where we spent an entire profitless day, since we could not agree, given so many different views, and had given up hope of ever finding a way to harmonize our discordant opinions. Having seen you from afar, and each of us judging from many signs that you were very much in love, we determined that if we could get any courtesy from you, we would ask you for the singular gift of advising us freely about what we are very much ignorant of, given our scant experience. Since each of us has determined to remain no longer without a lover, we ask what age and condition of lover we should choose. Also, how should we behave toward him before we make a free gift of ourselves in order to be certain whether we are really loved or whether he feigns love. We already know that since you are in love we could not have found more honest and true advice from anyone else. Now therefore, taking hope from your kindness, we await the answer we desire so much."[28]

Here the lovely lady stopped talking. After he saw the woman become quiet, Fabio let a large sigh out of his chest, and said, "My gracious ladies, the burden you have given me is much too important and should be carried by stronger shoulders than mine. It is true that I find myself in love, and maybe more than any of you may think, but I do not see how that would lend me the needed intelligence to deserve teaching you such important things. I will say this, however, dear ladies, that it seems to me that the way you saw and understood me—outside myself and almost looking like a dead man—should be an example to induce you to disentangle yourselves from the web of love rather than to labor to enter it. Think, my ladies, if as a man I suffer such bitter love pangs, how much more bitterly you women would feel the pain, since doubtlessly you have souls of lesser valor and strength than mine.

"God knows how much it pains me to say now what I am constrained to say, both because I will say things against my sex and because I will perturb your loving hearts. But I want to advise you faithfully. I say then, my lovely ladies, that although it appears, and indeed is the case, that in the laws of love there is little faith and less stability between lovers than customary elsewhere, nevertheless (I must say it), there is always less faith and more instability in men than in women. If you have no experience of this, the ancient

---

28. The love questions posited most often in sixteenth-century treatises followed an almost predictable format. Here are some sample questions from Betussi's *Il Raverta:* whether it is more difficult to feign love while not loving or to simulate not being in love while in love (86); whether reasonably the shy lover loves more or less than the bold one (94); whether woman or man is more constant (100); what more than perseverance constitutes a man's sign that a woman is loved (109); whether a lover can die of too much love (113); whether love gives wisdom to crazy men or works in the opposite direction (133), and so on. The model is of course Boccaccio's *Filocolo* in which questions such as whether love is a good or an evil thing or whether a lady should give her preference to the most valorous, the most courteous, or the wisest man are considered. What distinguishes Bigolina's take from that of the other writers is that her entire discussion about love ends with a marriage.

histories should reveal it to you, because many expose such amorous havoc; and each time you will see unhappy women complain of men's infidelity, whereas rarely does one see men have reason to fault women. This happens because of the influence of the most benign planets, as well as the greater presence of moister elements in women than in men, which makes women more benign and compassionate toward those who love them. As a result, you will find a thousand very unfaithful men to one unfaithful woman, and for every thousand faithful women there is hardly a faithful man.[29] Out of bad luck then this man will fall for the only unfaithful woman among a faithful thousand, as happened to my wretched self.

"The best advice one can give you then, my ladies, is to push this cruel love farther away from you rather than bring it closer. Nevertheless, since I see from your attitude that you are willing to do anything to follow it, I will try to give you the least harmful advice—although I am persuaded that love can only bring pain. I say then that although love is always dreadful (as I told you before), the person who wants to follow it should put all his care into making it as little awful as possible, and this will happen when a man takes the utmost care in choosing a woman and a woman does the same in choosing a man for a lover.

"I have listened carefully to your different opinions, all of which I am going to leave aside since you have not yet touched upon what should have been touched upon most of all. It does not appear to me that you have to worry about the age, nobility, or wealth of the man you want to select for a lover, but you should be much more concerned that he is graced with the best mores and has some particular virtues. Most of all, you have to be careful that this lover is not vain; namely, that he does not consider it clever to court all women. For it would be horrible, my ladies, if you were to stumble on lovers who would make you die of jealousy a thousand times a day. Their art being that of courting women, these men do not content themselves with one or two, but rather they want to get as quickly as possible to the tenth person, like merchants unhappy with one kind of merchandise who work to have many and varied things in their hands. Now you have to consider how much they can love any of these women, since the heart certainly cannot divide it-

---

29. The argument on women being moister than men comes from Aristotelian and humor-based Galenic understandings of the human body, in which dry and hot humors were said to be more prevalent in men and humid and cold ones in women. The argument that the inconstancy of men and the constancy of women is the result of humors was also made by the Magnifico Juliano in the *Courtier*: "For reason of its hot nature, the male sex possesses the qualities of lightness, movement and inconstancy, whereas from its coldness, the female sex derives its steadfast gravity and calm and is therefore more susceptible" (3.16).

self into many parts. As for me, were I a woman, rather than give myself as prey to any such man, a creditor of laziness and time, I cannot say what I would rather expose myself to.

"It would be a good thing, my ladies, following the opinion of some of you, if each could find a young, noble, and rich lover; but I would rather have these riches extend to good habits, a noble soul, and many virtues than to accumulated treasures, for the wise young man knows more than the old ignoramus. Nor can inexperience per se make an expert of one whose talent is buried in ignorance. Many times good advice is more important than great treasures, because the latter work for a moment and the former over time. I would very much prefer that his lovely soul be applied to some commendable work, as it would be in dealing with arms, gardening, hunting, music, or some activity customary among praiseworthy gentlemen, as long as he does not stay idle or pursue vice.[30]

"It is true that it would please me most if he were learned in Greek, Latin, or the vernacular and would regard them not as dead but on the contrary would always honorably exercise them. For you should know that it is much worse when a learned man comes close to vice, leaving aside the fruits produced by science, than when a simple and ignorant man does the same, even if he possesses ill will. Protect yourselves from these men, my dear ladies, as you would from fire.

"I would also prefer that the lover you select be modest and respectful, of few words, not puffed up with his own merits, and not too curious. By being naturally respectful and modest, he will bring you much respect and honor on every occasion, whereas, were he immoderate and presumptuous, he would never miss the opportunity to offend you. The same would happen if he by nature had a loose tongue, because he could easily trip over too many words and betray things about which he should remain silent. Equally, it could happen that were he vainglorious, no matter how many or great the favors you bestow on him, he would be spurred by an even larger desire to brag about them. Similarly, were he very curious, you could think that he would soon satiate himself with you, given the many and varied things he would want to see and try. But were he adorned of all those optimal traits I have mentioned, perhaps you could believe yourselves lucky in having this lover, if one could ever hope for any good to come out of Love.[31]

30. The model for the perfect gentleman who knows how to joust in war but also how to play music was offered in the *Courtier*, which soon became the standard manual on the subject.

31. Manuals on how to marry ("prender moglie") were common throughout the sixteenth century, although never written by a woman and thus with less of a sense that women should partic-

"It is true that I could not give you any rule by which you could assure yourselves of how much and with what kind of love the lover you selected loves you. This is especially true when he first starts to love, at which time all lovers, the false as well as the true, show themselves to be equally smoldering with the most burning flames of love toward you, and all are well behaved, adoring, and respectful. In short, there is no obsequious act they will not perform at that time, no honor or courtesy they do not show toward you, no task they abandon or forget (even though it may be tiring or may harm them) as long as it is valuable to little by little acquire your grace. Thus I conclude that it is not simply difficult but almost impossible, in the first throes of love, to know the men who love you from the ones who do not or whom you should or should not trust, because they all show themselves equally loving and observant of your honor and of their proffered faith.

"You can perceive how they really are soon after you make them masters, since the wicked ones will manifest right away their wickedness. If, however, they are naturally as they appeared at first, they will remain always in that relationship with you. It would not seem to me out of place to test their patience through some trials, because there is no one in the world more patient or tolerant toward a beloved than a true lover, whereas there is no weight more heavy or unbearable than patience and suffering for those men who feign love and do not love. Therefore I would say that you could inflict some

---

ipate actively in the choice of a partner. Here is an incomplete, but representative, list of texts on the subject published during the span of Bigolina's generation: Francesco Barbaro, *Prudentissimi, et gravi documenti circa la elettione della moglie . . . nuovamente dal Latino tradotti per Alberto Lollio* (Venice, 1548); Lodovico Dolce, *Dialogo della istitutione delle donne secondo li tre stati, che cadono nella vita humana;* Giovanni Della Casa, *Se s'abbia da prender moglie (An uxor sit ducenda),* written in the 1530s (Florence, 1946); Juan Luis Vives, *De l'ufficio del marito, come si debba portare verso la moglie. De l'istitutione de la femina christiana, vergine, maritata, o vedova,* trans P. Lauro (Venice, 1546); Giovanni Battista Modio, *Il convito overo del peso della moglie. Dove ragionando si conchiude, che non può la donna dishonesta far vergogna à l'huomo* (Rome, 1554); Antonio Brucioli, *Del matrimonio, Dell'officio della moglie,* and *Del governo della famiglia,* in *Dialoghi della morale philosophia* (Venice, 1538); Girolamo Muzio, *Operette morali . . . Trattati di matrimonio* (Venice, 1550); Paolo Caggio, *Iconomica . . . nella quale s'insegna brevemente per modo di dialogo il governo famigliare, come di se stesso, della moglie, de' figliuoli, de' servi, delle case, delle robbe, e d'ogni altra cosa à quella appartenente* (Venice, 1552); Sabba Castiglione, *Ricordi, overo ammaestramenti . . . ne i quali . . . si ragiona di tutte le materie honorate, che si ricercano a un vero gentil'huomo* (Venice, 1555); and Agostino Bucci, *Due lettere . . . Nel una delle quali si disputa quale sia maggior Amore o quello del padre verso il figlio, o quello dell'amante verso la donna amata. Nell'altra si lauda il matrimonio* (Turin, 1555). Leon Battista Alberti, *Il padre di famiglia* was written a bit earlier. For a fuller bibliography, see Daniela Frigo, "Dal caos all'ordine: Sulla questione del 'prendere moglie' nella trattatistica del sedicesimo secolo," in Zancan, 57–63; and *Il padre di famiglia: Governo della casa e governo civile nella tradizione dell' 'economica' tra Cinque e Seicento* (Rome: Bulzoni, 1985), chap. 3. For a discourse on marriage centered on the area around Venice, see Margaret King, "Caldiera and the Barbaros on Marriage and the Family: Humanist Reflections of Venetian Realities," *Journal of Medieval and Renaissance Studies* 6 (1976): 19–50.

light offense on those who love you to discern how much you are loved. Be careful, however, that such an offense is not the sort that would harm their honor, because then you would give them reason to no longer love you forever, even though they had loved you very much.

"Be careful not to offend men by loving another for any reason in the world, for if wicked jealousy enters their heads, they will no longer love you with that sincere love with which they loved you at first. But if the offense you cause them is neither of the two kinds that I have mentioned, you can very soon ascertain for yourselves how much they love you. If they do not love you a great deal, they will be taken by such furious disdain after the first or second offense that they will not want to be lovers or friends anymore. True lovers behave in such a way that they will patiently tolerate each offense you cause them. In fact, fearing abandonment, even if they have not offended you in any way, they willingly take upon themselves your faults, and if they do that you can be sure they hold you dearer than their own lives. But do not think that this way of hurting them should be used often and become a habit, because I can assure you that their suffering and patience will be wholly exhausted soon enough. Thereafter you will be (and with reason) avoided as proud and ungrateful, and you will be hated and dodged more than death. So as soon as you have understood how completely they love you after the second or maybe third wrong they have patiently suffered, leave behind every means of offending them and dispose yourselves with your whole heart always to please and love them. In so doing you will see the dear lovers keep you for a long time in amorous peace.

"It now seems to me, my kind ladies, that enough has been said on this subject. If I have not fully satisfied your desire in the counsel I have given, I pray you not to blame my will, which is faultless toward you, but my lack of knowledge. And if you have no other use of me at the moment, I beseech you to give me leave so I can return to my journey with your permission."

The women thanked him very much and praised highly the wise advice he had given them. They showed themselves very satisfied with his words and each desired to reward him for the benefit they believed they had received from him. Thus they all courteously forced him, by surrounding him, to remain with them for the rest of that day and the following night. Although Fabio would have welcomed solitude much more than company, he decided to accept their invitation, because he did not want to appear unappreciative of such sweetly entreating women by making them beg for his company. They stayed there a short time because the ladies' servants soon arrived with their horses. As evening was coming and they had a few miles to go, they all mounted at once and moved toward the palace of one of them that was nearby. When they arrived and dismounted, they put the kind Fabio in the middle of their group and walked through pleasant gardens for the remainder of the day. Now one and now the other held his hand, and they spent time in pleasing conversations much to their delight. Then, when evening came, and after a delightful dinner, they all went to bed.

How different the rest of that night was for the unhappy Urania than for all the others cannot be fully conveyed. Some of the women felt that they had already found the lover whom they wanted like the one Fabio had sketched the day before and had such joy and satisfaction in their hearts that they could not sleep. But Urania, who was excessively in love, was almost at the point of killing herself that night. She was assaulted by a larger passion than any felt before, since she knew that she alone was the one who truly loved a man possessing all the excellent virtues and habits that every true lover should have and knew likewise that she was worthy of his love. Yet she saw herself loved little or not at all and did not know what to blame if not her destiny for having made her so unwelcome to her Fabio. Still, helped by better counsel, she decided to live, hoping to find peace.[32]

When day came, she wanted by all means to depart, to the great sorrow of all those women who would have liked for him to remain always with them to give good counsel. And perhaps some of these women, knowing him to be adorned with such good habits and gracious manners, had become so enthralled that they would gladly have settled down with him and given up desiring to find someone elsewhere.

THE WORTH OF WOMEN

Now then, carried away by her fierce amorous passion, Urania had journeyed less than a mile from the palace when, as usual, she immersed herself in her inner thought of love. For this reason, she no longer cared about what she had done the day before, or about herself, or about her horse, or about holding the bridle. And so, wandering here and there for about four miles, she arrived at a meadow where a few young noblemen from Naples were trying out a handsome falcon. In seeing this person, whom they thought a young man, coming toward them on a horse so much dazed and out of himself, they were

---

32. This scene of quasi-suicide for love closely recalls a similar passage in Ariosto's *Furioso*, canto 32, in which Bradamante first morosely waits for Ruggiero and then one night decides to end her life because she feels that her love is no longer reciprocated. But she fails to stab herself because she forgot that she was still wearing her armor. She thus chooses to live and to start a quest to find out how things stand with him. We find her next in the Rocca di Tristano, in a scene that Bigolina will closely recreate two chapters from now.

seized by the greatest wonder. Therefore they abandoned their project with the falcon in order to investigate this unique situation and quickly surrounded the wretched Urania. Some of them started to shake her saddle, some grabbed her by the arms, and some shoved her back or her sides with the pommel of their swords. The unhappy one, although immersed beyond measure in her own amorous thought, came back to herself at once, having been struck by so many side blows and shoves. Seeing herself assaulted and abused by those men as if, in her judgment, by enemies, she had no time to feel shame, for her heart was at once filled with anger and disdain. Her face flushed with their color, she said to them, "If you are gentlemen, as your clothes declare, nature must not have made your hearts ever feel a spark of sweet love, because there never was a gentle lover who did not show himself similarly kind and courteous in all he did. It is hard to believe that one can still use such ill-mannered discourtesy as you showed me for no reason. Should we men not confess that women surpass us in many respects (I have to say so), but specifically with respect to courtesy? Here today I find myself treated exceedingly badly by you gentlemen, whereas when I was found not too far from here by five women no less beautiful than virtuous in the same condition as you, to my immense detriment, have found me, they brought me back to myself with no less courtesy than dexterity, as is the usual custom of every kind heart. They welcomed me among themselves and into their pleasing and wise discussions, they did not consent to my departure all day long yesterday, and only with great effort did they do so this morning. I will remember their immense courtesy as long as I live."

The young men, five in number and very dear friends and companions, were by chance in love with the already mentioned women. They were there, not too far from a palace of one of them, because they wanted to see the five women and try their luck, having learned that the women were nearby entertaining themselves. So each one of them felt their wounds reopened by the arrow of love. Submerged in a sea of shame at hearing their bad manners rebuked, they drew back and remained confused and speechless. But love was much stronger in them than shame when they realized that this young man could give them fresher news of their women. Even more, their hearts burned with a desire to know the kinds of discussions he had that he said were pleasant and wise. Thus one of them, more loquacious than the others, spoke to the young man, "Most kind young man, we frankly confess that our actions have been very discourteous, but we want to add that we did not exercise them maliciously. On the contrary, having judged you half dead, we acted without thinking further and only because we wanted to make you come back to life. Our good intentions—which now you will see revealed—can testify that we insulted you with no wicked thought. Not only do we confess ourselves unhappy and repentant for the offense we gave you, but we also offer to make any penance you think we deserve."

Hearing the young man's most humble words and surmising that they all repented of their acts, the sympathetic Urania, in whose heart never dwelled any discourtesy, could not avoid being moved, feeling very sorry for what she said. Forgetting any injury received, she made them understand with a proper and benign response that her life was governed by courtesy and kindness. Not satisfied at being forgiven and wishing more from her, namely, to know the nature of her discussions with their women the previous day, the young men pressed her closely and obliged her to remain for lunch that morning. They said that they would not believe she had forgiven them if she denied them such a small favor.

Not wanting to raise any suspicion about herself in the minds of the young men, Urania let herself be led willingly to the palace. When they arrived and dismounted, it seemed that the men could not stop welcoming and honoring her, so that she found herself favored and served at table better than she had ever been before. When they had finished eating their lavish meal, the young man who was a better talker than the others began to tempt her vaguely to reveal those conversations they wished to know about. But she, who was marvelously astute, guessed right away, as was in fact the case, that those five men were in love with the five women of the day before, and therefore she answered with a very pleasing demeanor, "Oh my, I understand that you would like me to open all my heart's secrets to you while you keep your own hearts shut and enclosed. This does not seem right, so I want you to know that if you do not reveal what you are about, you will not learn in any detail what I know. It would be unkind toward those courteous women to reveal their secrets behind their backs to those uninterested in them."

They realized that this other young man was shrewder than they and that he had guessed the source of their desires, so they smiled and with mutual good will disclosed their thoughts of love and their desires, passionately sighing from their hearts. They begged him humbly not to hide anything he had seen or known of those women, and each of them offered to do something more than the others for him. Urania felt a great happiness at having encountered the youths who were in love with those women, and thus she said to them, "Although I could truthfully call myself the most unhappy and unfortunate young man existing in the world today, nevertheless, I feel an infinite sorrow when I see virtuous men suffer the pain I suffer. Also, I take immense pleasure at knowing that their desires move toward a happy end, and I am even more pleased when I know that to some degree their happiness comes from me, as I hope will happen today with you. If you behave the way virtuous and faithful men should behave in the presence of the women they set out to love, I can assure you that all of you will fulfill your amorous desires soon and happily with the five women in question."

Then from beginning to end she divulged all the conversations between her and the women without leaving out a single word. It is difficult to convey the attention with which the young lovers listened to words so pleasing to them, and I truly believe that they never in their lives heard anything more delightful or sweeter. After she stopped talking and they individually and collectively thanked her so many times that it would be redundant to mention them one by one, the young man who had spoken earlier continued, "Most gallant young man, I cannot see what greater or more precious thing we could possess or what larger worth our lives could have that even if we could use both in your behalf we would truly have satisfied only the least part of our debt. To make ourselves even more obliged (if we can), we would kindly pray you to extend to us that great courtesy that you extended to those gentlewomen when you counseled and advised them about the condition and state of lover they should select for themselves, and advise us likewise, if it pleases you, about the state and condition of woman a man should choose to love. Earlier we believed that falling in love had to do only with the satisfaction of the senses and that we could remain inwardly calm and content as long as our eyes were satisfied at what they saw.[33]

"Considering that man is of greater perfection than woman—and indeed for some wise men the vilest and least worthy man on earth is more valuable than the most noble and valiant woman—I believe a man does not exist so wicked as to be unworthy of any woman. And yet you have directed women to carefully choose a love with such and such virtues. I disagree and judge that it is more important that a man use a greater diligence in choosing the least imperfect woman among many imperfect ones than it is for a woman to pick the best among many perfect men, because it is worse for women to be wrong than for men to be lucky even once."

"You are very badly informed and your understanding of the matter is even worse," Urania then answered. "Although you are such prudent young men, I am amazed that you have let such an obvious stupidity come out of your mouth, not realizing that those who said it first said it falsely, not moved by reason but goaded by passion. We are men, but reason does not allow us unjustly to defame and oppress women. I will not say that they are of the same perfection as men, but I will say that, at the least, they are only a bit less

33. As in Boccaccio's *Filocolo*, men think of love in terms of satisfaction of the senses, but women—Fiammetta in Boccaccio and Urania in Bigolina—emphasize that the only love worth pursuing and the only one which finds women interested is honest love, namely, as Fiammetta would say, the love that is "faithful."

perfect than we. Judging by the degrees of perfection in either sex, I believe that imperfect and wicked men greatly exceed in imperfection and wickedness the most depraved and imperfect women.[34] This truth I would like to establish with visible proofs.

"Let's talk first of perfections. We see that rarely does any noble art, high science, or virtue exist among men that is not also found among women—if not of equal perfection, then at least only a little less perfect—to the degree that it has been permissible for women to be involved. Therefore, if you praise men for piety by saying that many saints have expanded the Christian faith by spilling their blood in sacrifice to God Almighty, I will answer that many young virgins have made it no less large by showing themselves extremely steadfast in holy martyrdom. If you say that there have been many prophets among men, I would say that there has not been a lack of wise sibyls among women. If you say that there have been in the sciences many learned men of whom there was such a poet, such an orator, such a philosopher, and such a man endowed with such and such virtue, one could answer that there have been a Sappho, a Carmenta, or a Hortensia among women and many others only slightly less learned and wise than the men mentioned and that in Athens many women taught male scholars in the academies of philosophy.[35] If you then praise many valiant men for their greatness of soul and work, can-

34. The argument on perfection was typical of Aristotelian and Galenic discourses on the body in which the difference was on the degree of perfection (the woman being more inferior to the man in Aristotelian than in Galenic readings) rather than on the principle. The most common misogynist view was offered by the character Gasparo, citing Aristotle, in Castiglione's *Courtier*: "It is the opinion of very learned men that man is as the form and woman as the matter, and therefore just as form is more perfect than matter, and indeed gives it being, so man is far more perfect than woman" (3.14). Some courtiers rushed to praise women, but were unable to do a good job and in the end Emilia Pio, the lady in charge of the conversation, begged them to stop: "We can't at all understand your way of defending us" (3.17). On the interplay between Aristotelian and Galenic ideas of women in the period, see Maclean, *The Renaissance Notion of Woman*. For a study of the construction of the male body in Renaissance literature and culture and of the medical discourse that informed it, see Finucci, *The Manly Masquerade*.

35. Sappho of Lesbos, a Greek poet, lived in the sixth century B.C.E. and is credited with having invented a new way of versifying: the Sapphic verse. Carmenta, also called Nicostrata, was a learned woman and a seer, and at times she disclosed the future in verse; thus the Latins called her Carmenta (from *Carmen*, verse). Together with Evander, king of Arcadia, her son (or in other versions, her husband), she left Arcadia and reached the mouth of the Tiber in Italy to settle on the Palatine hill, which later became the site where Rome was founded. Aware that the people were illiterate, she established the original sixteen letters of the Latin alphabet. Hortensia was the eloquent daughter of Hortensius. She gave a speech to the triumvirs on behalf of Roman women against inordinate taxes. These women are all present in Boccaccio, *Famous Women*, respectively, chapters 47, 27, and 84. This book was translated into Italian and given a new circulation by Betuni in 1545.

not one answer that the four daughters of Amphion and Penthesilea and Tamyris merited no less honor and esteem?[36] Do you not believe that today in each of these professions there are many women among us who could put to shame men who think highly of themselves? Therefore, I conclude that there is no reason to say that the most vile and unworthy man is more worthy than the most worthy woman, a judgment truly stupid and insane.

"But to make you recognize further how the most wicked women have less imperfection and wickedness than the most wicked men, I ask you to consider fully from which of the two sexes come, most of the time, the many iniquities and wickedness filling the world. Where do deceits, usuries, betrayals, thefts, plunders, and homicides come from if not always from men? Laws so necessary among humans today would be of little usefulness if men lived with each other in loyalty and peace as women do."[37]

The young men had kept quiet until then, listening in rapt attention, but since it seemed to them that the young man's last words unduly blamed the male sex and were more partial to women than was appropriate, the youth who had spoken more than the others interrupted Urania in her speech and answered her: "You cause us great amazement, valiant young man, in your extreme affection toward women, in particular by not wanting to consent—as you let us understand by what you say—that they play any role, small or large, that is not all good, pure, and faithful. On the other hand, you ascribe all the worst villainies to men alone. We confess that the praise you gave them earlier in your conversation is just, since you have made your case with clear

36. Amphion and his proud wife, Niobe, had seven daughters (although in this version four), who died one after the other as the gods' punishment for their mother's vainglory in having given birth to so many children. See Ovid, *Metamorphoses*, 6.146–286; and Boccaccio, *Famous Women*, 15. Penthesilea, queen of the Amazons, forgot her beauty, covered her golden tresses with a helmet, armed her body, and was said to rout entire squadrons of armed men with her bow. She is credited with the invention of the ax. See Boccaccio, *Famous Women*, 32. Tamyris, queen of Scythia, stood up against the powerful king Cyrus when she was a widow. Feigning to flee his armies, she successfully encircled Cyrus, routed his men, and had his head cut off for a trophy. Boccaccio dedicates to her chapter 49 of his *Famous Women*. Lists of learned ancient women were also in texts more contemporary to Bigolina's writing, as in Galeazzo Flavio Capra, *Della eccellenza e dignità delle donne*, ed. Maria Luisa Doglio (Rome: Bulzoni, 2001), 90–93.

37. With this pointed attack on men, Bigolina paves the way for the more mordant one registered in Fonte's *The Worth of Women* a generation later: "even among themselves they [men] deceive one another, rob one another, destroy one another, and try to do each other down. Just think of all the assassinations, usurpations, perjuries, the blasphemy, gaming, gluttony, and other such vicious deeds they commit all the time! Not to mention the murders, assaults, and thefts, and other dissolute acts, all proceeding from men! And if they have so few scruples about committing these kind of excesses, think of what they are like where more minor vices are concerned: just give a thought to their ingratitude, faithlessness, falsity, cruelty, arrogance, lust, and dishonesty!" (61).

logic. But we do not believe you when you say they are of so great a perfection that they do not participate with us men in many villainies. We know very well, from personal experience, the depraved nature of many of them. We also know for certain that rarely does villainy, especially murder, come from any other cause than women, and we could give you many examples in our time.[38]

"But let us put today's examples aside because most are unknown, and let us consider the ancient ones known to the whole world, and above all the most noble Troy. Is it not true that the city was destroyed because of a poor little woman so that hardly one stone was left upon another? Was she not the reason why many armies took up arms? Was she not the reason why so many valiant men met their deaths, and of these one alone was worthier than all the women Mother Nature ever created?[39] Do we not have certain knowledge that women are amazingly vengeful and cruel and never appease themselves after a little injury made to them until they have exacted a cruel revenge?[40] Leaving aside modern women, tell me who can imagine a worse revenge than that of the cruelest old Medea and likewise that of Procne?[41] Nor would I say

38. Contemporary misogynistic treatises on the dangers posed by assertive women, although perhaps not as many in number as those that appeared later in the century, were widespread. See Vincenzo Maggi, *Un brieve trattato dell'eccellentia delle donne . . . Vi si è poi aggiunto un'essortatione a gli buomini perché non si lascino superare dalle donne, mostrandogli il gran danno che lor è per sopravenire* (Brescia, 1545); Michelangelo Biondo, *Dell'Angoscia, Doglia e Pena, le tre furie del Mondo. Nelle quali si contiene, ciò che si aspetta alla Donna* (Venice, 1546); and Lodovico Dolce, *Dialogo piacevole nel quale Messer Pietro Aretino parla in difesa di male aventurati mariti* (Venice, 1542).

39. The reference here is to Helen of Troy, wife of Menelaus, whose beauty was so unsurpassed that not even the best painters could catch it. She was first abducted by Theseus when very young, while exercising in the "palestra," as was the local custom. See Boccaccio, *Famous Women*, 37. Helen later married Menelaus, king of Sparta, and had a daughter, Hermione. Paris fell in love with her, seized her, and brought her to Troy. The enraged Greeks laid siege to the city, and what followed is told by Homer in the *Iliad*.

40. The idea that women are naturally more vengeful, jealous, mischievous, deceptive, and querulous than men was a given in culture. Aristotle had stated that much: "The female is softer in disposition, is more mischievous, less simple, more impulsive, and more attentive to the nurture of the young; the male, on the other hand, is more spirited, more savage, more simple and less cunning . . . . Woman is more compassionate than man, more easily moved to tears, at the same time is more jealous, more querulous, more apt to scold and to strike. She is, furthermore, more prone to despondency, and less hopeful than the man, more void of shame, more false of speech, more deceptive, and of more retentive memory. She is also more wakeful, more shrinking, more difficult to rouse to action, and requires a smaller quantity of nutriment." In *History of Animals*, 608b.1–13.

41. Medea, queen of Colchis, an expert on the properties of herbs, was said to have betrayed her own father to win the love of young Jason. She had her brother dismembered to delay her father's pursuit, and when Jason abandoned her, she killed their own two sons in front of him in vengeance. See Boccaccio, *Famous Women*, 17. Procne, married to Tereus, king of Thracia, killed her own son to vindicate her husband's rape of her sister, Philomela. The two sisters were changed into a swallow and a nightingale. Procne's story is told extensively in Ovid, *Metamor-*

that one should regard Circe less cruel than these, since she changed many charming and loving men into horrible and monstrous wild beasts as compensation for the pleasures she received.[42]

"Now please do not say any longer that women are so good that they can only do a good and never a wicked act, since we have made known to you how they can and actually do many evil things. Many, unable to resolve matters by themselves because of their weakness, try to give men reason to do so. From this one can conclude that women are always harmful and never are the reason that good things happen, unless you are their paid lawyer. Were such the case, you would have a great motivation to defend their reason valiantly, but even then we are not obliged to believe so lightly all you say in their favor."

"Undoubtedly you deceive yourselves not a little about me, gentlemen," Urania then answered, "feeling in your heart that all I have said in favor of women has been motivated by passion; on the contrary, please believe that reason—and reason alone—can move me to defend anyone. I believe I have spoken and demonstrated the truth, as you yourselves have already confessed, that women are, if not of the same perfection as we men, at least almost as much. Understand that I was talking of good women and not of bad ones, and not because I did not want to say that there are many among them who are evil and wicked. On the contrary, I tell you that were I to talk about their defects, as I have just been given reason to defend them, I would not keep silent about a single one I know.

"I was saying, I say, or at least I wanted to say, to those of you who want to compare the ugliness of the worst men with that of the worst women, that these are almost incomparable.[43] You say that women contrive to give men reason to do those evils they cannot effect by themselves and that they cause not one good thing but only bad ones. In truth, this argument lacks founda-

---

phoses, 6.439–674. For Dante, Procne's impious deed changed her form into the bird that most likes to sing (che mutò forma / ne l'uccel ch'a cantar più si diletta"). See *Purgatorio* 17, 19–20.

42. Circe was an extraordinarily beautiful woman, accused of changing men into animals. According to Boccaccio, she was very knowledgeable about herbs and very wanton. She is said to have had a son by Ulysses. See Boccaccio, *Famous Women*, 38. Fonte, however, offers a different biography. For her, Circe had a daughter with Ulysses, named appropriately Circetta, who was also an expert on magic, like her mother, but not wanton (in fact, "vergine pudica," 11.91), and unable to perform any cruelty. See Fonte, *Tredici canti del Floridoro*, cantos 5–12. In short, when women writers approach ancient myths not only do they rewrite them according to their more realistic views of women but they also uncover the male obsessions that preside over the creation of such stories of female monstrosity in the first place. See the introduction to Fonte by Finucci, xxxiv–xxxv.

43. Bigolina's "I was saying, I say, or at least I wanted to say" echoes Dante's famous "Cred'io ch'ei credette ch'io credesse" ("I think he thought I thought") in *Inferno* 13, 25.

tion, and I cannot guess what reason might move you to believe what you can neither know nor see. What you actually demonstrate is that you say this out of faulty thinking rather than any probable cause. But since you have adduced those examples of cruelty, vengefulness, and ruin caused by women out of scorn, I want to defend them using your very examples to make you realize that they are less cruel, less vengeful, and less the cause of any ruin than men.

"Earlier you said that the unhappy Troy was destroyed and many most valiant men were led to death because of Helen. But turn the order around, I pray; say, rather, that first, Paris's vain and disordered appetite, and second, his tenacious stubbornness caused every wrong and ruin. Have you ever read in any author that she went to Troy to invite the Trojan to love her? Rather you read everywhere that he went to Greece to lead her astray, and if he induced her to his pleasure with loving and sweet words, with alluring acts and grand offers, what do you then mean to say? I already know that you would say she would have been wise to close her ears to sweet entreaties and supplications.

"Oh, how stupid the opinion of many who, rarely seeing beneath the surface and having no knowledge of sensible things, do not even, by comparing them to things imperceptible, derive some true and proper understanding! These people never understand that a drop of water, the most soft and tender thing there is, still has the power to hollow out and pierce the hardest marble if it drips on it enough. How much more therefore will the heart of a kind woman yield when she sees in front of her a man who loves her, or who pretends love for her, telling her with warm tears, passionate sighs, and mournful, sweet words that he burns, is consumed, and yearns for her? Truly, to think of it, this unhappy female sex is persecuted by wretched fortune because of us men, and I want to be the one to say it, since no woman is present to hear me.

"No tall, strong tower could avoid complete collapse if it were to sustain half the blows women receive through men's solicitations, tricks, and deceptions. What is worse? If they surrender, they are denounced as women of bad habits by the same men who should be grateful to them. If, on the other hand, they show themselves stubborn and unyielding to their entreaties, they are called perfidious, cruel, unkind, ungrateful, and enemies of every virtue. I would not know what other less dangerous advice to give these unhappy ones in such cases except—and this is very unpleasant—that they should pray to God to make them physically unenticing and possessed of the least desired habits so that no man would take a fancy to them. Otherwise it is impossible for them to shield themselves from our evil tongues.

"But to go back to where I left off in their defense, having shown you that it was not the Greek woman but the Phrygian young man who brought about the destruction of ancient Troy, I still have to tell you how women have done many good and useful things and have been little inclined to evil. Tell me, did not the Jewish Judith greatly benefit her people by killing Holofernes with a manly spirit? Did Queen Esther do any less in providing her people with her wise talent and knowledge when she persuaded King Assuerus, her husband?[44] Were not the Sabine women's actions miraculous, since they had the strength and foresight to bring about a loving unity between two enemy peoples?[45] And what are we to think of that revered Roman Veturia, mother of the great Coriolanus, who alone had the power to obtain what so many great Roman delegates and ambassadors could not? She so humbled and softened her son's hard and depraved heart that Rome could not have escaped a serious and perhaps final massacre without her.[46] Does it seem to you that these benefits that men have received from women are small? I leave aside many others in order not to bore you.

"You also say that women are more vengeful and cruel than we men, but I tell you that we are much more cruel than they, and I would like to prove it to you. Tell me, I pray, where does vengeance start? I know you will answer that it comes from injuries received, and that is true. Now then, if women are vengeful, it necessarily follows that they have received offense from us in the first place, since injury always precedes vengeance. Therefore, we are the cruel ones and not they, because we first wronged those who did us no wrong. By taking vengeance on us, they cause injury to those by whom they were injured in the first place. If you tell me that Circe was cruel because, without having received any injury from those young men and lacking all piety, she changed them into various wild animals, I will say, as you do, that she was truly cruel. But on the other hand, we can attribute her great cruelty in large part to the inordinate love she had for herself. To allay her fear that those young men would reveal her too lascivious life, she prevented them from departing by means of enchantments. Now you see that she was not cruel, because were she cruel, she could just as well have killed them as changed them into beasts, but she did not. She was inclined to enchant them not by the hate she had for them, but by the love she had for herself.

"But tell me, I pray, for what reason do we want to defend men such as

44. Judith and Esther are two Jewish figures introduced by Bigolina. They do not appear in Boccaccio. As in the many representations of her in painting and sculpture, Judith beheaded her enemy Holofernes while he was asleep. Esther, wife of Assuerus, saved her people by revealing to her husband the plotting being done against the Jewish people by Aman, a royal favorite.

45. The Sabine women, abducted by Roman men, intervened to make peace in the battle between their people and the Romans by displaying to their kin the children born of their new relationships. See Livy, *A History of Rome*, 1.13.

46. Veturia, or Volumnia, a Roman matron, convinced her son Coriolanus not to attack Rome in revenge for having been exiled. See Boccaccio, *Famous Women*, chapter 55.

Marius, Sulla, Mezentius, Nero, Falari, Ezzelino, and many other extremely cruel tyrants who engaged in the most pitiless massacre of men without having received any injury from anyone and whose cruelty cannot be defended or excused for whatever reason?[47] Thus we should conclude, I think, that if women are not better than we men, at least they are not any worse. And we should also conclude that the man to whom the heavens have by chance given the most valiant woman for a companion can call himself blessed.

"So many and so good have been the reasons you have given in favor of women," the young man answered, "that we can now confess that what you have told us is wholly true and that we definitely erred when we expressed such a sinister opinion of them. I confess that I would forego a great treasure rather than hold on to the foolish belief that women could not be worth much except to accommodate themselves to our needs and stay some time with us so that we might escape idleness and for no other reason. Because of what you have said, I tell you that from now on I will hold them in that total veneration one should have for things almost sacred and divine."

"You are too precipitous," Urania answered the young man, "and you let your affections transport you to extremes far beyond reason. A while ago you did not want to admit that women had any worth, and now you want to worship them all, as if they were divine. I am quite glad that you are over that first mistake, but I would not like you to fall into perhaps a similar one because of that, for I believe it is equally bad to give excessive honor to those unworthy of it than not to honor those who merit it, and the reason is self-evident.

"You must know, gentlemen, that women worthy of being honored with true and perfect love are quite rare, although there are thousands who merit being honored because of their hereditary nobility. There are very few in this world, however, who merit honor not because it is derived from lineage, wealth, or the favors of friends, but because it is acquired through intrinsic worth, virtue, talent, and above all a very generous and fine soul.

"You have asked me to advise you of the qualifications you should look for in the beloved, a question that appears to me quite novel. You being the wise men you seem to be, I do not know why I should be so conceited as to believe I alone am qualified to teach the five of you. But in order to make you

---

47. The stories of the famous Roman tyrants Marius and Sulla are fully narrated by Plutarch. See *Lives*. The Roman emperor Nero has, through the centuries, come to represent the epitome of useless ferocity. The tyrant Mezentius, killed by Aeneas in a ferocious battle, appears prominently in Virgil's *Aeneid*. Ezzelino da Romano figures as an antichrist in popular medieval legends. He killed, among others, his own brother and attached his already killed nephews and nieces to the tails of horses. Being Padua's most ferocious tyrant, he also figures in the novella "Giulia," which is set in that city. Falari was indicted by Machiavelli as an infamous tyrant.

aware that I am pleased to please all virtuous men, I shall tell you what little I know.

"I say then that the wise man who has chosen to fall in love, which I believe happens only to a few men, since most are caught by surprise—I am referring here to the wise man who acts like the good merchant in wanting to see and know the merchandise first before buying it—this wise man in my judgment will need to be warned before putting his foot in the net of love, since, once entangled, it is not in his power to extricate himself when he wishes. On the contrary, once there, he is forced to remain, willing or not, even though many times it is clear that the woman for whom he pines is not a worthy subject. Oh, how many times do a beautiful braid and a pretty eye cover much perfidy or rudeness! How the one and the other are harmful I leave you to judge. But because I first have to speak of the rank the woman should have and then move on to the details, I think that in as many honorable as safe respects the wise man should not fall in love with a married woman, but only with a widow or a maiden, whichever of the two he likes more.[48]

"Above all I would like him to take care that she is judicious and adorned with a beautiful soul. If he does so, in addition to the delight he will receive in being with her, he will also be able to save himself and her from many dangers. More to the point, in questions of love I would judge more necessary to the preservation of the honor of both that the woman be much more careful than the man, since the honor of the one and the life of the other almost always depend on a woman's cautiousness and good behavior. How many we have seen tottering in their love and coming to a painful end! All things considered, it could be said that all the evil encountered proceeds from woman's negligence and lack of wisdom. The beloved woman should therefore be extraordinarily careful, but with a carefulness not accompanied by deceitfulness, duplicity, fraud, and other wicked qualities, as one often sees. From her prudence, the man can obtain another no less large benefit, which is that she will see her lover's worth better manifested and will know his value much better than would an ignorant and stupid woman. From this it follows that in knowing that he is more worthy, she will hold him in greater esteem and will love him more. This effect will bring about another no less large conse-

---

48. In Boccaccio's *Filocolo* too, question number 9—proposed by Feramonte, duke of Montorio—was on the merits of a relationship with a virgin, a married woman, or a widow (4.51–52). Bigolina herself, once widowed, did not remarry as far as we know. Among the treatises of the period that took up the problem of a new marriage, see Gian Giorgio Trissino, *Epistola de la vita che dee tenere una donna vedova* (Rome, 1524); and Lodovico Dolce, *Dialogo de la institution de le donne* (Venice, 1545).

quence in the man, that is, knowing himself so loved, he will burn with a double love and will rejoice with supreme happiness.

"The prudent man should also take care that the woman he has chosen not be totally vain, that is, that her heart not be pliant and ready to go wandering here and there, because if she keeps a changeable and unstable heart in her other actions, she will keep it changeable and unstable in matters of love. This constitutes the reason for many suspicions and for infinite mental turmoil. It would please me also if the woman were somewhat—or even greatly—learned in vernacular letters and enjoyed them a good deal and if she were acquainted with many ancient histories.[49] These things will have a most desirable result. By always being occupied in honorable mental exercise, her mind will not stray to thoughts of more dishonorable transactions, for in the end, there is no greater despoiler of good habits, diverter of good deeds, and destroyer of virtue than the awful idleness, which by itself supplants every vice. The human intellect cannot deny its own nature, which is to move continually and to form various images of itself as long as it is occupied in the various alterations of the senses—that is, in the occupations and exercises of the whole body. Thus, when the person is idle and the intellect desires to work its usual effect, it generates its concepts in that color with which it is tinged, because each seed produces fruit in conformity to its nature.

"By this I mean that the person not applying his soul to some virtuous

---

49. The recommendation to educate women was widespread in treatises on the excellence of women, especially for women of the upper class. But unlike Bigolina, who envisions a learned woman, female education was usually limited to readings of moral or practical value. Dolce argued for the importance of women reading the Bible. He also allowed them to read selections from Virgil, Horace, Cicero, and Seneca and to read Italian authors such as Dante and Petrarch, but not Boccaccio, and absolutely no reading of romances and novellas was envisioned. See *Dialogo de la institution de le donne*. On the scarce education reserved to early modern women, see Grendler, *Schooling in Renaissance Italy.* Convents were the usual place where poor girls were educated since no public school for girls existed until the end of the sixteenth century. Even then, the curriculum was limited to the catechism, reading, and sewing. See Angelo Turchini, *Sotto l'occhio del padre: Società confessionale e istruzione primaria nello Stato di Milano* (Bologna: Il Mulino, 1996), 283; Ludovica Lenzi, *Donne e madonne: L'educazione femminile nel primo Rinascimento* (Turin: Loescher, 1982); and Giulia Bologna, *Libri per un'educazione rinascimentale: Grammatica del Donato* (Milan: Comune di Milano, 1980). Unlike today, when writing and reading are learned together, in the early modern period the two educational moments were separate and writing was not introduced in the curriculum right away. This explains why some women kept signing their names with an X, as if they were illiterate, although they were able to read some religious books. For more on the subject, see Anne Jacobson Schutte's commentary to her edition and translation of Ferrazzi, *Autobiography of an Aspiring Saint* (Chicago: University of Chicago Press, 1996). On what women of the Venetian area read, see Federica Ambrosini, "Libri e lettrici in terra veneta nel sec. 16: Echi erasmiani e inclinazioni eterodosse," In *Erasmo, Venezia e la cultura padana del '500,* ed. Achille Olivieri (Rovigo: Minelliana, 1995).

deed is necessarily constrained to spend all the time left over from ordinary business either vainly or viciously. We see this by experience in those little women from the provinces who on holidays compete with each other in telling all they know of this and that woman after making a group or a circle among themselves. There are many who, in order to show that they know more than another, add things they do not know or cannot know. And thus it happens that often they come to reveal what should instead be denied, even under torture.

"Now you see that it is harmful and dangerous for both man and woman to remain idle. I say this with regard to those who are not virtuous, since the virtuous man is never idle, even if externally it does not appear that he is toiling. The vicious man, on the other hand, does not do much, since he does not intend to do anything that does not show up and does not bring praise to him.

"I will not tire of saying how much the woman needs to be chosen by the wise man for her modesty, good habits, humility, and good manners. For it is well-known that a woman in whom any of those qualities is missing would be like a tree without branches, a lawn without grass, or a fountain without water. Above everything else, if his good luck should grant this wise man the grace (given only rarely) to meet a woman in possession of all the good qualities about which I have spoken, I would advise him that, beyond counting himself lucky for being in her grace, he should conduct himself so as never to do the least wrong to upset her heart in any way; on the contrary, he should keep her always dear by being faithful and loving her sincerely."

As she was saying these last words she almost cried and held back her tears with great difficulty. They were coming from her heart so intensely because she felt that she herself was the person with all the above-mentioned qualities, the person her Fabio should have valued and loved more than any other woman. Yet she saw herself driven to wander through the world as a result of the little esteem he had for her. Therefore, seized at that point by an incomparable anxiety, she almost exposed her feelings against her will to those young men. But having a large heart, she strengthened herself and kept enclosed the amorous flame in her troubled heart.

Still, greatly desiring to depart so that she could cry and pour out aloud her bitter passion, she politely asked of those young men permission to leave. Although they would have been extremely happy for such a wise stranger to remain a few days with them, nevertheless, seeing that he was determined to go, they bade him good-bye after thanking him and offering him more courtesies. Then, to amend their previous rudeness, they also, against her wishes, kept her company for perhaps three miles.

LIFE WITH EMILIA

As the young men left her, the unhappy Urania went back to her bitter cry and lament more than ever before. Amid these tears, sighs, and wails, she went through many cities in Italy, stopping only a short time in each. Having arrived one day at the borders of Tuscany, she found herself more than ever assailed by such a fiery and cruel amorous passion—because she believed that she could no longer live without her Fabio—that she allowed herself to be conquered by desperation and decided no longer to eat and to let herself die.

Having ridden through populated places during most of the day, she entered an expansive, solitary valley in which she proceeded until evening without seeing anyone. As often happens to many who ask for and desire death every hour but then, when they see it close, try with all their might to escape it, so was the case of the unhappy Urania. As the night was approaching and she was alone in that solitary place, tired of riding and quite feeble because of her long fast, she felt her heart stung by such a great dread of her own pain that, had she known where to take refuge for the night to save her life, she would have done it very willingly, because she no longer wanted to die so basely for any reason in the world.

Therefore, spurring her horse, which had more desire to rest and eat than to trot, as her good luck would have it, at sunset she found an inn almost at the border of that valley. Once she saw it, she thought she had returned from death to a new life, such was the cheer she felt. She arrived, called to the innkeeper, and asked him for help in dismounting and for lodging. She was refused because a noble Florentine gentlewoman, young and widowed, who was going to Loreto with a large retinue of servants and maids, occupied the entire inn and had ordered that no one else be allowed to lodge there.

Upon hearing an answer so contrary to her expectation and need, Urania was assaulted by such a sudden and fierce pain that, unable to keep steady, she opened her arms and fell from her horse, as she cried in a high-pitched voice, "Alas! Wretched, unlucky me!"[50] Someone reported right away the news

---

50. This entire scene is a close imitation of an episode in Ariosto's *Orlando furioso* 32, already adumbrated by Bigolina in an earlier chapter, when Urania, like Bradamante, could not rest at night. In Ariosto, Bradamante leaves her home in the morning and rides all day in uninhabited places in the rain until she decides to take lodging for the night in the nearby Castle of Tristan. But she too is refused accommodation because of a tradition that requires that only one man per night can lodge in the castle with his retinue, unless the newcomer can fight the first male guest, or guests, already there. Bradamante accepts the courtly challenge and ends up jousting three kings to earn a place for the night for herself, which she eventually does. In both narratives the

of that accident to the beautiful Emilia, for this was the name of the young gentlewoman who had taken lodgings there. And she, who was very kind, having heard the pitiful case, went right away to where her servants, together with the host, moved by pity, were trying to revive Urania, but nothing they did helped.

As she arrived and saw such a handsome youth—whom she judged quite noble by his expensive clothes—led to those straits, the beautiful woman felt her heart moved by an unusual compassion and tenderness. Therefore, bidding her servants gently to remove him from the floor, she had him placed on the very bed prepared for her. Then, using her hands to rub his face with fresh water, in short order she made the youth come back to his senses. Her spirits having returned, and not fully aware of where she was because of her pain and distress, Urania began a loud wail accompanied by tears, cursing the luck that had kept her still alive in spite of herself and forced her to bear so much hardship.

Although the gentlewoman had seen him as if almost dead, nevertheless she liked his air so much that already she felt herself ignite with love for him. Wanting to comfort him as much as possible, she came closer to his bed, put her hand on his forehead, and said lovingly, "Handsome young man, I cannot imagine what sinister luck is pursuing you to make you scorn life and look for death. If I am not mistaken, from your gentle air and polite manners you seem of noble blood, wherefore I feel you must also be a noble soul. You should not allow yourself to be so tyrannized by the adverse blows of Fortune as to be led to such dire desperation. Whatever it is, since I have taken great pity on you and wish to proffer help and to be of comfort, I pray you please to reveal all your sad accidents as if I were your blood sister, and at the same time tell me who you are, where you come from, and for what reason you wander."

Seeing that beautiful young woman over her so sweetly comforting her, urging her to narrate her disgrace, and appearing more gentle and kind than any she had ever seen, Urania answered very humbly, after she had sighed even more deeply: "Most noble lady, if ever I had grounds to complain about my bad luck, I find that now, more than ever, I have reason to do so, because it has led me to the point where I cannot in any way repay with a worthy reward the great courtesy you show toward me. Never before having seen me, you have snatched me from death with such kindness and most gentle hands,

---

two women are cross-dressed as men and taken for such, but Urania's behavior is more feminine, or perhaps just more realistic, and therefore more in tune with the novella tradition. When she is told that she cannot take up lodging for the night, she faints.

and not yet satisfied with being good toward me, you offer still more help. Unable to do more, I will say at least this, that the little or much I am worth I wholly commit to your boundless courtesy and benevolence. Although I can reveal myself to you, my lady, the renown of my name is so little that to do so would make me no more known to you than if I said nothing. Nonetheless, since my intention is to obey, I will tell you. My lady, I am an unfortunate youth of very humble blood born in Salerno. My name is Fabio. Having experienced some bizarre luck as happens with men (the whole of which I pray you would not want to hear), I decided to run away from that angry fate and not stop until I found a virtuous gentleman or gentlewoman in whose service I could remain at least at peace, if not happy, for the rest of my life."

After Urania finished, the fair Emilia answered, shaking her head, "Alas, Fabio, you can hardly make me believe you are born of humble blood, as you say, because your noble manners and fine speech lead me to think that you are not just noble but very noble. God willing, I would not want these rare and desirable talents of yours to serve anyone, unless you wish otherwise, because they were given to you from the heavens not to serve others but to make you served and loved by others.

"I am a gentlewoman from Florence descended from noble ancestors. Just a year ago I became the widow of a knight, who left me heir to all his considerable wealth. Now I travel to Our Lady of Loreto to satisfy a vow I made during a severe illness I came down with a few months ago.[51] If you wish to join me, once I have satisfied my vow we shall return to Florence and you will be well served and honored by all. I shall regard you as my blood brother and would not want you to have less freedom than I have to dispose of my wealth at your will as freely as I do. I am induced to make such a generous offer by the gentle air and lovely and rare manners with which I see you adorned and which make me understand that you are just what my heart desires."

Urania gave infinite thanks to the kind gentlewoman, feeling that chance had prepared her for better luck than she herself could have imagined, since she could preserve herself from any shame with this woman and live comfortably until her amorous madness had departed her heart. She was

---

51. Loreto was a popular destination for pilgrimages in the middle of the sixteenth century, so much so that the Jesuits, who had a college there, began in 1554 to be responsible for the confessions of pilgrims as well. The number of pilgrims was immense by all accounts: 60,000, it has been said, confessed each year. According to Sergio Lavarda, Loreto was in third place as the most popular sanctuary for Paduans, after Assisi and San Lorenzo. See *L'anima a Dio e il corpo alla terra: Scelte testamentarie nella terraferma veneta, 1575–1631* (Venice: Istituto Veneto di Lettere, Scienze e Arti, 1998), 288. Such a narrative development in *Urania* is also heavily indebted to literature, specifically to Boccaccio's description of the pilgrimage of Lelio and Giulia Topazia to San Jacopo of Compostela at the beginning of *Filocolo*.

by now tired of so much wandering and was willing to rest. Therefore, after a thousand thanks rendered in pleasant ways, she accepted her kind proposal, offering herself to be a loving brother and faithful servant to the extent that her strength allowed.

A while later, after she got out of bed, they dined happily together. Early the next morning the beautiful Emilia became happier than ever on her journey because she had continually beside her such a fair youth. Meanwhile Urania, now having no other care than to make herself agreeable to the gentlewoman, kept the amorous torment buried deep in her heart and always rode next to her with the most cheerful face she could muster, striving to keep her pleased and entertained with sweet words and learned rhymes. By telling her sometimes about victories in love, she was able to keep her happy and content, so much so that Emilia's heart started to be doubly kindled with love toward her.

Traveling in such a pleasurable way, in due course they completed their trip and arrived in Florence, where in loving peace Emilia enjoyed her dear beloved's delightful company. Not many days went by before some of her relatives came to her house and asked her, in the name of a noble count, quite young and brave, to be his wife. Already for months he had been burning for her and had waited with the greatest yearning for the year of mourning for her dead husband to pass in order to ask her relatives for her hand. It never occurred to him that he would not obtain it, chiefly because he was noble and very rich. But as soon as the year had passed the lady began the journey to satisfy her vow and therefore he had to wait for her return. Having become aware of it, he went to her relatives. As I said, they came to her house with the request in the name of the count and beseeched her warmly to seize the opportunity for such a good match.

But she had her whole heart set on her dear Fabio, and since she was sufficiently rich, she felt no need to stop gratifying herself now and be pushed like a miser into gaining greater wealth by taking a husband she did not like. On the contrary, she desired (and almost felt it was her duty) to please herself more than anyone else in the world. Thus, putting on a good face, she made it quite clear to her relatives that she was not considering marriage at the moment. Thanking them very much for their kindness, she added that the match with that noble count was very agreeable to her and that whenever she had a mind to take a husband she would not exchange him for any other man in the world.

Her relatives tried hard to change her mind, but they did not succeed, for she remained firm in her original intention. Seeing that they could not satisfy the count's request as was their desire, they left unhappy. But she was doubly cheerful in realizing that she was now free of that obstacle to her greater happiness and could increase her pleasure tenfold. She felt that she had been the cause of all the pain she was suffering, for although she could find a remedy, she had been late in doing so. Now she no longer had to repress the flame of love burning in her heart for Fabio. She assured herself that she was loved back with the same kind of love she had for him, since she knew very well that he was perceptive and would have noticed how much and what kind of passionate love she had for him. She thought that he would not have hesitated to uncover his love for her, were it not for the great modesty she knew existed in him, as if he feared offending her with his words.

And therefore, both to remove this fear and doubt from her heart and because she believed she was providing a cure to her love pangs, that same day she drew him into her room. Having made him sit next to her, she said, "My dearest Fabio, since I know you to be very perceptive, I will not tire myself in convincing you of the boundless love I feel for you, for I am more than certain that you have already realized it, but now I have decided to confess my firm intention of loving you and keeping you dear as long as I live. You should know, my Fabio, that those relatives who came here today did not come for any other reason than to marry me to a noble and rich count, who already for a number of months has been deeply in love with me. But having given my heart to you, in whom all my desires and thoughts rest, I have dismissed them, though not without difficulty, intending firmly, at least for the moment, not to marry again.

"Now, my sweetest Fabio, it is up to you to accept a gracious offer presented by the woman who loves you more than herself. I know that you have such a noble heart that you could command gifts greater than this one, for you are worth all the good in the world. But I ask that you be kind enough to accept me as a wife, or rather as a servant, with whatever I possess in dowry, since my only desire is to serve you faithfully every day of my life. Take then this pain away from me, Fabio, I pray, and answer what your heart dictates you to do."

It would be difficult to say how much this offer that would have seemed extremely pleasant to any man was sour and bitter to Urania, for in seeing herself bound by these terms, she felt her heart gripped by an enormous anxiety. She seriously suspected that if she revealed herself to be a woman, Emilia would feel shame for the many amorous words and acts she made toward her and would begin to hate her, believing that she had been mocked. Even so, since Urania was uncommonly wise, without thinking too much she decided on the spot how to answer Emilia, and so she said, "Lady Emilia and my most honored mistress, I do not know whether I have to acknowledge this thing now revealed to me as the most memorable among the many and fierce assaults that my strange fortune has made in my days, although among the others there has been one so extreme as to send me away from my own country and house and make me go wandering in the world. Perhaps I would still be wandering if your mercy, together with your kind and loving nature, had not led me to a better life.

"I do not know whether the pain I feel now at not being allowed to accept your most gracious and liberal offer can be compared with the desperate reason that took me away from home. On the contrary, on reflection this really defeats and surpasses the other, since for that I alone was offended and felt the pain of my wound, but for this I feel the pain and grief for myself and for you, which weighs on me much more heavily.

"To reveal all my circumstances, my lady, and tell you what I did not want to reveal to you earlier, the judgment you first formed about me being noble is correct; you did not deceive yourself at all, since I come from a very noble family in Salerno. But I believe nature created no man in the world more unlucky than me, for I fell in love, as is typical of young men, with a most beautiful young lady. And as far as my judgment goes—and I know I do not deceive myself—she is most gentle and well mannered and possesses all sorts of beauties of the soul more than any other desirable woman. My good luck was such that for a while I was loved in return so much by this woman, whose name is Urania, that it seemed she was feeding and nourishing herself only with my presence and favor. This gave me so much pleasure that I felt myself the happiest lover in the world, and I would not have changed places with anyone else, however blessed.

"Not shy in bestowing any honest favor she could on me, this woman went as far to please me as to promise to be my wife. Alas, after some days, without my knowing the reason, she started to show herself averse to me, contrary to her usual behavior, and came later to the point of not allowing me to see her at all. I became so sad because of this strange predicament that I almost went mad and died of this wound. But seeing, to my greatest pain, that she did not change her unfavorable opinion of me, no matter what I did, I chose to leave my country as the lesser evil and in order to please her. I hoped that the extent of the hardship I was going to suffer would remove from my heart this passion of love.

"But I swear, my lady, this thought did not help me; on the contrary, the further I moved away from my beloved, the more I burned with a brighter flame and longed with a stronger desire to see her again. It is true that since your mercy, for which I shall be eternally obliged, brought me here, my pain has considerably diminished. My continuous mirroring in your rare and gentle ways and my continuous enjoyment of your great goodness and courtesy have been the reason why I have sought to become more yours than mine, even though little has remained free in me since that ungrateful one acquired most of me, no matter how scantily she appreciates such a purchase. Now therefore, my lady, you know how little free I am to accept your most courteous offer, but I give you all the thanks I can for your incredible kindness."

Oh, how sad! Oh, how horrible this unexpected answer seemed to the beautiful Emilia! With tears in her eyes she answered, "Alas, my sweetest Fabio, I knew very well that your merits were such that not I but a woman superior to me would be worthy of possessing you! Nevertheless, considering your goodness, I trusted in that, assuring myself that you would have respect not for my lowliness but for the magnitude of my sincere love. Such worth in your kind soul would have had the strength to make me equal to any woman of higher status. I am not so stupid, my Fabio, as to be unaware that what has caused you to refuse me—and this is my greatest pain—is your knowledge of my being unworthy of you and not another love occupying your heart. I cannot believe (I know you to be of such a noble soul) that you would ever throw yourself so basely after a woman who spurns your love, no matter how noble or beautiful. Be that as it may, I want only what pleases you, but I assure you that from now on no one will ever see me consoled or happy."

And here, shedding a sea of tears, she stopped. Urania saw herself led to straits so narrow that although she needed more than any other woman a similar consolation, she now beheld this other languish in front of her and did not know what choice to make. She felt that it was of little or no use to comfort her, nor was she in a position to give her help. Therefore, all perturbed in her soul and measuring the pain of the other with her own, crying and having no less pity for herself than for Emilia, she answered, "My lady, God knows how much pain I feel for not being able to satisfy our common wishes, but I suffer even more for the low esteem you have for me since, not having tied myself yet in marriage to another woman, you think I refuse you for a wife because I am such a proud and superior soul—you who would deserve not just me but any high-ranked prince. Besides, my obligation to you—for you have given me life—is such that not only would it please me to accept you as a very dear wife, as you have offered yourself to me, but it would make me a perpetual servant of your servants.

"I beseech and pray you now, lady Emilia, that if ever you gave your faith to a loyal man for a time, then you should give it to me, since I am the most loyal, and you should believe that I cannot unite myself in marriage to any woman. If I could, more than willingly I would do what you have asked me and I would not leave you in order to take any woman of higher station in the world. But if you would give me license to return to Salerno, were I to find her perhaps married and feeling that I were thus absolved and free, then you would see that you could do with me what pleases you most and I would consent gladly with double satisfaction on my part."

Being very wise, Emilia judged these last words to be said with no other intention than for Fabio to go away from her and never be seen again. She was certain that she was loved little, but Love does not lose its nature when it catches someone in his trap, even if the sad prisoner knows full well that he is liked little by the person he loves. Nor does this evil Love consent to his being freed, but on the contrary, because of love's natural force, the more the unhappy man sees his mistake and knows it, the more he plunges into it without regret. The tender Emilia acted likewise, for although well aware of how little she was desired or loved by Fabio with the love she wanted, still, burning with a stronger desire to make him hers in any way, she said,

"I could not fail, my Fabio, to believe all you have said, since I would not presume, given your rare virtues, that you would take pleasure in deceiving a simple woman like me. I believe you completely, and I very much approve the choice you have made to return to Salerno to see if perhaps your Urania is married. But as has always been the case for true lovers, I fear that you would simply not return, even if you were to find her married, and would be content to remain there, allured by the charm of your country and your kin. Thus I have decided that you cannot go without me, both to avoid this danger and because I wish more than anything else to see the woman who alone possesses that worth that many other women would like to possess, since she alone in the world is deserving of your love. I shall come dressed as a man in order to take away any shame and suspicion that people might have, and I do not wish for any other company for us except that of one faithful servant."

Urania wearied herself in dissuading Emilia from this thought of going with her, telling her of all the shame and damage that her going could bring, but in the end it all led to nothing. On the contrary, becoming more set in her purpose, she said that even if there were a thousand deaths to escape she still wanted to go with him and that by now he should no longer debate a matter in which all his efforts would be in vain.

Seeing that she could not do much else, Urania pretended to be pleased with whatever pleased Emilia, with the intention of unveiling herself as a woman once they arrived in Salerno. And so, very much consoled, Emilia had many rich and noble male clothes prepared in a few days for herself and Fabio. Then, affecting to go to the country for some months to entertain herself, she and her maids put her things in order, and early one morning she, Fabio, and a servant mounted on good horses and left for Salerno.

But let them go, because for the moment we have said enough about them, and let us return to the true Fabio in Salerno.[52] After he received Urania's letter from her servant, he tried to find peace as best he could, although it seemed strange to him to be deprived of someone he knew ardently loved him, and the pain was made worse by the fact that a woman of her status, worthy of being greatly desired and loved by everyone, had to go wandering so miserably because of him. Still he was aware that there was no remedy, having understood that she had already departed, and not knowing where she went.

Already earlier he had taken a fancy to a noble and beautiful maiden, and this new love was the reason for his behaving less affectionately toward Urania. It was to avoid this situation, and because she had no heart to suffer it, that Urania had chosen flight as the lesser evil. Now, since Urania had left, Fabio started to pursue with much more assiduousness and solicitude his affection for the beautiful young woman, whose name was Clorina.[53] Being very kind and clever—though not the equal of Urania by a long shot—and having become aware of Fabio's good ways and wise manners and finding them quite pleasing, she began also to burn with love for him. All the favors she honestly could give him she gave, since there was not in that period (as I said elsewhere) any shame in Salerno in young women being visited in their homes by all sorts of young men and conversing with them. Therefore, Fabio went to see her many times. Knowing from a number of signs that he was very much loved by her, he was so happy that in a few days he completely forgot the unhappy Urania, as if he had never seen her.

At this time, a young Sicilian gentleman came to reside at the court of Giufredi, prince of Salerno. He was handsome in build and brave and bold in person, but there were few other good aspects to his personality, and among the many bad ones he had was a wicked habit of bragging. Going here and there in the city, as was the custom of young men, by chance he noticed Clorina, and she pleased him much more than any woman he had seen there. To keep up his amorous practice, he decided to court her, although he was not

---

52. This technique of narrative *entrelacement*, with interruptions made at key moments to bring as seamlessly as possible the other narrative trends up to speed, was popularized by Ariosto, who used it masterfully to change subjects in his chivalric romance. See Daniel Javitch, *"Cantus interruptus* in the *Orlando furioso*," *Modern Language Notes* 95 (1980): 66–80.

53. Clorina, a variation perhaps of Clarina, Clori, or Cloride, was a popular female name at the time, especially in the pastoral genre. In mythological accounts, Zephyr ravished the veiled Clori as she was picking a flower and transformed her into Flora. In Botticelli's "Birth of Venus," Clori is represented as floating toward Venus thanks to the fecundative wind of Zephyr. Maddalena Campiglia's (1553–95) pastoral play *Clori* (1588) surprisingly has not only a character named Clori, but also one named Urania.

the sort of man to be caught in Love's net. And so seeing her sometimes in one place and sometimes in another, and always treating her with great honor, he did not rest until he had the occasion within a few days to visit her and converse agreeably with her, the way Fabio and some other men used to do.

Being not as bright as Urania and like many women, indeed the majority of them, considering a man's looks more than the reason why he is a man, Clorina felt that Menandro (such was the Sicilian's name) was a very handsome youth and physically well-endowed. Even more, he seemed to be a good talker and adapted every situation to his advantage (although more through deceitfulness than truth); but she liked those false ways so much that she turned her heart toward him only, without protecting herself. No longer did she appear to see anything engaging or good in Fabio, although she still made a great show of keeping him in high esteem.

But Fabio was very perceptive and realized quite soon that her love for him had cooled and that she loved Menandro more. Nevertheless, since, as I said elsewhere, Love does not allow unhappy lovers to untie themselves at their will when they make a mistake and know they are not loved, the wretched Fabio endured this great misfortune in silence for the sake of not annoying the woman who did not fear to annoy him. He had so much respect for her that in order not to aggravate her he feigned not to see what he could see only too clearly. And because she did not forbid him to go to her home any time he liked, he followed his earlier ways and often visited her as he had in the past, hoping that one day she would realize her mistake and would know that he was more worthy of being loved than Menandro. Thus, the enamored Fabio spent his life between doubt and fear, and very much dissatisfied.

THE DUCHESS

I have to leave these people for a while if I want to narrate fully the successful outcome of their loves, and speak about a very noble lady, in fact the Duchess of Calabria at the time. According to all those who had seen her, a woman more beautiful could not be found in the world. This striking lady was no more than twenty years old. A bit over a year earlier she had become a widow (with no child) and ruler of the state. She had little thought of remarrying, although she was continuously solicited by many noblemen and prominent princes and often beseeched by her people to do so. But having lived for two years through moments of enormous anxiety and bitter suffering with an old and very jealous husband, she had decided never again to marry, greatly fearing that she would stumble a second time, but always to live honorably in perpetual widowhood.

This woman (who was very Catholic and adorned with every good habit, but who was above all a recognized enemy of all sorts of vain love) had chosen as advisers four wise old men to whom she had turned over the government of the state and given all authority to rule. She did this so that she might spend her life quietly and far away from trouble. Among the four men, one was older and of more mature opinions than the others, and she honored and loved him as if he were her father and confided her major secrets to him more than to any other.

This fair lady had a particular passion, which was to have in her house the portraits of all the noble princes and princesses in the world. To do this, she kept on salary at her court the most famous painter of those times. Finding himself sometimes in one and sometimes in another court of princes, he would not depart without painting portraits of the ladies and gentlemen there. And upon returning home, after he had brought them to perfection through his artistry, he would give them to the duchess, his lady. With an almost miraculous contrivance she would have them framed in ivory, ebony, or some other material. Then after she had them exquisitely adorned with gold, pearls, and precious jewels according to their rank, she would have them put away in good order in a sumptuous room dearer to her than any other, which very few people (and those rarely) were given permission to enter. But she had the habit of going there at least once a day, and, by admiring now this and now that portrait, she entertained herself for a long time to her utter satisfaction.[54]

Now it happened that Love wanted to win and chastise this kind lady, who had lived until then very happily. And so by chance, whimsical Love, who rarely consented to humans presuming to fend off his power with their strength without making them know to their damage that all their strength is worth nothing against his power, which is infinite, decided to make her an example to others.

It happened, I say, that the painter, having traveled to many parts inside and outside Italy to gather portraits of various ladies and gentlemen to please his lady, came, fatefully rather than on purpose, to Salerno. Entering the city, as the horrible bad luck of his lady would have it, he met the most handsome, courteous, and kind prince in the entire world, that is, Giufredi, the most honorable prince of Salerno. The painter liked him so much that he felt he

---

54. Galleries of portraits, mostly male, were not rare in aristocratic households. But books of portraits of women were not rare either. For an example specific to the years Bigolina was writing, see Enea Vico, *Le imagini delle donne auguste intagliate in istampa di rame, con le vite, et isposizioni [. . .] sopra i riversi delle loro medaglie antiche* (Venice: V. Parmigiano and Vincenzo Valgrisio, 1557).

had never seen anyone in the world more charming, apart from the duchess, his lady. Therefore, remaining in Salerno for many more days, he painted him with extreme care, though without letting him realize it. Once he completed this portrait he decided to return to the duchess without going any further, even though he was committed by his lady to travel elsewhere to paint the portrait of another great prince.

Returning home cheerful and content, he appeared before the duchess and said to her, "My lady, what I have brought back with me this time is of greater value than anything with which I have returned on previous trips. Here is the portrait, my lady, a natural rendering of Giufredi, prince of Salerno, the most handsome, courteous, gracious, and kind gentleman I have ever painted. I do believe that neither nature nor heaven has ever produced anyone more handsome or distinguished. Henceforth you can relish having in your possession the portrait of one of the most handsome men in the world. And if I have succeeded in portraying on this canvas his grace, elegant ways, and courteous manners as I saw them with my own eyes, I swear, madam, that when you see them you yourself will remain astonished and surprised."

And then he praised so many particular features of that kind lord—those he had heard about and those he had seen—that the wretched lady, who had no thought of love, listening to the painter's very appreciative words with greater attention than perhaps would have been suitable, felt her heart punctured by something unfamiliar that she had never felt before. As she gazed at the portrait, it seemed to her that a sea of fire and a mountain of ice were pouring all over her at the same time, since Love, who until then had been late in manifesting his great power over her, had hidden himself in the handsome eyes of that portrait, not wanting to defer it any longer. Although they were lifeless, when Love looked through them the eyes achieved the same effect in her, in fact a greater one, than the prince's own live and animate eyes would have. Seeing them, she felt that her heart had been pierced by two thunderbolts, or rather by two sharp arrows.[55] Feeling extremely upset, contrary to her custom, this tender lady asked that the portrait of the handsome lord, the cause of her ruin, be placed in her room's most beautiful corner. She returned to look at it with greater attention and sensibility after the painter left, himself aware of the great change in her. The more she looked, the more handsome, gracious, and loving he appeared to her; hence she burned so inordinately that she felt like fainting out of love and desire.

---

55. The *topos* of love coming through the eye and the entire imagery of love with thunderbolts and arrows is heavily indebted to Petrarch and obsessively present in all Petrarchist Renaissance production, male and female.

Not many days passed before the lady, loving too much, almost came close to death, seeing continually before her eyes the reason for her pain and unable to hope for any relief. Many times she remembered the adventurous Pygmalion and offered countless prayers to the goddess of love as well as countless tears to obtain a gift similar to the one he had asked for.[56] But realizing that her prayers were in vain and finding it also undesirable to die, she decided to look for a remedy to save her life without ruining her honor, which she considered to be of greater worth than any treasure. Aware that by herself and with no good advice it would have been impossible to advance such an important business, she decided to have a meeting about it with her wisest, oldest, and most loved counselor and indeed to place the whole charge of this affair on his shoulders. Once she made such a determination, she summoned that good old man to her room. Bidding him to sit next to her, she said,

"Most honored father, I am well aware that you have been not a little amazed at the great change you have seen in me in the last few days. Since, as they say, we should not keep pain hidden from those who know and can or wish to give us some advice or remedy, so now realizing that the pain I suffer is bitter and treacherous and that I need good advice and a cure, I have chosen you, my father, to succor me with guidance, assistance, and much needed support. I have selected you alone because, being older and with more experience and knowledge, you can counsel me better than any other, and being more than anyone else a man of authority and power in my court, you can free yourself to find a solution to my problem without being observed or reproached. Lastly, being more loving and faithful than anyone else (as in truth I have always known you to be), you may be more inclined to assist me faithfully and lovingly with all your power and knowledge."

Having said this, she revealed with warm tears and passionate sighs the amorous torment she suffered for the love of Giufredi, prince of Salerno. Relating how his most fair portrait had been the cause, she added,

"My sweet father, you must believe that I had to force myself to make

---

56. According to Ovid, the sculptor Pygmalion did not like the lasciviousness of the female sex and chose to live as a celibate. In sculpting an ivory statue of a woman so beautiful that only modesty seemed to prevent her from coming alive, he narcissistically fell in love with the inanimate object and often touched it, not believing that it was just a statue. He then prayed the goddess Venus to have her come alive, and his wish was granted: "She was alive! The pulse beat in her veins!" See *Metamorphoses* 10.291. Bigolina may also have had in mind Petrarch's rendering of Pygmalion, in Sonnet 78: "Pygmalion, how glad you should be of your statue, since you received a thousand times what I yearn to have just once!" See *Lyric Poems* 78.178–79.

these thoughts of love manifest to you, since from the behavior you have observed in me until now I have no doubt that you know that I have never experienced amorous desire. Finding myself new to such passions, you can understand that I feel and bear them with much greater anguish than would another woman accustomed to them, and I make them known to you with a greater shame. Nevertheless, since I love you as a father and know myself to be similarly loved, rather than die (and I shall surely die, if you do not help me) I have brought myself to you to reveal my pain.

"What I desire is that you use your talent in a gracious effort to induce that prince of his own will and without his becoming aware that I desire him in any way, to ask me to be his wife. I would rather be asked by him and show myself reluctant and then make it appear that I consent because of your urging, since for no reason in the world do I want him to realize that I love him, and least of all to think that I seek him. Now then, my most honored father, you have heard all my need and desire and can understand how my life and death are in your hands. I am sure that if you want, you know how to do it and so can help me. Likewise, I can assure you that you will be forced to mourn my death if you do not help me right away."

The news seemed too enormous for the good old man to hear, chiefly because he had known her quiet and very modest nature up to that point. Thus for a good while he reflected without giving her an answer, while the beautiful lady continually cried bitter tears. Becoming aware of how important such an event was to her and knowing that admonitions and reproaches would have had no effect, feeling also respect toward her as his lady and bearing love for her as to a daughter, the old man then decided to help her with all his power. Breaking the long silence, he answered her, "My lady or my daughter, when I consider your age and beauty and especially when I look at your immense kindness, I am not amazed that Love has taken possession of your heart, because kindness is not just inclined toward but a very appropriate subject of love, just as youth and beauty are tilted by their very nature toward love. I, moreover, do not believe one can find any perfection in a heart in which love does not have a place; and I am amazed only that you have been late in falling in love, since you are truly a most beautiful, virtuous, and gentle woman. But when I fully consider the other side of the matter, I feel no surprise, for since it is true that one likes to move close to another similar in natural yearnings, you could not have fallen in love earlier because until now no one had appeared who was similar to you in beauty and virtue. Now that a comparable object has appeared, you could not escape burning for him. I am neither amazed nor do I reproach you, my lady, because I see you in love. You will see me indeed more than ready and eager to undertake the work necessary to reach the goal you desire so much. It is true that the way you want me to proceed seems difficult; yet if you agree that the painter also be aware and act on what I intend to do, my heart tells me that the matter will proceed the way you yourself desire."

It is impossible to relate the happiness and the joy the lady felt in hearing her own wise counselor reassure her so lovingly while also promising help. After she thanked him repeatedly, she told him that it would be very suitable to her if the painter was made aware of her secret desire, since she had always known him to be very faithful.

Asking permission to leave, and always eager to please her, the old man went to see the painter. Once he had his pledge of faith, he briefly told him about the great love their lady had for the prince of Salerno and also about what he had decided to do to bring her desire to a happy end. He wanted the clever painter to paint, with the greatest diligence he could muster, a masterful canvas of the judgment of Paris, that is, of the three goddesses and Paris with the golden apple, the cause of so much ruin. After much reflection he decided that the duchess of Borbone should take Juno's place and have the scepter in her hand and the crown on her head as queen of heaven. She was a very beautiful woman but also so full of charm that she could inspire a great desire to revere her, indeed to adore her, in whoever saw her. And he wanted the daughter of the king of Poland to be painted fully armed and with the lance in her hand, like Pallas. In those days she had a beautiful body and face but was impervious to all vain loves because she had consecrated her virginity to God and seemed to care for nothing but to be very learned.

Since he had heard many times from the departed duke, her husband, that there was nothing more beautiful in the world than the naked body of the duchess, his wife, he accordingly wanted the lady to be painted in the place of Venus with her graceful limbs partly exposed. A mantle, that is, a cover of red silk over the naked flesh, would wrap her left shoulder and coming down the right armpit would leave exposed the entire right shoulder and her bosom. To the left, her comely flank, part of the womb, the left thigh, both legs, and her most tiny feet would be shown naked. Such was the beauty and the whiteness coming out of those exquisite and well-formed parts that, as the painter worked, he was more than once mesmerized by them and came dangerously close to showing his excitement; nor could the white-haired old man, who was perhaps seventy years old, gaze upon the painting without feeling his soul and heart pierced many times. Nevertheless, using reason as a shield, both went ahead the best they could. The good old man also wanted the prince Giufredi painted in place of Paris, dressed as a shepherd, next to

the beautiful Venus.[57] The excellent painter portrayed him with such skill—
his eyes on the strikingly beautiful Venus's face offering her the apple—that
whoever looked at both of them was bound to feel touched by love.

After the painting was finished to perfection with the utmost diligence,
the painter boarded a ship leaving for Rome in order to arrive quickly, having
been given precise instructions by the old counselor regarding the method to
use in such a business, and in a few days he arrived in Salerno. Having disem-
barked and introduced himself with proper deportment to the prince, he paid
him the respect due him and then said, "Most noble lord, the renown of your
good looks led me here from the Spanish court not many months ago to draw
your likeness and then paint it. Thanks be to heaven, I achieved my purpose,
although your excellence was not aware of it in any way. Now the good repute
of your immense virtue and kindness brings me back. I always strove in my art,
my lord, if not to surpass at least to equal the most outstanding painters of my
time, and more than anything else I have enjoyed keeping with me the portraits of the most excellent and noble princes and of the most beautiful and
honorable ladies in the world. A year has just passed since, by lucky chance, I
was requested by an Italian nobleman to paint a portrait of his incomparably
beautiful wife, whom he wanted me to portray (overriding her objection)
from top to bottom with a cover of red silk voile over her naked flesh, partly
covering and partly leaving uncovered her fair limbs, a sight that generated
amazement in whoever beheld them. I swear, my lord, that in all my days I
never saw limbs more fine looking or better fit than those, nor do I believe that
Apelles and Zeuxis saw any similar to those, all part of the same body. Had

57. The detailed description of Bigolina's duchess, including the movement of the mantle over
her naked body, seems to be modeled on Titian's portrait of Heavenly Love represented as a
naked Venus with the flame of God's love in her left hand. This painting, "Sacred and Profane
Love," Titian's acknowledged masterpiece, was composed for the marriage of Nicolò Aurelius to
the Paduan noblewoman Laura Bagarotto in 1514 and therefore Bigolina may have seen it or
been aware of it. On this portrait and Bagarotto, see Rona Goffen, *Titian's Women* (New Haven:
Yale University Press, 1997) and Augusto Gentile, *Da Tiziano a Tiziano: Mito e allegoria nella cultura
veneziana del Cinquecento* (Milan: Feltrinelli, 1980). I thank Naomi Yavneh for this reference. Bigolina's composition of the three goddesses—Venus, Juno, and Pallas—also recalls another
mythological painting of Titian, "Venus Blindfolding Cupid" in the same gallery, which belongs
to the 1550s (but appears to have been completed ca. 1565). The "rustic" composition of Giufredi painted as a shepherd with Venus was also used in a number of Titian's "Venus and Adonis"
representations. Since Titian and Bigolina were friends, as is evident in two letters from Pietro
Aretino to her still extant, it is possible to speculate that she had acquired some familiarity with
his studio in Venice. For contemporary treatises on female beauty and on what feminine portraits should display (usually they were not mimetic in nature but the result of additions of the
most comely body parts of different women), see Agnolo Firenzuola, *On the Beauty of Women*
(1548); Gian Giorgio Trissino, *I ritratti del Trissino* (1524); and Federigo Luigini, *Il libro della bella
donna* (1554).

they seen any comparable, it would not have been necessary for Zeuxis to form a perfect body by collecting parts from so many beauties, for the woman of whom I speak has all of them in herself.

"After I portrayed her, that kind lord wanted to give me a suitable reward, but I did not want to accept anything; on the contrary, I begged him to please give me permission to make a similar portrait for myself, saying that were he to grant such a request, I would deem it the greatest compensation I could ever receive from him. On no account did that gentleman want to bestow such a grace on me; nevertheless, having given my promise that I would never reveal who was portrayed, he was mollified and agreed that I make another painting for myself, but secretly, so that the beautiful and kind lady would not know about it, since she would never have consented.

"Seeing myself rich with such a precious treasure, a new thought was born in me of wanting to paint a canvas of Paris's judgment of the three goddesses, because having with me that beautiful image, I felt she would make a most divine Venus. So I started to implement this new thought and put the very valiant duchess of Borbone in place of the goddess Juno. Feeling that this duchess was worthy of infinite honor, I gave her a place worthy of her dignity. Then I put the chaste and virtuous daughter of the king of Poland in place of Pallas and placed this other woman of whom I have spoken, who is no less kind and virtuous than beautiful, in place of Venus with the same dress with which I had portrayed her. But wishing to find a man for Paris's place in order to pair convincingly and in proportion to that strikingly beautiful Venus, I found myself quite uneasy, for in rummaging through my portraits I could not find any that I felt could merit being placed close to such a striking Venus. For this reason, despairing of ever finding one worthy of her, I almost ended the project I had begun.

"But finding myself a few months ago in Spain in conversation on this issue with a very dear friend, I was asked if I had ever seen Your Excellency. I answered no, and he replied, 'If you have never seen him, mourn your negligence, because you have not looked in the right place for what you want.' Then he dwelt so much on Your Excellency's courtesy, kindness, and good looks, putting such a desire in my heart to see the truth, that I set out the following day for your kingdom. Once I arrived, I realized that the reality very much surpassed the praise. The heavens were kind enough to give me the opportunity to portray you comfortably without making Your Excellency aware that I was doing so, and I perfected the portrait by using you, my lord, to compose my Paris. Considering your handsomeness and nobility, I felt that the portrait could not be better placed than if I were to make a present of it to Your Excellency. Thus, my lord, I brought it. Please accept

it as a small gift from your humble servant, who hands it to you with a faithful heart."

After he had finished speaking, the painter made a gesture to two servants close by to place the exquisite picture before him. In the meantime, the
kind prince thanked the painter very graciously for the many praises he had
given him and for the good will he had shown toward him. When the stately
painting was brought in, the painter said to him as he took off a silk cloth that
covered it, "My lord, here is the magnificent and noble painting, not noble
and magnificent because of my work, although I put all my craft into it, but
because of the great nobility one can see in its subjects. First admire, my lord,
I pray, the great majesty one can see in the face of this venerable Juno and of
this most wise Pallas. Whoever sees them is taken by surprise. Truly, though,
whoever considers the superhuman beauties of this Venus remains van-
quished, blinded, and confused.

"Please, look closely here, my lord, how the gold and curly hair seems
like a net to entrap a thousand hardened hearts. See the spacious and highly
polished forehead, the eyes, which resemble two stars, although one cannot
fully discern their natural liveliness, the lashes curly and black as ebony, the
well-proportioned nose, the rosy cheeks, the small mouth, the lips that surpass the corals in beauty; nor do I regret anything but having not been able
to paint so well those oriental pearls they enclose the way I saw them on her
and also the very proportionate chin, which is neither slight nor redundant
in any part. It seems that each says, 'Love has his kingdom here and not elsewhere.'[58]

"But what shall we say of this throat and chest that surpass the snow in
whiteness? And of that little protruding apple, which no one, admiring it
fully, can see without feeling his heart melt out of desire? My God, how
round and well-formed is this arm! I say nothing of the hand since it re-
sembles too well the one that often controls and holds the bow, the quiver
and the arrows of the boy Cupid.[59] I do not believe that envy could find any

---

58. Bigolina here seals her debt to Petrarch with a most close imitation of a line in his famous
Canzone 126: "Qui regna Amore" ("Here reigns Love"). See *Lyric Poems*, 247.

59. Bigolina is thoroughly indebted to Ariosto for this description of the fragmented female
body. Here I cite from the description of Alcina, which is also rendered in pictorial terms: "She
was so beautifully modelled, no painter, however much he applied himself, could have achieved
anything more perfect. Her long blond tresses were gathered in a knot: pure gold itself could
have no finer lustre . . . . Her serene brow was like polished ivory, and in perfect proportion. Beneath two of the thinnest black arches, two dark eyes—or rather, two bright suns; soft was their
look, gentle their movement. Love seemed to flit, frolicsome, about them . . . Down the midst
of the face, the nose—Envy herself could find no way of bettering it. Below this, the mouth set
between two dimples; it was imbued with native cinnabar . . . . Snow-white was her neck, milky

defect in the striking abdomen and the outlined flank, but please pay greater attention above all, my lord, to the extraordinary thigh.[60] Phidias or Polykleitos surely never sculpted another more beautiful. Finally, whoever sees and judges from head to toe, will say that the great Master Nature never created, nor could ever create, another body more perfect in beauty than this."[61]

While the painter was trying, through praise, to raise the excellence of these beautiful limbs in the eyes of the prince, the prince was staring fixedly at the portrait and sighing a thousand feverish sighs from his heart. The painter having become aware of it, believing that surely the prince had fallen in love with those singular beauties and feeling immense happiness on this account, worked hard to praise her all the more strongly. But to tell the truth something different was happening. For the past two years the good prince

---

her breast; the neck was round, the breast broad and full, . . . A pair of apples, not yet ripe, fashioned in ivory, rose and fell like the sea-swell at times when a gentle breeze stirs the ocean. . . . Her arms were justly proportioned, and her lily-white hands were often to be glimpsed: they were slender and tapering, and quite without a knot or swelling vein. A pair of small, neat, rounded feet completes the picture of this august person" (*Furioso* 7.11–15). Ariosto provides similar descriptions for Angelica and Olimpia. On the correspondence in the portrayal of female anatomical parts between literature and art during the first part of the sixteenth century, see Giorgio Padoan, "*Ut pictura poesis:* Le 'pitture' di Ariosto, le 'poetiche' di Tiziano," in *Momenti del Rinascimento Veneto,* ed. Giorgio Padoan (Padua: Antenore, 1978), 347–70; and Pozzi, "Il ritratto della donna nella poesia d'inizio Cinquecento e la pittura di Giorgione," *Lettere italiane* 21 (1979): 3–30. On the fragmentary nature of the Petrarchan portrait, see Nancy Vickers, "Diana Described: Scattered Woman and Scattered Rhyme," in *Writing and Sexual Difference,* ed. Elizabeth Adel (Chicago: University of Chicago Press, 1982); on the lack of individuality of the "bellissima donna," see Naomi Yavneh, "The Ambiguity of Beauty in Tasso and Petrarch," in *Sexuality and Gender in Early Modern Europe,* ed. James Grantham Turner (Cambridge; Cambridge University Press, 1993), 133–57.

60. In examining representations of female beauty in literature, Giovanni Pozzi identifies a short canon, which usually includes face, hands, and breast, and a long canon, as in this case, which depicts the entire body, feet included, and emphasizes proportions. See Pozzi, "Temi, topoi, stereotipi," in *Letteratura italiana I: Le forme del testo,* ed. Alberto Asor Rosa (Turin: Einaudi, 1984), 391–436; and Quondam, *Il naso di Laura: Lingua e poesia lirica nella tradizione del classicismo* (Modena: Panini, 1991), 291–328.

61. Phidias and Polykleitos were Greek sculptors who worked in the same period. Phidias supervised the decorations of the Parthenon. He was known for three colossal statues of Athena: the Athena Parthenos, made in gold and ivory and thirty-eight feet tall; the Athena Promachos, the largest statue ever erected in Athens, which was placed on the Acropolis; and the Lemnian Athena, made in bronze and sent to Lemnos. His colossal statue of Zeus for the temple of Zeus in Olympia was considered one of the seven wonders of the world. Polykleitos worked in bronze. The sculpted body of his athletes poised in what is known as chiastic balance dictated the standards of proportion for all later sculptors. As the sentence shows, Bigolina takes the description of Polykeleitos from Dante: "conobbi quella ripa intorno / . . . // esser di marmo candido e addorno / d'intagli sì, che non pur Policleto, / ma la natura lì avrebbe scorno" ("I perceived that the encircling bank . . . was of pure white marble, and was adorned with such carvings that not only Polykeleitos but Nature herself would there be put to shame." See *Purgatorio,* 10.29–33.

had been burning with love for a beautiful maiden, the daughter of a count, his vassal, who was called by everyone "the wise damsel" to please him. When he saw the great beauty in the limbs of that lovely lady he began to think and in fact firmly to believe that those of the damsel he loved so much were at least as beautiful and perhaps even more so. He thus burned with such a new and intense desire to see and enjoy them that not only did this cause those passionate sighs, but it was also the reason why, putting aside all reservations—and they were many—he determined that he would take her as his bride as soon as she returned from Naples, where some noble relatives had invited her to attend a wedding.

Oh, cursed be you forever, Love, since these are the good works you do! What help was it to that unhappy lady (you inhuman!) to show the beauty of her hidden and most noble limbs, if for your evil doing you turned what was meant to be helpful to her into usefulness for another to her damage and shame? Yet I am not amazed because, by depicting you as blind, you teach us—and it is your vengeance—that we are the blind ones, not you. But woe to those you like to ridicule and with whose pain you please yourself, the way you did with the unhappy lady I am talking about!

After the painter, having said more than enough, ended the many praises of his lady, and the prince, having looked at length, became satisfied, the prince, as most of us do, desired to know what was hidden from him, that is, the name of the beautiful lady portrayed in the painting. The painter, who had more desire to tell it than the prince had to hear it, revealed who and what she was after he let himself be implored for a while, and the prince pledged that it would never be repeated to anyone. He feigned that the duke, her husband, had had her painted in such a way fifteen days before his death, to her great displeasure. The prince was delighted to know who she was and held the beautiful painting infinitely dear. After he had it placed in his favorite room, he honored the painter handsomely and gave him a good welcome and some very honorable gifts, obliging him to remain with him for a few days. He did this because he wanted him to portray his damsel after the wedding, but he did not reveal anything about this plan to him.

No more than two days had gone by after the painter's arrival in Salerno when the duchess's old counselor also arrived, bringing along a beautiful rose garland, of a kind rarely seen in the world, made from the only plant of its kind in the duchess's garden, which had been brought to her from a country very far away. Such roses had a marvelous property, which was that beyond being most beautiful and with a strong pleasant smell, they also had the virtue of keeping their beauty and perfume perfectly for a whole year.

The old man having thus arrived in Salerno with the garland, presented himself to the prince. After making a suitable bow, he said to him, "Most excellent lord, I know that Your Excellency does not know me. For many years I have not been in these regions because, on becoming old, I remained at the court of Duke Federico, my lord, in Calabria. At his death, which took place just over a year ago, he heartily recommended to me his very beautiful, but even more virtuous bride, whose service I never left nor will I ever leave as long as I live. To tell Your Excellency briefly the reason that presently brings me before you, I say that, having to complete some business deals in Rome and having obtained permission from my lady to leave, I began a trip by land a few days ago, for I cannot suffer the sea much.

"My habit was to get up very early every day to make good progress before the sun with its rays makes the air and the land too hot. Now it happened two days ago that having risen out of bed, as I said, very early, and having started my journey ahead of all my servants in order better to recite my prayers without being disturbed, I had hardly ridden two miles along the bank of a stream when I found a beautiful young lady (from what I could tell) lying on the ground quite near death, wounded and wholly inundated by her own blood. Stopping at such a strange spectacle and feeling my heart moved by compassion, I dismounted my horse, and mercifully taking her in my arms, I asked what horrible destiny had led her to such a painful end. And she, who seemed now capable of lasting only a short time longer, answered me with great weariness, 'Most courteous gentleman, since I know for certain that my life will not last long enough for me to narrate the cruel reason leading a horrible knight to bring me to this most bitter end, it will be enough for you to know that I suffer this punishment unjustly. I beseech and pray you to the utmost, for all the kindness and piety in you, to please take me in your arms and throw me now into this stream. Do not have misgivings about throwing me in the river while I am still alive, because I will hardly be touched by those waters ere you will see a miraculous change in me.'

"Although it seemed to me that I had to perform a very inhuman act, nevertheless, seeing that she was firm in her wish and knowing how little more life she could lose, crying, I threw her in out of pity and to satisfy her. Oh, marvelous and almost incredible thing to hear, but I really saw it and will recount it! I swear, my lord, that I had hardly thrown her in that, as she went to the bottom, suddenly she came back up healthy, cheerful, and beautiful and with this very handsome box you see in my hand. She told me with a smiling face, 'Most courteous gentleman, I render you infinite thanks for the very large benefit I received from you, because I have reacquired my life through you. To express my gratitude with something more than simple words, for I have received a great gift and do not want to seem ungrateful, I want to give you a present. I think that you will perhaps judge it very small now, as not being a thing that suits you, but when you see the fruit that this present of mine will produce in a few days, you will hold it dearer than if I had granted you a large state. The gift I want to give you is a rose garland of marvelous beauty and great value. Its value is such that any man who bestows this garland upon any woman he loves and desires will awaken in her, as soon as she touches it, so much love for him who gave it that whatever he asks she will be unable to deny. Such love, never lacking, will always remain in her heart until the woman's death.'[62]

"'I know you will say, 'I am too old for such a present, and it would be unbecoming of me to find a woman ever to love me with such love.' But I give you this present particularly for this reason: knowing your courteous nature and how much more it pleases you to please others rather than yourself, you may give some help to the most handsome, kind, and courteous lord living today, namely, the very virtuous Giufredi, prince of Salerno. At your arrival (for I advise you to go straight to him), you will find him burning with so many amorous flames for the most worthy subject existing in the world that Mongibello hardly burns with a hotter blaze.[63] He does so with good reason, for the subject for whom he burns is worthy enough to convert a frozen heart into a burning one.'

"After she said these words, she pulled this handsome box over the bank of the stream, and then all of a sudden she plunged into the water. I never saw her again and remained so amazed that I am speechless even now. But later I realized, as she had said, that I should hold this present dearer than if she had granted me a large state, since I had been given the means, by way of this little gift, to make cheerful and happy such a rare lord as you, Your Excellency. Therefore, I suddenly turned my steps, which I had pointed in another direction, back toward Salerno, happier than ever. And so my lord, I make you a gift of this beautiful garland so that through it you may obtain whatever your heart desires from the woman you love most."

As he was saying this, having already taken the lovely garland from its

---

62. This scene is heavily indebted one more time to Ariosto, who in one of the most intriguing sex change narratives of Renaissance literature, had Ricciardetto recount how he saved a nymph from sure death and was told that he would be given a congruent reward for his help: she could transform him from woman to man so that he could satisfy the princess Fiordispina in bed, as was his desire. In both cases the nymph's role is to further amorous encounters through supernatural means: "It is not for nothing that you have saved me. You shall be richly rewarded and given as much as you ask for: I am a nymph and I live in this limpid lake. // I have the power to perform miracles, to coerce nature and the elements" (*Furioso* 25.61–62).

63. Mongibello is Mount Etna in Sicily. See a similar reference in Ariosto's *Orlando Furioso* 1.40.

beautiful box, the good old man put both reverently in the prince's hands. I cannot fully narrate the joy and happiness with which the prince accepted the present of the charming garland. Having understood very well what the shrewd old man had said, he judged that certainly the maiden who had given it to him was an enchantress who knew, he felt, that the merits of his wise damsel were infinite and that he loved her passionately. Therefore, she had conspired with the old man to deliver the garland in his hands. Feeling that heaven showed some care for his love, he sensed his burning heart on fire again with double flames and decided to take her by all means for his wife. He thus gave so many thanks and such a pleasant reception to the good old man that much less would have been sufficient to an emperor who had bestowed a kingdom on him. Then he added,

"My most honored father, before you depart, my heart tells me that I shall give you reason to say that the clever lady spoke wisely and truthfully, praising that very noble subject whom I love and to whom I intend to give the garland."

While he was saying this, the painter arrived and gave the old man a respectful welcome, feigning not to have seen him for many months and asking him how things were with the duchess, his lady. They then both passed the time in much honorable conversation about her, at which the prince remained present. But after he left to put some business in order and the two messengers of the duchess were alone, the painter told the old man all that had happened with the prince when he showed him the painting. He mentioned the fiery sighs the prince had emitted while looking at the duchess's limbs that he was praising, and for this reason he was almost certain that the prince would send the garland to no one else but her. The good old man felt supremely happy, and he did not believe any less than the painter that the matter would proceed as he had cleverly devised.

Having heard that his wise damsel would certainly return to Salerno within three days, the prince ordered—with more happiness than he ever felt—that his palace be decorated all over with the most ennobling hangings, and this order was executed right away. And to allow everyone to see and smell the perfume of those fragrant roses, he had the beautiful garland suspended from the ceiling of his large hall by a small gold chain.

THE LOVE TRIANGLE

As these things were happening—and already the news had spread through all Salerno of the loveliness and property of the garland together with the common opinion that the prince was only waiting for the return of his wise damsel to give it to her as a present—it also came about that the day after the garland arrived, Fabio and Menandro met, as chance allowed, while visiting at the same time their beloved Clorina, as they often used to do.

After they spoke to each other of this and that a good deal, they came to the subject of the garland, each of them stating that the prince would be giving it to his wise damsel as soon as she returned and that he would take her for a wife at the same time, since his having adorned the palace in such an exceptional way seemed to mean that there would be a wedding. Yet Clorina, who harbored a great envy and hatred of the wise damsel, thinking how lucky the damsel was to merit being so loved as to become a princess (although she was not in her view more noble or more beautiful than herself), became disdainful, and with a sigh coming from her heart toward those young men, she said, "O unhappy Salerno! I do not believe that whoever searched the whole of Italy could find another city so devoid of true lovers! I am amazed that you young men professing to be in love do not all hide for shame. How do you dare to look in the face the woman by whom each of you wishes to be loved, since having so close at hand a treasure such as that garland, which could make happy the man who gives it to his beloved, not one has been found among those who profess to be in love who has even tried to get it. If as many true as false lovers were to be found in this city, the whole of Salerno would be turned upside down (especially since the garland is in a convenient place to steal), for each man should make an effort to get it in order to give it to the woman he loves. But, alas, there is no lover brave and courteous in deeds rather than just in words. As for showing their love, they seem rather lame and stingy, and this applies to every one of them in my opinion. Today's youths do not want to suffer any inconvenience for the love of their beloved or to conquer them; on the contrary, they feel they do much and acquire infinite merit when they make a bow and pronounce words of good breeding upon seeing them, something that redounds to their honor and not to the women's.

"Today jousts, tournaments, or other kinds of valiant exploits are not held for the sake of displaying love, as was done in the past. Then, as we know, young men in love won their love through toil and by putting their lives in danger, but presently these victories are acquired in comfort and pleasure. To tell the truth, women themselves are the main culprits in this, because they are too loving and generous in granting men every favor. If I were beautiful or thought myself so, rather than regarding myself as the least attractive woman, I would not want a young man courting me in Salerno to miss such an occasion to show me, by trying to get the magnificent garland, that he loved me heartily, and if he did not I would not want him to dare appear again in my presence."

Both young men were struck dumb at these proud, indeed arrogant words, and for a good while they were lost in thought and said nothing. Being wise, Fabio took those words to heart more than the other because he fully understood that she had said them only for him, to dissuade him through them from visiting her again. Finding himself full of bitterness, without excusing himself otherwise and soon after taking leave from her, he went away.

But after he left and started to consider his great misfortune, how it had taken him away so abruptly from the heart of the woman he loved more than anyone else in the world and by whom he wished to be loved, he was overtaken by such anguish that, despairing of life and not considering that she had said those words as if she were his enemy, he firmly decided to try his luck and steal the lovely garland if he could and give it to her, the ungrateful one. He felt he would have acquired not a little, even if he were to die in the attempt, since he had no other desire except to make her fully aware that he loved her more passionately than Menandro and did not care otherwise whether he lived or died.

Having reached this decision, he borrowed some rags and a shabby hat from a scamp, paying him well. He then took off his noble and ornate clothes, covered his delicate limbs with those vile rags and hid his graceful head, the proper receptacle for the noblest intellect, under that tattered hat. He took a small lamp, lit a dim light in it, hid his sword among those rags, and went to the palace without saying anything to anyone. Walking here and there through it without being recognized, he saw some planks, a great number of which had been brought there in order to build a theater for the lavish wedding ceremony. He felt that those planks could be useful, and so when dusk came he hid behind them without being seen by anyone.[64]

Having seen Fabio leave Clorina so precipitously and so confused, and immediately imagining the reason, Menandro too took his leave from her. Feeling himself burning within with bitter anger for the great hatred he bore Fabio, he started to think of a way to follow him and disrupt his every plan. It thus came to his mind that he had established quite a familiarity with one of the prince's waiters, whose room, to crown it all, was facing the large hall. He found him right away and he was able to do and say so much—partly by giving him money and partly by promising more with kind words—that the

---

64. The preparation for a stage on which to recite comedies and perform dances ("moresche") was by this time a well-established custom for high-class weddings. Many Renaissance comedies in fact were performed on the occasion of the marriage of kings and noblemen, and many comedic plots centered on marriage because in a sense they reflected in the script the purpose for their own staging. Machiavelli's play, *The Mandrake*, for example, was first performed in Florence for the marriage of Lorenzo de' Medici in 1518.

waiter agreed to do what he wanted. Bringing him to the palace, he hid him
in his room until late into the night.

When it became very dark and everyone in the palace seemed to have
gone to bed, Fabio, who was hidden behind the planks, came out slowly.
Lighting the little lamp, he found some long ladders, which had been brought
there to arrange the tapestry, leaning against each other. He picked one up
with great difficulty because of its length and brought it to where the garland
was hanging. In danger of falling and breaking his neck, he climbed to the top,
detached the lovely garland, and put it on top of his vile hat to avoid spoiling
it. He was still ten long rungs from the bottom when Menandro, who, sword
in hand, had already entered the large hall with treasonous intentions toward
him, perceived that he was coming down the ladder. Knowing who he was
and thinking only to harm him, he shouted to Fabio, "Ah, traitor! I have caught
you, and you will not be given the grace to present the garland to Clorina as
was your intention; on the contrary, to spite you I will take away your unworthy life and acquire Clorina's love with the garland."

Hearing such arrogant words and realizing by his voice who the man
was, Fabio rapidly descended the few remaining steps. Taking his sword from
the ground where he had put it, he came toward Menandro at quite a disad-
vantage, because he had nothing else on to stave off the blows but those miserable rags, and Menandro, who was very well armed, would have taken his
life in a very short time. But as it pleased God, who did not want to have much
harm come to such a noble youth, Menandro's words had been heard and
recognized by some people in the palace who were still awake playing cards.
Taking up their arms right away, about six of them ran as fast as lightning toward the place where they had heard the voice and apprehended both before
they realized they had been seen. Both were at once taken before the prince,
who had awoken at the noise to find out the reason for it.

He soon recognized Menandro, but not Fabio, because of his rags and
tattered hat. He then asked Fabio who he was, but Fabio remained silent, not
wanting to give him any answer so as not to be recognized by the many
people there. But Menandro, who had his thought fixed on harming him, revealed that he was Fabio, and he recounted the whole business. He also said
that both were rivals for Clorina's love and added that having understood from
some signs of Fabio's intention to steal the garland and give it to Clorina, he
had hid in the palace to take it away from him by force and then return it to
His Excellency so that His Excellency would not receive such an insult.

But those who had caught them and had heard what Menandro had said,
told the prince all they had heard, because they loved Fabio more. With a
stern face, the prince said, "Ah! You renegade! I see that you are a traitor and

deserve a much worse punishment than this man, since he was driven to such an action by simple love, whereas you were incited by hate and malice to do evil. Nevertheless, both of you will go to prison, and you will not get out before having received a proper and suitable punishment."

That said, he had them taken to separate prisons, but first he had the lovely garland removed from Fabio and took better care of it afterward than he had earlier.

But after he returned to his room and started to think about the case, he felt great sympathy for Fabio, because he loved him highly for his virtues and knew that he was loved likewise by the whole city. He would more than willingly have freed him if he could have done it with honor while punishing the other. He had a great hatred for Menandro as a result of his reprobate ways and habits and for a while in the past he had looked for a good reason to punish him as he merited. But now that punishing him also involved punishing Fabio, he found himself extremely unhappy. Pondering all night long how to free Fabio and chastise Menandro without staining his own honor, he eventually thought of the perfect way to be judged merciful by being neither severe nor unjust.

Hardly had the following day brightened the morning than the whole of Salerno heard the news that Fabio and Menandro had been imprisoned for having wanted to steal the prince's garland during the night to give it to Clorina. Her father was so pained at this news that he felt sick, especially since his daughter was accused by all of being the reason for such a scandal, and he reproached her with harsh words. Fabio's relatives and many other gentlemen, his friends, all went together before the prince when they heard of his capture, beseeching him on their knees to have pity on Fabio because of his youth and the love that had led him astray, each offering to pay a large amount of money to ransom his life.

But the prince, who did not want to show himself partial (although no one had yet appeared in favor of Menandro), answered those who beseeched him, "My fathers and brothers, you all know how unsuitable it is for a just lord to forgo sound justice. You also know how partiality least suits a lord and judge, for it is often no less a cause of insult than of great harm, as many examples in the past have made clear. And therefore I pray you not to try to make your lord become unfair and drive him to injustice, since until now he has been known to act justly.

"When you consider all sides, you will see that each man's mistake is grave, and were I to punish them with the severity warranted by the crime committed, I would have both executed without delay. Nor would it be reasonable that because my citizens and you all plead in favor of Fabio I should show more condescension toward him than toward Menandro. You know I do not rejoice in being any less compassionate than just, and I prefer to show compassion when I know that the injury and the offense are directed at me rather than at other people, so that I alone in that case am injured (and beseeching me in that case would be useless). Therefore, for the love of you all and for Clorina, whom I know to be young, beautiful, well mannered, and discreet, I want to free them both, as I heard that both of them love her, giving a lead to the one (whoever he is) whom it will be understood she loves more than the other.

"I say then that for the love of her I will remit any injury committed against me by whichever of these two young men Clorina asks me to give her for a husband, and I want to give him to her as a free man. So that the other also gets something for having loved such a beautiful and worthy woman, I want him to be spared death and any other punishment incurred in loving her if another young lady will, for his love, cleverly steal a kiss from my wild woman. If he does not, within three days, find a young lady willing to expose herself to such a danger, I determine that he be sentenced, being unworthy of the love of any maiden, to the punishment he deserved when he hid himself in my palace. Moreover, he cannot have any other major dispensation from me except this: having deserved to die on the cross, he shall have his head cut off. And any man coming to ask mercy for him will, on the spot, receive the same punishment. Any woman or young lady asking such mercy from me will be whipped without let up three times around my palace with leather straps."[65]

The shrewd prince had settled on this sentence for no other reason than that he was almost sure Clorina would request Fabio for her husband. Thinking also that there would be no young lady willing to put herself through the danger of kissing the wild woman, Menandro alone would be punished. Nor was the prince alone in this opinion, but all those gentlemen, in fact the whole city, concurred in that conclusion, and they all rejoiced and gave countless thanks to the prince for such a sentence. Among all those rejoicing, Clorina's father showed himself the happiest and could hardly contain himself, for he too, thinking surely that she would demand Fabio, was delighted that his daughter would be relieved of her shame while he would get such a kind and virtuous son-in-law.

---

65. Renaissance manuals on punishments and ways to administer them clearly draw a line between the kinds of punishment that men and women can mete out. See Gallonio, *Trattato de gli instrumenti de martirio* (Rome: n.p., 1591). Women were more often than not just whipped, even in cases when they were denounced for magical practices.

Therefore, they all—father included—took leave of the prince and went to Clorina together and made her understand that Fabio's life was at her disposal. Each strongly implored her to go free him right away, since their lord showed himself so benign. Her father, exhorting his daughter to free him, added many other words so laudatory of Fabio that he made clear to all how much more he wished Fabio rather than Menandro to become his son-in-law.

Having until then grieved bitterly for such a strange accident and hearing now the good news—that she alone had the power to free the one whom she liked most—raising her hands to heaven and releasing in joy those very tears that earlier she had shed in fiery passion, Clorina went to the prince with her mother and the other matrons who had assembled there, dressed as she was and taking her veils along. She was followed by all those gentlemen but did not state her preference to anyone. Curtseying properly, she said to the prince, "Most illustrious and excellent lord, how good it has been for all of us, your subjects, to find ourselves governed by such a just and benevolent prince is very openly shown by our quiet lifestyle unconstrained by any tyranny. But what can also please many even more is the fact that in addition to the justice and mercy that are known to reside abundantly in you, you are also a true expert on how much the darts of love prick youthful breasts. The young men now in prison for the error they committed of trying to steal the garland and I as well could give true evidence of this. The two young men deserved a grave punishment for having shown you little respect when they used violence in the very palace of their kind lord, and I as well, because I have given them reason. Nevertheless, being extremely benign, you have provided us all with the solution to save ourselves, for, as I said, you know how strong an amorous desire can be in a youthful breast. I deeply feel that I am unworthy of this extremely compassionate gift and do not know how to thank you sufficiently for your goodness and my indebtedness to you. But I dare to hope that your knowledge of how much power the flame of love has will be the cause not only of Your Excellency's excusing me if I do not choose the groom whom I know all those present here expect me to choose, but also that you will defend my behavior in front of them.

"I do not doubt, my lord, that my father, and whoever else is here, and also perhaps Your Excellency with them, hold for certain that I should ask for Fabio as a husband. I reasonably should do so, had I not learned from you, my lord, how to be just and kind. I know that Fabio's nobility, his rare virtues and manners, his singular good looks, and more than anything else the fact that we are both citizens of the same country, give you reason to believe that I should want him and not Menandro. But to tell the truth, such causes are the very ones that give me grounds to act differently from what everyone expects.

"My motivation is that, finding myself, as is known, greatly loved by these young men, both of whom are noble, kind, and virtuous (a state of affairs which leads me to love both indifferently), but knowing how much Fabio is loved by the whole of Salerno for his great merits, which is not the case with Menandro because he is a foreigner, I feel that it is right and just, both because I love him dearly and because I know that he would not find here a woman who would put herself in danger by kissing the wild woman, that I should free him rather than Fabio by asking for him as a groom. I am more than certain that there will be no scarcity here in Salerno of many noble young women who will compete with each other to free Fabio, while I am sure that none of them would do so for Menandro, and thus both will be free because of me.

"Therefore, my lord, since your kindness of heart makes it possible that one of the two, by becoming my husband, is freed thanks to me and it is my choice to free the one I like most, I pray you, my lord, to agree to give me Menandro for a groom. At the same time please excuse me before all these gentlemen and reconcile me with my father, whom I know will be fiercely upset with me because I have asked for Menandro rather than for Fabio. I also know that I will be no less hated than believed stupid by everyone. Still I trust that when all will have considered the result of this choice, they will praise more than blame me, since I know that by freeing Menandro there will be no shortage of women, perhaps more deserving than me, to offer themselves to free Fabio."

How unexpected this request of Clorina seemed to the prince and all the others cannot be truly narrated. Moved by infinite pain, all the gentlemen shouted that she was a foolish girl. Totally breathless, her own old father was ruder than anyone else toward her, threatening to make her repent her bad choice unless she revoked it.

Although it pained him in his inmost heart to see the matter move in this direction, still not wanting to be considered by any as partial and unjust, the prince asked her father and the others to reconcile themselves to the desire of the foolish Clorina. He had more than once and with loving words advised her that it would have been much more honorable and useful for her to take Fabio rather than the other for a husband, but had seen her remain steady, fixed in her opinion and strongly determined.

Requesting that Menandro be led out of prison right away, he had Clorina marry Menandro then and there in his presence. Making everybody leave soon after with great regret on the part of Clorina's father and of Fabio's relatives and friends, he issued an edict—a painful one for him—that any young lady, noble or not, who through cunning or artfulness could, within three days, get a kiss from his wild woman, would be given the gentle Fabio for a husband, together with a dowry of ten thousand ducats from the prince himself.[66]

Having heard of the edict, many poor girls came to try their luck and see whether they could get such a valiant man for themselves, but when they got even a little close to the wild woman they became so frightened and ran away from that horrible monster, as they would have done even if they were sure of acquiring the whole world. To reveal the reason why the wild woman was so frightening, I will tell you that, together with her wild man, she had been given as a gift to the prince two years earlier. The man was so scornful and unpleasant that he would have killed for little or nothing and was therefore always kept strongly chained by his feet. The same was not true of the wild woman, who, having become almost sociable, would go here and there in a familiar way through the palace with the servants of the prince's mother. Still she felt such boundless love for the wild man that she would not let an hour go by without coming to see him and would kiss him a thousand times with great affection.

Now it happened, as with children who often have strange wishes, that a prince's page, wanting to laugh at him and have a good time, had a great desire to upset the wild man. He more than once watched how best to catch him alone, and as chance would have it, he found him one day that way. For neither the wild woman nor anyone else was around, and he was all by himself, scornful as usual. The page then being in a better humor and happier than ever, taking a long staff which he had prepared for this purpose a few days earlier, started to provoke the wild man, all the while keeping his distance. He did this so well and with such agility that although he kept poking now at his eyes, now at his ears, and now at some other part of the body,

---

66. During those years, a very good middle-class dowry amounted to 1,500 or 2,000 ducats in Venice and Padua, with the ceiling of 5,000 established by sumptuary laws. Bartolomeo Salvatico's wife, for example, brought a dowry of 2,000 ducats. For more on dowries in Padua, see Lavarda; for dowries in nearby Venice, see Chojnacki, "Nobility, Women and the State: Marriage Regulation in Venice, 1420–1535," In *Marriage in Italy, 1300–1650*, ed. Trevor Dean and K. J. P. Love (Cambridge: Cambridge University Press, 1998). On early Venetian legislation to control dowries, see Donald Queller and Thomas Madden, "Father of the Bride: Fathers, Daughters, and Dowries in Late Medieval and Early Renaissance Venice," *Renaissance Quarterly* 46 (1993): 685–711; for similar cases in Florence, see Christiane Klapisch-Zuber, "The 'Cruel Mother': Maternity, Widowhood, and Dowry in Florence in the Fourteenth and Fifteenth Century," in *Women, Family, and Ritual in Renaissance Italy* (Chicago: University of Chicago Press, 1985), 117–31; and more generally, Manlio Bellomo, *La condizione giuridica della donna in Italia* (Turin: Einaudi, 1970).

the wild man could never escape the insolent page, until finally he became blinded by the most ferocious rage. Strongly provoked but powerless to defend himself, and unable to take vengeance against the one who was offending him, he turned against his own person and began to eat his own hands with the most appalling screams.[67]

It happened by chance that a woman of the palace, walking by and hearing the incredible noise being made inside, entered the room to observe what was happening. Seeing that horrible spectacle and that the wild man had almost eaten both hands and was all smeared by his own blood, she took a large cane in her hands with which the wild man's guardian was often able to keep him in his place. After she managed to drive away the page with the most reproachful words, she began to hit the wild man as strongly as she could to make him stop devouring himself.

But as bad luck would have it, the wild woman, who had not seen her man for a good while and was coming back eager to visit him, heard the horrible screams he was making from far away. Rushing into the room where he was kept, she saw that poor woman hitting him with the cane. Seeing him without hands and all bloodied, she thought that the woman had reduced him to that state, so she hurled herself onto her with wild fury to kill her. She would have done it soon enough, had not the governor and many court servants heard the screams the three of them were making, arrived quickly, and stopped the assault. They took the unfortunate woman away alive, but with her face so ripped up that she died within a few hours. And the same happened to the wild man, who ended his life in a very short time, between the pain he felt for the hands he had eaten and the ferocious indignation he had generated in himself.

Having fixed in her mind that a woman and no one else was responsible for her being deprived of her dearest companion, the wild woman became so hateful and such an enemy of her sex that she would have violently killed any woman who came within close proximity to her. But she too was put right away under the same restraints that earlier kept her man, that is, with chains on her feet.

This was the reason why I said earlier that all of the young women who wanted to kiss her in order to free Fabio ran away from her frightened, for whenever one came close she ground her teeth so monstrously that many

---

67. The figure of the hardly human, possibly non-European, *homo sylvestris* resorting to cannibalism was one about whom early modern culture liked to fantasize. Here, however, Bigolina makes the wild man a victim of the young page of courtly society, who by poking him with a staff—a much more proper wielding club than the one with which the savage was typically associated—pushes the uncivilized foreigner to become a masochistic anthropophagite.

swooned frightfully in shock. There was one who dressed as a man thinking to deceive her, since she pined hugely after men, but as she drew near the wild woman, who possessed a highly responsive sense of smell, immediately realized that she was a woman. Having come so close that she could not step back, the wild woman tore her apart with her hands and teeth, and it was not possible to get the young lady away from her, either through force or various entreaties, until she was dead. For this reason, all the young women, whether rich or poor, became so frightened that none could be found courageous enough even to look her in the face.[68] Thus the prince, Fabio's relatives, and in the end the whole of Salerno, were weeping, realizing that there was no remedy left for him. Two days had already gone by, and all waited with extreme grief for the third while cursing the cruel Clorina.

In prison, the young Fabio was given the news that only for the love of him had the kind prince given Clorina so much authority to free the one of the two young men whom she liked most and take him for a husband, with the firm belief that she would ask for him and not Menandro. Having also heard how the badly advised young woman had asked for, and indeed obtained, Menandro and not him for a husband, he fell into such a bitter state of mind that he would have killed himself to get out of the anguish he felt had he had the chance. In this extreme torment the endless and faithful love Urania used to have for him came back into his mind, and he recalled how he had been unappreciative of such a love, although she had given him no reason to leave her for another woman, even one more beautiful. Still he had been so blind that not only had he stopped loving someone who loved him very much for the sake of his most cruel enemy, but he had also given her reason to go wandering in the world and perhaps become lost.

So he started to mutter with a faint voice accompanied by sighs and tears, "For pity's sake, Urania, already so faithful toward me, why was it not my destiny to know your worthy and constant love while you were close to me and I was so loved as I am realizing now that you are far away and perhaps feel hatred for me—and for good reason? Alas, if I had understood it I would not have found myself (I know it for certain) in this miserable state. For it is well-known that you are so judicious and kind (if you are still alive and the unjust torment I gave you has not brought you to death) that I would not

---

68. The portrayal of the wild woman as the aberration of femininity, an old crone unnatural even in her desire for men, given her age, has many literary antecedents in the misogynist topos of the *vituperatio vetulae*. The ugly old woman was very often used in poetic parodies to subvert the established Petrarchan canon of proportion-bound beauty. A contemporary sonnet by Anton Francesco Doni, for example, in *I marmi* (1552), parodies a woman whose "face is wrinkled, her breast is black and withered" (71–72).

have fallen into such a shameful blunder with you around. I can truthfully affirm that while I loved you I never had to suffer the smallest humiliation. In fact, I want to add that I remember you as so gracious, loving, and compassionate, that were you here in Salerno now or in a place sufficiently close to hear my great misery in time to help, I have no doubt that you would put on wings to come where I am and try every possible means to free me, even if you knew that I was led to such a miserable end because I was trying to please another ungrateful woman.

"But alas, poor me, what am I saying? How much am I out of myself not to consider that one of two things necessarily must have happened: either she is already dead (for she could not have lasted long in such a bitter life, given the endless sorrow she expressed in the tender letter she sent me at her departure), or, if she is still alive, she no longer loves me (for one cannot escape the suffering caused by many discomforts, as when undertaking long trips). Recalling my cruelty that caused her to suffer so many inconveniences and such anguish for no fault of her own, I think she must have become so full of pity toward herself that she must have developed a strong hatred for me, since I am the reason for her pain.

"On the other hand, perhaps there was another man wiser than me who, in displaying a better knowledge of her worth and virtues than I did, has so honored and respected her that she—all loving and yielding to honest and kind demands—now loves him wholly. It is indeed much better to love when love is reciprocal than when one hopes for nothing better than ungratefulness and contempt (which she received from me). Considering that, I deserve a punishment equal to my ungratefulness. I do not believe that I have met this bad luck for any sin of mine except for the cruelty I unjustly displayed toward the woman who loved me so much. Rather than loving someone who loved me more than her own self and deserved to be loved, I wanted to love and follow one who was unworthy of my love and did not appreciate me. Now, unhappy Fabio, take the bitter and appropriate pill coming from the disordered love you had for Clorina."

The troubled Fabio was muttering these and similar painful words, and by now he was bereft of any hope. Since being put in prison he had never closed his eyes in slumber, and now being extremely tired, he was overtaken by the deepest sleep. In his dream he seemed to be inside a lovely garden, accompanied only by a devoted little dog flattering him with the most endearing and affectionate behavior imaginable. He seemed to take great pleasure in those pleasing allurements. While enjoying them to the utmost, he saw a lovely maiden appear on the other side of the garden, coming toward him with great strides. Once he become aware of her, hardly appreciating the dog anymore, he started to walk toward her, all smiles. But the little dog felt that he was wrong in spurning her and tried as much as she could to stop him by pulling at his clothes with her teeth, but to no avail. On the contrary, he, having become quite eager to draw close to the charming maiden and feeling that the devoted little dog was somewhat delaying his willing steps with her frequent pulling, began to kick her far away, full of indignation and forgetting how pleasurable her company had been. But the affectionate dog again came back to pull at his clothes, and again he drove her away with little consideration. When the dog realized that he cared no more about her once he had come near the maiden who received him with many blandishments, she painfully removed herself from his presence, crying and yelping in her own idiom, and hid well inside the garden.

After she left, Fabio seemed to be very happy to have remained in the company of that fair maiden. Taking him by the hand, she said, "Listen, Fabio, I know you are burning with love and desire to take pleasure in this life of mine. You will find me most ready to serve your pleasure after you in exchange render me a great service. Needing a few small birds that are in a nest on the top of that tall thin tree in front of us in the middle of the garden, as you can see, I would like for you to climb to the top to get them so that I can take them from your hands; as soon as I have received them from you, I swear that you may dispose of my life as if it were yours. Now decide what you would like to do."

Fabio seemed to feel great happiness at the maiden's words, and therefore he answered, "Fair maiden, you have guessed right that I find myself burning with the most fiery flames of love for you and desire only to be worthy of acquiring your grace. To gain your love, not only will it be easy for me to climb to the top of that tree to get your desired birds, but I would try to go still higher in the sky to get anything that would please you. Thus, let us go there right away, for I have no other care than to please and obey you."

And so they went toward the tall thin tree. Once there, it seemed to him that he could climb it quite easily. But as soon as he came close to the top and near the nest, he felt the tree shaking at the foot. Looking down along its trunk, he saw something that terrified him beyond measure, for it seemed that the maiden, who a little earlier appeared so beautiful, had the body of the ugliest serpent from the waist down. And she had taken from the base of the tree so much dirt with one of those tools used to till the soil that the tree, almost dug up, was shaking strongly. He seemed also to see an ugly faun at the foot of the tree leaning on a large staff and looking at the monstrous woman who was working so well at kicking the tree to make it fall. When she felt that she had taken enough soil away that any tiny shake could have sent the tree to the ground, she put away the tool with which she was working and turning to the faun, she said, "Does it seem to you, my dear, that I have reassured you today of the great love I have for this man of whom you lived in great suspicion? Now you see how I have brought him, to please you, where he cannot with all his craft run away from death. Let us go then to enjoy the sweetest fruits of our love and leave him up there with his misfortune."

At that moment both of them vanished from his sight, hugging each other. He remained so confused and scared that he did not know what to do, for it appeared that if he moved, even a bit, the shaking tree would fall to the ground to his extreme ruin, but his remaining up there was also certain death. Therefore, he seemed to be bitterly crying over his misfortune, unable to do anything else. While he was thus distressed he saw the devoted little dog come from the place where she had earlier hidden and move straight to the tree. Once there, it seemed that she was grieving greatly for his pain with a whining congruent to her nature. After grieving for a while she looked up, moved by that supreme affection she ardently had for the young man, and started with claws and muzzle to replace the earth around the tree. She was so successful that in a short time the tree seemed to have become firm and solid enough for Fabio to come down calmly and easily. When he reached the ground, realizing that his life had been saved by that dog, indeed the very one he had driven away many times to follow the scheming woman, he took her in his arms with affection. As he hugged her to his breast, such was the pleasure he felt in stroking her that his sleep broke, conquered by an utter sweetness.

When he woke up and considered the dream for a while, he figured that he could take it not for a dream but for a vision. He also realized that the monstrous maiden could not signify anyone other than the false Clorina, who had led him with arrogant cajoling into danger, and that the faun indicated none other than the Menandro loved and freed by her. But the very faithful dog, which he had wrongly driven away, he felt should stand for Urania.[69] Therefore, considering how the dog had freed him from that danger, he began firmly to hope that his Urania, for whom his love had already returned, likewise would come to free him from his dire circumstances. And although only one day of the three was left, after which he would be sentenced to death, he took so much comfort from this vision that he felt certain he could no longer die of that death which he had feared so strongly shortly before.

---

69. Fabio interprets his dream as a premonitory one, and thus makes it easy to interpret. A Freudian reading would put the emphasis on the phallic elements (the tall thin tree), the sexual ones (the maiden changed into a serpent, Medusa-like), the predatory ones (the instrument that uproots the tree), and the compensatory ones (the female dog with the utmost fidelity).

But let us leave him for a while, comforted somewhat by this new hope, for it will be good to return to talk about the disheartened Urania, who was riding in great haste with the loving Emilia toward Salerno.

RETURN TO SALERNO

Dressed as a man like the fair Emilia, Urania started her journey with the intention of going incognito to Salerno so as not to be recognized by any relative or friend. Once she had the opportunity to see her Fabio, she would tell Emilia that she was a woman and would reveal all her misfortune to her. If Emilia was then still pleased to keep her in her retinue, she had decided never to abandon her for the rest of her days. As she arrived in Salerno she decided to lodge at an inn in order not to be recognized by anyone. But she had hardly dismounted her horse when the awful news of Fabio's plight reached her, since in the whole of Salerno there was no other subject of conversation than that cruel case. It was almost vespers that day, the third, and not seeing much possibility up to that point for his escape, everyone was sure that he would die the following day. Hence he was greatly lamented, for everyone loved him.

As Urania heard the horrible news and became certain that the person assaulted by such a cruel fate was truly her beloved Fabio—the one who was also her spirit, her soul, her heart, and her life, the one for whom her wretched self had suffered so many worries and hardships and without whom she could hardly bear to live—hearing now, I say, how he was led to that extreme condition for the love of the ungrateful Clorina, the pain to her poor heart was so great and piercing that, abandoned by her vital spirits and without saying a word, she let herself fall anguished to the floor. Emilia, seeing this, could not believe that this Fabio could grieve so much for the horrible destiny of another Fabio as to allow himself to be led to such an ending, even if he were his brother. It took her some time and much hard work to revive Urania's lost spirits. Moved by compassion and love and crying hard, Emilia said to her, "Alas, Fabio, only hope of my soul, what is distressing you so much? Who could this man be over whose impending death you suffer so much that it seems you want to die before him? If I had not heard him called by your very name, I would believe he was your brother. Whoever he is, I pray you, my dear Fabio, for the love I bear you, to share the reason why you torment yourself so bitterly over the loss of this man. Being myself a loving and faithful companion, I should be given the chance to grieve with you both for the reason and the pain it causes. You know well that loving you as passionately as I do, there can be no pain in you that is not pain and anguish in me, as every occasion for cheerfulness in you would likewise be reason enough for my sheer happiness."

Won by Emilia's sweet words, Urania, after she had recovered her ability to speak, answered, "Lady Emilia, my honored mistress, I see once again how much you love me out of kindness and without my being worthy of it in any way. This distresses me no less than all my other discontents, because I know I cannot ever deserve your love for me, no matter how long I might live. My greatest pain is seeing how this miserable life of mine is affecting you. If I could make you a present of it, I would at least be able to satisfy some part of my debt, but I cannot do so, for if earlier I was prevented by love from doing so, at the moment I am prevented by death. I will tell you why I decided to end this very unhappy life of mine and with it my pain: this Fabio, who at present finds himself in danger of death under such strange circumstances, is so tied to me, not by blood but by love, that you could hardly imagine his worth to me. This Fabio, my lady, is my much beloved Urania's brother, and there is nothing in the world that she holds more dear or loves and appreciates more completely than him, nor should one doubt that were he to die she would die as well, and if she dies, do not think that I could live even one hour after her death. Now you can understand, lady Emilia, how important this man's life and death are to me and how much reason I have to grieve."

Hearing, with great affliction, her beloved Fabio say these words and knowing very well that she was not loved with the love she wished he had for her, the fair Emilia still could not stop loving him ardently and wishing his happiness rather than hers. Thus she said with tears in her eyes, "Alas! Fabio, cursed be that cruel destiny that forces you to follow one who does not love you, who perhaps could in the end be the reason for your death and who makes you run away from another who values you more than her own life and with whom you could abundantly enjoy all the amenities and pleasures that can be desired in this world. Nevertheless, since your destiny and mine seem to be that each of us will always follow the worst path, being myself not good enough to make you mine, I have decided to let you know at least how genuine my love for you is. I want to try to free this Fabio, if I can, by kissing the wild woman, so that, since I cannot have any happiness through you, at least you can obtain yours through me. If it happens that by way of enticements, as I think I know how to do them, I could have a kiss from the wild woman by which Fabio would be delivered from death, the first thing I would tell him is to please make Urania your wife. Having thus obtained your purpose with my help, it will not displease you, as I change my Florence with your Salerno, to have me at least as your dearest sister-in-law, since it did not please you to love me as your bride."

Urania did not like these last words very much, since she did not want any woman other than herself to have power over her most beloved Fabio. Therefore, her face upset, she answered, "Would that it not please God, lady Emilia, that anyone other than myself were to give life back to my sweet Urania's brother, for although I cannot save him by kissing the wild woman since I am a man, still it may be possible for me to discover some other way to save him by using my talent and love. It would be a great sin to put your beautiful face in danger of being rent by that most ugly monster; still, if you please, let us go to the palace to see what is being said on the subject."

"My sweetest Fabio," Emilia answered, "I said those words with the intention of helping you and not of injuring you, even though from your haughty answer you appear to have taken them as an insult. Do as you like in this and in anything else, dear Fabio, for I like everything that makes you happy."

Urania, whose heart was pressed by a larger care than the words this woman was saying, without giving her any answer, took the innkeeper aside and persuaded him to help her find the kind of garment worn by a brigand, greasy and filthy and smelling strongly of perspiration. Having obtained it, she rubbed her neck, face, and hands all over with the greasiest part until she became nauseated with herself, and then having found likewise a dirty shabby hat which, like the garment, was well greased and covered her face almost entirely, she donned both the garment and the hat.[70] Thus suitably decked out, she returned to the lovely Emilia, to whom she said she had dressed so in order not to be recognized. Then both, having gone to the palace, found the wild woman in a fury because a young woman a short time before had tried to kiss her, and her appearance was rousing terror in everyone. As Emilia, who was very delicate, saw that horrible look, she took such a fright that, coming close to Urania, she said to her, "For pity's sake, my Fabio! Let us leave right away, for I swear that despite the love I have for you, fear so surrounds my soul and heart in seeing this ugly beast that I have lost interest not only in helping Fabio, as I had offered to do, but even my father and mother. If they were in danger of dying and I could save them only by coming close

70. This scene is close to one in the *Furioso*, with the gender of the quester reversed. In Ariosto's text, Lucina is kept prisoner while the faithful king Norandino, who, like the equally faithful Urania, has decided either to get his beloved or to die ("he had no will to go on living, unless he rescued her," 17.37), tries desperately to free her by going to the Orcus's den. In his makeshift prison, the Orcus separates women and men because, like the wild woman in *Urania*, he recognizes the difference between sexes from the smell: "He will tell them apart by smell" (17.42). To avoid being recognized, Norandino smears his body with the grease of goats and sheep: "[he] ran and rubbed it all over himself, from top to toe, till it overpowered his own natural odour" (17.45).

to her, I would rather leave them to die than draw any nearer to the horrible monster. Hence, my Fabio, I pray that we set out at once from here, for you will surely find another, less dangerous means to obtain your dear Urania."

Urania smiled slightly at these words and then said, "Tell me, lady Emilia, I pray, if, like Fabio, I were to find myself in the same danger of death, would you at least try to kiss her in order to make me yours and save me now that you have seen the dreadfulness of this wild woman's face? Or rather, would you let me die, frightened by enormous dread as you are now?"

"My Fabio," Emilia answered, "to tell you the truth, I myself do not know what I would do in such a case, so infinitely do I find myself frightened at the moment. I can tell you this: to make you mine or to free you from a similar danger, I would go through the hottest fire or suffer the danger of a rapid current, but this monster is truly frightening and ugly beyond any human conception. I swear, my Fabio, that although you can see that I am so far away from her, I feel my heart beat and my hair curl so much in terror that I have no doubt that, were I to come closer, I would die."

Hearing Emilia say such words and letting out a passionate sigh, Urania said to her, "Ah, lady Emilia, there are many who love and countless others who call themselves subjects of love, but there are only few who can be called true lovers and know how to love well or, in other words, want to make those demonstrations of love that a true lover always needs to make. Believe me, the man or woman who just feigns love runs away with almost everything he has from the beloved at a time of need or danger. Therefore I deem it a sign of love when a true lover tries with whatever he has to make himself appreciated by his beloved since, for things of the slightest value, in fact very often for something that causes damage and shame, we see treasures destroyed and dissipated every day as a result of badly regulated appetites. Rest assured, the man or the woman who flees from saving the life or the honor of the beloved with his or her life does not truly love but pretends to.[71] And if he or she loves, that love is superficial and should not be highly esteemed, nor should the beloved place any trust in such a lover.

"I know well, lady Emilia, that at present it seems to you that you would not run away from water and fire to make me yours or to save me from death. Still I believe just as fully that if you should find yourself so close to the fire that burns and the water that chokes as you find yourself close to this wild

71. In this, Urania follows King Norandino, who in the episode I referred above in the *Furioso* declares his love and faithfulness toward the entrapped Lucina: "I am here by my own wish, and not by mistake, to die beside my wife" (modified trans.). Giulia Camposampiero too chose to risk her life, like Urania, for the man she loved even though in both cases the man was (or was rumored to be) in love with another woman.

woman, you would depart as much or more frightened by those as you are by this woman now. But I know what I would do to acquire what I love, and perhaps we will not leave this palace today before you see a major illustration of it. First I shall try to humiliate this wild woman to keep her quiet afterwards, if by chance some other young lady comes along to kiss her, because I know that she likes men inordinately."

"Alas, my Fabio," Emilia said, "since your help will not avail in rescuing that other Fabio from death, leave her, I pray, and do not give me so much grief as I shall feel when I see you close to that ugly beast. Your mistake in being sure I do not love you as much as a true lover would does not diminish in any way the great love I have for you nor lessen in me that fear of losing you today that presses my heart more than ever before."

"Do not fear losing me today, my lady," Urania answered, "because I assure you that you will not lose me before you and I will be known by everyone as similar and almost like each other. Still do not deny me a chance to do all I want to do for this day alone."

"I desire nothing else from you," Emilia answered, "but that we will both be known by everyone as similar, because were it to happen, I have no doubt that you would become my husband soon. Therefore, do all you would like to do, as you said, for this day."

While she was saying this, Urania was moving very slowly closer to the wild woman, trying a thousand ways to charm her. When she drew so near that the woman could smell the powerful stench of the old garment she was wearing, she found it to be the natural smell of man. Since she delighted in men a lot, she became more cheerful and beckoned Urania to come closer. Seeing this, Urania took the greatest comfort and solace. Putting her confidence in her ardent faith and love for Fabio, without fearing anymore, she came closer and gave the woman a big kiss on her hairy cheeks. But the woman, who believed Urania to be a man because of the smell of her garment, unsatisfied with just one kiss, and her appetites awakened, pulled Urania to her breast with both arms and with such a fury that it is a wonder she did not deprive Salerno of one to whom all its inhabitants were indebted. Many wild, indeed feral kisses she gave her so that more than once Urania thought she would not emerge alive from the encounter.

Many people, noblemen and others, were assembled in that place, drawn both by the turmoil those nearby were creating because of the danger in which they saw Urania (whom they considered a pretty stupid young man for having placed himself in such danger to no purpose) and the bitter weeping of the lovely Emilia. When Emilia saw her beloved Fabio being treated so roughly by such a loathsome woman, she felt her own heart had burst and weeping loudly she screamed, "Help! Help!" But there was no one who wanted to help the miserable Urania, for each was saying, "If he is crazy, let him do what he wants, for then he will perhaps recover from his foolishness."

After the wild woman had kissed Urania for a good while, she gave her up in the end, thank God, more tired than sated, and Urania, although very tired and bruised, extracted herself with dexterity. As the lovely Emilia saw her dear Fabio freed from so great a danger, she threw herself on the man's neck, crying out in utter happiness, while all those present partly reproached and partly derided Fabio, saying that his folly had been immense for having put himself needlessly at the discretion of that wild fury.

Caring little for what they were saying, Urania answered them, "You have said what you wanted, but not because you know anything. I would be perpetually indebted to you all if I could be led before the prince, in whose presence I would like to speak to the wretched Fabio on behalf of a maiden who loved him most passionately."

There was no lack of people to lead him to the prince right away in the hope that this was good news for Fabio. As they came before him, Urania bowed and said, "Your Excellency, I am on no errand that would warrant my presenting myself before Your Excellency, but I was asked to do so by a young woman who, for all I could guess, seemed to have been more in love than anyone else. I was asked by her to come to Salerno for her sake and say some words in her name to a lover of hers named Fabio who, from what I have understood, is in prison and sentenced to death by Your Excellency. Since I cannot give him this news secretly as I was asked to do, I hope Your Excellency will be satisfied if I reveal it to him in your presence as best I can."

Feeling a great affliction in seeing that every road was shut to free Fabio (since he did not want to be held less than just) and hoping that perhaps this was news that would enable him at least to prolong his life if not rescue him from death, the prince told the young man that he was more than happy for him to speak to Fabio of whatever he liked and for as long as he wished. He was praying to God that the news he was bringing was such as to give him reason to help Fabio because he could not have had any greater happiness in the world than to be able to free him. He had Fabio brought before him right away.

Fabio had remained quite unhappy in prison, having lost more than half his hope, seeing that it was almost evening and that neither Urania, as he had started to hope thanks to his vision, nor anyone else had appeared to help him. But hearing now that a young man wanted to talk to him in the name of a young lady and that for this reason the prince had taken him out of prison, he went before the prince slightly happier, comforted somewhat by a new hope.

As Urania, who had left him happy and handsome at her departure from Salerno, saw him presently so sad and with the gloomiest air, her heart became so heavy that it almost caused her to reveal who she was more through her reactions than her words. Still, with great strength she forced herself to hold back the feelings engulfing her. The courteous prince (also moved at seeing Fabio) said to her, putting on a good face, as Urania had done, "Move closer, young man, if you want to say anything to Fabio."

Coming somewhat closer to Fabio and disguising her voice, she then said to him, "Most noble young man, God knows how much I regret having to bring you sad news, as I regretted seeing the reason for such news with these eyes. Having ascertained for myself, as soon as I entered this city, of your rare, indeed singular qualities and having heard at the same time of your misadventure, I feel doubly sorry to have to be the bearer of such unhappy tidings. Yet, since I promised to do so, I will say what I know against my will, for the sake of keeping faith.

"I am the young son of a rich merchant from Bologna. Being sent by my father to Venice, which is often the case, to hasten some business connected to his trade, and having completed my mission, I wanted to return to Bologna not by water, as I usually do, but by land, in order to see more things. One day, riding through the Euganea region alongside a river that flows into the Brenta and that I believe is called Bacchiglione, a quite lamentable voice reached my ears.[72] And as it is almost a universal desire of everyone, but particularly of young people, to follow up on such matters, I had a great desire to know who was moaning so loudly.

"Moving away from the main road—for I felt the voice was coming far away from it—and riding after the voice, I followed it into a verdant lawn in the middle of which there was a charming pond. A young man was sitting all alone on its bank letting out a pitiful moan while keeping his eyes fixed on it. Moved by the sadness, I came closer and began to ask him softly to please reveal the reason for his bitter cry. The young man, who had not become aware of me, raised his gaze from where he had it fixed as he heard me talk and said to me, 'For pity's sake, young man, I pray you in God's name to please continue your trip. Do not stay if you do not live here, since it will do you little or no good to hear of my misfortune, while it will pain me infinitely to accommodate you in the place where I have decided to put an end to my troubles. This pond will be my burial ground. Depart soon, I beg you.'

---

72. The Bacchiglione is a narrow river that runs through Padua; the Euganea region lies south of Padua and is important literarily because it was the place where Petrarch settled. Bigolina used it as the fictional setting for her novella, "Giulia."

"This was such a strange thing to hear that I felt I would on no account leave without exerting all my powers to steer that young man away from putting an end to his own life. Therefore, dismounting my horse and coming closer to him, with all the kind words I could use and weeping out of compassion, I beseeched him to tell me the reason for such desperation. Being truly kind, he replied, 'Most courteous young man, since heaven made you so compassionate I will yield to your polite requests and tell you what you want to know about me, but I pray you, since you are so kind, to make me a promise. If you promise it to me, having decided by all means to die today in this place, I swear that I will go to the other world happier perhaps than I have been in this world for some time.'

"Having at that time no greater desire than to please the sorrowful young man, I offered to do everything I possibly could for his benefit and asked him to command me with no reticence. After I said this to him, he replied, 'I have no doubt, courteous young man, that you believe I am a man like you, but to reveal myself, you should know that I am not a man but a woman and a woman of noble blood born in Salerno. Because of the immense cruelty received from a young nobleman, whom I held dear and loved much more than my own soul and to whom I gave numerous favors, for a year I have moved about like a lost soul and have now arrived at this miserable end. The favor I would like from you and that would please me most, since I see you ready to please me, is that you go to Salerno and find there the cruel beloved of whom I am speaking, named Fabio, and tell him how Urania, who so passionately loved him and who said and did so much for him, is reduced because of him—indeed because of his cruelty—to the painful end that you will witness me act out before you leave. Were he not to believe these things about me, give him this ring, which he gave me as a token of his love when I was happiest, as a sign that you tell the truth.'

"And so she gave me the ring, which now in obedience to her I give you, Fabio. Then she detailed the love affair between them from beginning to end, weeping profusely. I swear I listened to those words with great pain, but she had hardly said them that, without myself realizing it, she stabbed herself in her bosom with a dagger she had with her, saying, 'It should not please God, dear Fabio, that I remain alive very long without you.'

"Realizing this, crying and screaming to dissuade her from the cruel act, I took her in my right arm. And she, though almost near death, said to me with a feeble voice, 'Alas, dear brother, if you have pity—and you seem to possess it—I pray you not to disturb me any longer but, as you promised, to start right away your journey to Salerno.'

"Seeing that such was her desire and that I could no longer give help and in order to please her, I began my journey here right away, more than a little upset. I arrived today and heard what truly torments and afflicts me with redoubled pain."

Being unable to hold back her tears in saying these words, the unhappy Urania fell silent. Fabio, who earlier had worried only about himself, seeing his problem now surpassed by this new one, which he knew had come from him alone, and with a pain so sharp that a human heart cannot feel a greater one, turned to the prince and said,

"Alas, merciful and just lord! I beseech and pray you to please carry out without delay your just sentence against me, for if you hurry, my lord, I swear that I will judge you no less merciful in giving me a quick death than others would judge you just in taking away this unworthy life of mine. Today I confess myself worthy of the most cruel death, since my wretched self has caused the death of someone who did not deserve it."

The prince had been chagrined in the past because he did not understand the real reason why Urania had secretly left Salerno. Moved by pity for both, he said to Fabio, almost crying, "Alas, Fabio, is it possible that you were the reason why Urania, whom we valued so much, left us with no explanation, and why she was then led to desperate death, as this young man affirms? You used to be so benign, kind, and gentle (I know it for sure), and I cannot imagine how you came to show yourself rude and malicious only toward her. I wished very much at the time to know why she departed so suddenly, and thus I entreat you to please tell me if she gave you any reason to become so cruel that she was led to depart in such a desperate state.

"Please temper your grief and affliction and flee despair, for as you know, despair keeps company not with generous and strong souls, but with the cowardly and feeble. Do not fear, I pray, for you do not know what help heaven suddenly might send, and this I would welcome more than if I were to see another state added to my domain. God knows, although I should not say it, that when I passed this cruel sentence, which is both your misfortune and mine, I believed, indeed I held it for certain, that that miserable Clorina would ask for you as a husband, and not Menandro.

"But this business has moved in a direction very different from the one I had anticipated. Having developed a good deal of contempt toward Menandro for his bad manners and holding you more dear than any other young man in this city because you deserve it, I thought of saving you while sending him away without any infamy on my part. Whence I want to believe that God permitted this bad luck to fall on me to punish me, so that I might never again dare to pass sentence if my soul is not wholly free of passion. And I do not regret any other thing except that I am not the only one punished, because I alone deserve it, rather than you with me, for you have not deserved it. Do not believe, Fabio, that if you should die (may God not allow it), my punishment is less than yours even though I remain alive, because I will have procured myself a perpetual and eternal discontent if I have been the cause of your sudden and undeserved death."

"Most benign lord," Fabio answered, "these words of yours are so sweet, kind, and loving that they will make my death less hard than I prefer it to appear to me. When I consider that I disobeyed and insulted such a benign and loving lord, for whom I should have died a thousand times rather than fail once, and that I offended and abused a woman who merited being loved and helped for the rest of my days for her worth and for the immense love she had for me, and even more for the infinite favors I received from her, then just one death would not be sufficient to punish such an error of mine, given the great punishment I deserve.

"It is true, my most loving lord, that as long as this brief life of mine remains with me—and it has to be very short in any case—I shall never stop praising and blessing your immense kindness. If from the other world I am granted the power to pray for your health, just as I shall praise you continuously on earth until this life of mine ends, believe for certain, my lord, that I will offer my prayers so warmly that you will become much better aware of the signs of my true love than you have been aware of those of my faith while I was down here.[73] Since you wish to know the reason why Urania, already mine, upset with me, left Salerno, although, my lord, I do not know much, I will tell you all I imagine has happened. To tell the truth, I never had a wish to insult her, but I wanted to honor and love her always while I lived.

"I say then, my lord, that I loved Urania very much, although only for a short while, in which time she never stopped showing me all her kindnesses and favors, and I gave back very much the same, although briefly. But as often happens, I began to love this damned Clorina, and not because Urania had left my heart. I no sooner started to pursue this new love than Urania became aware of it and complained vociferously to me, now on paper and now

---

73. This passage is a good indication, among many in the text, of how intimately a writer like Bigolina, whom we presume had no official schooling, knew Dante. The section "as long as this brief life of mine remains with me—and it has to be very short in any case" recalls Dante's Ulysses in *Inferno* 26.114–15: "a questa tanto picciola vigilia / d'i nostri sensi ch'è del rimanente." The section "if from the other world I am granted the power to pray for your health" recalls Francesca in *Inferno* 5.91–92: "se fosse amico il re de l'universo, / noi pregheremo lui de la tua pace." Finally, the section "you will become much better aware of the signs of my true love" echoes Dante's words to Virgil as he readies to meet Beatrice in the Earthly Paradise in *Purgatorio* 30.48, itself an echo of Virgil's Dido: "Conosco i segni de l'antica fiamma." Italian quotations of *Urania* in Finucci, ed., *Urania*, 180.

in person, but I always denied it all with a straight face. Having become, however, a less acute observer than she was as a result of my new love and my visits to her consequently having become rarer and less fervent, I think she left perhaps because her heart would not suffer to see how the great love I used to have for her was somewhat diminished for the sake of a woman less worthy than she. After sending me a letter, which would have moved a tiger to love her, and without otherwise waiting for my answer, she disappeared dressed as a man.

"I swear, my lord, that I was moved so strongly by that letter that after I read it I would have taken away from her any reason to leave, had she delayed a bit her departure for me to proffer a remedy, and never again would she have had grounds to complain about me. But woe on me, what goodwill of mine can help now that the heartbroken one has taken her life, being much more faithful than I and unable to live without my love, and I, who betrayed her, have given her reason for doing it? I must die, and if justice is delayed too long in giving me the death for which I was sentenced by Your Excellency, my hand will not be long in inflicting a death upon myself that my cruelty toward the wretched Urania makes me deserve."

Urania, seeing that her Fabio so bitterly regretted his destiny, unable to suffer his distress any longer, threw down that filthy shabby hat and running to hug him, said in the sweetest way, "Here you see, my most desired Fabio, that your beloved Urania, whom you mourn as dead, is not dead but alive, and not only does she still live, but risking her life she has also saved yours. Do not believe that for no reason, my sweetest Fabio, the heavens, notwithstanding my desire, kept me alive, protecting me against a thousand deaths so that this humble life of mine might be of use in saving yours, which is more valiant and worthy than any other, and so that my sincere and inviolable faith could be manifested to you."

As she said this, taking her arms from around the neck of Fabio who was beside himself and as if dead, she turned to the prince, "Most excellent lord, you must be amazed at the incredible boldness that led a young woman to close her eyes to reason so completely that, dressed as a man and leaving her home, she went wandering in many parts of the world, and after she returned incognito and came before her lord, she did not hesitate in his presence to embrace the man whom she had made her heart's idol. On the other hand, I do not doubt that such amazement will soon dissipate, for knowing how much the force of love can do in human hearts, as I know you do, I am more than sure that Your Excellency will defend and praise rather than accuse and reproach me for such behavior.

"I believe, my lord, that you have already realized that I am Urania. I am the one who, led by extreme despair because I felt I was not loved for my worth by my sweetest Fabio, or perhaps to say it better, for my wish to be loved, left these parts with a firm intention never to see them again. I now believe that it has been God's will that in his extreme need I arrived in time to save his life, which invites me to live a new life. So, my lord, I ask whether the law made by Your Excellency regarding the freeing of Fabio could apply to me as it would have to other maidens, for not only have I saved him from death but I can also say that I have made him mine, having received not one but a thousand and more kisses from the wild woman, as those here can testify."

All confirmed with the utmost joy that her words were true. Having almost gone out of his mind at this series of accidents, the prince soon regained his composure and felt his heart fill with so much happiness that he embraced Urania lovingly. Leaving aside any ceremony, he said to her, "Blessed be you, Urania, and blessed the arrow that stung your heart so deeply for Fabio! Blessed be your most faithful perseverance, and blessed be all the torment, hardship, sorrow, and torture you suffered for him, since now all of troubled Salerno will become merrier and more joyful than ever![74] It is just, most beloved Urania, that your dearest Fabio be given back to you a free man, and it is also just for him to make himself a very loving present to you as your ransom."

That said, taking Fabio—still astonished, lost, and unable to say anything—by one arm and moving him closer to Urania, he made it possible for him to come back to himself. Hugging her tightly, Fabio said so many loving and sweet words to her that it would be too time-consuming to recount them. Among those who were there admiring such a novel situation, the lovely Emilia was finding herself so extremely confused that she did not know whether she was asleep or whether, dreaming while awake, she was seeing and hearing all this.

Having become aware of Emilia's predicament and regretting it very much, the kind Urania decided to help free her from the suspicion in which her Fabio would have fallen with everyone else if she were to leave them with the impression that the handsome man with whom she had come to Salerno

74. For Petrarch, the blessing of Laura, or rather, of his love for Laura, changed the lover into a poet: "and blessed be the first sweet trouble I felt on being made one with Love, and the bow and the arrow that pierced me, and the wounds that reach my heart! // Blessed be the many words I have scattered calling the name of my lady, and the sighs and the tears and the desire; // and blessed be all the pages where I gain fame for her, and my thoughts, which are only of her, so that no other has part in them!" In *Petrarch's Lyric Poems*, 61.5–14. Bigolina has already said that being in love with Fabio was for Urania the means by which she constituted herself as a poet; here we hear from the voice of political authority in Salerno that her love for Fabio has a patriotic value in that it saved Salerno.

was a man and not a woman like herself.[75] Therefore, putting an end to her sweet exchanges with Fabio, and thanking the courteous prince, she added, "Most noble lord, and you, my kind Fabio, since Fortune, reconciled with me, has led me back to a place to which I thought I would never again return, I must describe briefly what my trip was like, so that I can also talk about the company I kept during my return.

"After I entrusted to the hands of my servant the letter that you, my Fabio, confessed having received, I left Salerno at once dressed as a man and alone, with the intention never in my life to return to this region, never indeed to stop in any place, but to roam through the world, always wandering. Pursuing such an aim and passing through Naples without stopping, I did the same from land to land until I arrived at the borders of Tuscany. There one day I let myself be overcome by such a sharp pain that, desperate, I decided to die of hunger.

"As my destiny would have it, I entered then a large and deserted plain and had not fully passed through it before I regretted wanting to end my life so miserably—although I hardly had a pleasant one—because I was frightened at the possibility of that death that already I felt I was seeing sculpted before my eyes. For this reason, hastening my steps more than before, as it pleased God, I arrived toward the end of the day at the border of this plain and there found a very comfortable hostel. Taking no little comfort in the thought that I would find a certain welcome there—that being the usual behavior of innkeepers—I knocked at the inn's door and asked for lodging. But I was given a response so contrary to what I expected that the memory of such a bitter rejoinder still makes my blood freeze in my veins. I was told by the host that it was impossible for anyone else to lodge there because a noble young Florentine gentlewoman, a widow going to Loreto to fulfill some vows, had filled all the quarters for herself and her retinue. Hearing such an adverse answer and doubting ever to be able to find anything good in my life, my heart tightened with such extreme anguish that I fell from my horse in a swoon without saying a word. I believe I would have died there because that beast of a host took no more care in giving me the help I needed at that time than he would have had I been an ugly animal.

"Having learned the news of such a strange accident, the gentle lady,

---

75. Emilia's confusion matches the reader's confusion, in that her love seems at this point trivialized, and she indeed fears having been duped by Urania. On the difficulty women writers had in modifying the plots available for them to imitate in light of the fact that their main character was a woman doing men's things, see Finucci's introduction to Fonte's *Tredici canti del Floridoro*, IX–XXXIX. For more in general, see Nancy Miller, "Emphasis Added: Plots and Plausibility in Women's Fiction," *Proceedings of the Modern Language Association* 96 (1981): 36–47.

whose name is Emilia, being benevolent to the extreme, immediately came to the place where I was lying like a dead person. Seeing that everyone had abandoned me, her kind heart was moved to pity, and since it was not honorable for her to put her hands on me because she judged me a man, she arranged for an elderly maid of hers to bring back my lost spirits, which she did after a while with fresh water and other remedies. When the kind lady saw me returned to good health, she called on some of her servants before departing and commanded them under penalty of punishment to take good care of me for that night.

"But wishing to die rather than see even my clothes touched by those peasants, I felt it was better to disclose who I was to this gentle lady. Thus beseeching her to come closer, I revealed that I was a woman and what my condition was. Hearing this and assuring herself that what I was saying was true, she proved so welcoming that I do not believe that, had her own sister shown up, she could have given her greater demonstrations of kindness and lovingness than she gave to me. She and her maid, each taking one arm, lovingly brought me into the room prepared for her and laid me down on her bed. There the gentlewoman wanted me to recount everything about myself, and I swear I saw her cry out of compassion for my miseries as if some of mine had befallen her.[76]

"After I finished talking, she comforted me with so much tenderness and so many kind words that she was able, in large part, to lessen my bitter passion, for in the end a friend means the most when desperation deprives us of the light of reason. She then added that she accepted me as a most loving sister and would never consent that I leave her. She made so many courteous and affectionate offers to me that it would take too long to recount them. Seeing then how these manly clothes were of no use and could bring her much shame, she begged me sweetly to dress again in more suitable women's clothes, because doing this would give me greater ease and her greater happiness.[77] Knowing how much I was obliged to her and how right her request

76. The story Urania tells of her acquaintance with Emilia is clearly a story *ad hominem*, in that the cunning changes in her retelling are made to please the bien-pensant types of the court and guarantee Emilia a suitable match, if she chooses to remain in Salerno.

77. This scene closely recalls one in *Orlando furioso*, in which Fiordispina has Bradamante, dressed as a man, don feminine clothes to avoid any blame: "Here Fiordispina made much of my sister; she dressed her once more in feminine attire and made plain to one and all that her guest was a woman. / Realizing how little benefit she derived from Bradamant's apparent masculinity, Fiordispina did not want any blame to attach to herself on her guest's account. In addition, she nurtured the hope that the sickness already implanted in her as a result of Bradamant's male aspect might be dispelled by a dose of femininity to show how matters really stood" (25.40–41). For a reading of this episode of cross-dressing in the *Furioso*, see Finucci, *The Lady Vanishes*, chap. 5.

was, from that moment on I dedicated all my actions to her pleasure. To conclude, I went with her to Loreto honorably treated, and after that I set out with her toward Florence, where I found myself honored and well accepted by everyone no more and no less than herself.

"But since the wound that Love first made in me for you, my Fabio, had passed down to the very roots of my heart, and thus was incurable, its fire growing in me ever hotter and I being powerless when away from you, I decided in the end to return to Salerno dressed as a man. That most chaste lady, Emilia, had often shamefully reproached those who allow themselves to be inflamed by any sort of insane fire of love, and I wanted, my dear Fabio, at least to put a brake on the very ardent desire I had to see you again. This consumed me day and night, for I no longer was able to place the obstacle of reason against the great yearning in my heart to see you once more. I made a firm resolve in any case to leave forever after I had seen you once.

"When I revealed my decision to lady Emilia, she reproached me in strong but tempered language. But seeing that her reproaches or persuasions had no leverage with me and that I was firmly determined to return to see my dear Fabio, she added to her admonitions that since I was so foolish as to decide to return to find what was killing me, she would not suffer me to make this trip without her, given the great love she had for me, for her being with me would constitute a check to my life and honor.

"I did and said much to make her want to remain behind, but in the end my words were useless, for she too wanted to come dressed as a man like me. And so having made such an arrangement between us, we soon set out on the road dressed in honorable clothes and riding two good horses, accompanied only by a trusted servant. As it pleased God, we arrived in Salerno earlier today, in sufficient time to complete the most honorable act that anyone ever performed in the world.

"Now, most loving lord, and you Fabio, loved by me above all others, you should know that the lady who is with me and whom you have perhaps judged a young man is a woman like me, who will reveal herself, as you get to know her, to be well-bred and of a valiant and kind soul."

It seemed strange to the gentle Emilia to find herself deceived by Urania, yet she knew that there was no remedy for past events and she saw how ingeniously Urania had taken away from her any shame—in fact she had so well fashioned her speech that what everyone upon hearing the truth would have thought shameful, was now turned into her highest praise and acquired for her the name of merciful. Being very wise, coming close to the prince, she made a deep bow, for she could do nothing but accommodate herself to the occasion.

Being very courteous himself, as has often been said of him, the prince embraced her with great tenderness and said, "Be welcome a thousand times, most valiant young woman, and may God reward you for the great benefit we have all received from your having kept alive the one who was destined to bring us life and happiness, for I confess that I am for the most part unworthy to satisfy such a debt."

Fabio added to the prince's kind words similar ones most loving and tender, and the gentle Emilia rendered suitable thanks to both of them with obliging and adroit words.

Wishing to see complete happiness in his court, the prince said, turning to Fabio, "Since this wise young woman is without a husband, I very much wish that she always remain with us by marrying in Salerno. It would be good, were she to like it, and it would bring me great happiness, if Hortensio, your brother—a very handsome and kind young man—should take her for a wife, so that she and Urania could live forever as very loving sisters-in-law, having been until now the most faithful companions."

Fabio liked the prince's advice very much and wanted to know from Emilia whether she was satisfied with this. Seeing that she could do no better at this point, she answered that she would do whatever pleased the prince and him, as long as she was not separated from her beloved Urania. As such words were said, all Fabio's relatives arrived together with many gentlemen who had heard the good news of his freedom. They had hardly arrived there ere they were overtaken by Urania's mother and many of her relatives, who had all come with great happiness to see and rejoice with her, having heard that their relative had freed Fabio from death.

There is no one who can relate fully how loving were the embraces and welcomes from both sides. Since dusk was coming, the courteous prince wanted all to dine with him that evening in order to demonstrate that he was just as happy for their joy as they were, and he further ordered that all the weddings were to be performed in his palace and at his expense. Urania had some beautiful clothes and jewels brought from her home for herself and the lovely Emilia, and they both dressed again as women, spending that evening very happily together. Emilia had seen the young Hortensio, Fabio's brother, and having liked him very much because he was quite handsome, she was so happy to have him as a husband as to be almost beside herself.

The good prince, wanting to redouble the pleasure in himself and in everyone, called the following day for the duchess's old adviser, who had given him the rose garland (the reason for such grief), and said to him, "My father, my past troubles have prevented me until now from showing you what I desired most, namely, the worthy and noble subject to whom I have destined the lovely garland you have given me. But now that things have turned out much better than I myself could have wished with the help of someone able to bring all this about, let us go happily and merrily to satisfy my most proper desire."

That said, he called the painter, Fabio, and many other gentlemen and went with the garland in tow to the house of the wise damsel, who had just returned from Naples. When her father opened the door, he asked for his daughter in marriage. No one can say how unexpected and marvelous this seemed to the count. With infinite pleasure and with reverence he answered his lord that since he belonged to His Excellency with whatever he possessed, his lord could dispose of the whole any way he liked and added to these many other honorable words.

Hearing this and embracing him with love as a father, the prince went with him to the wise damsel. Once there, he asked whether it would please her to be his bride. Full of joy, she answered that she was ready to do everything that pleased her lord, for which he, who was not expecting a different answer, tightly hugging and kissing her, put the lovely garland on her head saying, "And I accept you, my wise and most loving lady, for my beloved bride."[78] Then he added, turning toward the old man, "Do you feel, my honored father, that my judgment in electing a beautiful and valiant bride has been such that no one could object to it? Have I shown how the subject to whom I have given the garland is marvelously worthy and precious? Tell me what you think, I pray you."

The good old man, to whom truly it seemed that this woman could be compared to his incredibly beautiful lady only as the stars to the moon or the moon to the sun, was full of bitter disdain and of surprise, but he said in a dissimulating tone, "My lord, to tell the truth, I do not believe that another man can be found in the world similar to you in judgment, nor do I know of any who could oppose you in this decision. Therefore, I pray God, our Lord, to bring as much happiness and contentment to this union of yours as indeed my heart desires for you."

After these words he made a sign to the painter, and leaving that place most loathsome to them, both the painter and the old man departed Salerno right away. But when they found themselves where their harshest indignation could be expressed without disrespect, they let their tongues loose in so

---

78. This kind of marriage, in which a couple marries because such is their natural desire, will soon be superseded by new Counter-Reformation rules made to reduce the number of marriages decided on the spur of the moment and with no respect, presumably, for family alliances. The new rules required, among other things, that the banns be posted for forty days prior to the wedding and that a parish priest preside over the ceremony.

many words of insult against that good prince that whoever might have heard them would have had pity on him because for no reason they accused the poor prince of bad judgment, base spirit, and ingratitude. This came about because his looking at the most beautiful members of the duchess, their lady, had not extinguished the fire burning in his heart for his wise damsel and had not kindled any love for their lady. For them it was as if the love with which a man loves a woman and a woman a man was similar to the love one has for a good horse, a lovely jewel, or a good possession—the kind of love that can easily replace something less beautiful with something more beautiful. But this is a stupid opinion, for it does not take into account the fact that the matter, which has already taken one form, cannot so easily transform itself into another, as likewise a cloth of one color can only with great difficulty be changed into another.

After they had verbally abused that poor prince at leisure, they began to counsel each other about what to say to their unlucky lady so that the insult she had received would pass with the least trouble. They rejected many possible explanations and eventually concluded that the best strategy was to feign that they did not want to give him the garland, having seen many vices in that most kind lord, so that she would not be obliged to become the wife of such a vicious prince. Thus they threw the beautiful garland into the sea in contempt.

As they arrived in due course at the palace of the unhappy duchess who, with a tender desire, was waiting for them, they labored to make her believe the tale they had invented, causing her infinite displeasure. For she was wise and sensitive, and although feigning to believe them wholly, she judged quite correctly that the heart of that lord was elsewhere, that he cared little for her rare beauty, and that they had said what they did thinking that through the abuses heaped upon him they could take him out of her heart, as the many praises heard of him earlier had been able to put him there. But they showed themselves to have very little experience of the effects of love, which is of such a nature that the more one hears the loved one blamed the more love grows. Just as a man does not believe that the woman he loves has any defect, so he hates the one speaking badly of her, and moving toward the beloved in pity, he redoubles his love.

So this unlucky duchess, being unable to tolerate them speaking so badly of her beloved prince and without believing anything they said, started to hate them in the extreme. Considering that she had shown her most beautiful body naked with such a scant reward, the anguish and the love grew in her so quickly that, not daring to disclose the bitter pain destroying her heart to anyone who could have given her comfort, in a few days she ended her unhappy life. And this happens to all who readily allow their desire to be perceived behind the tortuous ford of love, for having to come back, they do not know where to start the journey.

But enough of this. Let us return to the kind prince of Salerno who, happier and more joyful than any man of his day, had a very honorable wedding prepared, sufficient for a great king, indeed for an emperor. The prince also wanted everyone to be married the same day: he to his wise damsel, Fabio to the valiant Urania, and Hortensio to the lovely Emilia. For the sake of having a larger celebration and of manifesting even more his kindness, he wanted Clorina also married anew that day with her Menandro, each side forgetting all affronts. Realizing in the middle of the wedding that the old man with the garland and the painter were nowhere to be found, the prince regretted very much their absence. Still, knowing that this had not happened because of any rudeness on his part, he almost guessed what they had been up to. He hid the whole thing in his heart and gave it little thought, and thus happy and satisfied, he enjoyed the wedding and his beloved bride.

After a few months went by and all celebrations had ended, the news came to Salerno that that most beautiful duchess had lost her life quite suddenly, assaulted by some unknown passion. The prince regretted it very much and suffered in his heart, persuaded that such a strange end had been met because of the love she felt for him. Still, not seeing how he could remedy the misfortune that had followed, and not revealing the matter to anyone except Fabio, he made peace with himself by wisely attending to other matters. And so from then on, he and his wise damsel, Fabio and Urania, Hortensio and Emilia, and Menandro and his Clorina lived long and happy lives.[79]

79. All romances and fairy tales typically end with a marriage, but in women's narratives the final euphoria leads very often to double and triple weddings, all dutifully aligned with social classes. Here the four marriages, each carefully spelled out twice, make the reader think of equally famous double marriages in Jane Austen's novels, written more than two hundred fifty years later.

SERIES EDITORS'
BIBLIOGRAPHY

PRIMARY SOURCES

Alberti, Leon Battista. *The Family in Renaissance Florence.* Trans. Renée Neu Watkins. Columbia, SC: University of South Carolina Press, 1969.

Arenal, Electa, and Stacey Schlau, eds. *Untold Sisters: Hispanic Nuns in Their Own Works.* Trans. Amanda Powell. Albuquerque, NM: University of New Mexico Press, 1989.

Astell, Mary. *The First English Feminist: Reflections on Marriage and Other Writings.* Ed. and intro. Bridget Hill. New York: St. Martin's Press, 1986.

Atherton, Margaret, ed. *Women Philosophers of the Early Modern Period.* Indianapolis, IN: Hackett Publishing Co., 1994.

Aughterson, Kate, ed. *Renaissance Woman: Constructions of Femininity in England: A Source Book.* London and New York: Routledge, 1995.

Barbaro, Francesco. *On Wifely Duties.* Trans. Benjamin Kohl. In *The Earthly Republic,* ed. Benjamin Kohl and R. G. Witt. Philadelphia: University of Pennsylvania Press, 1978, 179–228. Translation of the preface and book 2.

Behn, Aphra. *The Works of Aphra Behn.* Ed. Janet Todd. 7 vols. Columbus, OH: Ohio State University Press, 1992–96.

Boccaccio, Giovanni. *Famous Women.* Ed. and trans. Virginia Brown. The I Tatti Renaissance Library. Cambridge, MA: Harvard University Press, 2001.

———. *Corbaccio or the Labyrinth of Love.* Trans. Anthony K. Cassell. Second revised edition. Binghamton, NY: Medieval and Renaissance Texts and Studies, 1993.

Brown, Sylvia. *Women's Writing in Stuart England: The Mother's Legacies of Dorothy Leigh, Elizabeth Joscelin and Elizabeth Richardson.* Thrupp, Stroud, Gloceter: Sutton, 1999.

Bruni, Leonardo. "On the Study of Literature (1405) to Lady Battista Malatesta of Montefeltro." In *The Humanism of Leonardo Bruni: Selected Texts.* Trans. and intro. Gordon Griffiths, James Hankins, and David Thompson. Binghamton, NY: Medieval and Renaissance Texts and Studies, 1987, 240–51.

Castiglione, Baldassare. *The Book of the Courtier.* Trans. George Bull. New York: Penguin, 1967.

Christine de Pizan. *The Book of the City of Ladies.* Trans. Earl Jeffrey Richards. Foreward by Marina Warner. New York: Persea Books, 1982.

———. *The Treasure of the City of Ladies.* Trans. Sarah Lawson. New York: Viking Penguin, 1985. Also trans. and intro. Charity Cannon Willard. Ed. and intro. Madeleine P. Cosman. New York: Persea Books, 1989.

Clarke, Danielle, ed. *Isabella Whitney, Mary Sidney and Aemilia Lanyer: Renaissance Women Poets.* New York: Penguin Books, 2000.

Crawford, Patricia and Laura Gowing, eds. *Women's Worlds in Seventeenth-Century England: A Source Book.* London and New York: Routledge, 2000.

Daybell, James, ed. *Early Modern Women's Letter Writing, 1450–1700.* Houndmills, UK, and New York: Palgrave, 2001.

Elizabeth I: Collected Works. Ed. Leah S. Marcus, Janel Mueller, and Mary Beth Rose. Chicago: University of Chicago Press, 2000.

Elyot, Thomas. *Defence of Good Women: The Feminist Controversy of the Renaissance.* Facsimile Reproductions. Ed. Diane Bornstein. New York: Delmar, 1980.

Erasmus, Desiderius. *Erasmus on Women.* Ed. Erika Rummel. Toronto: University of Toronto Press, 1996.

Female and Male Voices in Early Modern England: An Anthology of Renaissance Writing. Ed. Betty S. Travitsky and Anne Lake Prescott. New York: Columbia University Press, 2000.

Ferguson, Moira, ed. *First Feminists: British Women Writers 1578–1799.* Bloomington, IN: Indiana University Press, 1985.

Galilei, Maria Celeste. *Sister Maria Celeste's Letters to Her father, Galileo.* Ed. and trans. Rinaldina Russell. Lincoln, NE, and New York: Writers Club Press of Universe.com, 2000.

Gethner, Perry, ed. *The Lunatic Lover and Other Plays by French Women of the 17th and 18th Centuries.* Portsmouth, NH: Heinemann, 1994.

Glückel of Hameln. *The Memoirs of Glückel of Hameln.* Trans. Marvin Lowenthal. New intro. Robert Rosen. New York: Schocken Books, 1977.

Henderson, Katherine Usher, and Barbara F. McManus, eds. *Half Humankind: Contexts and Texts of the Controversy about Women in England, 1540–1640.* Urbana, IL: University of Illinois Press, 1985.

Hoby, Margaret. *The Private Life of an Elizabethan Lady: The Diary of Lady Margaret Hoby 1599–1605.* Phoenix Mill, UK: Sutton Publishing, 1998.

Humanist Educational Treatises. Ed. and trans. Craig W. Kallendorf. The I Tatti Renaissance Library. Cambridge, MA: Harvard University Press, 2002.

Joscelin, Elizabeth. *The Mother's Legacy to Her Unborn Childe.* Ed. Jean leDrew Metcalfe. Toronto: University of Toronto Press, 2000.

Kaminsky, Amy Katz, ed. *Water Lilies, Flores del agua: An Anthology of Spanish Women Writers from the Fifteenth through the Nineteenth Century.* Minneapolis, MN: University of Minnesota Press, 1996.

Kempe, Margery (1373–1439). *The Book of Margery Kempe.* Trans. and ed. Lynn Staley. A Norton Critical Edition. New York: W.W. Norton, 2001.

King, Margaret L., and Albert Rabil, Jr., eds. *Her Immaculate Hand: Selected Works by and about the Women Humanists of Quattrocento Italy.* Binghamton, NY: Medieval and Renaissance Texts and Studies, 1983. Second revised paperback edition, 1991.

Klein, Joan Larsen, ed. *Daughters, Wives, and Widows: Writings by Men about Women and Marriage in England, 1500–1640.* Urbana, IL: University of Illinois Press, 1992.

Knox, John. *The Political Writings of John Knox: The First Blast of the Trumpet against the Monstrous Regiment of Women and Other Selected Works.* Ed. Marvin A. Breslow. Washington: Folger Shakespeare Library, 1985.

Kors, Alan C., and Edward Peters, eds. *Witchcraft in Europe, 400–1700: A Documentary History.* Philadelphia: University of Pennsylvania Press, 2000.

Krämer, Heinrich, and Jacob Sprenger. *Malleus Maleficarum* (ca. 1487). Trans. Montague Summers. London: Pushkin Press, 1928. Reprint New York: Dover, 1971.

Larsen, Anne R., and Colette H. Winn, eds. *Writings by Pre-Revolutionary French Women: From Marie de France to Elizabeth Vigée-Le Brun*. New York and London: Garland Publishing Co., 2000.

de Lorris, William, and Jean de Meun. *The Romance of the Rose*. Trans. Charles Dahlbert. Princeton: Princeton University Press, 1971. Reprint University Press of New England, 1983.

Marguerite d'Angoulême, queen of Navarre. *The Heptameron*. Trans. P. A. Chilton. New York: Viking Penguin, 1984.

Mary of Agreda. *The Divine Life of the Most Holy Virgin*. Abridgment of *The Mystical City of God*. Abr. Fr. Bonaventure Amedeo de Caesarea, M.C. Trans. from French by Abbé Joseph A. Boullan. Rockford, IL: TAN Books, 1997.

Myers, Kathleen A., and Amanda Powell, eds. *A Wild Country Out in the Garden: The Spiritual Journals of a Colonial Mexican Nun*. Bloomington, IN: Indiana University Press, 1999.

Teresa of Avila, Saint. *The Life of Saint Teresa of Avila by Herself*. Trans. J. M. Cohen. New York: Viking Penguin, 1957.

Weyer, Johann. *Witches, Devils, and Doctors in the Renaissance: Johann Weyer, De praestigiis daemonum*. Ed. George Mora with Benjamin G. Kohl, Erik Midelfort, and Helen Bacon. Trans. John Shea. Binghamton, NY: Medieval and Renaissance Texts and Studies, 1991.

Wilson, Katharina M., ed. *Medieval Women Writers*. Athens, GA: University of Georgia Press, 1984.

———, ed. *Women Writers of the Renaissance and Reformation*. Athens, GA: University of Georgia Press, 1987.

Wilson, Katharina M., and Frank J. Warnke, eds. *Women Writers of the Seventeenth Century*. Athens, GA: University of Georgia Press, 1989.

Wollstonecraft, Mary. *A Vindication of the Rights of Men and a Vindication of the Rights of Women*. Ed. Sylvana Tomaselli. Cambridge: Cambridge University Press, 1995. Also *The Vindications of the Rights of Men, the Rights of Women*. Ed. D. L. Macdonald and Kathleen Scherf. Peterborough, Ontario: Broadview Press, 1997.

Women Critics 1660–1820: An Anthology. Edited by the Folger Collective on Early Women Critics. Bloomington, IN: Indiana University Press, 1995.

Women Writers in English 1350–1850. 15 volumes published through 1999 (projected 30-volume series suspended). Oxford: Oxford University Press.

Wroth, Lady Mary. *The Countess of Montgomery's Urania*. 2 parts. Ed. Josephine A. Roberts. Tempe, AZ: Medieval Renaissance Texts and Studies, 1995, 1999.

———. *Lady Mary Wroth's "Love's Victory": The Penshurst Manuscript*. Ed. Michael G. Brennan. London: The Roxburghe Club, 1988.

———. *The Poems of Lady Mary Wroth*. Ed. Josephine A. Roberts. Baton Rouge, LA: Louisiana State University Press, 1983.

de Zayas Maria. *The Disenchantments of Love*. Trans. H. Patsy Boyer. Albany, NY: State University of New York Press, 1997.

———. *The Enchantments of Love: Amorous and Exemplary Novels*. Trans. H. Patsy Boyer. Berkeley, CA: University of California Press, 1990.

SECONDARY SOURCES

Ahlgren, Gillian. *Teresa of Avila and the Politics of Sanctity.* Ithaca: Cornell University Press, 1996.

Akkerman, Tjitske, and Siep Sturman, eds. *Feminist Thought in European History, 1400–2000.* London & New York: Routledge, 1997.

Allen, Sister Prudence, R.S.M. *The Concept of Woman: The Aristotelian Revolution, 750 B.C.–A.D. 1250.* Grand Rapids, MI: William B. Eerdmans Publishing Company, 1997.

———. *The Concept of Woman: Volume II: The Early Humanist Reformation, 1250–1500.* Grand Rapids, MI: William B. Eerdmans Publishing Company, 2002.

Andreadis, Harriette. *Sappho in Early Modern England: Female Same-Sex Literary Erotics 1550–1714.* Chicago: University of Chicago Press, 2001.

Armon, Shifra. *Picking Wedlock: Women and the Courtship Novel in Spain.* New York: Rowman & Littlefield Publishers, Inc., 2002.

Backer, Anne Liot Backer. *Precious Women.* New York: Basic Books, 1974.

Ballaster, Ros. *Seductive Forms.* New York: Oxford University Press, 1992.

Barash, Carol. *English Women's Poetry, 1649–1714: Politics, Community, and Linguistic Authority.* New York & Oxford: Oxford University Press, 1996.

Battigelli, Anna. *Margaret Cavendish and the Exiles of the Mind.* Lexington, KY: University of Kentucky Press, 1998.

Beasley, Faith. *Revising Memory: Women's Fiction and Memoirs in Seventeenth-Century France.* New Brunswick: Rutgers University Press, 1990.

Beilin, Elaine V. *Redeeming Eve: Women Writers of the English Renaissance.* Princeton: Princeton University Press, 1987.

Benson, Pamela Joseph. *The Invention of Renaissance Woman: The Challenge of Female Independence in the Literature and Thought of Italy and England.* University Park, PA: Pennsylvania State University Press, 1992.

——— and Victoria Kirkham, eds. *Strong Voices, Weak History? Medieval and Renaissance Women in their Literary Canons: England, France, Italy.* Ann Arbor: University of Michigan Press, 2003.

Bilinkoff, Jodi. *The Avila of Saint Teresa: Religious Reform in a Sixteenth-Century City.* Ithaca: Cornell University Press, 1989.

Bissell, R. Ward. *Artemisia Gentileschi and the Authority of Art.* University Park, PA: Pennsylvania State University Press, 2000.

Blain, Virginia, Isobel Grundy, & Patricia Clements, eds. *The Feminist Companion to Literature in English: Women Writers from the Middle Ages to the Present.* New Haven: Yale University Press, 1990.

Bloch, R. Howard. *Medieval Misogyny and the Invention of Western Romantic Love.* Chicago: University of Chicago Press, 1991.

Bornstein, Daniel, and Roberto Rusconi, eds. *Women and Religion in Medieval and Renaissance Italy.* Trans. Margery J. Schneider. Chicago: University of Chicago Press, 1996.

Brant, Clare, and Diane Purkiss, eds. *Women, Texts and Histories, 1575–1760.* London & New York: Routledge, 1992.

Briggs, Robin. *Witches and Neighbours: The Social and Cultural Context of European Witchcraft.* New York: HarperCollins, 1995.

Brink, Jean R., ed. *Female Scholars: A Tradition of Learned Women before 1800.* Montréal: Eden Press Women's Publications, 1980.

Broude, Norma, and Mary D. Garrard, eds. *The Expanding Discourse: Feminism and Art History.* New York: HarperCollins, 1992.

Brown, Judith C. *Immodest Acts: The Life of a Lesbian Nun in Renaissance Italy.* New York: Oxford University Press, 1986.

Brown, Judith C., and Robert C. Davis, eds. *Gender and Society in Renaisance Italy.* London: Addison Wesley Longman, 1998.

Bynum, Carolyn Walker. *Fragmentation and Redemption: Essays on Gender and the Human Body in Medieval Religion.* New York: Zone Books, 1992.

———. *Holy Feast and Holy Fast: The Religious Significance of Food to Medieval Women.* Berkeley: University of California Press, 1987.

Cambridge Guide to Women's Writing in English. Ed. Lorna Sage. Cambridge: Cambridge University Press, 1999.

Cavanagh, Sheila T. *Cherished Torment: The Emotional Geography of Lady Mary Wroth's Urania.* Pittsburgh: Duquesne University Press, 2001.

Cerasano, S. P., and Marion Wynne-Davies, eds. *Readings in Renaissance Women's Drama: Criticism, History, and Performance 1594–1998.* London and New York: Routledge, 1998.

Cervigni, Dino S., ed. *Women Mystic Writers. Annali d'Italianistica* 13 (1995) (entire issue).

Cervigni, Dino S., and Rebecca West, eds. *Women's Voices in Italian Literature. Annali d'Italianistica* 7 (1989) (entire issue).

Charlton, Kenneth. *Women, Religion and Education in Early Modern England.* London and New York: Routledge, 1999.

Chojnacka, Monica. *Working Women in Early Modern Venice.* Baltimore: Johns Hopkins University Press, 2001.

Chojnacki, Stanley. *Women and Men in Renaissance Venice: Twelve Essays on Patrician Society.* Baltimore: Johns Hopkins University Press, 2000.

Cholakian, Patricia Francis. *Rape and Writing in the* Heptameron *of Marguerite de Navarre.* Carbondale and Edwardsville, IL: Southern Illinois University Press, 1991.

———. *Women and the Politics of Self-Representation in Seventeenth-Century France.* Newark: University of Delaware Press, 2000.

Christine de Pizan: A Casebook. Ed. Barbara K. Altmann and Deborah L. McGrady. New York: Routledge, 2003.

Clogan, Paul Maruice, ed. *Medievali et Humanistica: Literacy and the Lay Reader.* Lanham, MD: Rowman & Littlefield, 2000.

Clubb, Louise George. *Italian Drama in Shakespeare's Time.* New Haven: Yale University Press, 1989.

Conley, John J., S.J. *The Suspicion of Virtue: Women Philosophers in Neoclassical France.* Ithaca, NY: Cornell University Press, 2002.

Crabb, Ann. *The Strozzi of Florence: Widowhood and Family Solidarity in the Renaissance.* Ann Arbor University of Michigan Press, 2000.

Cruz, Anne J., and Mary Elizabeth Perry, eds. *Culture and Control in Counter-Reformation Spain.* Minneapolis: University of Minnesota Press, 1992.

Davis, Natalie Zemon. *Society and Culture in Early Modern France.* Stanford: Stanford University Press, 1975. Especially chapters 3 and 5.

———. *Women on the Margins: Three Seventeenth-Century Lives.* Cambridge, MA: Harvard University Press, 1995.

DeJean, Joan. *Ancients against Moderns: Culture Wars and the Making of a Fin de Siècle.* Chicago: University of Chicago Press, 1997.

————. *Fictions of Sappho, 1546–1937.* Chicago: University of Chicago Press, 1989.

————. *The Reinvention of Obscenity: Sex, Lies, and Tabloids in Early Modern France.* Chicago: University of Chicago Press, 2002.

————. *Tender Geographies: Women and the Origins of the Novel in France.* New York: Columbia University Press, 1991.

————. *The Reinvention of Obscenity: Sex, Lies, and Tabloids in Early Modern France.* Chicago: University of Chicago Press, 2002.

Dictionary of Russian Women Writers. Ed. Marina Ledkovsky, Charlotte Rosenthal, and Mary Zirin. Westport, CT: Greenwood Press, 1994.

Dixon, Laurinda S. *Perilous Chastity: Women and Illness in Pre-Enlightenment Art and Medicine.* Ithaca, NY: Cornell Universitiy Press, 1995.

Dolan, Frances, E. *Whores of Babylon: Catholicism, Gender and Seventeenth-Century Print Culture.* Ithaca, NY: Cornell University Press, 1999.

Donovan, Josephine. *Women and the Rise of the Novel, 1405–1726.* New York: St. Martin's Press, 1999.

Encyclopedia of Continental Women Writers. Ed. Katharina Wilson. 2 vols. New York: Garland, 1991.

De Erauso, Catalina. *Lieutenant Nun: Memoir of a Basque Transvestite in the New World.* Trans. Michele Ttepto and Gabriel Stepto; foreword by Marjorie Garber. Boston: Beacon Press, 1995.

Erdmann, Axel. *My Gracious Silence: Women in the Mirror of Sixteenth-Century Printing in Western Europe.* Luzern: Gilhofer and Rauschberg, 1999.

Erickson, Amy Louise. *Women and Property in Early Modern England.* London & New York: Routledge, 1993.

Ezell, Margaret J. M. *The Patriarch's Wife: Literary Evidence and the History of the Family.* Chapel Hill, NC: University of North Carolina Press, 1987.

————. *Social Authorship and the Advent of Print.* Baltimore: Johns Hopkins University Press, 1999.

————. *Writing Women's Literary History.* Baltimore: Johns Hopkins University Press, 1993.

Farrell, Michèle Longino. *Performing Motherhood: The Sévigné Correspondence.* Hanover, NH, and London: University Press of New England, 1991.

The Feminist Companion to Literature in English: Women Writers from the Middle Ages to the Present. Ed. Virginia Blain, Isobel Grundy, and Patricia Clements. New Haven, CT: Yale University Press, 1990.

The Feminist Encyclopedia of German Literature. Ed. Friederike Eigler and Susanne Kord. Westport, CT: Greenwood Press, 1997.

Feminist Encyclopedia of Italian Literature. Ed. Rinaldina Russell. Westport, CT: Greenwood Press, 1997.

Ferguson, Margaret W., Maureen Quilligan, and Nancy J. Vickers, eds. *Rewriting the Renaissance: The Discourses of Sexual Difference in Early Modern Europe.* Chicago: University of Chicago Press, 1987.

Ferraro, Joanne M. *Marriage Wars in Late Renaissance Venice.* Oxford: Oxford University Press, 2001.

Fletcher, Anthony. *Gender, Sex and Subordination in England, 1500–1800.* New Haven: Yale University Press, 1995.

French Women Writers: A Bio-Bibliographical Source Book. Ed. Eva Martin Sartori and Dorothy Wynne Zimmerman. Westport, CT: Greenwood Press, 1991.

Frye, Susan, and Karen Robertson, eds. *Maids and Mistresses, Cousins and Queens: Women's Alliances in Early Modern England.* Oxford: Oxford University Press, 1999.

Gallagher, Catherine. *Nobody's Story: The Vanishing Acts of Women Writers in the Marketplace, 1670–1820.* Berkeley: University of California Press, 1994.

Garrard, Mary D. *Artemisia Gentileschi: The Image of the Female Hero in Italian Baroque Art.* Princeton: Princeton University Press, 1989.

Gelbart, Nina Rattner. *The King's Midwife: A History and Mystery of Madame du Coudray.* Berkeley: University of California Press, 1998.

Glenn, Cheryl. *Rhetoric Retold: Regendering the Tradition from Antiquity Through the Renaissance.* Carbondale and Edwardsville, IL: Southern Illinois University Press, 1997.

Goffen, Rona. *Titian's Women.* New Haven: Yale University Press, 1997.

Goldberg, Jonathan. *Desiring Women Writing: English Renaissance Examples.* Stanford: Stanford University Press, 1997.

Goldsmith, Elizabeth C. *Exclusive Conversations: The Art of Interaction in Seventeenth-Century France.* Philadelphia: University of Pennsylvania Press, 1988.

———, ed. *Writing the Female Voice.* Boston: Northeastern University Press, 1989.

Goldsmith, Elizabeth C., and Dena Goodman, eds. *Going Public: Women and Publishing in Early Modern France.* Ithaca, NY: Cornell University Press, 1995.

Grafton, Anthony, and Lisa Jardine. *From Humanism to the Humanities: Education and the Liberal Arts in Fifteenth- and Sixteenth-Century Europe.* London: Duckworth, 1986.

Greer, Margaret Rich. *Maria de Zayas Tells Baroque Tales of Love and the Cruelty of Men.* University Park, PA: Pennsylvania State University Press, 2000.

Hackett, Helen. *Women and Romance Fiction in the English Renaissance.* Cambridge: Cambridge University Press, 2000.

Hall, Kim F. *Things of Darkness: Economies of Race and Gender in Early Modern England.* Ithaca, NY: Cornell University Press, 1995.

Hampton, Timothy. *Literature and the Nation in the Sixteenth Century: Inventing Renaissance France.* Ithaca, NY: Cornell University Press, 2001.

Hannay, Margaret, ed. *Silent but for the Word.* Kent, OH: Kent State University Press, 1985.

Hardwick, Julie. *The Practice of Patriarchy: Gender and the Politics of Household Authority in Early Modern France.* University Park, PA: Pennsylvania State University Press, 1998.

Harris, Barbara J. *English Aristocratic Women, 1450–1550: Marriage and Family, Property and Careers.* New York: Oxford University Press, 2002.

Harth, Erica. *Ideology and Culture in Seventeenth-Century France.* Ithaca: Cornell University Press, 1983.

———. *Cartesian Women. Versions and Subversions of Rational Discourse in the Old Regime.* Ithaca, NY: Cornell University Press, 1992.

Harvey, Elizabeth D. *Ventriloquized Voices: Feminist Theory and English Renaissance Texts.* London and New York: Routledge, 1992.

Haselkorn, Anne M., and Betty Travitsky, eds. *The Renaissance Englishwoman in Print: Counterbalancing the Canon.* Amherst, MA: University of Massachusetts Press, 1990.

Herlihy, David. "Did Women Have a Renaissance? A Reconsideration." *Medievalia et Humanistica,* n.s. 13 (1985): 1–22.

Hill, Bridget. *The Republican Virago: The Life and Times of Catharine Macaulay, Historian.* New York: Oxford University Press, 1992.

A History of Central European Women's Writing. Ed. Celia Hawkesworth. New York: Palgrave Press, 2001.

A History of Women in the West.

Volume 1: *From Ancient Goddesses to Christian Saints.* Ed. Pauline Schmitt Pantel. Cambridge, MA: Harvard University Press, 1992.

Volume 2: *Silences of the Middle Ages.* Ed. Christiane Klapisch-Zuber. Cambridge, MA: Harvard University Press, 1992.

Volume 3: *Renaissance and Enlightenment Paradoxes.* Ed. Natalie Zemon Davis and Arlette Farge. Cambridge, MA: Harvard University Press, 1993.

A History of Women's Writing in Russia. Ed.Alele Marie Barker and Jehanne M. Gheith. Cambridge: Cambridge University Press, 2002.

Hobby, Elaine. *Virtue of Necessity: English Women's Writing 1646–1688.* London: Virago Press, 1988.

Horowitz, Maryanne Cline. "Aristotle and Women." *Journal of the History of Biology* 9 (1976): 183–213.

Howell, Martha. *The Marriage Exchange: Property, Social Place, and Gender in Cities of the Low Countries, 1300–1550.* Chicago: University of Chicago Press, 1998.

Hufton, Olwen H. *The Prospect before Her: A History of Women in Western Europe, 1: 1500–1800.* New York: HarperCollins, 1996.

Hull, Suzanne W. *Chaste, Silent, and Obedient: English Books for Women, 1475–1640.* San Marino, CA: The Huntington Library, 1982.

Hunt, Lynn, ed. *The Invention of Pornography: Obscenity and the Origins of Modernity, 1500–1800.* New York: Zone Books, 1996.

Hutner, Heidi, ed. *Rereading Aphra Behn: History, Theory, and Criticism.* Charlottesville, VA: University Press of Virginia, 1993.

Hutson, Lorna, ed. *Feminism and Renaissance Studies.* New York: Oxford University Press, 1999.

Italian Women Writers: A Bio-Bibliographical Sourcebook. Ed. Rinaldina Russell. Westport, CT: Greenwood Press, 1994.

Jaffe, Irma B., with Gernando Colombardo. *Shining Eyes, Cruel Fortune: The Lives and Loves of Italian Renaissance Women Poets.* New York: Fordham University Press, 2002.

James, Susan E. *Kateryn Parr: The Making of a Queen.* Aldershot and Brookfield, UK: Ashgate Publishing Co., 1999.

Jankowski, Theodora A. *Women in Power in the Early Modern Drama.* Urbana, IL: University of Illinois Press, 1992.

Jansen, Katherine Ludwig. *The Making of the Magdalen: Preaching and Popular Devotion in the Later Middle Ages.* Princeton: Princeton University Press, 2000.

Jed, Stephanie H. *Chaste Thinking: The Rape of Lucretia and the Birth of Humanism.* Bloomington, IN: Indiana University Press, 1989.

Jordan, Constance. *Renaissance Feminism: Literary Texts and Political Models.* Ithaca: Cornell University Press, 1990.

Kagan, Richard L. *Lucrecia's Dreams: Politics and Prophecy in Sixteenth-Century Spain.* Berkeley: University of California Press, 1990.

Kehler, Dorothea, and Laurel Amtower, eds. *The Single Woman in Medieval and Early Modern England: Her Life and Representation.* Tempe, AZ: Medieval Renaissance Texts and Studies, 2002.

Kelly, Joan. "Did Women Have a Renaissance?" In *Women, History, and Theory.* Chicago: University of Chicago Press, 1984. Also in *Becoming Visible: Women in European History,* ed. Renate Bridenthal, Claudia Koonz, and Susan M. Stuard. Third edition. Boston: Houghton Mifflin, 1998.

——. "Early Feminist Theory and the *Querelle des Femmes.*" In *Women, History, and Theory.*

Kelso, Ruth. *Doctrine for the Lady of the Renaissance.* Foreword by Katharine M. Rogers. Urbana, IL: University of Illinois Press, 1956, 1978.

King, Carole. *Renaissance Women Patrons: Wives and Widows in Italy, c. 1300–1550.* New York and Manchester: Manchester University Press, 1998.

King, Margaret L. *Women of the Renaissance.* Foreword by Catharine R. Stimpson. Chicago: University of Chicago Press, 1991.

Krontiris, Tina. *Oppositional Voices: Women as Writers and Translators of Literature in the English Renaissance.* London & New York: Routledge, 1992.

Kuehn, Thomas. *Law, Family, and Women: Toward a Legal Anthropology of Renaissance Italy.* Chicago: University of Chicago Press, 1991.

Kunze, Bonnelyn Young. *Margaret Fell and the Rise of Quakerism.* Stanford: Stanford University Press, 1994.

Labalme, Patricia A., ed. *Beyond Their Sex: Learned Women of the European Past.* New York: New York University Press, 1980.

Laqueur, Thomas. *Making Sex: Body and Gender from the Greeks to Freud.* Cambridge, MA: Harvard University Press, 1990.

Larsen, Anne R., and Colette H. Winn, eds. *Renaissance Women Writers: French Texts/American Contexts.* Detroit, MI: Wayne State University Press, 1994.

Lerner, Gerda. *The Creation of Patriarchy* and *Creation of Feminist Consciousness, 1000–1870.* New York: Oxford University Press, 1986, 1994.

Levin, Carole, and Jeanie Watson, eds. *Ambiguous Realities: Women in the Middle Ages and Renaissance.* Detroit: Wayne State University Press, 1987.

Levin, Carole, et al. *Extraordinary Women of the Medieval and Renaissance World: A Biographical Dictionary.* Westport, CT: Greenwood Press, 2000.

Lewalsky, Barbara Kiefer. *Writing Women in Jacobean England.* Cambridge, MA: Harvard University Press, 1993.

Lewis, Jayne Elizabeth. *Mary Queen of Scots: Romance and Nation.* London: Routledge, 1998.

Lindsey, Karen. *Divorced Beheaded Survived: A Feminist Reinterpretation of the Wives of Henry VIII.* Reading, MA: Addison-Wesley Publishing Co., 1995.

Lochrie, Karma. *Margery Kempe and Translations of the Flesh.* Philadelphia: University of Pennsylvania Press, 1992.

Lougee, Carolyn C. *Le Paradis des Femmes: Women, Salons, and Social Stratification in Seventeenth-Century France.* Princeton: Princeton University Press, 1976.

Love, Harold. *The Culture and Commerce of Texts: Scribal Publication in Seventeenth-Century England.* Amherst, MA: University of Massachusetts Press, 1993.

MacCarthy, Bridget G. *The Female Pen: Women Writers and Novelists 1621–1818*. Preface by Janet Todd. New York: New York University Press, 1994. Originally published by Cork University Press, 1946–47.

Maclean, Ian. *Woman Triumphant: Feminism in French Literature, 1610–1652*. Oxford: Clarendon Press, 1977.

———. *The Renaissance Notion of Woman: A Study of the Fortunes of Scholasticism and Medical Science in European Intellectual Life*. Cambridge: Cambridge University Press, 1980.

Maggi, Armando. *Uttering the Word: The Mystical Performances of Maria Maddalena de' Pazzi, a Renaissance Visionary*. Albany: State University of New York Press, 1998.

Marshall, Sherrin. *Women in Reformation and Counter-Reformation Europe: Public and Private Worlds*. Bloomington, IN: Indiana University Press, 1989.

Matter, E. Ann, and John Coakley, eds. *Creative Women in Medieval and Early Modern Italy*. Philadelphia: University of Pennsylvania Press, 1994.

McLeod, Glenda. *Virtue and Venom: Catalogs of Women from Antiquity to the Renaissance*. Ann Arbor: University of Michigan Press, 1991.

Medwick, Cathleen. *Teresa of Avila: The Progress of a Soul*. New York: Alfred A. Knopf, 2000.

Meek, Christine, ed. *Women in Renaissance and Early Modern Europe*. Dublin and Portland: Four Courts Press, 2000.

Mendelson, Sara, and Patricia Crawford. *Women in Early Modern England, 1550–1720*. Oxford: Clarendon Press, 1998.

Merchant, Carolyn. *The Death of Nature: Women, Ecology and the Scientific Revolution*. New York: HarperCollins, 1980.

Merrim, Stephanie. *Early Modern Women's Writing and Sor Juana Inés de la Cruz*. Nashville, TN: Vanderbilt University Press, 1999.

Messbarger, Rebecca. *The Century of Women: The Representations of Women in Eighteenth-Century Italian Public Discourse*. Toronto: University of Toronto Press, 2002.

Miller, Nancy K. *The Heroine's Text: Readings in the French and English Novel, 1722–1782*. New York: Columbia University Press, 1980.

Miller, Naomi J. *Changing the Subject: Mary Wroth and Figurations of Gender in Early Modern England*. Lexington, KY: University Press of Kentucky, 1996.

Miller, Naomi J., and Gary Waller, eds. *Reading Mary Wroth: Representing Alternatives in Early Modern England*. Knoxville, TN: University of Tennessee Press, 1991.

Monson, Craig A., ed. *The Crannied Wall: Women, Religion, and the Arts in Early Modern Europe*. Ann Arbor: University of Michigan Press, 1992.

Musacchio, Jacqueline Marie. *The Art and Ritual of Childbirth in Renaissance Italy*. New Haven: Yale University Press, 1999.

Newman, Barbara. *God and the Goddesses: Vision, Poetry, and Belief in the Middle Ages*. Philadelphia: University of Pennsylvania Press, 2003.

Newman, Karen. *Fashioning Femininity and English Renaissance Drama*. Chicago and London: University of Chicago Press, 1991.

Okin, Susan Moller. *Women in Western Political Thought*. Princeton: Princeton University Press, 1979.

Ozment, Steven. *The Bürgermeister's Daughter: Scandal in a Sixteenth-Century German Town*. New York: St. Martin's Press, 1995.

Pacheco, Anita, ed. *Early [English] Women Writers: 1600–1720*. New York and London: Longman, 1998.

Pagels, Elaine. *Adam, Eve, and the Serpent.* New York: Harper Collins, 1988.

Panizza, Letizia, ed. *Women in Italian Renaissance Culture and Society.* Oxford: European Humanities Research Centre, 2000.

Panizza, Letizia, and Sharon Wood, eds. *A History of Women's Writing in Italy.* Cambridge: University Press, 2000.

Parker, Patricia. *Literary Fat Ladies: Rhetoric, Gender and Property.* London and New York: Methuen, 1987.

Pernoud, Regine, and Marie-Veronique Clin. *Joan of Arc: Her Story.* Rev. and trans. Jeremy DuQuesnay Adams. New York: St. Martin's Press, 1998. French original, 1986.

Perry, Mary Elizabeth. *Crime and Society in Early Modern Seville.* Hanover, NH: University Press of New England, 1980.

———. *Gender and Disorder in Early Modern Seville.* Princeton: Princeton University Press, 1990.

Petroff, Elizabeth Alvilda, ed. *Medieval Women's Visionary Literature.* New York: Oxford University Press, 1986.

Perry, Ruth. *The Celebrated Mary Astell: An Early English Feminist.* Chicago: University of Chicago Press, 1986.

Rabil, Albert. *Laura Cereta: Quattrocento Humanist.* Binghamton, NY: Medieval Renaissance Texts and Studies, 1981.

Ranft, Patricia. *Women in Western Intellectual Culture, 600–1500.* New York: Palgrave, 2002.

Rapley, Elizabeth. *A Social History of the Cloister: Daily Life in the Teaching Monasteries of the Old Regime.* Montreal: McGill-Queen's University Press, 2001.

Raven, James, Helen Small, and Naomi Tadmor, eds. *The Practice and Representation of Reading in England.* Cambridge: University Press, 1996.

Reardon, Colleen. *Holy Concord within Sacred Walls: Nuns and Music in Siena, 1575–1700.* Oxford: Oxford University Press, 2001.

Reiss, Sheryl E., and David G. Wilkins, ed. *Beyond Isabella: Secular Women Patrons of Art in Renaissance Italy.* Kirksville, MO: Turman State University Press, 2001.

Rheubottom, David. *Age, Marriage, and Politics in Fifteenth-Century Ragusa.* Oxford: Oxford University Press, 2000.

Richardson, Brian. *Printing, Writers and Readers in Renaissance Italy.* Cambridge: University Press, 1999.

Riddle, John M. *Contraception and Abortion from the Ancient World to the Renaissance.* Cambridge, MA: Harvard University Press, 1992.

———. *Eve's Herbs: A History of Contraception and Abortion in the West.* Cambridge, MA: Harvard University Press, 1997.

Rose, Mary Beth. *The Expense of Spirit: Love and Sexuality in English Renaissance Drama.* Ithaca, NY: Cornell University Press, 1988.

———. *Gender and Heroism in Early Modern English Literature.* Chicago: University of Chicago Press, 2002.

———, ed. *Women in the Middle Ages and the Renaissance: Literary and Historical Perspectives.* Syracuse: Syracuse University Press, 1986.

Rosenthal, Margaret F. *The Honest Courtesan: Veronica Franco, Citizen and Writer in Sixteenth-Century Venice.* Foreword by Catharine R. Stimpson. Chicago: University of Chicago Press, 1992.

Sackville-West, Vita. *Daughter of France: The Life of La Grande Mademoiselle.* Garden City, NY: Doubleday, 1959.

Sánchez, Magdalena S. *The Empress, the Queen, and the Nun: Women and Power at the Court of Philip III of Spain.* Baltimore: Johns Hopkins University Press, 1998.

Schiebinger, Londa. *The Mind Has No Sex?: Women in the Origins of Modern Science.* Cambridge, MA: Harvard University Press, 1991.

————. *Nature's Body: Gender in the Making of Modern Science.* Boston: Beacon Press, 1993.

Schutte, Anne Jacobson, Thomas Kuehn, and Silvana Seidel Menchi, eds. *Time, Space, and Women's Lives in Early Modern Europe.* Kirksville, MO: Truman State University Press, 2001.

Schofield, Mary Anne, and Cecilia Macheski, eds. *Fetter'd or Free? British Women Novelists, 1670–1815.* Athens, OH: Ohio University Press, 1986.

Shannon, Laurie. *Sovereign Amity: Figures of Friendship in Shakespearean Contexts.* Chicago: University of Chicago Press, 2002.

Shemek, Deanna. *Ladies Errant: Wayward Women and Social Order in Early Modern Italy.* Durham, NC: Duke University Press, 1998.

Smith, Hilda L. *Reason's Disciples: Seventeenth-Century English Feminists.* Urbana, IL: University of Illinois Press, 1982.

————, ed. *Women Writers and the Early Modern British Political Tradition.* Cambridge: Cambridge University Press, 1998.

Sobel, Dava. *Galileo's Daughter: A Historical Memoir of Science, Faith, and Love.* New York: Penguin Books, 2000.

Sommerville, Margaret R. *Sex and Subjection: Attitudes to Women in Early-Modern Society.* London: Arnold, 1995.

Soufas, Teresa Scott. *Dramas of Distinction: A Study of Plays by Golden Age Women.* Lexington, KY: The University Press of Kentucky, 1997.

Spencer, Jane. *The Rise of the Woman Novelist: From Aphra Behn to Jane Austen.* Oxford: Basil Blackwell, 1986.

Spender, Dale. *Mothers of the Novel: 100 Good Women Writers before Jane Austen.* London and New York: Routledge, 1986.

Sperling, Jutta Gisela. *Convents and the Body Politic in Late Renaissance Venice.* Foreword by Catharine R. Stimpson. Chicago: University of Chicago Press, 1999.

Steinbrügge, Lieselotte. *The Moral Sex: Woman's Nature in the French Enlightenment.* Trans. Pamela E. Selwyn. New York: Oxford University Press, 1995.

Stephens, Sonya, ed. *A History of Women's Writing in France.* Cambridge: Cambridge University Press, 2000.

Stocker, Margarita. *Judith, Sexual Warrior: Women and Power in Western Culture.* New Haven: Yale University Press, 1998.

Stretton, Timothy. *Women Waging Law in Elizabethan England.* Cambridge: Cambridge University Press, 1998.

Stuard, Susan M. "The Dominion of Gender: Women's Fortunes in the High Middle Ages." In *Becoming Visible: Women in European History,* ed. Renate Bridenthal, Claudia Koonz, and Susan M. Stuard. Third edition. Boston: Houghton Mifflin, 1998.

Summit, Jennifer. *Lost Property: The Woman Writer and English Literary History, 1380–1589.* Chicago: University of Chicago Press, 2000.

Surtz, Ronald E. *The Guitar of God: Gender, Power, and Authority in the Visionary World of Mother Juana de la Cruz (1481–1534).* Philadelphia: University of Pennsylvania Press, 1991.

———. *Writing Women in Late Medieval and Early Modern Spain: The Mothers of Saint Teresa of Avila.* Philadelphia: University of Pennsylvania Press, 1995.

Teague, Frances. *Bathsua Makin, Woman of Learning.* Lewisburg, PA: Bucknell University Press, 1999.

Tinagli, Paola. *Women in Italian Renaissance Art: Gender, Representation, Identity.* Manchester: Manchester University Press, 1997.

Todd, Janet. *The Secret Life of Aphra Behn.* London, New York, and Sydney: Pandora, 2000.

———. *The Sign of Angelica: Women, Writing and Fiction, 1660–1800.* New York: Columbia University Press, 1989.

Valenze, Deborah. *The First Industrial Woman.* New York: Oxford University Press, 1995.

Van Dijk, Susan, Lia van Gemert, and Sheila Ottway, eds. *Writing the History of Women's Writing: Toward an International Approach.* Proceedings of the Colloquium, Amsterdam, 9–11 September. Amsterdam: Royal Netherlands Academy of Arts and Sciences, 2001.

Vickery, Amanda. *The Gentleman's Daughter: Women's Lives in Georgian England.* New Haven: Yale University Press, 1998.

Vollendorf, Lisa, ed. *Recovering Spain's Feminist Tradition.* New York: Modern Language Association, 2001.

Waithe, Mary Ellen, ed. *A History of Women Philosophers.* 3 vols. Dordrecht: Martinus Nijhoff, 1987.

Walker, Claire. *Gender and Politics in Early Modern Europe: English Convents in France and the Low Countries.* New York: Palgrave, 2003.

Wall, Wendy. *The Imprint of Gender: Authorship and Publication in the English Renaissance.* Ithaca, NY: Cornell University Press, 1993.

Walsh, William T. *St. Teresa of Avila: A Biography.* Rockford, IL: TAN Books, 1987.

Warner, Marina. *Alone of All Her Sex: The Myth and Cult of the Virgin Mary.* New York: Knopf, 1976.

Warnicke, Retha M. *The Marrying of Anne of Cleves: Royal Protocol in Tudor England.* Cambridge: Cambridge University Press, 2000.

Watt, Diane. *Secretaries of God: Women Prophets in Late Medieval and Early Modern England.* Cambridge: D. S. Brewer, 1997.

Weber, Alison. *Teresa of Avila and the Rhetoric of Femininity.* Princeton: Princeton University Press, 1990.

Welles, Marcia L. *Persephone's Girdle: Narratives of Rape in Seventeenth-Century Spanish Literature.* Nashville, TN: Vanderbilt University Press, 2000.

Whitehead, Barbara J., ed. *Women's Education in Early Modern Europe: A History, 1500–1800.* New York and London: Garland Publishing Co., 1999.

Wiesner, Merry E. *Women and Gender in Early Modern Europe.* Cambridge: Cambridge University Press, 1993.

———. *Working Women in Renaissance Germany.* New Brunswick, NJ: Rutgers University Press, 1986.

Willard, Charity Cannon. *Christine de Pizan: Her Life and Works.* New York: Persea Books, 1984.

Winn, Colette, and Donna Kuizenga, eds. *Women Writers in Pre-Revolutionary France.* New York: Garland Publishing, 1997.

Woodbridge, Linda. *Women and the English Renaissance: Literature and the Nature of Womankind, 1540–1620.* Urbana, IL: University of Illinois Press, 1984.

Woods, Susanne. *Lanyer: A Renaissance Woman Poet.* New York: Oxford University Press, 1999.

Woods, Susanne, and Margaret P. Hannay, eds. *Teaching Tudor and Stuart Women Writers.* New York: Modern Language Association, 2000.

INDEX